To my dear pals
Ken and Karen.

I hope you enjoy
my book.

Best,

Harold Breen

The Last Stonecaster

by Howard J. Breen

 FriesenPress

Suite 300 - 990 Fort St
Victoria, BC, Canada, V8V 3K2
www.friesenpress.com

Copyright © 2015 by Howard J. Breen
First Edition — 2015

No part of this book may be reproduced, stored in retrieval system, or transmitted by any means without the written permission of the author.

This is a work of fiction. Names, characters, businesses, organizations, places, events, and incidents are either the product of the author's imagination or are used fictitiously. Any resemblance to actual persons, living or dead, events, or locales is entirely coincidental.

ISBN
978-1-4602-7358-6 (Hardcover)
978-1-4602-7359-3 (Paperback)
978-1-4602-7360-9 (eBook)

1. Fiction, Fairy Tales, Folk Tales, Legends & Mythology

Distributed to the trade by The Ingram Book Company

This story is dedicated to my darling Martha...

Introduction

Runic symbols, some of which have been carbon dated to five thousand years, have been found throughout Europe and Scandinavia, which is not surprising given their Germanic origin and the Viking invasions of Russia, France, Spain, Portugal, England, and Ireland. However, what is intriguing has been runic symbols discovered across the Eastern coast of Canada and in the United States throughout Maine, Rhode Island, and as far inland as Kensington, Minnesota. In 1898, a farmer named Olof Ohman discovered the Kensington Rune, a ninety-kilogram sandstone stele. For over a century the Kensington Rune was considered a forgery until archaeologists and scientists verified its authenticity using more reliable carbon aging analysis, a better geological comprehension of pre-fifteenth-century waterways in North America, and an improved linguistic analysis. Geographically connecting these North American runic glyphs reveals a map of vast exploration of America long before its recorded discovery by Columbus in 1492.

Beyond being used as an alphabet to record events, runes and their distinctive glyphs are believed to serve a mystical purpose. Norse mythology tells that Odin first acknowledged their connection to the

Divine. The God of Gods understood that each runic symbol represented a story that could foretell the future. He instilled an ability to interpret the runes into a select group of mortals. These mystical practitioners, called Stonecasters, were venerated and feared as a conduit to the Gods and oracles of things to come even after Christianity was accepted across Scandinavia.

Runes

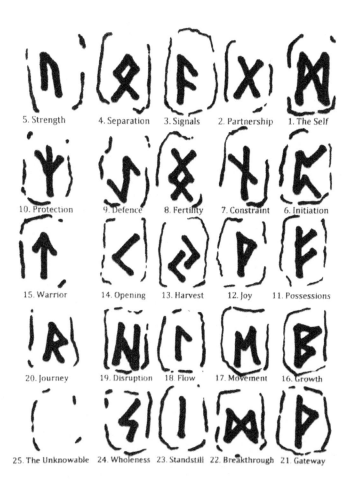

Prologue

Gotland Island
1942

"She's different from the others," the middle-aged woman stated, as she cautiously lowered the wick inside the hurricane lantern and crawled beneath the thick duvet on their four-poster bed. "Our neighbours gawk when she passes and speak ill of her." A deep chill in the air and the wailing of the on-shore winds foretold a storm approaching. Winds coming from the southwest across the Baltic whipped violently across Gotland like the mythical tempest of Norse legend trying to lower their island back into the sea. The woman with the long, flowing flaxen hair glanced towards the window shutters to ensure they were securely fastened.

"Shh, speak quieter Birgitta, or the others will hear you," her much older husband admonished, aware of the thinness of the walls that separated their own bedroom from those paying guests in the adjoining rooms. "As the youngest of five daughters, is not Ingegard supposed to be different? You were the youngest. Weren't you shown the way of the runes because you were the chosen one and different from your sisters?"

His wife's cold feet were like blocks of ice and the man shuddered when his mate of twenty-five years sought out the heat of his warm calves. Birgitta lowered her voice below a whisper and shifted closer.

"I was the youngest of three daughters. My mother was the youngest of two. Norse legend tells of the powers that are blessed upon the youngest of *five* daughters. Our fifth girl has unusual gifts akin to my great-grandmother's great-grandmother. My ancestor Sigrid Gustavson was the youngest of five daughters and did not just cast the runes and read them—she saw the future through them. I've told you Sigrid foretold the invasion of Gotland in 1361. There has never been another like her until our daughter, whose skills make mine child's play. Ingegard's power of sight is growing and she's yet to have her first monthly bleed."

The man exhaled slowly and listened to the rumble of thunder. Truth be told, his youngest daughter was odd. He had watched her talking with unseen creatures of the spirit world as easily as she communed with the animals in the barnyard or birds in the sky. She had already fashioned her own set of runes by painting the mystical symbols on flat pebbles. Just last June she had dreamt that the sea swallowed a neighbour by grabbing his foot. A week later, Lars Johansson's boot caught in the nettings and he was dragged overboard to his death. Ingegard had shared dreams her sister would marry an Islander with blue skin. Within a month a sheep farmer arrived from the east asking to board for the night. His hands and forearms were covered in blue paint, which he employed on his sheep to identify them from neighbouring flocks. A year later Bjorn Larson became his son-in-law. Ingrid's dreams and visions were often muddled and unclear, which her mother attributed to youth. Some visions were nightmares filled with violence so extreme that she would lash out at unseen villains and scream to the Gods for help.

"What do your runes say about our girl's future, Birgitta?" he inquired nervously.

His wife rolled away and folded a pillow within her arms. She realized she had forgotten to braid her hair. It would be matted in the morning, something Birgitta abhorred.

"My interpretations for Ingrid are always the same... which in its own right is cause for concern. The Gods have crafted a destiny for her that will be rife with danger and hardship. Ingegard's journey through life will not be an easy one. Our youngest will encounter hostility and violence, frightful changes, heart-wrenching loss, and then, with time, peace. She will find and lose great love. Ingegard will not remain on Gotland much longer and will journey afar to a land strong with the spirit world. It's hard to read any more into my runes, Lonegrin. I don't have Ingrid's sight."

"And you've told her of this?"

"No."

"Why not?"

His wife bit her lip and shifted so that she was lying parallel to her husband, both on their backs.

"If Ingrid is indeed a true Stonecaster with Sigrid's sight, then nothing I interpret should matter."

The man listened to the winds as they pounded the side of their stone house. From the sound of the tempest, he knew that the city's seawall would be underwater and hoped that the moorings of the town's fishing trawlers would remain fast. When the storm moved inland, the sea would ebb back from the shore. He doubted there would be fishing. The day would be spent repairing the damage. Their boarding house would be overrun with bored fishermen with nothing to do but eat and sit around the fire in the dining room. It would be a busy cooking day for Birgitta, but a good day for the money it would bring. Absentmindedly, Lonegrin felt a stirring as his cock stiffened. Hoping for satisfaction, he slipped his hand towards his wife's midsection and let it rest gently on the mound between her legs.

"No, not tonight," she replied, shifting away. His hand returned to his side and the two remained quiet until his disappointment subsided and he thought of something.

"Why cannot she see what you have interpreted?" he asked, and it was a sound question.

"Our daughter's inexperience and youth limit her. Ingrid sees glimpses of dreams, which confuse and frighten her. She can see little things in the near future but her youth holds back the sight. The runes must belong to the seer for them to unlock the full comprehension of her deeper vision. At least that's what the legend of my ancestors says."

"So what will you do, Birgitta?" he inquired quietly, spooning with his wife. He understood her shivers were not from the cold or the approaching storm.

"I will continue to teach her as my mother taught me. I will turn over my ancestral runes and she will become the Stonecaster. By then she will have matured, and that wisdom will help her understand her visions."

The man's breathing turned heavy as he fell asleep. Soon his snoring drowned out the winds of the approaching storm. Birgitta remained awake, staring intently into the dark as paranoia filled her thoughts. The woman had not shared with her husband everything her own mother had told her of Sigrid Gustavson.

In the mid-fourteenth century, the island of Gotland was under Swedish rule and Visby had become a deep-water port for ships from Russia, Germany, Denmark, Norway, the Swedish mainland, and anywhere else accessible by the Baltic Sea. The walled city of Visby prospered with shipping, the production of iron, and fishing. A treacherous warlord chieftain named Jakob Pleskov, who begrudgingly paid fealty and taxes to Sweden for its protection and trade agreements, ruled the entire western coast of the island. His council of business and religious leaders included a Stonecaster of great repute named Valifrid Gustavson, a raven-haired beauty from a lineage of rune readers and Oracles. The Shaman was both revered and feared by her fellow Vikings and looked the part with fierce blackened eyes, a flowing fur cape, and wolf-skull-topped oak staff. Widowed when the sea swallowed her husband's long ship, Valifrid was left alone to care for their five daughters.

In the spring of 1342, the Stonecaster forewarned the council of a deadly snake that would attack Gotland, killing thousands before the beast would be burned with fire. She insisted Jakob remove his household from Visby. Taking her own family, she hid in a cave in the volcanic mountains to the east. Valifrid and her five girls remained there for twelve full moons as people on the island died horrible deaths. On the island of Gotland, the Black Plague of 1342 killed eight thousand Gutes, but not Jakob Pleskov, nor the members of his council. From that day on, the Stonecaster's predictions were never questioned.

One unusually warm spring day in 1351, Valifrid's youngest daughter was summoned to the Great Hall. Sigrid Gustavson was twelve when she was roughly escorted through the palisade and along the rampart to the hall. Undaunted, she was paraded through the awaiting throng to her Chieftain, a shrewd man notorious for his cold-blooded approach to justice. Jakob had been informed of Valifrid's daughter's witch-like behaviour—talking to invisible entities and phantoms, summoning farm animals to her side, warning neighbours of accidents befalling them in days to come, and, most disturbing to him, her fabrication of an enemy invasion before the next year. The Chieftain could not abide such fear mongering.

The headstrong child walked unshod along the flat stone floor, past the torches that lit the otherwise dark and imposing hall. Eight braziers were positioned throughout the large room but only two were lit, casting an eerie glow that was enhanced by a dozen lanterns hanging from the rafters. A thick cloud of dust and smoke filled the air, making the room clammy and surreal.

Valifrid's youngest daughter approached the raised dais and looked up at her liege Lord, his lady, and the imposing host of heavily armed guards surrounding him. Suspended from the walls about Jakob were fifty or sixty shields and an innumerable number of spears. Two immense steel battle-axes were suspended behind the chieftain's large throne chair. It was an imposing site for any Viking, let alone a young girl who weighed less than any of the weapons on display.

Jakob was bemused with the tiny, frail-looking waif standing before him. Valifrid's daughter did not have her mother's beauty, but her gentle cherubic face was perfectly symmetrical, with piercing womanly green eyes that shone like emeralds in the flickering light emanating from the braziers. Her complexion was luminescent, and waves of long yellow hair cascaded to her waist. The fifth of five daughters stood patiently, dwarfed by the two heavily muscled and armed warriors who escorted her. After several minutes, the leader of Western Gotland stopped talking to the Earls and absentmindedly looked towards the Stonecaster's daughter, which she took as an invitation to speak.

"May the Gods be with you today," she pronounced eloquently, bowing deeply at the waist.

Jakob had already determined to put the girl in her place so that any incendiary suggestion of an invasion could be put to rest.

"I understand you are making claims that are upsetting my people," he accused loudly, for all to hear. He signalled to one of his men to get more mead. "What are you, a witch?"

Sigrid confidently stepped forward and calmly announced she had dreamt of a pending invasion from the north that would see the slaughter of many Gutes including the Chieftain, his council, and her mother. Her vision was of an overwhelming slaughter and much devastation. When probed when such an invasion would occur, Sigrid replied "before the rivers freeze."

"And will you be massacred as well, my little troublemaker?" Jakob teased playfully, winking at those standing closest to the throne, sparking laughter.

"No sir, I will survive and bear my king five daughters," Sigrid replied succinctly, staring determinedly at the inquisitor, without so much as blinking an eye.

Jakob Pleskov was surprised by her arrogance, but instead of reacting angrily, played his part and laughed, inciting all around to join in.

"You insignificant, petulant imp. Who, aside from Odin himself, would attack Gotland when we are under the protectorate of Sweden?" he called out rhetorically, to the hundred Gutes occupying the hall. "Who would attack a walled city with a standing army of two thousand warriors with garrisons to the south? Perhaps you can enlighten us."

"I do not know," the slip of a girl answered truthfully, "but by Thor's winds, eagles will fly to Visby and feast upon the Gutish army."

The laughter in the Great Hall tapered to silence and the Chieftain felt the shift in mood of his highly superstitious and gullible clansmen. He became cautiously aware that every eye in the room was upon him.

"And through this invasion of scatter-brained birds, do I distinguish myself in battle?" he mocked derisively, unsheathing his dagger and slashing the air at their would-be attackers. Those fearing him most laughed the hardiest, hiding their deep-seeded trepidation of any prediction from the Stonecaster's youngest of five.

"My Lord Chieftain," Sigrid responded deliberately. "The goddess, Freyja, told me that eagles will find you cowering amongst the hogs and sheep. She warned that cowards never enter the halls of Valhalla. Freyja said that even your Christian God will look away and you will wander through eternity a despised man."

You could have heard a pin drop in the dimly lit hall.

Valifrid Gustavson was mortified by her daughter's rash prediction but stood paralyzed, awaiting the fury that was about to be unleashed upon her child like an avalanche from on high. A claim of cowardice was the greatest insult to a Viking.

Sigrid's casually spoken prediction enraged the Chieftain and overwhelmed his political acumen. Violently, he grabbed the child by the hair and slapped her face repeatedly with both front and back of his hand, his iron rings slicing like shards of glass into her tender flesh. When he felt her go limp, he flung the tiny body down the length of uneven stone steps and then reached for the hilt of his weapon.

"By the Gods, show mercy. That child is the Stonecaster's daughter," trembling voices called out, cautioning him against committing an unspeakable act in the face of Odin.

A perplexed Jakob Pleskov stood, paralyzed in the most awkward of situations. A claim of cowardice warranted the tip of his great sword, but Runic law protected the child of a Stonecaster. He thought quickly.

"I will spare this life out of reverence for the runes," the Chieftain pronounced loudly. "Chain her by the neck to the killing post amongst the swine. If they feast on her, then her death is the will of the Odin and not my doing."

Off to the side of one of the braziers, Valifrid Gustavson raised the fur cowl of her cape and slipped away unnoticed into the shadows. Her youngest daughter's death sentence could easily be extended to the entire family. For Valifrid, self-preservation was paramount. If something happened to Sigrid, she would still have four other daughters. What was the loss of one?

In the darkest hours of that very night, when the Great Hall calmed and the people had either gone home or found a place to sleep around the hearths of the well-stoked fires, Jakob summoned Valifrid to bring her charm pouch. Without warning, the heavily inebriated Chieftain slapped his Stonecaster and pushed her to the stone floor. Before she could recover, the giant Viking clutched one hand around her windpipe and with the other used his dagger to cut away her fur cape and the thin white shift she wore beneath. Jakob stared lasciviously at her nakedness and threw his knife to the side where it clattered down to the bottom of the steps.

"This is your daughter's doing," he growled, as he indignantly drove himself into her like she was one of his slave whores. With every humiliating and painful thrust, the Stonecaster silently cursed her daughter. Excessive drink depressed the chieftain's legendary stamina, causing him to quickly spill his seed.

"Is there any truth in your daughter's predictions?" he spat out angrily. Valifrid Gustavson covered herself, withdrew her charm pouch, and cast her stones at their feet. She stared down at those stones whose symbols faced upward. Determined not to reveal her embarrassment, she ignored the rape and interpreted the carvings, recognizing the paramount need for prudence.

"No, my Liege, it is nonsense," she reassured, staring at the upturned stones. "Look, I will show you." Valifrid explained that the symbols of *Kano, Dagaz, Inguz,* and *Uruz* roughly carved into the ivory runes showed joy, wholeness, fertility and strength. "You are in no danger Lord. This will be a prosperous year for you and those close to you. I don't know why my daughter has been so foolish and disrespectful."

Jakob reached over and took Valifrid by the chin. The Stonecaster flinched, expecting to be slapped again. The Chieftain leaned forward until their noses touched.

"You had better hope that bitch you spawned dies quickly," Jakob hissed, a sinister look creeping into his eyes, "or you will find yourself taking her place at the post. Now strip off that robe and bend over. You did not think I was through with you?"

As the summer passed into autumn, the townsfolk of Visby became obsessed with Valifrid's daughter. The child with the startling green eyes inexplicably continued to survive. No victim chained to the post had managed to live more than three days before the swine had feasted upon their flesh and bones. Sigrid Gustavson stood talking with her would-be executioners who rooted about her feet, allowing her to scratch behind their floppy pink ears. At night they surrounded the post, allowing her to sleep amongst them and share in the warmth of their bodies.

"She's a witch," the locals shared quietly, fearing retribution if her claims proved to be true.

Each day Sigrid lived gave credence to her predictions of doom. By November the superstitious Gutes pled with Jakob Pleskov to fortify the defenses in case Valifrid's youngest was right. Unlike the town people, the Stonecaster judiciously avoided her daughter, lest any resentment come her way.

One night when the city slept and a harvest moon shone intensely overhead, four of Jakob Pleskov's personal guards approached the swine pen where Sigrid Gustavson was chained. The Vikings carried oak-slatted buckets teaming with the warm blood of two goats just slaughtered. The four assassins heaved the thick gooey red atop the girl until her blond hair and fair skin were drenched.

"Let us see how long these bastards leave you alone now," one growled. The waif of a child clucked her tongue oddly and spoke indiscernibly to the animals with which she shared the enclosure. The four guardsmen found themselves amidst the riled herd of swine that viciously attacked from all sides. The hideously inhuman screeching preceding their deaths awoke the entirety of Visby. By the time the closest-dwelling Gutes had gathered, the frightening screams had been replaced with the grunting sounds of the ovine beasts voraciously devouring Jakob's kinsmen, munching on bones, skulls, armour, weaponry, and the blood-lined oak buckets. Standing by the post, observing it all, was a peaceful but blood-drenched Sigrid Gustavson staring languidly towards the moon, watching a lone eagle circling against the white orb.

"It is time," she announced, and looking about the crowd of horrified onlookers, she saw her mother hanging back in the shadow of a doorway leaning heavily on her staff. Their eyes locked and Valifrid clearly heard her daughter whisper, directly at her, "It is your time."

The following night was unseasonably cold with the smell of snow in the air. The sky was crystal clear and yet the November gales raced across the Bering Sea carrying a fleet of thirty long ships transporting 2,400 blood-seeking Vikings from a fjord in Denmark, their billowing sails emblazoned with the brightly painted image of an eagle in full flight with talons extended. Valdemar, a warrior son of a generation of battle-hardened Norsemen, led the invaders. The war-hungry Danes landed unmolested and met little resistance as the protectorate of Visby slept. Within a day of stepping ashore, King Valdemar IV, through his prayers and sacrifices to Odin, conquered Visby and the four remaining harbours of Western Gotland. Thousands of Gutes were hideously slaughtered in the lightening attack that swept the coast. Valdemar lost only twenty-five men and yet their loss grieved him deeply. Jakob Pleskov was found hiding in a barn amongst the sheep. After being paraded in chains through Visby, the Chieftain was drawn and quartered and his headless corpse hung atop the city wall. The council members shared the same fate—except for the Stonecaster who was dragged into the Great Hall.

Brought before the new king, Valifrid dropped to her knees, pled for mercy and swore allegiance. Valdemar stared a long time before expressing surprise at having met such a weak resistance when the Chieftain possessed a "seer" of such renown.

The Stonecaster with the long midnight black hair was shaking visibly. The uncontrolled sound of jeering from those in attendance drowned out her quivering response. Several Gute prisoners shouted of the prediction made by Valifrid's daughter.

"And where is this young seer?" the giant warrior with the flaming red hair inquired, and the conquered people told him. His face filled with disdain and he leapt from his chair.

"You would idly stand by while your child suffered such a horrifying fate?" he admonished the woman kneeling before him. "Bring me the daughter."

Ten minutes later, a yet blood-covered Sigrid Gustavson staggered into the Great Hall and was brought before him. When the king arose, the Great Hall fell silent.

"I have been waiting for you," the young woman-child offered, and the genuine excitement she exuded—and the depth of what he could feel behind the green eyes—touched the King's heart. Sigrid warned of a counterattack from Visby's trading partner: Germany. Despite a weakened state, which made it difficult for her to maintain her balance, the young girl directed him to fortify the western stone wall and anchor oil-laden ships in the harbour that could be put to flame amongst the German fleet which would arrive in a fortnight.

Valdemar scrutinized the fearless Gute standing before him.

"Thank the Gods that the lame resistance we encountered on this island didn't have your courage and conviction," he stated loudly, for all to hear. "Shall I reward you with treasure?"

"No," she stated adamantly, as if the thought of treasure was beneath her. "I want only what's mine—the ancestral runes hanging in the charm pouch around that treacherous woman's neck."

The Viking with the thick red beard and shoulders like a giant boar commanded the girl with the green eyes be given the runes.

"But by runic tradition they must stay in my possession while I live," Valifrid Gustavson protested, all too feebly. "My king, you know a Stonecaster's life is held sacred?"

"I do know that," Valdemar declared. "We Danes honour our Gods. Far be it from me to do anything that would grieve Freyja, Thor, or Odin."

Valifrid's expression eased and she nodded thankfully . . . too soon.

"But you of the raven hair are not my Stonecaster. You were Jakob Pleskov's Stonecaster and he is no more. This girl with the green eyes and true vision of our victory is *my* Stonecaster and will be the Oracle to future victories. And the ancestral runes within that charm pouch around your neck will belong to her presently."

His warriors cheered raucously as Valifrid was dragged by her hair to the to the post amongst the swine where she was chained by the neck. Screaming out threats and curses, Valifrid Gustavson only drew the attention of the animals that had protected Sigrid.

"They will not harm me," the raven-haired Stonecaster exclaimed, holding forth her oak staff. The swine felt otherwise and rendered her to pieces.

When the filth had been washed from her, the conquering warriors wrapped Sigrid in a large wolf pelt and gently escorted her to the right hand of Gotland's new king. Clutching her charm pouch and carved runes to her heart, she approached the conquering Viking.

"I will bear you five daughters but not be your queen," the young Stonecaster told him. "With me by your side you will never be defeated in battle and will die peacefully in your bed a contented old man that history will remember well."

And those predictions came to pass, and Sigrid's legend was born.

Birgitta listened as the storm unleashed its torrential rains upon Visby and the entire western coast of Gotland. The flashes of lightning and the rumbling sounds of thunder reminded her to pray. The hail sounded as if a million stones were being flung at their house and Birgitta was thankful for the shutters or her glass windows would have doubtlessly shattered. Her husband's unconcerned snoring had reached a new crescendo and she marvelled how he could abide such a tempest. As Thor blew his storm inland, Birgitta's eyes grew heavy and her breaths deeper as she dreamt of Sigrid and the fate of her own child.

Chapter One

August 2014

The day retained the last vestiges of an incredibly beautiful summer as the immaculately clean Audi RS 5 Coupe sped quietly along the eight-lane freeway towards Toronto's Pearson Airport. With less traffic the driver would have employed more of the 450 horsepower than his current speed of eighty-two required. The peaceful silence of the new vehicle was disrupted by the ping of his passenger's cell. Benoit Duval glanced in the rear-view mirror. Benoit had driven Charlie Langdon for five years and knew something disquieting was on the mind of his customarily cheerful and talkative client.

The message accompanying the ping confirmed Charlie's boss was anxiously waiting at the gate. Irv Telfer was one of the co-owners of the advertising agency where Charlie had begun his illustrious and highly successful career seven years earlier. Like Charlie, Irv would have passed a sleepless night in the anticipation of what awaited them in Chicago.

The powerful V8 of the Audi hummed as the chauffeur slowed to jockey curbside. Other black limos of varying lengths cut in and out before Benoit took advantage of an opening.

The ruggedly handsome executive with the shark blue eyes, strong chin, and wavy dark blond hair had flown to Chicago every week for five years since winning the agency's new business pitch for Daily Planet Foods. It had been the biggest coup in the Canadian Ad Industry in a decade with a small privately-owned Canadian shop out-pitching five major USA agency networks for the coveted creative account. As the team leader, it was Charlie Langdon's role to hire and direct a diversely talented team of sixty and pull those sixty into a cohesive unit managing and directing deadlines, budgets, and deliverables expected of the agency. And for five years the Daily Planet Foods account had run smoothly, with Telfer Stuart's reward being additional assignments and considerably more revenue. But the adage that "all good things must come to an end" was proven with the arrival of a new Chief Marketing Officer named Tom Potter.

"Same pickup tonight?" Duval asked, as was habit. "Eight on the button?"

His client hesitated with the uncertainty of the next six hours.

"Check with Kathy later this afternoon," the adman responded deliberately.

The driver, formerly from Montreal, glanced in the rear-view mirror and could see the visible strain on his passenger's face.

"Problems in the windy city, Mr. Langdon?"

His passenger forced a smile, nodded and hopped out.

As Charles Michael Langdon approached security, his mind recalled the previous evening's disastrous phone call. Tom Potter, in his new role as Chief Marketing Officer, bluntly announced he was making changes in Daily Planet Food's agency roster, and his first action was to upgrade Telfer Stuart with a better agency. What an unusual way of putting it—upgrading. There was no discussion, just an insensitive and arrogant "I need a top-ranked agency that understands our needs and puts us first."

It was mind-blowing that the agency's largest and highest profile client could make such a pronouncement after an incredibly successful and prosperous five-year relationship that saw Telfer Stuart's Daily Planet Foods' brands break all sales records and win an unprecedented number of industry awards. As recently as two months ago, Telfer Stuart had won the industry's most prestigious award—Advertising Age's Creative Agency of the year—notably for its awareness-building advertising on Daily Planet Foods. But the hiring of a new Chief Marketing Officer had consequences for suppliers, and Tom Potter had lived up to his notorious reputation as a hard ass, arrogant CMO looking to inflate his stature.

Potter's first meeting with the agency had been an unmitigated disaster. A foolhardy Irv Telfer boasted that Telfer Stuart was "bulletproof" given their track record and extremely tight relationship with Tom's boss, the Chief Executive Officer. Potter smiled wryly, and it was apparent to everyone that Irv had crossed the line, which as a weak-minded, paranoid, unimpressive businessman he was apt to do. From that meeting, the new CMO resolved himself to exterminate Telfer Stuart despite the agency's outstanding contribution. Ignoring the shortcomings and bumbling miscues of his own marketing team, a backstabbing and hostile Tom Potter publicly blamed the agency, questioning about their ability to play in the USA advertising league.

And then came last night's summary firing.

After the phone call ended, a red-faced Irv Telfer accused the agency's team leader of incompetence, negligence, and a complete dereliction of duty. Any element of blame slid off Telfer's shoulders like water off a mallard. At twenty-nine, Charlie had learned that there are times to duck and times not to duck—this was the latter. He sat stoically as his undeserving boss ranted like a mad man. After shouting himself hoarse, a thoroughly deflated Irv Telfer slumped down in his swivel chair and buried his face in his hands. It irked Langdon that Telfer was such a dim-witted lightweight with so much money. If Irv's father hadn't started their agency, the younger Telfer would have been lucky to get a job selling sneakers in a bargain basement department store.

"Pull together copies of every document from DPF's marketing guys that we can use to show how inept they have been. If that arrogant prick refuses to budge, then I'm going over his head to Jack. If he wants a war, I'll give him one."

Charlie chose his words carefully and spoke calmly.

"Agencies do not win wars with clients. Jack Reeseborough has to fully support his new CMO. It's not likely that Potter fired us without discussing it with his boss. We have to bend over and drop our pants. Our only way out is to show Tom we'll do things his way and that he, and not Jack, is the boss. If we do that, Potter might allow us to keep some assignments."

Reluctantly, Irv nodded and picked up the phone to call Kevin Stuart, the other principal whose name was on the letterhead.

"I need a moment. Go run the financials and show me how this revenue loss will hurt us. Get me on your flight tomorrow. If we need to kiss ass then we'll kiss ass like ass has never been kissed before. If we don't pull this off, we'll be firing a lot of people, and our other clients will start looking at us like we must be broken."

"Will do," was all Charlie replied.

Langdon exited his boss' office and raced towards his own. His well-heeled assistant was standing at the door and Charlie's expression was one Kathy Graham knew meant trouble. Removing her glasses, she scrunched up her face.

"Ugly?" she whispered, as he approached.

"Hideous. Daily Planet just canned us. Tom Potter wants us out so he can give our business to other agency pals," Charlie explained. "Book Irv on my flight tomorrow and get our boarding passes. Have Jan and Tim put together a case showing how Tom's marketing managers have been fucking us around with timeline, budget, and last-minute briefing changes. I need it tonight by six and I want it iron-clad."

Without response, Kathy hustled to her desk. Graham had lived through agency firings and her heart was pounding. Firings brought layoffs, and layoffs meant finding a new job in a Canadian advertising arena rife with unemployment. The industry had gone down the wrong path decades earlier as privately owned shops sold out to American, British, and French communication holding companies. The owners who sold cashed out big, but their agencies suffered. Now, the Canadian arms of those global networks were nothing more than satellite offices, often doing little more than adapting global creative to local government regulations and French adaptation for Quebec consumers. Telfer Stuart had yet to be acquired, and a loss of their major client would negate that happening.

The financial projections that Charlie's team pulled together were abysmal, requiring at least thirty employees be fired in order to protect the agency's bottom-line profitability.

And that is why neither Charlie Langdon, nor his boss Irv Telfer, got much sleep the night before and were flying to Chicago as if they were Doug Flutie sailing a Hail Mary pass to the end zone at the end of the fourth quarter.

Charlie retrieved his passport and boarding pass from his left jacket pocket. If he could somehow manage to keep Irv's ego in check and have Tom believe their sincerity and crow eating, the day might be saved.

An elderly couple were directly ahead as he approached the scanners. The two octogenarians took forever painstakingly removing their shoes, his keys, her jewellery, his belt, her hat, and then their sweaters. It would have been comical if Charlie's head had not been pounding and his disgruntled boss already at the gate. After finally clearing security, Langdon hustled to Starbucks and ordered a Grande Pike and a buttered cinnamon raisin bagel. The Chicago gate was directly across the hall where Irv paced like a caged tiger, cell phone glued to his ear.

Charlie was dry-swallowing two Tylenol gel tablets when an overhead LG monitor caught his attention. The morning business analyst, John Walker, was talking about NovaRose International Research (NIR), a company headed by Charlie's best friend, Alexander Fanning. NIR was an investor's darling and often headline news but not with the word EMBEZZLEMENT printed in bright red capital letters beneath its logo.

Charlie stepped forward, straining to hear.

"NovaRose International Research leaves investors in the lurch. Chief Executive Officer and company founder, Alexander Baron Fanning, and Chief Financial Officer Jay Andrew Datrem, have been accused of bilking investors out of $285 million. Medical executives at NIR have contacted the United States Securities and Exchange Commission with allegations that Fanning and Datrem withheld negative testing results of the company's revolutionary cancer-fighting cream.

'Dermmexx5' received approval from the FDA to proceed to Phase Two human clinical trials after highly successful results retarding melanoma cancer strains. That announcement rocketed NIR's share price on the NYSE from $45 to $245. The CEO and CFO were fully aware that Dermmexx5 failed Phase Two testing and actually acted as a catalyst to spur more rapid growth of cancer cells. Bench warrants for their arrest have been issued."

Walker removed his glasses and lowered his eyes for dramatic effect.

"Watch for NIR stock price to plummet like a rock as investors line up to see what can be salvaged. I expect trading will be suspended by noon."

Charlie left his coffee on the counter, raced towards the closest newsstand, and desperately clutched for a Wall Street Journal. The front-page headline took his breath.

"Christ Almighty," he stated aloud. Dermmexx5 was supposed to have been the goose that laid his golden egg. Now it was going to be the goose that shat on his head from on high because Charlie Langdon had put every cent he and his wife owned into NovaRose International.

He glanced over at the gate. His boss stood by the flight attendant, urgently waving at him to hurry.

Charlie Langdon's feet felt as if they were encased in cement, and his body began to sweat profusely as he thought of his wife. Kyla had no idea that he had invested all of their savings in NIR. She and Alex Fanning hated each other's guts. He grabbed his iPhone and pressed number one on speed-dial. Alexander's cell went straight to voicemail.

"Call me. What the fuck is going on?"

Charlie pressed number two—Alex at home. Again straight to voicemail and he left the same message.

He pressed number three—Alex's executive assistant Carole Harris. Her line didn't even ring.

No longer thinking of Chicago, Daily Planet Foods, or even his arm-flapping boss, Charlie extricated his feet from the figurative block of cement and raced down the corridor towards security. He had to find Alex. His friend's family was enormously wealthy and they could make this all right before Kyla found out. As he ran towards the exit, he could hear Irv calling after him.

Charlie hopped into a limo that had just deposited its fare. His phone rang.

"Where the fuck are you going?" an irate voice screamed profanely.

"Kyla's been in an accident. I've got to get to the hospital." The lie slid easily from his lips.

"Kyla," Irv echoed, his tone quiet. "What's happened?"

"I don't know. I've got to get to Sunnybrook Hospital. If everything is okay, I'll take the next flight."

"Alright. Let me know," Irv directed, and Charlie quickly hung up as Telfer was telling him not to miss the next flight.

"Fuck me," Charlie cried aloud, and the driver looked at him in the rear-view mirror.

"She'll be fine mister. Don't worry. I'll get us there fast."

It took forty minutes of intense traffic as Charlie's fear and frustration mounted with every unanswered call he made to NovaRose's CEO. It took another ten calls to direct his broker to immediately sell his holdings of NIR.

"It's sinking faster than the Lusitania," David Chan exclaimed. "We've never seen a stock tank so badly. I'll be lucky to get you ten cents on the buck."

"Ten cents?" Charlie screamed, startling the driver. "Are you fucking kidding me? Get off the phone and *sell it*."

A confused driver wondered what his customer was talking about and why he had been directed to a downtown office tower and not Sunnybrook Hospital where the man's injured wife had been taken.

It took forever to get to the fourteenth floor, and when he exited the elevator, Kathy Graham was standing in reception talking to a creative director. Her vibrant smile disappeared.

"Charlie, what are you doing here?" his startled, long-time assistant asked incredulously, as he bolted from the elevator. She glanced at her watch. "Your plane is in the air." Graham was milling amongst a number of his employees, including two creative writers.

Her boss hustled past and pointed at one of her co-workers standing there.

"Johnny, how's that new copy coming for White's Vodka?" he asked indifferently, trying to appear as natural as his exploding insides would allow.

The writer with the shaggy hair and ripped blue jeans said something about needing more time but Charlie was already halfway down the hallway, Kathy following at heel. His assistant grabbed him by the back of his coat.

"Charlie, what is going on? Where's Irv?"

Langdon looked at Kathy's panicked expression and took a deep breath.

"Kathy, Irv went on ahead. See what later flights are available."

His conservatively dressed assistant looked perplexed.

"What about Daily Planet? You told me Potter can't stand Irv's guts and the only chance we had was you."

"Irv will do fine."

"What do I say when people phone?" his assistant persisted. "Your staff has been asking if they should be getting their resumes on the street. You've had five phone calls from the press. It's all over the street that we've been canned by Daily Planet."

Charlie rubbed her shoulder.

"Kathy, check on flights. I need a pot of coffee and some phone time."

After abruptly closing his office door, he booted up his desktop, wondering how many other NovaRose investors were being decimated. There on his desk was a framed photo of Charlie and his best friend Alex Fanning at their grade twelve commencement, and another at a College Football game where they were both standing completely inebriated on the sidelines looking as if they had the world by the balls. Charlie was so perplexed as to how this man, his best friend, could be the same person being vilified on the news. He remembered their first meeting in High School like it was yesterday.

Charles Michael Langdon had been an odd duck when he walked into grade nine at Toronto Northern Secondary. Having accelerated twice, he was two years younger than the other students and barely touched five feet in height and weighed 104 pounds soaking wet. His parents told him to adapt by using his great sense of self-deprecating humour and his relentless determination to help whatever team would allow him to play. Langdon was the smallest guy in any sport he played but he never gave up and worked harder than anyone else. He chased down every ball, tackled opponents twice his size, and kept running until his nose bled. And for those reasons the older, bigger students left him alone and considered the Langdon kid a decent go-to guy.

On the same day that Charlie arrived from elementary school, another odd duck named Alexander Baron Fanning showed up from The Stanwick Academy—Toronto's premier private boys' school. Despite his parents' protestations Alex refused to continue at Stanwick, demanding the public school system so that he could learn how to interact with kids from "normal" families. His father Ernest Fanning was a Senior Partner at Blackmore, Craig and Fanning, one of the top law firms in the country. Alex's father came from wealth and was one of the country's most formidable legal minds with a well-earned reputation for brilliance and ruthlessness. His business and political connections were the envy of Bay Street. Alex's mother, Bettina, was an exceptional woman—beautiful, well bred, and highly educated. Dr. Bettina Fanning was an obstetrician at Toronto Hospital. Her family's wealth and position far exceeded that of her husband's. As a power couple Alex's parents were on the "A-list" of Toronto's wealthiest citizens.

Alex Fanning had put all that good breeding and those incredible genes to their proper use until, in his parents' estimation, he had "lost it," opting for the public school system. When he arrived, Alex stood apart from the other students like a one-eyed giant in the land of the blind. He didn't look or dress as any other thirteen year old. His black hair was gelled perfectly in place above an acne-free face that was so handsome it looked airbrushed. Crystal blue eyes smouldered despite his youth. Fanning was tall, lean, and very fit with a fitness plan that included a healthy diet, regular yoga, Pilates, and Tai Chi.

Day one: Alexander Fanning arrived at school wearing a blue Brooks Brothers' blazer, designer jeans, and a light gray Ferragamo cashmere V-neck. His shoes were high-top Johnston Murphy with leather soles, and his left wrist was adorned with a Patek-Phillipe, which was a collector's item from the 1960s that was worth more than most of the other students' fathers' yearly salaries. Walking through the hallway, Alex looked like a GQ model on his way to a photo shoot. Female students from all grades grew weak at the knees and giggled to one another. The boys stared in seething jealousy.

As it turned out, Alex and Charlie shared a number of classes and within weeks showed themselves academically strong—although Charlie studied like a dog while Alex could glance at any book and instantly memorize and fully comprehend it.

"I'm a polymath," Alex told Charlie, after a surprise Algebra test on which he scored perfect. "I can't help it. My mind applies itself to everything very quickly. Sort of like Sherlock Holmes and his powers of observation and deduction."

Within weeks Alex also proved himself as capable an athlete as he was an academic. He could outrun, outshoot, and out-throw any other student. Again, it all seemed to come to the rich kid with the greatest of ease and the least amount of effort. Coaches competed with each other to snare the new "golden boy" for their team.

Every female student in the building fawned over Fanning's movie star looks, and by October the "perfect young man" was on the hate list of every male at Northern whose raging hormones erupted towards physically vindictive reactions. One day after rugby practice, Alex rushed into the boys' change room to shower and stripped off his clothing. From out of nowhere five guys grabbed him and pinned him against the lockers.

"What the hell?" he cried out, glaring into the throng of angry faces—some of whom he recognized from older grades. "Get the fuck off me."

Silently, punches flew at him from all directions, connecting hard against his face and stomach. The wind was pounded from him, but the cowards stood Fanning up to continue the beating.

"You're a prick, Fanning," the boys growled, their mob-mentality bravery heightened in numbers. "Go back to your little private school, you cocksucker. You're not welcome here."

A buzzing sound came from his left and one of the kids stepped forward with a barber's hair clipper. Alexander freed a hand but was unable to stop them as the hair clipper shaved a swath, taking hair and skin.

One tormentor held up a plastic container of liquid that he poured all over Alex's genitals.

"It's peacock blue ink," the kid screamed out, in laughter. "Get it? Pea*cock* blue!"

"You cowards," Alex cursed through gritted teeth. "How about one at a time?"

And then as chunks of gelled black hair dropped to the floor, someone rushed into the room swatting a lacrosse stick at the boys swarming Fanning. Grunts and cries of pain filled the air as the smallest grade nine student cracked heads and shoulders with all the might he could muster. It didn't take long until the lacrosse stick was grabbed and Charlie was corralled, thumped, and crammed upside down inside a locker.

That ended it. A naked and pummelled Alex Fanning slumped on a bench, looking quite the mess with a buzzed, bleeding head and blue ink splattered from his waist down. His nose was bleeding and his face was badly bruised. A cut on his lower lip bled profusely. The boys around him laughed like hyenas. When one kid pulled out his cell phone camera, another had the decency to tell him to put it away.

"Now you're not such a pretty boy," the older student with ginger-coloured hair commanded, his voice hardly audible over the noise of Langdon kicking and hammering from within the locker.

When the assailants finally skulked out of the locker room, Alex struggled to his feet and opened the locker. A beet-red-faced Charlie fell out and the two stood facing each other, panting loudly. Despite the pain, fear, and embarrassment, Alex's bright blue privates caused them both to burst out laughing.

"Thanks for showing up," Fanning said, and he held out his right hand. "You've got guts."

And that is how Charles Michael Langdon and Alexander Baron Fanning became best friends.

When Ernest Fanning learned of the assault, he unleashed the power of his law firm on the assailants, their parents, the school administration, and the Board of Education. His fury knew no limits. Within forty-eight hours, four of the assailants involved in the attack were charged as young offenders, suspended, and transferred to another school. As minors, four of them could not be formally charged, but given Fanning's connections their parents could be sued for emotional damage, which they were. The fifth boy with the ginger hair was sixteen and Fanning had him charged as an adult.

Nothing more came of the locker room incident after the novelty wore off and it became yesterday's news. Alex kept his hair short, starting a school-wide fashion trend for buzz cuts. By senior year, Fanning was captain of every team on which he played. While Charlie was a "B+" student, his pal was an "A+." But through high school, the two were inseparable, with Fanning spending more quality time at the Langdon's house than with his own dysfunctional family. Alexander grew to love Charlie's parents, wishing they were his.

Bill Langdon was an accountant and worked with three partners in tax preparation. Unlike his own father, Charlie's dad was one of those "salt of the earth" guys with whom you could walk into any alley and know he'd never leave you to harm. Bill's wife had graduated with her

MBA from Ivey at the University of Western Ontario and was immediately hired by a large communication company. Rose was the nicest and most caring woman Alex had ever met. Charlie's mom actually hugged him every time he showed up at their house. He couldn't remember the last time his own mother had ever hugged him. Rose Langdon baked him the first birthday cake he had ever had.

Charlie's parents recognized Alex's home shortcomings and tried to fill in the gaps without making a big deal about it. Rose became a surrogate mother and Bill set Alex straight when he needed to be talked to.

But then in their senior year, Rose Langdon underwent a double mastectomy. Encouraging post surgery results waned as she lost her appetite and ability to find sleep at night. The Langdons found themselves living a nightmarish hell of hospitals, chemo, radiation, and "not knowing." Alex went to his parents for help and Dr. Bettina Fanning used every connection she had to bring the top experts in the country to Rose's bedside but by October the cancer migrated to her lungs. Bill's wife's immune system deserted her, and a simple, innocuous pneumonia crippled her respiratory system. On December 23rd Rose Langdon lost her battle, and Charlie and Alex lost their mother.

For the next four years at Queen's University in Kingston, Ontario, the two boys lived, studied, and partied together. They didn't speak of Rose, but her passing scarred each of them in very different ways. Their friendship strengthened with each passing year, and when Alex's arrogance and mouth got him into trouble, it was Charlie who stepped in like the cavalry. Fanning threw insults and Langdon threw punches. At the end of their fourth year Charlie graduated in the top five percentile of his business class. Alex Fanning graduated first, took the gold medal for Sciences, and won fellowships to medical universities across the States.

Despite Ernest and Bettina Fanning's determined efforts, their only son snubbed the school offers and incorporated a company under the banner of NovaRose International Research—NIR. The "Rose" was Alex's tribute to the mother he loved. Within three years, and considerable financial assistance from his father, Alex's company boasted new corporate offices, a staff of sixty, and financial statements that were the envy of every start up company in North America.

One evening over drinks in a popular watering hole on the Toronto waterfront, Alex handed Charlie an envelope.

"What's this?" Charlie asked curiously.

"Open it," Alex directed, as he took off the jacket of his Armani and folded it neatly over the back of the empty chair beside them. He glanced across the room taking in every person. His eyes lingered on two very attractive, expensively dressed thirty-year-old women nursing glasses of white wine. In an instant, he garnered that the one on the right in the extremely short blue dress was a time waster. However, her long-legged companion with the short black hair had a look revealing she would happily accept the drinks he'd send over later. Alexander Fanning decided that without much effort he'd be getting to see the inside of her apartment.

Charlie Langdon, unlike his lascivious pal, hadn't even noticed the two women eying them. He opened the envelope that contained ten officious-looking stock certificates for NovaRose International Research. At the top of each certificate was printed "$15,000."

Charlie's face showed confusion, and Alex leaned forward.

"You've got to give me your word you won't repeat what I'm about to say or I could end up in jail."

Charlie nodded, looking around to make sure no one could hear.

Alex leaned even closer and took Charlie by the forearm.

"Buddy, we're going public six months from today. NIR will be one of the biggest IPO's to hit the NYSE this year. I want you to profit from it."

"What do I do?" Charlie inquired, trying to curb his excitement.

"Here's how it will go," Alex clarified. "In the next two days you buy these stock certificates for $150,000. Get a loan if you have to. The appraised price per share of each stock is fifteen dollars . . . so you own ten thousand shares. With me?"

"So far," Charlie responded anxiously.

"When NIR hits the street, the analysts are going to set the stock price per share at seventy-five dollars, so on the very first day of us going public, you will earn five times your investment. I'd recommend you let that ride for at least two years, because we have outstanding research that will take the stock three times over the opening price. That will make your return on investment just shy of three million dollars. So, are you in?"

A hesitating flicker of Charlie's eyes brought an instant reaction from his friend. "What, you have to check with your boss?" Alex challenged.

"Hey, you're not married yet pal. I need to discuss it with my wife."

"I don't see why," Alex continued. "You're a full-grown man."

"It's half her money."

"Hardly. Just because she's now 'Kyla' and a real estate agent doesn't change the fact she is a couple of years off the farm. Last year Francine—oops, I mean Kyla—was scraping plaque off people's teeth."

Charlie sat back. His best friend could be a nasty, arrogant bastard when he wanted to be.

"You're talking about my wife."

"I know who I'm talking about," Alex countered sharply, and he lifted his hand to signal for the waiter to bring another round of drinks as well as to take a bottle of wine to the two attractive ladies sitting alone at the table by the piano.

"I need an answer by tomorrow night," Fanning said, as he eyed the recipients who were both looking his direction and smiling. The shorthaired woman on the left shifted in her seat, allowing him a very clear look at her and he knew the deal was locked. "Dad will buy these if you won't."

More Scotch arrived and the two sat quietly. Charlie stirred the ice cubes with his finger while Alex pretended to scrape at a stain on his tie.

"Sorry," Alex apologized slowly. "I just want to help you out, and this is sure money."

Charlie quickly accepted the apology.

"You'll like her someday, I know you will."

"No I won't, but as long as she doesn't interfere in our friendship, I really don't give two shits about her," Alex stated matter-of-factly.

"You know I think you married a money-grabbing, ladder-climbing hick from bum-fuck Ontario, but who am I to judge? Mark my words Charlie, she'll bolt on you the minute she sees a better meal ticket."

Alex clapped his pal on the shoulder and told him to go home to the old ball and chain. Charlie watched as his best friend crossed the room and introduced himself to the two women.

A knock at Charlie's office door brought him back to the present. Kathy Graham poked her head inside. Her hair was dishevelled and her eyes strained.

"Mr. Telfer is on the phone and he's cursing a blue streak. I told him you weren't here."

"Good girl," Charlie responded slowly. "Sorry to put you through this."

Charlie phoned his accountant and then his lawyer. The message was the same—Alex Fanning deserved to be tarred and feathered. More whistle-blowers were coming forward with damning evidence. It was a heyday for CNN and an unmitigated disaster for Charles Michael Langdon.

There was still one more person he had to phone.

"Ernest," he said aloud, as he worked up the courage to phone Alex's father at the law firm. Ernest and Bettina Fanning had always been hugely supportive. Alex's father had been generous with a marked reserve, in keeping with his reputation as one of the top corporate lawyers in the country. He dialled the number, and to Charlie's surprise, Ernest Fanning answered the phone. After exchanging pleasantries, Charlie got to the point.

"Sir, can you shed some light on what's going on with Alex?" Charlie asked nervously, trying not to sound desperate.

Ernest Fanning had built a highly successful and lucrative legal career that spanned four decades heading up both the Corporate and International Law departments of the firm. He had received three honorary doctorates and his net worth was reputed to be several hundreds of millions.

"Charlie, you know how the media loves a feeding frenzy. This news story is the flavour of the day. By tomorrow everything will have settled down and there'll be some new crisis in Korea or Syria that will let NovaRose slip off the radar. Alex is keeping his head down until this insanity blows over."

The young adman took a breath, but after another five minutes of Ernest's ramblings Charlie was ready to bang his head against the wall. "May I ask one last question sir?" he interrupted politely.

"Of course," the silver-haired lawyer replied, his voice echoing well-rehearsed sincerity. Charlie imagined him sitting in his oversized leather wing-backed chair behind the large mahogany desk that had once been used by Canada's first Prime Minister, John A. MacDonald. The lawyer would be leaning back with a large cigar in one of his hands as he looked out his forty-seventh floor corner office. A buxom secretary with a short skirt would be sitting somewhere in the room to service his every need. Alex's father's assistants were notoriously big-breasted and small-brained. The old man's reputation as a womanizer was legendary, and Charlie, like most others, wondered why Alex's remarkable mother chose to stick around.

"Sir, you were an initial investor in Alex's start-up. Aren't you concerned that you're going to lose your investment? I've lost pretty well everything."

There was a deafening silence.

"I don't make it a practice to discuss my investments but with you I'll make an exception."

"Thank you sir."

"I pulled out of NIR about four months ago. I needed an influx of capital for a real estate deal in Dubai. I netted post capital gains tax almost twenty times my initial investment in NIR. Not bad in this economy."

"No, not bad at all," Charlie conceded, realizing Alex had given his father a heads up.

"I know a lot of investors will be burned badly. But Charlie, perhaps this is a lesson, albeit a hard one, that you need to go through. Never invest what you can't afford to lose."

That was all Charlie needed to hear. Advice from the father who had made a fortune before his crook of a son had skipped town.

"Give me a call in a couple of months and Bettina and I will have you to the club. You know how special you are to my wife." Fanning hung up without saying more.

Kathy deposited a large mug of coffee on Charlie's desk and stood there uncomfortably.

"Mr. Telfer has left me a dozen e-mails," she interjected urgently. "I have five voice mails from him. I can't keep ignoring him or it will cost me my job."

"I know," Graham's boss replied. "I'm sorry about all this."

The middle-aged co-worker removed her glasses and began cleaning one lens on the front of her blouse.

"We're not keeping Daily Planet Foods, are we?" she inquired softly, intense strain beneath her question.

"No, we are not."

"No chance to keep anything?"

"Not that I can see," he responded honestly, and his assistant took a deep breath.

"Am I going to lose my job?" Kathy inquired hesitatingly, tears welling up in her eyes. She had two kids in pre-school and a husband on workman's compensation. He hated seeing the strain under which his co-worker and friend was struggling.

"No Kath, I'll make sure you don't lose your job," he promised sincerely. "They'll take out the younger employees and a couple of the senior account people."

"You?" she asked. Charlie nodded his head and smirked.

"I'm walking dead. I'd be surprised if I'm around on Monday."

Kathy touched his shoulder and walked out of the room, feeling much better than when she had entered. It would be unfortunate to lose such a great boss but if Charlie had fucked up, then it wasn't fair if he dragged her down with him. Once outside his office, Kathy Graham bent over and exhaled deeply.

Charlie pulled up his online banking file and logged in. For several minutes he stared at the numbers as if something would magically happen and the words NovaRose International Research would disappear from his statements. His $3.5 million investment in NIR was practically worthless. Had David Chen said ten cents on the dollar? Even if they found Alex and Jay, it would be years of trials and appeals. And then lawyers and accountants would grab their share before anyone else had a chance. Charlie sat staring out the window for another twenty minutes and then stood up and stretched. His iPhone had been buzzing steadily. His boss would be sitting in Chicago fuming like a five-year-old boy told he couldn't have any dessert.

Charles Michael Langdon considered what was worse—that he had lost his money, that his best friend had fucked him over, or that he would have to own up the disaster to an intimidating wife who had no idea how much they had invested in NovaRose—a company headed by a man she detested.

Chapter Two

The sun hung high above the pine and spruce trees and there wasn't a cloud within miles in the cerulean sky. It seemed to enjoy this particular lake and reflected its rays across the top of the ripples, making them dance. This body of water born of a natural spring had been originally called Gichi-Manidoo-Giizis but had long since been translated from its Ojibwe name into Great Spirit Moon Lake.

The lake was about three hours north of Toronto in Ontario's region of the Canadian Shield called the Muskokas. It was a throwback in time with most of the cottages reflecting the 1960s with fifty to sixty foot frontages. Great Spirit Moon Lake had avoided being taken over by the nouveau riche who had inundated most of the other lakes in the area with their spacious, architecturally stunning "summer homes" featuring interlocking bricked driveways lined with Lexus and Mercedes SUVs. Neighbours on this lake knew each other by first name, and more than half had grown up on Great Spirit Moon Lake spending every childhood summer boating, fishing, canoeing, and swimming. The water was undeniably clean and drinkable, and had miraculously escaped the damaging effects of acid rain carried airborne from the northern states. Cottagers were respectful of the lake and took great care to protect it and the fish and animals that shared the water, the neighbouring forests, and the surrounding farms. Fishing licenses were restricted to people owning property along the water's edge, and both trespassers and poachers were prosecuted to the full extent of the law.

Long before Canadian women had the vote, Great Spirit Moon Lake had been the home of a tribe of Ojibwe who, for generations, had fished the pristine lake, trapped the rivers, and hunted the endless acres of unblemished forest. At one point in time, this great nation of Aboriginals had extended from the deserts of New Mexico to the forests of northern Canada. The Ojibwe had vigorously defended their Canadian lands from warring tribes of Huron, Iroquois, and Algonquin. Never defeated, some found peace in the Muskokas, generously sharing their land with white settlers who eventually did everything they could to steal it away.

But the passage of time into the early twentieth century brought with it the progressive era of new towns, roadways, and greater numbers of people migrating from southern Ontario to the regions north of Toronto. With the population growing, real estate purchases were executed that contravened land treaties signed between the federal government and Aboriginal tribes. Without a voice to be heard, those who depended on fishing, hunting, and trapping to put food on the table found their lands sold and their lives dismantled. The government ignored requests to create a reservation with formal boundaries as had been outlined in the Simcoe Indian Treaty of 1880. Instead, the Ojibwe families were illegally ordered from their properties and forced to relocate north or east onto ill-equipped reservations in Quebec.

Now into the twenty-first century, only four Ojibwe families still inhabited the northern shore of Great Spirit Moon Lake. Their cottages and Chevy pickups were a far cry from the wigwams and canoes that had spotted the area only a hundred years earlier. They found construction work in Bracebridge or Huntsville, working nine to five jobs with time and a half for overtime. Their otter and beaver traps and .22 hunting rifles gathered dust in sheds or back room closets, along with ceremonial robes and cherished memories of a now forgotten history.

But this morning, away from the inequities of history, the familiar sunrise brought Gichi-Manidoo-Giizis to life, as it had since the beginning of time. Fishing boats with their powerful Evinrude motors had been out since dawn to see if the lake trout, walleye, pike, and striped bass could be tempted to chase down a three-pronged lure or bait of live crawfish. Half a dozen small white sails captured the slight breeze that wafted lightly from the southwest. Along the shoreline the happy sound of children's uninhibited laughter echoed wondrously across the ripple of waves. Dogs barked in response to each other and cicadas hummed their death song as the mid-morning thermometer edged north of eighty degrees Celsius.

Along the southwest shore of the lake stood a singularly magnificent property with close to two hundred feet of waterline. Its location and immaculately tended garden were the envy of the region. Stone walkways throughout the property were lined with overflowing yet masterfully manicured bushes of roses and lavender. Back forty feet from the water stood a two-story stone house that shouted of the craftsman's talent who had constructed it sixty years earlier. The house stood encircled by four majestic oak trees whose limbs reached across to one another like a heavenly canopy existing to ward off the weather. The property was idyllic except for the old, half-submerged cement dock that jutted out into the lake from the front of the garden. The dilapidated mooring was at complete odds with the picturesque settings depicted in *Better Homes and Gardens*.

The architect and guardian of this property with the immaculate garden was an elderly, unusually petite lady who moved deftly amongst her knee-high lavender bushes while wearing oversized Wellingtons and a wide-brimmed sun hat that covered shoulder-length, snow-white hair. Her skin was tanned but not in that unhealthy, leathery look. Her face exuded character and was engraved with deep wrinkles that gave her a wizened rather than an aged appearance. Her eyes were the brightest emerald green and seemed to observe everything. For being well into her eighties, the longest-dwelling inhabitant of

Great Spirit Moon Lake moved about the garden with the agility and grace of a ballerina floating effortlessly across a stage.

Awake before the sun had peaked out from the Heavens, the lady had carried a mug of coffee out to her back porch and set it on the wicker table. Taking a match from a box sitting there, she lit the hurricane lantern that her husband had purchased a half a century before. Glancing up at the moon she muttered a greeting to Gmot the Norse god of the moon. In her left hand she clutched a small leather charm pouch that had been held by her female ancestors. She took a drink of the strong black coffee, savouring the rich hazelnut taste. Ignoring the arthritis that had plagued her for a decade, her tiny hand reached inside the sacred pouch and began fingering the ivory. There were twenty-five tablets, each measuring one-inch by one-and one-half inches. One was blank but the other twenty-four displayed carved symbols. She carefully withdrew and arranged six of the tiles on the table in front of her, each visible by the light of the lantern. The roughly carved symbols looked back at her and she studied them, noting the direction of each rune's symbol since almost half of the tiles were asymmetrical.

Of Swedish decent, the white-haired gardener had read these runes every day from the time her mother's instruction began shortly after her twelfth birthday. The worn tiles had been held by the most famous of her ancestors, Sigrid Gustavson. Their strange, roughly carved symbols had guided her and unlocked visions, showing her a journey that had taken her halfway around the world. Now, nearing the end of her physical days, her visions no longer came and she was at a loss at what to do. An impatient spirit filled her soul as she longed to once again be in the arms of her husband and those who had gone before her.

A red bird landed on the railing of the porch and she warned the tiny creature to be careful to avoid the danger of the hot hurricane lantern. Heeding her words, the bird flitted to safety. Ingrid took a piece of toast from her left apron pocket and offered it to her friend.

"Eat this and then take the rest to your family." Her ability to converse with nature had remained with her long after her visions of the future had deserted just before the deaths of her children.

Comfortably, the small cardinal snatched the first tasty morsel in his beak and had eaten heartily. When he clutched the second crust in his beak, he looked at the woman, chirped his thanks, and then flew off into the pines to share this morning treasure with his mate and offspring. The Swede leaned over and blew out the flame within the lantern before looking back at the six white tiles on her table. The message was consistent with her previous readings.

The first rune, in the position of "past," was *Berkana*. The rune of growth faced inward showing a fruitful and tumultuous life. She smiled.

The second rune, *Isa*, made the Swede laugh because it was the symbol of "standstill."

"Of course I am at a standstill. I do not have a place on this earth anymore. I do not belong in the past, I do not belong in the present, and given my age and rotten health, I do not belong to the future."

The third tile, *Halgaz*, the symbol of disruption, was in the position of near future. *Halgaz* signified death. Being of Viking ancestry, the Stonecaster's earthly death was only another journey to a life in Valhalla with those loved ones awaiting her.

The fourth position was the foundation of what was to come, or the forces affecting what was going on in a life. That rune was *Gebo*, the symbol of partnership and unity.

"I'm going to meet someone new?" she asked aloud. "A stranger or messenger will come into my life who needs me and whom I need. Why in the name of the Gods do I need anyone else coming into my life?"

She glanced back at the *Halgaz* tile.

"Ah, is it this person who has gone through much disruption? Maybe it is not my life that gets turned upside down this time."

The fifth rune was in the position of understanding the challenge to be faced or obstacles to be overcome. The symbol in the fifth position was *Othilla*, which signified separation or a radical severing of relationships and possessions that are no longer important. This rune of shedding meant that you had to walk away from your past in order to grow and find happiness.

The final tile brought a sense of relief to the Stonecaster. It was *Jera*, the symbol of harvest, and this rune and its positioning could not be misinterpreted. As her mother had taught her more than seven decades ago, finding *Jera* in the future meant that everything would fall into its proper place and that you would eventually find joy and happiness if you had patience and understanding.

"Vor help me to be patient," she prayed aloud to the God of Wisdom. Vor was inconsistent in hearing her prayers.

The six tiles intrigued her. She had been praying to Odin and Freyja to give her some sign that would break the paralysis she was experiencing. Only the Gods could determine when it was time for her to take her place in Valhalla. The runes she had stared at earlier that morning had told her someone in great need would come to her and together they would help each other shed the past and find happiness.

The red bird flitted back to the table and she took another crust from a pocket. She warned him of a pigeon hawk circling in the sky off to the west. If birds could smile, he certainly did as he accepted her offering and flew off on a southward course.

"I do not know that I can wait much longer to meet some stranger," she stated aloud.

Arthritic fingers had gathered the six runes and returned them to the charm pouch. As was her custom, she raised the pouch to her nose, smelled it, and whispered a prayer. It had been over seventy years since this pouch had been in another's hands, but her mother's scent remained. A smile touched her lips and she rubbed the silver amulet that hung around her neck.

"I smell you, Mother," she whispered, and then something caught her attention.

A fat, calico cat meandered slyly from beneath her front porch and stretched lazily. He looked at the old woman and purred.

"You old rat-catcher," the woman laughed, as she reached inside her apron pocket and withdrew a small piece of cheese wrapped in a napkin. "The red bird has already come and gone twice with his breakfast. Unfortunately for you, he knows you are too lazy to be a threat. Remember I told you to leave him alone."

The contented visitor with four white mittens took his time moseying towards her and then paraded back and forth, kneading the side of his whiskered face across the lady's bare calves. Eventually, he reached up a soft paw to touch the woman's knee. Tenderly avoiding nipping her fingers, the cat took the piece of cheese and withdrew to one of the larger rhododendron bushes. He glanced back over his shoulder and then disappeared into the wild looking for quarry to torment and eat.

As she had for six decades, the old woman walked around to the front of her house and peered across Great Spirit Moon Lake just as the sun began to peek over the stand of maples and poplars. The fresh smell of her apple and pear tree orchard brought a smile her face. Her roses were just awakening, and a tiny brown rabbit with a white tail was perched on his haunches below one of her many lavender bushes. Overhead a gaggle of Canada geese flew northward to the marsh just past her lake. Their honking reached down in greeting to her and the gardener waved happily in reply.

Questions muddled her peace of mind. Would the Gods finally permit her to see those she loved, or would they force her to remain in this painful existence on earth? Were her ancestors angry that she had not borne five daughters to carry on the tradition of being the Stonecaster? Had they deserted her because she had cursed them and lost faith? Why was Odin's face filling her dreams every night? Who was the stranger coming into her life?

Chapter Three

Ernest Fanning's father Goodwin Thompson Fanning had built his fortune on brilliance, tenacity, cunning, and the ruthlessness of an eighteenth-century pirate. Goodwin Fanning had taken over an already successful machine parts and drills factory in west-end Montreal and driven it five times over by the time he was thirty. World War II had helped when the war effort drove demand for machinery and ball bearings through the roof. With well-placed bribes to key government procurement managers, Goodwin illegally secured an exclusive contract with the Canadian Armed Forces worth tens of millions. Between 1939 and 1945, Fanning Machine Parts ran three eight-hour shifts each day, seven days a week. The factory employed 385 full-time employees, the majority of whom were women. This was a godsend to a lecherous predator like Goodwin Fanning.

As an only child, Ernest was raised with a silver spoon in his mouth under the guidance of a revolving door of governesses and nannies. As a child, his daily meals were in the nursery, away from the formal dining room where his parents would eat in complete silence. At twelve, he was permitted to sit in total silence at the dining room table. At the age of fifteen he was allowed to speak at the dining room table but only if spoken to. His father would engage his tall and gangly son in conversation, or rather, one-way lectures on Canadian and American politics and the stock market. His mother was a socialite who had more time for bridge and afternoon teas than for her son. His father worked long hours, but when he did happen across his boy in their spacious Westmount, Montreal mansion, the bespectacled, heavy-set CEO would thrust his thumbs inside his vest pockets and spout fatherly pearls of wisdom.

"Never give a sucker an even break," Goodwin Fanning would state officiously. "Take before someone takes it from you. There is no serious problem if it can be solved with money. The only difference between telling the truth and telling a lie is getting caught. Never negotiate a deal without having knowledge in your pocket that can damage your opponent's reputation. Avoid narcotics and hard liquor or suffer the damnations of Satan's Hell. Never have bareback sex with a woman. When you've got somebody by the balls, squeeze until you feel them burst and then squeeze harder. Women will have sex the minute they realize it will profit or hurt them. And never forget that a female's worth is what you tell her it is."

Ernest would listen attentively, while his mother would sit without making comment. Hearing his father's lessons was one thing, but witnessing first hand how his father intimidated and controlled women to get what he wanted was altogether revealing.

One Saturday morning, Ernest was sitting on the floor reading *In Cold Blood*, Truman Capote's non-fiction bestseller about the 1959 massacre of a family in Holcomb, Kansas by two drifters. Goodwin Fanning prohibited such violence in the house so his son borrowed a copy from a friend and read it, hidden in that corner of the library. His peace was disturbed when the new downstairs' maid entered the room and began dusting the books on the opposite wall. Her name was Jeanne Valois and she was eighteen and exceptionally pretty. Weeks after her arrival from northern Quebec Jeanne was scooped up off the factory floor and offered a job as a maid at the Fanning mansion. For a girl raised on the edge of poverty, this was a dream. Working at the Fanning estate would give her a steady income, regular hours, decent food, and a chance to upgrade her English. Ernest took little interest in the household staff who cooked, cleaned, chauffeured, tended the gardens, and made life easy. But the attractive Jeanne Valois caught his eye, which was not unusual for a fifteen year old whose hormones were raging.

But then his father entered the library, and the boy dog-eared his novel and began to stand to say hello but his father's next action made him quickly retreat to his place of hiding. Goodwin Fanning approached Jeanne, wrapped her in his arms, and began kissing her neck. The maid from Jonquiere reacted in shock, pleading in broken English to be left alone as the patriarch of the family reached under the back of the girl's dress and took a firm hold of her buttocks.

"What a firm bottom you have."

Ernest watched and marvelled as his father took complete control of Jeanne's life by threatening to accuse her of theft. Even at his youthful age, the boy was aware that a servant fired for stealing would never be employable again.

"Mais, monsieur, I do not take nothing," the girl with the black hair and hazel eyes protested, a look of shock appearing on her face.

"Innocence is of no matter," Ernest's father replied cruelly. "Why do you think I plucked you from the factory floor . . . to dust my shelves? Your body is not made to work amongst machinery. It's made for other things, *n'est-ce pas*? Now be in my change room in ten minutes or I will inform my wife that money is missing from my desk and the blame will fall on you. Your next job will be walking the streets of Montreal for five dollars a go. Do you understand my English?"

"Oui," she responded, her eyes brimming with tears.

"Good, I will see you presently."

The Fanning child stole from the library and raced up the servants' stairwell. He snuck into his father's wardrobe just as the whimpering maid entered the room. Jeanne Valois stood with her hands folded as if waiting for an inspection. Moments later his father entered the room and locked the door. With no hesitation he ordered her to undress and get on the settee. The downstairs' maid stared at her feet.

"Monsieur, I am Catholic. I am virgin," Jeanne pled unreservedly. "Please, monsieur, you are a gentleman."

"Well, that's where you are totally wrong because I am no gentleman and you, young lady, are no virgin."

Goodwin Fanning's lecherous face betrayed no remorse as he undid the buttons on the maid's blouse. When he tossed it on the floor, Jeanne quickly bent down and scooped it up so it would not wrinkle. And then, as he had directed, she removed her clothing. Jeanne was still protesting when he led her to the settee, undid the front of his smartly tailored blue pinstriped trousers, and unceremoniously mounted her. Watching from the wardrobe, a thoroughly fascinated Ernest was mesmerized. Goodwin grunted loudly and then stood, zipped up his pants, and handed Jeanne forty dollars. The maid was still panting hard but stared incredulously at the money. Forty dollars was a week's pay, and she greedily clutched the bills.

"Hardly a virgin, are we?" he commented, as he pulled her legs apart and took one last look at her body. "You've had a lot of practise. I'm sure this money will do."

"I keep my job?" Jeanne asked quickly, not hurrying to cover her nakedness.

"Oui, if you are willing to be here same time next week."

Jeanne's innocence fell faster than dried out autumn leaves on a dying maple.

"Forty dollars *chaque fois*?" she demanded hastily. She had never been paid more than ten.

Her employer chuckled approvingly as his eyes roamed across her body. Goodwin had marked both bills with a tiny blue "F" in the bottom right corner. If the girl changed her mind or caused any problems he'd revert to having her fired for theft.

When the master of the house left the room, Jeanne Valois burst out laughing, kissing the two twenty dollar bills like they were bars of chocolate. When she began collecting her clothes, her employers' son stepped out of the wardrobe in the corner. Turning away, her heart raced with the realization of what Ernest had witnessed.

"You are bad," she admonished, quickly stepping into her dress and shoving the cash into the front pocket of her crisp, white cotton apron. "Your papa will beat you. Leave me alone."

Ernest walked towards her, gathering his courage with each step.

Goodwin would have been proud of his son as he countered quietly, "when I tell Mother what you just did with my father, she will fire you. And when your family in Jonquiere learns you are not a virgin, they will disown you. Do you understand my English?"

The maid's mouth fell open and she spewed something under her breath in French. Despite living in Montreal, the Fanning children had not been taught French but Ernest took her meaning from the tone.

"Do—you—understand—my—English?" the teen repeated slowly.

Jeanne Valois defiantly folded her arms across her chest.

"You will not tell your mama. I will go to your father. We see."

Ernest laughed, aware that he was dizzy with anticipation. Until the last few minutes he had only read about what men and women did. Now he knew.

"I just heard him drive off."

The new maid unfolded her arms and exhaled. Reluctantly, she withdrew one of the bills and held it out.

"We share?" she reluctantly offered. Ernest shook his head and pointed at his privates.

"You crazy? Twenty dollars is a lot."

Ernest slowly walked over to the settee and with great courage for such a youthful blackmailer began to undo his belt.

Jeanne flushed and began to sway in indecision from one foot to another.

"*Seulement cette fois?*" the maid asked sheepishly, holding up her index finger, and Ernest's innocent nod concealed the deceitful intentions already forming in his brain.

* * *

Jeanne Valois continued her weekly tryst with Goodwin followed by ten minutes with his son—until the day she unabashedly announced she was "*enceinte.*" To avoid scandal, Ernest's mother bribed the chauffeur to claim accountability and then promptly fired him. The downstairs' maid and her unborn child were sent packing. Goodwin, believing himself to be the father, slipped her $1,500 and a train ticket for Quebec City.

Ernest was distraught. Without his weekly encounter, he remained uncomfortably erect most of his waking hours. And then as great fortune would have it, he happened to overhear his mother talking with a friend who was married to the mayor of Montreal. It appeared the friend was having an adulterous affair with her husband's brother. Within the week Ernest who had just celebrated his sixteenth birthday appeared unannounced at the woman's front door, and when escorted into the library, threatened her with a public scandal. Having found the perfect incentive to exert control, Goodwin's son found himself in *flagrant delicto* with the mayor's wife. Ernest learned volumes from the lusty woman and remained in her bed until her husband was voted out of office. By that time Ernest was old enough to have a job, required only until his dear father's demise, and the extensive Goodwin Fanning estate and fortune passed to his only son and heir.

"Never make your wife the beneficiary in your will," the old man warned. "Puts a bulls-eye on your chest if she ever decides she's had enough of you."

Much to his father's disgruntlement, Ernest Fanning did not want to work at the factory. He despised the smell of oil and found the workers beneath him. He did promise his father that when the time came, he would drop whatever he was doing and return to Montreal to take up his father's mantel at the factory. That was a promise he never intended to keep.

Of all of his parents' guests, he found those friends who practised the law of business to be the most appealing and interesting. To Ernest, Corporate Law was the area of law in which he wanted to play. It was a highly intelligent game, and if you understood the rules, you could be successful, especially if you held your scruples close to your chest. After being called to the Bar, Goodwin's son gained a reputation for representing clients whose business interests spanned the globe. Many had achieved wealth operating just on the edge of the law, exactly where Fanning thrived. Like his father before him, Ernest succeeded, and his practice at Blackmore and Craig LLP flourished. The employers for whom he worked turned a blind eye given the enormous billings their rising star generated and the blue chip list of international clients he was adding to their roster.

Working in a firm with a secretarial pool was like having a personal harem. As the years passed and more females entered the firm, Ernest Fanning deftly employed the despicable lesson of extortion his father had shown him with that young maid in his dressing room. It was so easy to find a victim with debts, a restricted salary, and few job options. Through those filters, Ernest Fanning culled his targets for successful entrapments.

At the urging of the senior lawyers of Blackmore and Craig LLP, Fanning married the only daughter of a colleague's excessively wealthy client. Bettina Robertson was a stunningly beautiful woman who, at the age of twenty-nine, had a successful medical practice and sterling credentials. His new wife was sexually curious and willing to indulge him. Best of all, Bettina was as gullible as his own mother and took him at his word. She would never believe him capable of being an adulterer or a sexual predator. Ernest determined he could have his cake and eat it too if he was discreet and didn't bring home any sexually communicable diseases.

As he sat at his desk in the law offices of Blackmore, Craig and Fanning, Ernest stared out the window thinking about Charlie Langdon. Typically, Ernest didn't give a damn about anyone except himself and lying was second nature. But the Langdon kid was different. The lawyer knew that Charlie and his parents had been a solid influence on his mercurial son. When bullies had taken a shot at Alex, Charlie had intervened. When their son had the weight of the world on his shoulders, Bill and Rose Langdon set him back on course. Even after Rose had succumbed to cancer, Bill had been there whenever Alex needed a father.

There were not many Charlie Langdons in Alex's world. Lying to the boy had left an unfamiliar dirty taste in his mouth.

Ernest's assistant of two months entered his office, placed two manila folders on his desk and retrieved the empty coffee cup sitting by his phone. He had developed a taste for younger women and had insisted Tara Kirkpatrick be hired despite having limited experience in a law firm. He had no intention of bedding her but took great pleasure at teasing her and watching the reaction.

"That's a fetching dress Tara," Fanning offered, unconcerned with his blatant breach of the firm's code of sexual conduct. "It certainly catches you in all the right places and, my Lord, do you have all the right places."

Ignoring him, Tara Kirkpatrick slipped from the room, knowing the old man's eyes were locked on her behind.

Ernest giggled like a schoolboy and momentarily mused that when Bettina was much younger she had had an exceptional figure too. Thinking of that had reminded him of the night before when their son had unexpectedly appeared at their bedroom door.

Alex had disarmed the house alarm and made his way up the servants' staircase to the master bedroom. Bettina had been reading in bed when the youngest Fanning stepped through the door. His hair was dishevelled, his face unshaven, and it was obvious he had been drinking.

"Alexander?" his mother had announced in surprise. "Is something wrong?

Without being invited, their son crossed the room and perched on the king-sized bed. He reached for his mother's hand and held it.

"We need to talk," he slurred, and then confessed the lies, the fraud, the breach of trust, and the embezzlement.

"It's going to be a massacre in the press tomorrow morning," he revealed, unreservedly, "a goddamned massacre."

His mother's horrified stare had conveyed her bewilderment and disappointment. As Alex spoke, Bettina Fanning had turned towards Ernest who was standing quietly by her dresser. Despite acting like a drunk, her son's choice of words and phrases were too well rehearsed and might as well have been coming out of her husband's mouth. As her son's story continued, Bettina's eyes filled with disdain. Ernest had always played her for a fool and with the passage of time she had come to accept that role. But it cut her to the quick that Alex was now doing the same thing. Had the son become the father?

Ernest understood that Bettina Fanning despised him for the lies, deceit, and womanizing and had considered leaving him. As the years passed, Ernest knew his wife had stayed for Alex's sake, but when the boy left for university she continued to use her son as an excuse for staying. She threw herself into her practise, but when Ernest took up with another woman Bettina would rant and rave and threaten to walk out all over again. But she was a coward and could not face such a scandal.

"Don't smoke in the bedroom," Bettina demanded, as the silver-haired lawyer withdrew a cigarette from his night table. Looking through her like Ernest knew exactly what she was thinking, he clicked a sterling silver lighter upon which his initials were engraved.

"So what's your plan?" Ernest asked, as he inhaled deeply, Bettina settled back into her pillows and let their rehearsed performance continue.

Alex moved from the bed and sat in the second wingchair. Slowly, he had laid out a plan that his mother unfortunately recognized as vintage Ernest Fanning.

"Son, this is wrong and unethical," she interrupted forcefully. "Let's stop this charade. You're letting your father lead you by the nose. There is no way this is going to turn out right until you face what you've done and come clean."

Alex opened his mouth to speak but his mother had held up her hand and stopped him short.

"Don't!" she exclaimed. "You're making a grave error."

Bettina Fanning pushed back the duvet and chose her words calmly.

"Son, this isn't you. It's your father speaking and he is 100% wrong. Alexander, you still have time to own up to what you've done. If you follow your father's plan you will lose your name and your future. The money you plan to steal will never compensate for that."

Alex lowered his head. "I'm not as strong as you. As a doctor, you make decisions of life and death on a daily basis. I can't undo what I've done and, regardless of Dad, I'm not going to go to prison. I have to get out of here. This is the only way."

Totally distraught, Bettina Fanning leaned away.

"And I suppose you were able to get our money out before the news is made public tomorrow?"

The silver-haired lawyer nodded. "We are perfectly safe."

Bettina reached towards her night table and turned off the light. Without acknowledging her son, she rolled over and pulled the duvet up around her shoulders.

Closing her tear-filled eyes she had gritted her teeth. "Get out, both of you. Leave me alone."

Chapter Four

At noon, Charles Langdon was slumped in his high-back chair like a defeated man. It hurt badly to learn that Alex had pre-warned his father but his best friend had left him to drown with the other rats on the sinking ship. An hour earlier, David Chen phoned to confirm that before NovaRose trading had been halted he had dumped Charlie's stock at twenty-three dollars per share, recouping a little more than $300,000—less than a tenth of what his client had invested. More than $3.2 million had vanished along with the CEO for whom Charlie would have given his life. By now, the meeting at Daily Planet Foods was over and Tom Potter would have maintained his position. An irate Irv Telfer would have contacted Kevin Stuart to immediately begin the staff terminations. Charlie had no doubt whose name topped the list.

The soon-to-be fired adman knew he had delayed too long in telling his wife. Kyla would be working out of her home office given her time productivity analysis that revealed she never closed a sale on a Friday. His wife hadn't become one of the top real estate agents in Toronto by wasting time. She adjusted her schedule so that

Fridays were spent clearing paperwork, following up on closed deals, and exercising.

Charlie looked at the silver-framed wedding photo on his credenza and then glanced over to the wall at a more recent real estate magazine cover picture of his wife. They were the same woman but different names, hair colour, teeth, and personality.

The beautiful, wholesome-looking bride in the wedding photo was Francine Marie Powell—his wife's birth name. Francine had been raised on dairy farm just outside Clinton, Ontario. Her parents were good, hard-working people who scraped out a living for their brood of six, with Francine being the youngest. From an early age, Francine had fostered an unrelenting desire to escape the drudgery of rural life, which included getting up at four-thirty in the morning to complete her chores before catching a school bus at the end of their lane. Unlike her siblings, who seemed contented with the quieter life of a farm, Francine had dreamt of living in city and sleeping in until seven. From her earliest years her head had exploded with visions of fabulous designer clothing, restaurants, dancing with complete strangers, and a bedroom that she didn't have to share with two older sisters. A keen brain, great looks, a hatful of confidence, and a three-year college scholarship paved the way for that dream, and at eighteen she had bolted on a Greyhound bus to Toronto to attend college at George Brown. After graduating top of her class, she had secured a job as a dental hygienist and revelled in not having to look at cows or siblings.

Charlie could distinctly remember the first time he set eyes on his future wife. The seventeen year old was sitting back in the dentist chair when an attractive girl in a white smock entered the room and asked if he was flossing regularly. In Francine Powell, he saw a beautiful older woman whose smile made his heart skip a beat. Francine became that fantasy woman about whom he dreamt. When Rose Langdon died, Francine kept in touch with Charlie after he headed off to Queen's University. She e-mailed, phoned, sent letters of encouragement, and care packages. The two celebrated when Charlie graduated. When the new graduate was applying for a job at Telfer Stuart Advertising, Francine practised his interview responses.

After securing the entry position at Telfer Stuart, Charlie asked her out. Their first date was a movie and the two got along like old friends. After six months, the two wed in a quiet ceremony and everything fell into place. Charlie's career took off and the agency exploded with growth. With the arrival of new clients came title changes, bigger offices, salary increases, and more responsibilities. A bigger apartment closer to her job negated subway travel and entertaining clients meant an exciting nightlife. Francine told him that their marriage had made her dreams come true.

But then as time passed their marriage took an odd turn as Charlie's success came at them like a double-edged sword with more money but less time together. Charlie travelled, worked until midnight, and was too tired for the exciting nightlife that Francine craved. He didn't appreciate that he had relegated his wife to going to work and coming home to eat alone in front of *Wheel of Fortune*. When he realized she was bored he suggested she take a course or join a club. He only half heard when she announced she had hired a personal life consultant named Suzanne Weston. Before Charlie knew it, Francine quit her job and over nine months transformed into one of the most stunningly beautiful and impressive women he had ever laid eyes on. Unfortunately, her attitude and personality made Kim Kardashian look like a shrinking violet. It was as if his wife's brain had been geared for aggression and manipulation. And then Francine announced she had changed her name to Kyla Victoria Langdon and had attained her real estate license and a new job. Six months later, she had "cracked the code" and her earnings were at par with his. A year after that, "Kyla" was out-earning him and the two were nothing more than housemates who booked time to discuss their finances.

"I'm going home, Kathy," Charlie announced as he hurried past his assistant's desk.

Graham looked up from her computer. "Are you going to tell me what's going on?"

"I will later. I've got to talk with Kyla."

To avoid meeting people in the elevator, Charlie raced down the steps and flagged down a cab. After giving the address, he closed his eyes and reviewed the morning's disastrous turn of events. It seemed only a moment had elapsed when he was delivered home. His wife's brand new mystic white Mercedes SLS, plated "KYLA ONE," was parked in the driveway. Charlie paid in cash and trudged apprehensively towards the front steps like a man en route to having a root canal. This was going to be excruciatingly painful. Charlie procrastinated even further by inspecting the wilting brown geraniums that lined the driveway.

Reflecting momentarily, he thought it wise to anticipate the discussion and reviewed their holdings. There was the $300,000 that David Chen had recouped in the NovaRose stock sale, the house worth around $725,000 after paying the $700,000 mortgage, Kyla's Mercedes at $300,000, his 911 at $95,000 after the lease buyout, his sports' paraphernalia and collectibles $25,000, Kyla's jewellery maybe $20,000, and a couple of thousand in the bank. He kicked himself for having transferred the gold certificates into NIR stock.

An elderly neighbour with bluish-white hair walked by leading her salt and pepper Labradoodle. Eleanor Harris called out, "Charlie, your geraniums need watering," and as if on cue, the mutt lifted his rear leg and obliged her.

Charlie waved but was consumed with angst. Close to a year ago, he had misled his wife into signing investment papers that dramatically increased their holdings in NovaRose International. Francine would have understood and forgiven. Kyla would not.

Discovering he had left his house keys at work, Charlie walked to the side door and reached for the emergency key stuck behind the mailbox. Journey's "Anyway You Want It" assaulted his eardrums the moment he opened the door. Loud music meant his wife was downstairs in their home gym, fully outfitted with floor to ceiling mirrors, a sixty-four inch flat screen Samsung high-definition Smart TV, an Ironman treadmill, a stair climber, an elliptical machine, and enough free weights to exhaust Duane "The Rock" Johnson. Kick boxing equipment filled one corner with a seventy-five pound Everlast punching bag suspended from the ceiling. Lord, how his wife could kick that bag. The floors were protected with heavy rubber tiling that also muffled the sounds of dropped weights. Charlie's framed sports paraphernalia adorned every other wall.

"Jesus Christ," he muttered, as he reached the bottom step. Taking a deep breath and dreading what had to be done, he forced an awkward smile and stepped into the exercise room. What he saw hit him like a freight train and he froze.

Two bizarrely clad people were aggressively fucking on the weight-lifting bench. The mirrored walls reflected the scene from every possible angle. The man was freakishly enormous and the much tinier woman was bucking and thrashing about like a wild bronco. But what made the scene bizarre beyond belief was that the behemoth was wearing Tom Brady's New England jersey with his signature "12" emblazoned on the front and back. Atop his head was a white football helmet. Naked from the waist down, heavily muscled legs were tattooed Patriot's red, white, and blue lightning bolts along with the chisel-chinned mascot and logo, "Pat Patriot." The logo and lightning leapt up and down with every thrust. Tattoos of similarly collared lightning bolts adorned the man's backside and thighs. His body thrust back and forth like a colourful racecar revving at the starting line.

The woman had unnaturally long wavy bright red hair and, in keeping with the football motif, was wearing the cheerleader costume of the Dallas Cowboys—white boots, a long-sleeved blue blouse, and a white bolero vest complete with blue stars. Dangling from her hands were blue and silver tinselled pompoms. The alluring Dallas Cowboy cheerleader was incredibly built and, judging by her unbridled screams, was either delirious in her ecstasy or the most incredible actress on the planet.

"Harder Tom, you're in the end zone," the redhead moaned.

Mortified that he had somehow walked into the wrong house, Charlie began backing up, desperate to avoid being detected. At that exact moment, Steve Perry's song ended and his voice was replaced by the animalistic sounds of rutting lovers.

"I'm coming Tom," the enraptured female called out, and then, true to her word, she did—loudly and uncontrollably.

Looking past the mating frenzy, Charlie's eyes locked on a framed autographed photo of Derek Jeter. To the left of Derek were Babe Ruth and Ted Williams. He took a closer look at the cheerleader and his insides felt like they had been sliced apart with a chainsaw. When he gasped audibly the two lovers turned in unison and looked directly at him.

The three shared an uncomfortable silence until the Cowboy cheerleader pulled away from the man mountain and struggled to her feet. The long red wig fell to the floor as she stood there desperately trying to catch her breath.

"What are you doing here Charlie?" she asked brashly, in her highly recognizable staccato clip, taking the offensive, as his wife was prone to do.

The Tom Brady wannabe rose to his full height and his helmet was mere inches off the ceiling. His black, Atlas-like body was glistening with sweat and seemed to fill the entire room. Charlie couldn't help but stare at the man's mid-section where an inhumanly large pecker hung. The gargantuan yanked off the helmet and bellowed like a cornered bear.

Charlie Langdon instantly recognized Duane Michaels as one of his all-time favourite NFL players. Michaels was the former star linebacker for the New England Patriots for thirteen seasons. Before that he was "All American" at Alabama under legendary coach Abe Waters. In his storied career, Michaels had been elected to six Pro-Bowls and won the NFL Defensive Player of the Year in 2006 and 2008. As irony can be cruel, Charlie had an autographed jersey of Duane Michaels hanging beside his pool table just twenty feet down the hall.

"Shit," Duane Michaels exclaimed, angry not at being caught with another man's wife but because of the testicle-numbing discomfort of coitus interruptus.

"You the husband?" he inquired. Down the hallway his deep baritone voice echoed, *"you the husband?"*

Charlie ignored him and stared at Kyla. His wife's face was flushed with that glow of having just climaxed but her eyes were filled with anger as if he had done something wrong in surprising them. Kyla dropped her hands to her side revealing her nakedness.

"Duane, this is my husband Charlie. Charlie, this is Duane Michaels."

"I know who he is," Charlie responded, turning to face the man who had been one of the most feared linebackers in the NFL. "Get out of my house!"

Michaels' straightened to his full six feet, eight inches. Every Herculean muscle of his 265-pound machine flexed like they were about to explode.

"No one speaks to Duane like that," Kyla's lover hissed.

Kyla stepped forward and put a hand on her lover's heaving chest.

"Get dressed," Kyla whispered calmly, and then looked at her dumbfounded husband.

"Go upstairs Charlie, I'll be there in a minute. Go on now."

Bill and Rose Langdon's son slowly turned and retraced his steps to the kitchen . . . his head exploding with every step. He leaned against the counter and wondered what else could go wrong.

Five minutes later Duane Michaels had shed Tom Brady's uniform and walked up the stairs looking more menacing than before. Abnormally sized shoulders and freakishly ripped abs defined the contour of his shirt like fake plastic Halloween body armour. His neck and arms bristled with steroid-enhanced muscles. He strode across the tiled floor to the kitchen and took out a stick of Juicy Fruit.

"You know who I am?" he inquired, as if his name and reputation would make everything right. He was one of those disgusting gum chewers who keep their mouth open so you could see the gum being masticated amongst their teeth. Duane Michaels had exceptionally white teeth, just like Kyla.

"I know who you are," Charlie responded. "For Christ's sake, I've got one of your autographed jerseys on my wall downstairs. If you hadn't been so busy playing Tom Brady with my wife you might have seen it."

The ex-NFLer stopped chewing and walked forward until Charlie's face came to the top of his chest. Charlie tensed his body and gritted his teeth.

"You've got Duane Michaels' autographed jersey?"

Charlie nodded, hearing the third person reference.

"It must be in the pool room. Hey Kyla baby," he shouted back down the stairs. "Your husband has Duane's jersey. How's that for a coincidence?"

The former Patriot turned and put his baseball mitt sized hand on Charlie's left shoulder.

"Duane's really sorry," Michaels offered apologetically. "You're a big fan and here I am fucking your wife in your own house. That's just not cool."

Charlie felt his head moving in agreement and had to force himself to stop.

"I feel lousy about all this. Your name is Charlie, right?"

Again the uncontrollable head bobbing.

"How about a signed helmet and game jersey? Duane will have them sent over tomorrow. Oh, by the way, it would make Duane Michaels furious if you hurt Kyla. You understand?"

Duane's hand squeezed Charlie's shoulder shooting pain through his neck and upper arm.

"And Duane won't send over the autographed stuff."

Momentarily, the vicelike grip eased and Duane smiled.

"Duane, Kyla and I have to talk," Charlie stated quietly. "Please go."

Just then, Kyla raced up the stairs wearing Kate Hudson white yoga pants and a bright red tee shirt with a picture of Lady Gaga splashed across the front. Her blond hair was coiffed beautifully and her makeup was flawless. It was a rapid transformation from the redheaded cheerleader on the exercise bench having her brains rearranged. The former farm girl looked drop-dead gorgeous and somehow managed to smile as she saw the two men together.

"Nothing odd about this!" she remarked carelessly.

Duane pulled out the pack of Juicy Fruit and offered a stick to Charlie who took it.

"Duane was a football player for the Bears," Kyla boasted, uncomfortable in the silence.

"Patriots," the two men corrected in unison, and Duane gently elbowed Charlie's upper arm.

The ex-NFLer remembered Charlie's request and headed towards the door.

"Hey Kyla baby, remember this house closes two weeks from today," he called out over his shoulder, and then pointing at her husband added, "Charlie, Duane will send you over a big box of autographed stuff tomorrow. Stay cool."

The pile of muscles walked through the door and was gone.

"Aren't you supposed to be in Chicago?" Kyla asked casually.

Charlie Langdon could only stared at her unwavering audacity.

"Why *are* you home?" she repeated indignantly.

Charlie had momentarily forgotten about Chicago.

"Duane Michaels?" he asked rhetorically, his voice quiet and distant. "Has this been going on long?"

"No, not long," she lied easily. "I sold him and his wife Evangeline a house five months ago. It was the biggest sale of the year for me." Kyla decided it was better not to tell him that only yesterday she had closed the deal on the purchase of a $10.45 million property on the Bridal Path, one of Toronto's most exclusive neighbourhoods. Kyla had earned over $250,000 on the one commission. In the earlier days, she would have rushed to phone Charlie and they would have celebrated. Instead, she had phoned her accountant inquiring how the money could be transferred from her real estate operation to a completely separate holding company. Kyla had no intention of sharing one cent of her money with Charlie.

"Did you start having sex with him before, or after, you got him to buy the house?" Charlie inquired.

Kyla calmly began tucking in her shirt.

"Grow up Charlie," she retorted, the question hanging in the air.

His over-confident wife strutted past him like a Paris runway model. There was no hint of the sweet Francine Marie Powell from Clinton, Ontario.

"How long has it been going on?" the adman rephrased, not certain he really wanted to know.

Kyla filled a blue mug adorned with yellow butterflies with coffee, added some skim milk and took a long, slow sip. Her deceptive mind quickly connived how much to admit.

"About two months," Kyla responded, when in fact it was closer to six months ago when Duane and Evangeline Michaels had made her promise to participate in a threesome the day they inked the real estate papers. She had eagerly agreed and earned the biggest commission of her career. After placing the signed real estate contract in her briefcase, Kyla had followed the Michaels upstairs to their bedroom. As Evangeline, a stunningly attractive flight attendant for American Airlines, led her to the king-sized bed, Duane watched excitedly as his nubile wife undressed an obviously uncomfortable newbie. After that, Kyla Langdon had lost track of who was doing what to whom.

After that first encounter, Kyla was hooked on the Michaels as if they were crack cocaine. She engaged in sex with one—or both—of them at least twice weekly. Carnal time spent with the Michaels was complete with costumes, role-playing, sexual paraphernalia, and toys. Duane and Evangeline were physical machines with insatiable desires and few inhibitions.

Kyla realized Charlie had asked her a question. Just thinking about the Michaels drew her to distraction.

"What?" she asked.

"So you've been screwing around for two months? And from what I saw, he wasn't wearing protection."

His wife took another sip and moved her neck from side to side as if trying to un-strain a muscle pull.

"What did you expect? You're always working and I can't remember the last time you showed any interest in sex with me."

Charlie suddenly recalled Duane's final words.

"What did he mean about our house closing in two weeks?"

"Well," she began slowly, as if she was talking to an eight-year-old child, "the house is in my name. Duane's parents are moving from St. Kitts, so he bought them our house and takes possession in two weeks. Isn't that considerate of him?"

Charlie's eyes widened.

"Kyla, he bought our house? You sold him *our* house?" he asked, without looking up.

"No, I sold *my* house," she responded, emphasizing the ownership word.

Kyla slowly licked her lips and pulled her hair out of her face. "Charlie, let's face it. We aren't compatible anymore, and you're holding me back. I don't want to be cruel, but I don't find you sexually attractive anymore. Being with a man like Duane Michaels has shown me what I've been missing."

Charlie wondered where this was headed.

"Look at us. My career is rocketing and yours has completely stalled," she continued. "My earnings are going through the roof and you're losing clients. I'm a winner, Charlie. You used to be a winner, but you aren't anymore. I can't have people holding me back. I need someone to help me be my best, and it isn't you."

Charlie groaned and rolled his eyes.

"Kyla, you sound like your life consultant Suzanne Weston. I guess your mentor taught you that cheating on your husband and fucking a married man is being your best?"

His wife aggressively turned on him.

"Let's cut to the chase. I want a divorce," she stated bluntly. "My lawyer has drawn up papers."

"A lawyer?" Charlie interrupted. "When—"

"There's no need to drag this out," she interrupted, holding up her right hand like a stop sign. "He'll courier the papers to you tonight."

Charlie stood up and Alex's warning about Francine "dumping him for a better meal ticket" came flooding back.

"So you decide our future?"

"Charlie, my mind is made up," Kyla responded in monotone clip. "Let's be grown up about this. Without kids, divorce is easy. We split everything down the middle and go separate ways. There doesn't have to be animosity between us. There was a time we were best friends. All you have to do is sign the papers and we get on with new lives."

Charlie walked to the fridge, pulled out a Corona and took a seat on their leather sofa. He knew Kyla hated when he ate or drank anything on the white kid leather sofas. He waited for her rebuke but she held her tongue. For several minutes, neither spoke. He knew that Kyla Victoria Langdon was as moveable as a two-ton slab of cold cement once her mind was set.

"Out of curiosity, why are you home?" she inquired again, as she ran her fingers through her hair.

After a long drink, Charlie wiped his mouth on his right sleeve and undid his tie. He was no longer afraid of telling her about the money.

"Well," he began slowly, "it's been a rather disturbing day, even before I walked in on you and Duane Michaels. My trip to Chicago was to beg Daily Planet Foods to recant their decision to fire us. I missed the flight."

Kyla's stopped toying with her hair and sat in one of the wing-backed chairs by the fireplace.

"Why did you miss the flight?" Kyla asked, and Charlie took another swig, letting time pass for effect.

"Something awful happened this morning when I arrived at the airport."

"Bill?" Kyla inquired hastily, genuine concern registering across her face that something had happened to Charlie's father.

"No, he's fine, and thanks for your concern."

"Then why?" she repeated impatiently.

He began sticking his middle finger in and out of the lip of the bottle—a habit that thoroughly ticked off his wife. "Well, you're not going to like what happened."

Kyla stood and planted her hands on her hips. "Enough of the cat and mouse game. What the fuck is going on?" she demanded sharply.

Charlie placed his beer bottle on the glass table.

"I came home from the airport to tell you that we lost a lot of money today—a *lot* of money."

"How much money?" Kyla asked slowly, as she sat back down, crossed her legs, and began rocking her foot like it was an uncontrollable appendage with a life of its own.

Charlie blurted it out.

"We lost our entire investment portfolio and most of our savings. We still have whatever money you netted from selling our house to Duane, the two cars, your jewellery, our paintings, my sports collectibles, and about $4,225 cash. I don't know what monies you have in your company. We'll need to go over your books."

Kyla's face distorted like her cheekbones had melted and she bit her lip hard. There would be no going over her books.

"You're not making any sense. What are you talking about?"

Charlie Langdon didn't have to look to know that his wife's skin would be doing the "red" thing. When Kyla got angry, the skin on her upper chest and neck turned blotchy red and then the blotchiness migrated up to her cheeks and forehead. Right now, "crimson" would be zooming up her face like mercury in a thermometer that had been tossed in the fireplace.

He got up and walked into the kitchen. After depositing the empty in the recycle bin beneath the sink he went to the fridge and pulled out a second Corona. He could feel the heat coming off Kyla's body as she followed him into the kitchen. As anticipated, her chest, neck, and face were the colour of a harvest tomato.

He unscrewed the cap.

"You've been too busy playing cheerleader with Tom Brady to have heard any news this morning, but NovaRose International Research has gone bust. Alex falsified research results, embezzled the money, and then took off. I can't even remember all the charges being levelled against him but there's a warrant out for his arrest."

"Alex faked cancer results and then embezzled from his company?"

"He and his CFO took off with everything," he replied factually.

Charlie could smell the rubber burning inside Kyla's brain. Her eyes turned ice cold.

"You're just fucking with me because you caught me downstairs."

Charlie stared directly at her and his wife started pacing.

"Okay, so we lost money in your asshole friend's company," Kyla stated, with some conviction. "The majority of our holdings are in tech and pharmaceuticals. NovaRose was around $125 thousand. So we lost the $125 grand?"

Her husband's silence revealed that there was much more to it.

"We only lost $125 thousand. You didn't invest more, did you?"

Charlie's mouth opened but nothing came out.

"You did!" she accused loudly, and the red exploded from ear to ear. "Exactly how much?"

He took a deep breath. "Over $3 million," Charlie announced, and some part of him felt good to saying it. "I transferred our entire portfolio, including the money I invested in gold certificates, into NovaRose International Research."

Kyla's eyelids blinked uncontrollably which was a nervous trait of Francine's that Kyla had yet to overcome. "Over $3 million, including our gold investment?"

"Yes."

Kyla clasped her fingers and began cracking her knuckles—another of Francine's nervous traits.

"But I didn't agree to transfer any funds," she stammered. "We still have a joint investment account. David Chen needed both our signatures to sell the gold certificates or even reallocate any of our stock holdings."

Charlie knew this part was dicey.

"We both signed the paperwork to transfer our funds solely into NovaRose International Research," he stated factually. "Your signature is on the broker directions beside mine."

Kyla cocked her head.

"I didn't sign any papers," she avowed firmly. "I would never have agreed to put more money into NIR. I fucking hate Alexander Fanning."

"Well," he countered slowly, "you did. You obviously were too distracted with Duane Michaels."

Kyla's knuckles continued to snap while she tried to quickly process her husband's words. She stared at him and watched as a stream of sweat trickled down the side of his forehead. "You're lying."

"Well you did sign the papers," he insisted, not giving any ground.

Kyla ran to her office and fetched her BlackBerry. Skipping through her meticulously organized calendar she locked on a date. "The only financial papers I've signed with you were exactly five months ago this week. I was rushing out to close a sale. I've got the date right here. It was raining and I was late. You had some banking papers that required our signatures on record for cheque-signing security. Beyond that, I haven't signed any papers for David Chen in well over a year."

Charlie sat quietly staring at the piece of art above the fireplace. It was a Phillip Craig that depicted a quiet stream along the Canadian Shield in Northern Ontario. Kyla exhaled and put the BlackBerry in her back pocket.

"They weren't banking papers and our signatures had nothing to do with cheque signing security. You had me co-sign the authorization for our funds to be transferred into NovaRose International. You deceived me when you knew I was in a frantic rush and running late," she hissed. "My lawyer will have a field day with this. You can forget any fifty-fifty divorce."

Charlie scratched an imaginary itch, returned to the kitchen and leaned against the island. Kyla followed and stood by the fridge.

"Threaten all you like, but your signature is on the papers and legally, that's all that counts. You can say you didn't know what you were signing and I will say you did. It's a moot point since we've lost the money."

"No," Kyla responded, her mouth twisted and her eyes ablaze. "You lost our money."

The frantic eye blinking returned and his wife began puffing erratically. Charlie was afraid she might be having a heart attack and took a step towards her. But it was no heart attack. His wife was urging an adrenaline flow. Without any warning and with extreme deftness, Kyla drove her right knee violently into Charlie's groin. The pain was instantaneous, sucking the air out of his lungs, blurring his vision and buckling him forward. Instinctively his hands clutched at his testicles as Kyla's right elbow flew towards his face. Charlie's head propelled upward as his wife's elbow caught him squarely on the jaw. Recoiling to the right, Kyla's cupped left hand rocketed towards her victim's right ear. The unimaginably painful impact slammed Charlie like he had been hit with a sledge hammer and his body fell sideways into the stainless steel door of the fridge. He slumped to the floor, gasping for air.

Kyla stepped towards him.

"So I was wasting my time with strength training and martial arts," she mocked remorselessly. "The only time I wasted was in sticking with you." Through blurred eyes he watched her walk over to the counter and pick up a porcelain vase filled with orchids.

Charlie's jaw and eardrum were exploding. His testicles were screaming with pain. Crawling up on one elbow he watched as his wife raised the orchids above her head. He had no time to react as the vase and its contents smashed across his head, slicing a six-inch gap across his forehead. Staring at the red puddle forming on the floor, he vomited and passed out.

Thirty minutes passed before Charlie regained consciousness. His jaw felt like it was broken. His testicles were whimpering in agony and there was an odd two-note ringing in his ear. He struggled to the sink and picked up a dishtowel. Folding it several times, Charlie pressed it against his forehead to stave off the bleeding.

There was a repeated thumping sound on the hallway steps—*thud, thud, thud*—and then the unmistakeable clickety-click of high heels walking across the marble tiled floor. Kyla appeared in the doorway wearing a bright yellow strapless sundress with matching shoes. Looking past her down the hallway Charlie saw the two oversized suitcases she dragged noisily down the stairs. Ignoring his injuries and the blood and vomit on the kitchen floor, Kyla walked over to the counter and scooped up her car keys.

"Clean that up. I'll be back later tonight for the rest of my things," she stated as she dropped her keys into her purse, which was yellow like the dress and heels.

"You'd better have someone look at that," she remarked offhandedly, looking at her handiwork. "You need stitches."

Kyla gavotted from the kitchen then turned slowly.

"Can you understand me Charlie?" she asked, and her husband nodded.

"I want you to understand that I phoned my lawyer and told him you walked in on Duane and me. I cried when I told him you slapped me and that when I demanded a divorce you threatened to kill me so I had to defend myself and barely got out of the house. He wanted to send the police but I told him to hold off. I told him about the stock loss and how you deceived me into signing the investment papers. He recommended we rewrite the divorce papers and take every cent. I agreed."

Charlie leaned on the island and removed the towel to see if the bleeding had stopped.

"Are you getting this?" she asked, staring into his cloudy eyes. "Do you understand me?"

"Yes," he responded coldly, his jaw aching with every word.

"My lawyer is redrafting the divorce papers. You sign whatever he sends you or we'll call the police and have you arrested for battery. Every person we know including the owners of your agency, all your clients, and every player in your advertising world will hear that you were arrested for wife abuse. You won't be able to get a job writing jingles for toothpicks."

Charlie raised his eyes.

"You'd do that to me?" he asked incredulously, and Kyla laughed.

"Charlie, you just lost me $3 million."

Kyla dragged her suitcases to the front door.

"Sign the divorce papers or I'll make your life a blood-sucking misery."

The front door slammed and Kyla Victoria Langdon's Mercedes squealed from the driveway. Charlie picked up the dishtowel and pressed it against his forehead. "You've already done that."

* * *

The elderly gardener living on the southwest shores of Great Spirit Moon Lake finished her yard work and stood back to admire it. Content with her effort, she walked to the wicker rocking chair on the front porch. The old cat had returned from his day of hunting and rubbed up against her legs before finding a shaded resting place amongst the flower-filled pots that resided everywhere. She said something to the cat and he seemed to reply. Anyone looking at the porch would have thought that the two were engaged in a conversation. A pitcher of lemonade sat on a nearby table. She poured a glass and took a long drink, savouring the flavour of the fresh lemons. It had been a happy day, and she wondered if it was to be her last. The elderly lady with the shoulder-length white hair arose and walked into her kitchen to prepare what might be her last supper depending on what Odin decided to do the next morning when she forced his hand.

Chapter Five

After Kyla sped off, Charlie painstakingly hobbled upstairs and found Johnson & Johnson medical gauze, which he taped to his forehead. He discovered his wife's closet was empty. She had even taken the wooden hangers. She'd obviously been removing her clothing over the last couple few days. The two suitcases Kyla had just carted out were the last remnants.

Gingerly, the embattled adman crawled out of his vomit, blood, and soil-covered clothing and stepped into the shower. It was disconcerting watching the blood circle down the drain between his feet. Upon inspection he discovered his testicles had inflated to the size of billiard balls and touching them made him grimace. He pulled on a clean tee shirt, Levis, and a pair of Nikes and, fearing a concussion, he determined to drive to the nearest hospital. Careful to not get any blood on the leather seats of the Porsche 911 Turbo S, Charlie drove off slowly. He had 550 horsepower at his beck and call but the best he could do with the 3.8 litre engine was the city speed limit of fifty kilometres per hour.

As luck would have it, he found an empty parking spot and holding a towel to his bandaged head entered "Emergency." The stout receptionist sitting behind the Plexiglas barrier gave him a once over and asked for his health and insurance cards.

"Charles Michael Langdon. Mugging?"

Charlie stared awkwardly with a throbbing head, ringing ears, and a jaw that felt broken.

"No. I need stitches and I might have a concussion."

Not seeing anything life threatening, the nurse pointed towards the waiting room. "Take a seat. I'll call you."

Charlie found a seat in the corner and reluctantly reached for his iPhone. He had sixty-five messages including at least fifteen from his boss. The messages began with Irv's concern for Kyla. Then, as the client meeting neared, his boss' messages showed greater urgency. After the disastrous meeting, Telfer's e-mails were vitriolic. The most recent read:

"We've lost DPF. No ninety-day termination clause. I have instructed Kevin and HR to commence firings. Be in my office tomorrow 9:00 a.m. sharp."

Charlie glanced at the industrial-sized wall clock. Four and a half hours had passed since he sat down.

"Charles Langdon," a voice announced calmly over the intercom. Charlie stood up and had to momentarily steady himself before he walked past the receptionist who pointed towards an examining room off to the left.

"Hi," the youngish doctor with greasy hair and dark black circles under his eyes offered. Without inviting Charlie to sit down or any hesitation, he immediately removed the gauze covering Charlie's wounded forehead. The cut had formed a light scab but the skin surrounding it was covered in blood.

"Yikes, that must have hurt. So, what happened, sir?" the doctor inquired with a strong British accent which Charlie determined made people sound smarter even when they weren't.

He gave a rehearsed answer.

"I was gardening underneath the back balcony when our cat bumped up against one of the pots. It came crashing down on my head. I think I've got a concussion."

The doctor opened the wound and then squeezed the folds of skin together. Charlie grimaced.

"How long ago did this happen?"

"I was in the waiting room over four hours. It happened about an hour before that."

A middle-aged nurse with unusually clean white Sketchers entered the room and asked if the resident needed assistance. The woman's face looked like a Mr. Potato Head creation including a mole the size of Cleveland on her chin. Charlie averted his eyes.

"Dizziness?" the resident inquired. "Nausea?"

"Yes. I think I might have passed out when the pot first hit me. There was a lot of blood and I vomited."

Taking a penlight from the breast pocket of his white smock, the doctor moved and it back and forth in front of Charlie's face directing him not to move his head but follow the light with his eyes. He reached up and felt around Charlie's temples, ears, neck, and throat.

"Any heart conditions I should know about?"

"No."

"On any prescribed medication including Viagra?"

"No."

"Taking any drugs of any sort?"

"No."

"Did you urinate or void your bowels while you were out?"

"No."

"You certain?"

"Yes."

More scribbled notes.

"What's this bruising around your eye and here on your chin?"

Charlie recoiled when the doctor touched both painful spots.

"I must have hit my head when I passed out," he responded lamely.

"I can smell alcohol on your breath and you've got blood in your right ear," the resident remarked judgmentally, without lifting his eyes.

"I had a beer when I was gardening. It was hot as hell out," Charlie responded, "but that was hours ago."

The nurse with Mount Vesuvius on her chin peered closely at his forehead.

"Sir, your injuries are consistent with having been assaulted. We can call the police if you'd like."

"No, it was a plant, actually, an orchid in a porcelain vase," he corrected, staring at her forehead to avoid the chin.

It took two needles to freeze the site, nine staples, and a tetanus shot.

"Good job," the resident stated, admiring his handiwork. "I don't think any plastic surgeon could have done better. No alcohol, driving, or heavy lifting for the next twenty-four hours. I don't want you falling asleep until late tonight. No napping."

"Don't I need an X-ray or an MRI to check for a concussion?"

The resident shook his head as he scribbled notes.

"I think you took a very bad clobbering but I don't see any evidence of a concussion. You are going to have a severe headache for the next twenty-four hours. If your head is still sore Sunday then come back and we'll run some tests. Do you have someone who can take you home?"

Charlie lied that a friend was waiting before getting the prescription for painkillers filled at the pharmacy. He immediately opened the bottle of Tylenol 3's and popped two in his mouth. The drive home took longer as Friday night rush hour traffic slowed to a snail's pace. He was glad to get out of the Porsche and be home. But the moment he walked through the front door that feeling disappeared.

The first floor of the house had been emptied out except for one lamp sitting on the floor beside the fireplace. The leather sofa, love seat, and two wing-backed chairs were gone. Kyla's antique display cabinet containing her collection of twenty Russian lacquer boxes and fifteen antique silver snuff boxes had been removed. The walls were bare of all paintings and light sconces. Black cables protruded above the fireplace where the LG high-definition TV had earlier hung. The twenty-five square foot Chinese carpet was gone, giving the entire floor a naked appearance.

Charlie turned and looked around the kitchen. There was nothing in it. As he hastened anxiously through the house, he discovered Kyla had emptied the dining room and her office. Hurrying down the basement steps sent him into conniptions when he found the lower floor empty too. Kyla had removed all of his autographed jerseys including Ted Williams, Willie Mays, Joe DiMaggio, Sandy Koufax, Derek Jeter, Michael Jordan, Wayne Gretzky, and Walter Payton. She'd made off with over thirty boxes of trading cards most of which were pre-1970. Same with his revered baseballs signed by Babe Ruth, Joe DiMaggio, Ted Williams, Sandy Koufax, and Willie Mays. Only one piece of sports' paraphernalia had been left behind—the autographed jersey of Duane Michaels. Every piece of exercise equipment, all the free weights, and the big screen TVs were gone.

"You fucking bitch," his scream of rage echoed, through the barren house causing a throbbing implosion inside his head.

The second floor was no different and had been emptied save for a single bed mattress on the guest room floor along with a scattered pile of his clothes. As nausea set upon him, he perched on the edge of the bathtub and vomited in the toilet.

And that's when it dawned on him that his wife already had a new place to live and had orchestrated the movers for the day he was supposed to be in Chicago. Langdon crawled onto the mattress and despite the doctor's warning fell into a coma-like sleep.

* * *

A giddy Charlie Langdon was waiting impatiently amongst a mob of extremely excited and obnoxiously loud baseball enthusiasts all of whom had happily queued for hours. Standing on tiptoes he could almost catch a glimpse of the legendary Yankee autographing cards, photos, hats, baseball bats, and jerseys. It was nearly Charlie's turn and he inched forward one agonizing mini-step at a time. Around him the atmosphere was electric, buzzing with anticipation. And then, as a lifelong dream came true he found himself face to face with his all-time baseball hero—the Great Bambino.

"Mr. Ruth," Charlie cried out, his voice cracking like a prepubescent boy. "Babe, you're my all-time favourite Yankee. Would you please autograph these?"

George Herman Ruth Jr. looked up as he took the baseball cards.

"Your favourite Yankee? I'm not your favourite ballplayer?" he kidded as he chewed on a slug of tobacco wedged deeply into the side of his mouth.

Somewhere behind them an annoying sound caught the attention of the Yankee born in Baltimore, Maryland.

"Charles Michael Langdon," the New York Yankee exclaimed, "can't you make that annoying sound stop?"

Charlie giggled like a little girl. The Sultan of Swat with four World Series rings knew his name.

"Stop that damn drilling sound," Ruth commanded, to a trainer standing off to the side. "I've got to sign these cards before that bitch Kyla beats the shit out of Charlie again."

Bitch Kyla beats the shit out of Charlie again?

Charlie opened his eyes and sat upright. The Babe was gone. The annoying sound from the dream was his cell phone vibrating loudly on the hardwood floor. He grabbed it and muttered a drowsy, "Hello."

"Charlie, do you know the time?" Irv Telfer spat out through teeth gritted in frustration.

Charlie looked at his watch. It was 9:20 a.m. and he'd been asleep over fourteen hours.

The beginning of a lame excuse was interrupted.

"I told you to be here at 9:00 a.m. sharp."

His boss's raspy voice sounded like he hadn't been to bed.

"I'm sorry," he responded genuinely, "I can be there in twenty."

"Forget it. Tom Potter crucified me. I've never been so humiliated in my entire fucking career. I don't know what happened to you or Kyla and frankly I don't give a damn."

"Irv, I had—" Charlie tried to interrupt, but Telfer was not in a listening mood.

"Do you realize how many people are losing their jobs because of you?"

Charlie had to pee and could not hold it in. He painfully walked into the bathroom. Quietly he lifted the toilet seat and sat down. As urine painfully streamed out he observed that his testicles had ballooned to the size of tennis balls.

There was deafening silence on the other end of the phone as Charlie continued peeing against the porcelain side of the bowl.

"Langdon, we pulled the trigger on ten people yesterday afternoon and another twenty will be fired Monday. I was going to do this in person, but let's save time. I'll make it official. You're fired. Leslie will work you through your termination papers."

Leslie Ingram was Telfer Stuart's Vice President of Human Resources. Charlie and Leslie had worked together from the first day of his arrival. Having to be involved with this many terminations would be unbearably hard on her.

"I'm sorry the way this turned out."

"Too little, too late," Irv offered dismissively, and the line clicked dead.

Thirty minutes later a thoroughly disheartened Charles Langdon had shaved and showered. A streak of purplish-blue had appeared below and around his swollen right eye. His jaw ached from Kyla's elbow smack and his head was ringing like a church bell on Sunday. A patch of red now showed on the bandage the nurse had applied to his forehead.

The ex-adman gingerly zipped his pants avoiding any pressure on his privates but failed.

"Oh Christ." He grimaced when the front of his pants rubbed his privates.

Charlie discovered the fridge contained some cheese, a half-litre of milk, four pieces of bread, and a cucumber. Sitting at the kitchen counter he finished off a cheese sandwich and considered he might as well get the hell out of Dodge before something else went wrong. In less than twenty-four hours he had lost his wife, his job, his best friend, and, if Kyla's lawyer was worth his salt, pretty well every remaining dollar. Funny to think that on Thursday night he was agonizing over the phone call from Tom Potter. That now seemed laughable.

Hopping into his Porsche he lowered the roof, donned his sunglasses, and let the sun pour on his face. Saturday morning traffic was light and he soon left behind all the skyscrapers in exchange for wide-sweeping vistas of corn stalks and stunning yellow fields of canola. After two hours he couldn't remember taking any exits, passing any cars, or seeing any signage. The engine purred, running free on the open road in the middle of the Canadian Shield. Uncountable coniferous forests and roadways cut a swath through a maze of boulders. Magnificent, entreating lakes would suddenly jump out of nowhere along Highway 11 like a landscape portrait by Tom Thomson or any of the Group of Seven painters. Along with each lake appeared cottages and boats and people fishing, canoeing, and swimming. And then in a moment they were in the rear view mirror and the 911 would cruise another twenty miles of the barrens touched only by paved highway and telephone wires before another body of water would appear.

The beauty of the day and breath-taking Northern Ontario Canadian Shield vistas distracted Charles Michael Langdon from dwelling on having lost everything he valued.

Chapter Six

Ingrid Petersson awoke very early that Saturday morning as Charlie Langdon's Porsche 911 sped northward from Toronto. So early did she rise that as she looked out her window, twinkling stars still adorned the heavens. The Swede breathed deeply and looked up at the dreamcatcher that hung above her bed.

Today, Saturday August 29th would have been her seventieth wedding anniversary. Twenty-five difficult years had passed since Henrik had entered Valhalla. It didn't matter that she was beloved and a fixture in the community surrounding Great Spirit Moon Lake. Her heart ached for Henrik and the people with whom she had shared life and laughter. As she approached her ninetieth year her health was deteriorating, her eyesight was weakening, her cholesterol levels were dangerous, her good ear was deafening, and there was that whole nasty business with the eight-inch aneurysm doctors had discovered on her renal artery. They had described it as being like a thin finger-shaped balloon that would grow until it ruptured, sending blood from the artery into her body cavity. When asked, "how long?" the two female doctors had given each other sideways glances and arrived at a timeframe of no more than two years.

That conversation had occurred twenty-two months earlier and Ingrid hadn't told a soul, not even her beloved goddaughter Cassandra Turner.

The Swedish gardener was appreciative that August 29th had finally arrived. Her runes had told her that this day, her seventieth anniversary would be the day to offer her life to the Gods. Ingrid Petersson had no intention of committing suicide because no Viking could take their life and expect to be welcomed in Valhalla. Rather, the Swede would leave it up to Odin whether she was to continue on Earth or enter Valhalla. Her intent was to force a decision to be taken one way or the other.

Ingrid crawled out of bed and dressed. As was her custom, she took a cup of coffee out onto the back porch and interpreted her runes, which strengthened her resolve to proceed with her plan. There was no cleaning or baking to be done. Her house was immaculate and over the past two days she had baked enough pies and cookies to feed an army. Her neighbours would serve these at her wake if the Gods chose to accept her into Valhalla so she could reunite with her husband and children.

The morning passed slowly and at 10:00 a.m. Ingrid walked to the chicken coop. She glanced down the lake and saw sailboats and canoes taking advantage of yet another glorious day. Opening the wire door, she reached down and asked one of her brown hens to step forward.

"Come my lady," she cooed to the hen, "I apologize but I need you," and with an expert flick of her wrists snapped its neck while she walked towards her orchard. Ingrid hung the fowl from her favourite tree and slit its throat. Blood trickled onto her right index finger and she drew a red line across her forehead and down each cheek.

Kneeling beneath the tree, Ingrid pulled her ancestors' runes from their leather charm pouch for the second time that morning. The Norse symbols were a comfort as she felt each piece. She selected twelve and cast them on the ground beneath the dead fowl. Praying to Odin and Thor she asked for grace and courage. Ingrid noticed that once again the symbols foretold of a stranger's arrival.

"Well, if you are coming into my life you had better do it quickly," the elderly Swede suggested aloud, but the only response was the chattering of a chipmunk somewhere near the pear trees. Gathering up her runes she replaced them in the charm pouch. It grieved her that she had no daughter to whom she would leave her runes. Ingrid Signalda Holmberg Petersson was the last Stonecaster of her ancestral line, and if Odin chose to take her to Valhalla, seven hundred years of tradition would come to an end this very day.

"Odin, hear me. My life is in your hands," Ingrid prayed, reaching inside her shirt for the two medallions that hung around her neck. Her fingers easily recognized the outline of a horse and a hammer. The horse was Odin's steed called Sleipnir and the hammer was Thor's weapon, Mjolnir. She rubbed them and repeated her prayers.

The last Stonecaster knelt and continued praying as the morning drew on and the sun moved to the south. As the hour of noon approached she arose and walked into her house. Ingrid placed the charm pouch on the fireplace mantel before letting her eyes wander across all her cherished possessions.

"It is time," she whispered. "Freyja, please give me courage."

* * *

After Irv Telfer had fired Charlie Langdon he looked across the desk at the well-dressed middle-aged woman sitting there. Leslie Ingram's drawn complexion showed the strain of having fired ten employees the previous afternoon. It cut her to the quick to have to inform hard working and loyal employees they were being terminated for no fault of their own. Five had almost broken down in the brief meetings, but all had conducted themselves with professionalism.

The stern expression on her face revealed that the VP of Human Resources hadn't been impressed by the way Irv had fired Charlie Langdon. Leslie reached across the desk and angrily slapped his forearm.

"Irv, sometimes you can be an asshole," she exclaimed, and her superior stared at her audacity.

Leslie walked across the room and looked out the window. A Dash-8 was taking off from the Billy Bishop Island Airport on its way to New York or Boston. She shook her head in great frustration.

"You and Kevin have made a rash decision to fire Langdon without fully understanding how this will hurt the agency."

"That's crap. Kevin and I totally get it," Telfer shot back, as he cleared off his desk. He had a golf game at noon and a Jays' game that started at 7:05 p.m. The Cardinals were in town.

"Well Irv, we've lost all this revenue and are about to terminate a team of very loyal, smart people. So just who do you think will help get us back on track and win new clients? You just fired the best guy for the job. Where do you think he'll go? Come on, use that pea-brain and think about it. Where will he go?"

Irv ignored her rudeness and Leslie continued.

"Directly across the street to our competitors. Not only did you hurt our new business chances by firing him but you've handed our competition a loaded gun which they will use against us. Good luck trying to sell this broken company to a multi-national."

Telfer knew it would be desperately hard to rebuild the agency. A client loss of this magnitude needed a scapegoat. Firing Charlie would hurt their chances at regaining the lost revenue, but it was a necessity to protect himself from wearing any of the blame. It was a simple act of self-preservation. Besides, he had done nothing to contribute to Potter's decision to fire the agency. Why should any of this fall to him?

* * *

The Porsche 911 Turbo S hugged the curves of the winding road and whipped briskly along the highway. Charlie had stopped to pick up a couple of cheeseburgers, onion rings, and a chocolate shake. The purplish bruising on his face had worsened making him look like someone had taken a baseball bat to him. His forehead throbbed and there was a ringing in his ear that varied across two notes.

The sun-filled skies shone as sounds of Bruno Mars played on the 911's Bose system, drowning out any semblance of reality. The nightmare of the previous twenty-four hours was foggy at best as he sat in the comfort and safety of the Porsche's cockpit. There were no thoughts of Kyla, divorce, Duane Michaels, Irv Telfer, or Alex Fanning. It was just good tunes, the incredible northern scenery, and the open road. As the small picturesque tourist town of Huntsville drew closer, Charlie considered getting a motel for a couple of days. It was not as if he had anywhere to be. The first thing he'd do after checking in was to phone his father.

A most charming setting appeared ahead as a lake revealed itself just beyond an array of spruce and oak trees. Charlie was captivated by the scene and pulled over to the gravelled shoulder of the road. The bright blue water was speckled with white sails and the lake seemed to be alive amongst a forest of richly greened trees. He turned off the motor and flicked on the emergency flashers.

Beyond the blinking of the flashers, outboard motors hummed as boats scooted across the lake perhaps a hundred metres from where the Porsche sat. Langdon could see people canoeing and sail boats everywhere. The view was exceptional. He pulled out his iPhone to take a picture when a very faint sound caught his attention. Charlie strained to hear. It took a moment but again he heard a plaintive, urgent cry for help.

Hopping over the passenger door, Charlie raced down the gravel siding of the road and barrelled through a bed of cattails whose sun-drenched stalks cut like hundreds of tiny razors at his bare arms. It took all of twenty seconds before he found himself standing on the grassy shoreline looking across a finger of the lake at a little girl with unusually long blond hair. The child wore a blue dress and was frantically pointing and calling out.

"Help!" the child screamed. "She's there in the water. Get her. Get her please!"

Charlie couldn't see anybody in the water yet the girl continued to call frantically.

"She's disappearing to the bottom. Nyk will get her. Hurry!"

The look of abject panic on the child's face convinced him this was no prank. Pulling off his sneakers, shirt, and pants he hastily waded into the water. The bottom was squishy and weedy.

"She's drowning," the child desperately shouted, and Charlie dove into the murky water, looking over at the girl for guidance. Visibility was four or five feet as he descended. A diluted ray of sunshine caught a flicker of yellow below him but his lungs demanded air forcing him to surface.

"Go get help," he shouted desperately at the child, unable to stop choking down water.

Kicking frantically, he re-descended to the weed-covered bottom of the lake. Where was the yellow? His instincts ordered him to surface for air but he kept hearing the girl, "she's ahead of you, don't give up." Unable to see anything, he clutched through the murkiness of the reeds that wrapped dangerously about his legs and arms. And then suddenly his fingers touched something rubbery. It was a yellow rain coat, inside of which was an old lady with long pale white hair that was undulating ghostlike with the movement of the water. Holding tightly to the collar of her coat, Langdon pulled towards the surface fighting the death clutch of the weeds. The drowning woman thrashed and clutched at his right arm until her face was within inches of his left shoulder. A tiny hand reached up and poked at his upper arm. For an instant their eyes locked through the brackish water and the two froze motionless in time. Then, simultaneously, they clutched each other and kicked for the surface. The sunlight was knifing through the water like a runway to the life-saving oxygen that awaited them. Charlie could feel life ebbing from his body but the girl's voice urged him.

"A little further Charles Michael. Don't let go of her," she encouraged.

But his lungs were finished and death was gripping him as he involuntarily began swallowing water. Convulsing uncontrollably, he shoved the woman's body above towards the surface, which in turn propelled him deeper. His last memory was of the woman's body being pulled from the water. After that he floated dreamlike until someone grabbed him by the hair. The next few minutes were a blur with people screaming, someone pushing on his chest, and water spewing from his lungs.

"He'll be okay," a voice shouted loudly. "Swallowed half the goddamn lake, eh." Charlie opened his eyes and found himself face down on a boat. A portly middle-aged man with a bad toupee was patting his back. His rescuer was in his early fifties, dressed in chinos and a blue Tiger Woods golf shirt. His nose was hawkish and too large for his unshaven face.

"The woman with the white hair," Charlie gasped. "Did you get the old woman?"

"Barrett got her to shore and Doc Miller is with her. You just 'bout drank half the lake, eh. I'm Phil Henderson."

Charlie took the offered towel and wiped his face. There was blood on it and he realized his forehead was bleeding. Henderson handed him a pair of sweat pants and a T-shirt. As Charlie pulled them on over his boxers he realized they were in the middle of a flotilla of small crafts. He looked past the boats to find the little girl on the shoreline.

"There was a girl who called for help."

"Little girl, eh? How old?" Phil Henderson asked, with a puzzled expression.

Charlie had to think a moment.

"I don't know, maybe eight or nine with long blond hair and a blue dress."

Phil shrugged his shoulders and lit a Marlboro which he deeply inhaled like it was to be his last. When he exhaled the stream of smoke seemed never-ending and continued to seep disgustingly from his nostrils as he responded. His own grandfather had smoked the same way, and when Charlie had asked to try, the old man had acquiesced on the condition that Charlie had to smoke a cigar. After vomiting for an hour and listening to the old man's laughter, Charlie Langdon vowed never to smoke again. A promise he had kept.

"I've lived here most of my life and know every cottager, eh. There's no kid like that here."

Charlie suddenly remembered what Phil had just done.

"You saved my life. Thank you."

Henderson grinned and blushed a little. "No big deal, eh?"

As Phil piloted his twenty-one-foot Malibu Wakesetter towards shore he chatted about the woman Charlie had just pulled from the water.

"The woman you saved is Ingrid Petersson and she and her husband settled on the lake around 1949. Back then, there were still about a hundred Ojibwe living off the land at the far end," Phil stated, pointing up the lake. "Most people think Ingrid is either monstrously eccentric or completely daffy because she believes in elves, fairies, and Gods like Odin and Thor. Talks up a storm with animals and birds like they were her friends."

More boats, canoes, and kayaks continued to arrive to see what all the excitement was about. A pair of Bombardier Jet Skis zoomed up sending a spray of water into the air.

Phil ran the Malibu Wakesetter up beside a half-submerged cement dock and tossed a rope around an old post on the shore. Twenty to thirty crafts of various sizes and makes had now congregated along the shoreline. As Charlie stepped unsteadily onto dry land, he noticed a small pail suspended by a hook on a post just at the water's edge. It was filled to the brim with small finishing nails. The man who caught the rope tossed by Phil introduced himself as Barrett Sanford. His unkempt mop of hair looked like it hadn't encountered a brush or comb this century. Barrett was stocky with broad shoulders and a swarthy complexion that spoke of countless hours under the sun without any UV protection. Unlike Henderson's sporty wardrobe, Sanford wore work jeans with a rip at one knee topped with a round-necked cotton T-shirt sprinkled with what might have been oil stains. He looked like he had seen better days and pointed at the bucket of nails.

"The nails sc-sc-scare away evil sp-spirits," he clarified, with a pronounced stutter. The man had a friendly face and sported the unmistakeable smell of *Old Spice*. When a more youthful Charles Langdon had spent summers at his grandfather's cottage he'd come across lots of men like Barrett—poorly educated and not too bright, but willing to give you the shirt off their back.

The adman cocked his head.

"Come again sir?"

Barrett chuckled quietly at the mention of *sir* and looked over at Phil Henderson who had disembarked and come over to join them.

"Our Ingrid b-believes whole-heartedly in sp-spirits. We know they d-don't exist b-but to Ingrid they are as real as you and m-me."

The dapper man with the toupee added his two cents worth.

"At night the old girl leaves food on her back porch for some abominable ghost named Tomte who oversees her property. And that bucket of nails Barrett was telling you about. Whenever Ingrid walks near the lake she tosses a nail in the water and curses a mean streak at some villain named 'Nyk.' It seems you scare him away by tossing a piece of steel at him. She's almost ninety and a bit addled, eh." Henderson touched an index finger to his forehead to emphasize his point.

Charlie selected a nail and tossed it in the water.

"Can't hurt," he supposed, as Barrett stared at Charlie's forehead.

"Doc Miller will f-fix your c-cut. He's st-st-stitched up m-more k-kids on this lake than you can sh-sh-shake a st-st-st-stick at."

"What's your name son?" Phil inquired, casually reaching up his right hand to ensure his toupee was sitting properly. Charlie noticed that the man's nails looked manicured with a light coat of nail lacquer.

"Charlie Langdon."

"Where from?"

"Toronto."

Henderson cupped his hands and shouted, "Hey everyone, listen up, eh. First of all, Ingrid's okay. She will come out spitting mad if you trample her garden so for Christ sakes don't go near her roses. Second, don't forget about the free hot dogs and sodas at my dealership tomorrow from ten 'til six. Got some great deals on Escorts and Escapes. You should think about it with your kids heading off to university. Oh yeah, and here's Charlie Langston from Toronto. He pulled Ingrid out of the lake."

Charlie didn't correct the emcee before a cacophony of cheers arose. Air horns blasted in competition with one another until Phil raised his hands to hush the crowd. Charlie wondered if he might be the mayor.

"Anyone got a ten-year-old blond girl wearing a blue dress visiting with them?"

The cottagers milling about stared blankly and others started their motors wafting white clouds of exhaust into the air. A few pulled away from the flotilla creating a chorus of wave swells against the shore.

"My car is somewhere over there," Charlie mumbled, pointing absently. "I'm not sure where I went in but my clothes and my keys are somewhere over there."

"I'll t-take care of it," Barrett promised, before hustling off along the shoreline like the White Rabbit hurrying to avoid being late.

People crowded around Charlie and some shook his hand or planted kisses on his cheek. It seemed everyone knew the white-haired lady in the yellow jacket.

Out of his peripheral vision he saw someone approaching fast. It was an attractive middle-aged woman who looked totally out of place from the crowd that had gathered. She was dressed as if she was going to a party wearing mid-height heels and a bright floral dress that hugged her plump figure too tightly at the waist and then flared out like those skirts women wore in the 1950s. As she made a beeline towards him her hips swivelled like she was dancing across the yard. Like every other red-blooded male on the property, his eyes locked on six-inch cleavage and breasts that spilled out from a low cut top. The newcomer smiled revealing incredibly white teeth that shone like a lighthouse beacon from a heavily made-up face. Her lips had that awkward puffiness from too much filler and her eyebrows reached unnaturally upward betraying a forehead lift. She wore shoulder-length hair that was far too black for her age. The intense smell of her perfume preceded her. Coco Chanel would have not have embraced how liberally her namesake fragrance had been applied.

"What's your name again? I couldn't make out what Phil was yattering about," the woman asked in a very nasal tone as she stepped directly into Charlie, elbowing two other cottagers out of the way. They relented, oblivious to the rudeness they had come to expect from her.

"Charlie Langdon."

"Well Charlie Langdon, I'm Lizzie Grant. Aren't you the hero," the woman exclaimed. "In my book, heroes deserve to be kissed."

With that, Lizzie took Charlie by the face and kissed him directly on the mouth, slowly pressing her body against his chest.

"Lizzie, that's enough, eh," Henderson admonished sharply. "Let the man breathe."

The woman eased her grip and flashed her eyes indignantly towards Henderson.

"Jealous Philly? Marge should have mentioned that your toupee is on backwards," she taunted, and as Lizzie Grant sashayed off, she turned and coyly blew Charlie a kiss. "You're a hero Charlie Langdon."

Both men quietly stared at her as she disappeared around the corner of the stone house.

"Ya, the woman's got a killer body but she's the biggest tease on the lake, so watch yourself around her. Her husband Roy is one of my best friends and one of the most decent men you'll ever meet, eh? But he'd have to say the same," Henderson observed, as he meandered off, secretively ensuring his toupee was sitting correctly atop his head. The remaining cottagers shook Charlie's hand and then headed back to their crafts now that the excitement and commotion had ebbed. The adman from Toronto found himself standing alone in the Swedish woman's front yard.

It was a large stone house with two stories and a big old-fashioned porch that wrapped completely around the front and sides. Well-painted, sturdy storm shutters bracketed every window. A porch swing moved back and forth with the slight breeze coming down the lake. A stone walkway made of thousands of carefully selected pebbles led from the water's edge towards the front steps. On either side of the walkway were waist-high bushes of bright purple lavender that led to climbing rose bushes that lapped the railings of the porch. Some of the stems on the rose bushes were thicker than his wrist.

Four humongous oaks stood like sentinels guarding each corner of the house. Their branches reached across to the others like they were holding hands, protecting what stood beneath.

By now, most of the boats had departed, leaving enough gasoline exhaust to choke a horse. A short, rotund man with a cigar clamped in his mouth appeared in the front doorway. He was bald as a cue ball and motioned Charlie to come to the house. When Charlie drew near, the man withdrew a lighter and set the large cigar aflame. He looked intently at the blood-encrusted cut across Charlie's forehead and then gently poked at the bruise on his cheek, his swollen jaw and the scrape across his nose.

"That's quite a gash. Good stitch-work, but it's been torn open. You get a tetanus shot and X-ray?" the cigar-smoking doctor asked in a very raspy voice. His horrific breath was crippling.

"Yes to shot, no to X-ray. The doctor in Toronto told me to come back if my headaches lasted until Sunday," Charlie replied, turning his head to avoid the invasive acrid smell of the cigar smoke. The doctor was one of those men who could talk, breathe, and exhale all at the same time. "Is the lady going to be okay?"

"Yes Ingrid will be fine. She's one tough old bird and won't be worse for the wear after her ordeal today. What happened to your face?"

"Pot of flowers fell on my head yesterday morning."

Doc Miller inspected the wound and reached into a black case that was brought to him by another of the locals introduced as Pete Duffield. The doctor's eyes betrayed scepticism.

"Pot of flowers, eh?" he questioned. "Angle of the bruising tells me you were either on the ground or it was pitched directly at your face from someone standing above you. And this bruising around your cheekbone and jaw coupled with the dried blood in your ear tells me the flowerpot must have hit you several times. You must have really pissed off those flowers."

Charlie's facial expression revealed nothing, but the doctor knew that discretion was the better part of valour.

"You've got some ripped stitching I'll have to fix up. It won't take a minute."

Miller pulled on a pair of blue latex gloves and ripped open a white package containing a sterilized needle and stitching thread. Pete Duffield returned carrying a mickey of Old Hickory and after Miller took a slug he handed it to Charlie and motioned for him to do the same.

"You look tough enough and Old Hickory is the best calming agent I know. I'm not going to waste time with freezing and I'll be doing it the old fashion way without a staple gun so don't move unless you want an eye-full of needle. This'll hurt like hell for about fifteen seconds, so 'man up.'"

Despite the intense pain of having a needle stuck in and out of his forehead, Charlie did not budge. His eyes involuntarily began to water.

"I'm going to spray antiseptic and then bandage you up," he advised. "My three stitches aren't going to dissolve like the originals. You're going to have to go to your doctor and have them removed in ten days. No booze or driving for a couple of days. This new bandage will have to be changed in two days. If you have a severe headache I want you to go immediately to the hospital. Got it?"

"Got it sir. What do I owe you?"

The bald man with the girth of a sumo wrestler and the breath of an ashtray laughed.

"Folks would lynch me if I charged the man who pulled Ingrid Petersson from the lake," Miller retorted. "This one's on me."

A familiar face arrived and handed Charlie his clothes and car keys.

"That's some P-Por-Porsche," Barrett smiled, his face flushed from hustling back around the lake. "T-typical confusing German vehicle. Why? B-b-because it t-took me t-ten min-minutes to get it st-started and then another f-five to p-put the d-d-damned roof up."

"Where is it now?" Charlie inquired nervously as he gratefully accepted his belongings.

"Phil's lot. B-be p-p-perfectly s-safe."

"Lucky that doctor lives close," Charlie commented, as the bald-headed cigar smoker climbed into his fifteen-foot aluminum boat.

"D-Doc Miller's lived here for years. B-best ve-vet in the area."

Charlie looked sideways.

"He's a veterinarian, not a doctor?"

"How b-be we g-go inside?" Barrett suggested, ignoring the question. "Ingrid will have something t-tasty in the p-pantry. It's ab-bout t-time you g-got introduced."

* * *

Alex Fanning squirmed on the toilet seat cradling the plastic-bag lined waste paper basket in his hands. His eyes were bloodshot, his hair askew, his mouth tasted like vomit, and his haggard face gave the appearance of a much older man who hadn't slept for a week. For all of his public bravado and ice-king confidence his insides were paying the price for bolting from his responsibility as CEO of NovaRose International Research and escaping an arrest warrant. Now, as he crouched on the toilet, his bowels unleashed a painful stream of water.

Alex regretted the way the conversation with his mother had ended. He knew she was right. Bill and Rose Langdon would have told him the same thing—never run from a problem. But his father had convinced him that there was only one course of action. The younger Fanning male had no intention of losing hundreds of millions of dollars and having a gorilla-sized cellmate rent out his backside for a pack of cigarettes.

There was a knock at the bathroom door as his fellow embezzler asked if there was anything he needed. Alex mumbled thanks and told his CFO to take Linda for breakfast. There was a diner just down the street. Alex, Jay, and his wife Linda were sharing a room in the Lakeview Motel on the seedier outskirts of Toronto. It wasn't exactly lodgings to which they were accustomed. The Lakeview rented rooms by the hour, so when Jay's alluring wife rented the room, the pock-faced manager smelling of weed thought nothing of it. The place was poorly constructed, and the three listened through a sleepless night to sounds of the local working girls earning their money.

The trio had four more hours to kill until the private jet would fly them to a restricted airstrip south of Dubai. It was Ernest's long time friendship with the Chairman of one of the United Arab Emirates' largest banking conglomerates, CFMT, that had been brought to bear.

Richard Strickland didn't blink an eye when asked to make the travel arrangements for the embezzlers' escape.

"Wear a hat and sunglasses, Jay," Alex ordered. "Linda, cover your hair. Our faces are all over the news. Don't be talking with anyone and don't do anything stupid."

"Can we bring you back something to eat?"

The thought of eggs turned his stomach and Alex lurched and dry vomited into the wastebasket. He no longer even tried to conceal the sound of his retching.

Chapter Seven

Intriguing sensations touched Charles Langdon the moment he stepped through Mrs. Petersson's front screen door. A floor of ten-inch wide oak planks spanned the length of the house leading to the most incredible fireplace. The hearth was easily six feet tall, seven feet wide, and three feet deep. It was the olden kind of fireplace where "women-folk" did the cooking. The stonework was artistic with each shape and colour carefully selected and expertly mortared in place. The craftsmanship was like nothing he had ever seen.

Six feet above the base of the fireplace top was a twelve-foot wide oak mantel on which a plethora of objects rested. There was a book on the *History of Sweden*, what appeared to be a golden golf ball, two pairs of baby-sized moccasins, a bowl of acorns, a leather-encased compass, and, a World War II German army knife complete with a swastika on the handle. Suspended on the wall above were old-fashioned sets of steel fur traps, a shotgun, a two-bladed axe with a broken handle, and a framed photograph of a merchant ship.

Charlie turned from the fireplace. Every corner, nook and cranny had something of interest that caught his attention. There were duck decoys, wooden canoe paddles and snowshoes, ceramic flower pots, toboggans and skates, fishing equipment, a pile of odd-shaped stones and rocks sitting in a wooden box to the right of the fireplace, a wall of firewood and kindling sitting to the left of the fireplace, and wolf pelts hanging over the backs of hand-crafted oak rocking chairs. He picked up one of the larger pelts that had to have come from an enormous black wolf.

Each of the non-fireplace walls was adorned with paintings, some of which Charlie recognized as Norse symbols. There were other more rustic paintings on flattened birch bark showing various scenes of what Charlie surmised to be Great Spirit Moon Lake and the surrounding area. Most interestingly to him were five portraits of stern-faced Aboriginals dressed in full regalia. The quality of the artist's skill was exceptional.

A sudden fatigue overwhelmed Charlie as he became aware of people talking in the room beside the kitchen. With some effort, he walked on rubbery legs across the oak floor into a sparkling clean kitchen with a pine table and six chairs. Yet another stellar view of the lake was revealed through an enormous bay window that stretched across the kitchen. The counters overflowed with pies, thickly iced cakes, and Tupperware containers filled with cookies.

Being early afternoon, the sun was heading towards the west making the cottage bright and comfortably toasty. Sunbeams streamed through large front windows that were adorned with colourful dangling beads, Christmas decorations, and crystal chandelier prisms that grabbed the sunbeams and transformed them into a tapestry of rainbows across the east wall. It was living art that recreated itself with every shift of the clouds and filtering of the sun through the window accessories.

As the chatter from the adjoining room tapered off a steady stream of women unexpectedly flooded out and made their way to the front door. Along the way, each stopped to shake his hand and offer thanks. One, who introduced herself as Anne-Marie Downey, advised him that Ingrid was resting in her bedroom and wanted to thank him.

Charlie nodded politely and tepidly walked towards the room beside the kitchen.

"Come in," a tiny voice called from within.

Charlie stepped forward but hesitated at the doorway.

"Well, are you coming in?" asked the lady propped up by a phalange of fluffy white pillows that looked like they were swallowing her whole. A duvet was pulled up to her waist despite the heat in the house. An oxygen tank stood beside the bed. A long plastic tube wound its way towards a pillow where the oxygen mask rested. The bedroom reflected the decor of the living room and was crammed to the hilt with a lifetime of things of interest.

Charlie walked to the end of the bed and put his hands on one of the four corner brass knobs and smiled. The lady in the bed looked like an old grandmother who had aged gracefully. She had high cheekbones, a perfectly sculpted nose, a gentle chin, and distinctively vibrant green eyes that revealed a clever mind yet exuded calmness and tranquility. Her skin was tanned and taut but not wrinkly like most old people. Well-defined age lines framed her eyes and mouth. Two silver combs with ornate carvings held long hair in place. What a delicate beauty she must have been in her youth.

"Do you always stare so intently at people when you have yet to be introduced?" the white-haired Swede inquired, interrupting the moment.

"How rude of me," he responded contritely, his cheeks blushing in embarrassment, "my name is Charlie."

"Just plain Charlie? Is there more than that, perhaps?"

Charlie laughed, stepped to the side of the bed and held out his right hand.

"My name is Charles Michael Langdon. I'm from Toronto and I work in the advertising industry."

The lady tilted her head as if she had not heard him and her eyes widened. She took his hand with a surprisingly strong grip. She had a silver ring on every finger including her thumb.

"Could you repeat that? I am hard of hearing on my left side," she asked.

"My name is Charles Michael Langdon. I'm from Toronto," he spoke slowly and louder this time, enunciating each word more clearly.

The woman in the sea of pillows looked perplexed.

"Charles Michael? That is truly your name?" she repeated slowly. "How the Gods play with us."

The woman cleared her throat and leaned forward, trying to put his name aside for a moment.

"My name is Ingegard Signilda Holmberg Petersson," she announced almost lyrically, and her eyes flashed the most incredible shade of the sea.

The handsome young man standing before her smiled. "That's a mouthful. I see why people call you Ingrid."

Ingegard Petersson pursed her lips and lay back into her pillows but didn't let go of Charlie's hand, gently pulling forward until he was perched on the side of the bed. Now it was her turn to stare, her eyes scrutinizing each feature of his face like she was preparing to paint his portrait. She ignored the bandage across his forehead and the bruising beneath his eyes and around his jaw. There was a story he would tell when he was ready.

"Swedes have many names. Signilda was my grandmother. Holmberg was my parents' surname. It means "Island Mountain" since I was raised on the island of Gotland in the Bering Sea. My ancestors lived on the side of a volcanic mountain when Vikings struck terror into your ancestors. Petersson was my husband's family name."

Charlie could hear a more pronounced Scandinavian accent as she spoke her names.

"Charles Michael, you are how tall?"

"Six feet, two inches," he answered.

"My husband was inches taller than you with mammoth shoulders and arms like a mid-sized oak tree. He could lift the front of our truck two feet off the ground. When we built this house he constructed the doorways to be seven feet tall. Did you notice?"

Charlie looked back at the door, now noticing its abnormal height.

"My husband's name was Henrik Olaf Petersson. We were married forty-five years. It would have been seventy this very day if he were still alive."

"That's a long time," Charlie answered as he considered his own shattered marital situation.

"Not long enough," Ingrid reflected. "My Henko has been gone twenty-five years, died at the age of eighty-five on Christmas Day in '88. His heart gave out while he was chopping firewood."

"I'm sorry," Charlie responded sincerely, and the woman saw that he was.

"Yes, you truly are. Your name is honestly Charles Michael?"

"Yes ma'am."

"I have the feeling that you have been experiencing hardships lately and I am not referring to you jumping in the lake to save my life. Perhaps the injuries I see are reminders of those troubles?"

Langdon cocked his head in response to her odd yet intuitive question.

"I've had easier times," he responded truthfully with a deep sigh that brought a smile to the tiny face.

"And now that you are here, you will have easier times again," she responded, accepting that the stranger foretold in her runes had just come into her life.

The two remained silent for several minutes looking out her window. Like the other rooms, the window was adorned with colourful beads and prisms with, of course, the strange bowls of acorns on the windowsill.

Curiosity got the better of him and Charlie let his eyes wander. He counted twelve dreamcatchers in various sizes and colours and an equal number of nosegays of lavender hanging from the ceiling. On the table by her bed was an oversized knife the size of a small machete. The hilt was richly leather bound and the knife was encased in a beaded sheathe.

Ingrid allowed her guest to inspect her inner sanctum. It was a pleasure to watch him take an interest in her belongings.

"That knife belonged to Niigaanii, one of our first Ojibwe friends," she explained, a touch of fatigue and perhaps even melancholy behind her words. "His wife Miigwaans was my Canadian sister."

Charlie realized that while his hostess needed to rest she seemed intent on having a conversation.

"Niigaanii saved me and my husband from certain death," Ingrid continued, and she tenderly patted his arm. "And today, you delivered me from Nykkjen who was soon to claim my soul. Perhaps Freyja sent you since I gave sacrifice this morning. When I saw Odin's image on your shoulder, I knew you were sent from the Gods. But now your name only adds to the puzzle."

Charlie sat staring politely at her.

Ingrid understood his confusion. "There is much to explain, and I realize that I must be sounding senile, perhaps?"

Charlie shook his head.

"No ma'am, we're both tired," he responded politely. "Can I tell you something?"

"Of course," the lady replied curiously.

Charlie leaned over the side of the bed. "When we were underwater I didn't know if I could save us both. Those guys in the boats are the heroes, not me."

Ingrid squeezed Charlie's hand tightly.

"But you did not let go of me to save yourself . . . did you?"

He lowered his eyes and shook his head.

"And you thrust me upward to safety realizing it might be the end of you?"

Charles lowered his eyes and nodded.

"And because of you, are we not here talking about our adventure?"

"Yes we are," Charlie answered, with a grateful smile.

Ingrid's face had a lovely warm glow and her eyes twinkled.

"Viking tradition says that when one saves another's life they join as family for eternity. But you know that."

"I know that?" the adman inquired.

"You have knowledge of Norse ways. Odin's face is burned onto your shoulder."

Charlie was surprised. It was his tattoo that had caught the woman's eye below the surface when he first clutched her yellow coat. But it was hardly what she thought it was.

In the fall term of grade twelve, an inebriated Charlie Langdon and eight school chums agreed to get a tattoo of their championship High School team, the Northern Vikings. By the time he woke the next morning he had a vicious hangover and absolutely no recollection of the previous night's escapades. When he staggered into his bathroom he discovered a large white bandage adhered to his left shoulder. As the horribly hung-over teenager removed the bandage, his father walked into the bathroom and both stared at the tri-colour tattoo of an angry-looking Viking. Bill Langdon even poked the inflamed shoulder.

"Tender?" his father asked facetiously, and Charlie winced in agony.

"Jesus Christ," he cried out in pain. "Don't touch it."

His dad inspected at the workmanship trusting that his son had at least gone to a reputable tattoo artist. "Well, it's done now, so there's not much to talk about," Bill commented, before walking out of the room. Charlie returned to his mirror and studied the angry Norseman with the fantastic beard and steel-tough eyes.

And now, more than ten years later, an old Swedish lady living in the Muskokas mistook him for having Norse blood because of it.

Charlie clarified, "This tattoo is the symbol of my high school football team: the Northern Vikings."

Ingrid smiled. His explanation was inconsequential. She had prayed to the Gods and dreamt of Odin's face seven nights passing.

"No matter," she whispered, as she placed the clear plastic oxygen mask over her nose and mouth. She inhaled deeply, and the inside of her plastic oxygen mask clouded with condensation. Momentarily, she asked him a question.

"By the way, Charles Michael, how did you know I was in the water? You could not see the front of my property from the highway."

Charlie looked into her eyes. "I stopped my car to admire the view and heard screaming. There was a little girl in a blue dress standing on the shore opposite your house. She pointed to where you were and I dove in."

Ingrid leaned forward.

"A pretty girl in a blue dress with long blond hair?" the muffled voice asked.

"Yes, blond hair and a blue dress."

"With long sleeves?" Ingrid clarified.

"Yes, now that you mention it. I remember wondering why she was wearing a dress on such a hot day."

Ingrid's eyes began to water and her head shook slowly from side to side.

"Did I say something wrong?" he asked concernedly.

Ingrid reached for a tissue from the side table and dabbed her eyes.

"Charles, we have much to talk about. But for now, go put on a pot of coffee and pull down the Tupperware container on the top of the fridge. You like cookies, perhaps?"

He nodded and glanced at his watch. He had to find a motel or plan on a long drive back to the city.

"Good," she sniffled. "Lizzie Grant offered to bring our dinner at six. It will be just you and me. Doc will stop in before bedtime. You will be staying tonight and I do not have the strength to argue. Anne-Marie put clean sheets on the bed and fresh towels in the bathroom. If you do not have a shaving kit or pyjamas, Lizzie will bring over some of Roy's."

Charlie opened his mouth to argue.

"I am not asking. Phone whoever is expecting you and tell them you are staying with a friend on Great Spirit Moon Lake. Now, see about that coffee while I check the inside of my eyelids for cracks."

Ingrid retrieved an iPod from under her pillow. Popping the white buds in her ears she touched the screen. Puccini filled her head as the oxygen-masked face reclined into the pillows. How the Gods were playing with her. Odin's face appearing in her dreams, the runes telling her of a stranger coming into her life, Odin's image burnt on the man's shoulder, his given names, and a phantom of her long-dead daughter being the portal to her rescue. Ingrid closed her eyes as *La Boheme* lulled her to sleep.

When Charlie Langdon returned with the coffee and cookies the old woman's breathing was deep and steady. Careful not to slam the screen door, he went out onto the porch and set the tray down on the wicker table. Pouring a cup he wondered about the blond-haired girl in the blue dress and why the old lady had found his name so peculiar. The last twenty-four hours had been like a bizarre episode of *The Twilight Zone.* He kept expecting to awaken.

Chapter Eight

"Listen to me please. You don't understand what he is capable of," the older woman offered cautiously, but her only child had long since stopped listening. Her daughter could be so infuriating when she adopted her know-it-all attitude. The thin, gaunt-looking mother raised her hand and snapped her fingers to get Tessa's attention. "He won't think twice about ruining you like he did me. What if this goes wrong and he discovers your connection to me?"

Her twenty-four-year-old daughter looked in the mirror, happy with the attractive reflection. Her makeup was flawless, her bobbed auburn hair was perfect, and the expensive Vera Wang navy blue suit was a spectacular fit and very thinning. It cut her two inches above the knee. At five feet, two inches, Tessa had to make every inch count. She looked at her mother and wondered how Phaidra had come up this outfit and all the others in the closet.

"I look great," she boasted confidently, turning to the side to admire her butt. "Tell me I don't. Mom, where did you get these fabulous clothes? What did you have to do?"

Phaidra McTavish would never own up to what she had done in return for the beautiful outfit Tessa modelled or the nine others in the closet. Her child looked supremely professional but feminine with her trim figure, lean legs, and slight hips. It was the perfect outfit for her daughter's first day of her new job at Blackmore, Craig and Fanning LLP on Monday.

Phaidra McTavish remembered a time twenty years ago when she wore outfits just like this, and truth be told she had worn them better. She had boasted a fuller more womanly body. At Tessa's age, Phaidra couldn't walk down the street without being propositioned. Phaidra had learned how to act, walk, smile, and tease like a woman by the time she was eighteen. No backseats and boy-men for her. She set out to find a man who could satisfy her physically, emotionally, and financially. After securing her first job at Blackmore and Craig LLP, Phaidra thought she had hit pay dirt. The young partner's name was Ernest Fanning and he came from a stinking rich family. He had been practising law for seven years and looked the way a man should. He was handsome beyond belief in $2,000 suits and was built like a professional athlete. The other office girls chatted that he got around which, to Phaidra, was more of a challenge. While studying to be an executive secretary she spent most of her day plotting on how to get the firm's star junior partner into her bed. Ernest Fanning's recent society-page marriage didn't hamper Phaidra's ambitions, or the bridegroom's lustful nature.

They became lovers. Phaidra's lawyer showered her with expensive presents and approached lovemaking with a vivid imagination. For months, the two revelled in their illicit and symbiotic relationship. Their affair could have gone on indefinitely, but in a split second, Phaidra blew it with just enough cocaine for a couple of lines. She thought Fanning might like to try some to heighten his sexual gratification but her lover's reaction was visceral. The thought of drugs enraged him, given the risk it posed to his name and career. After flushing the cocaine down the toilet, his temper exploded like a volcano erupting. Despite Phaidra's heartfelt apology and tears, Ernest told her to never contact him again. A day later she was fired for incompetence when a file mysteriously disappeared from her desk, despite her having locked it within her desk the night before. Being dismissed for negligence from Blackmore and Craig LLP was a death knell to her career. Her life spiralled downward at an incredible velocity. Without a steady income, she blew through her savings account, pawned all the jewellery Ernest had given her, downsized her apartment, and sold all of her furniture. She discovered that parties were a great place to make a few bucks from sexually frustrated husbands. But soon she had to lay off wild nights when her health took a turn and she was unable to keep anything inside. Phaidra scoured the wanted ads and accepted a secretarial post at a small family accounting firm. The work was easy, except that the two older Ukrainian partners expected something "extra" in exchange for her bi-weekly paycheque.

And now, a much older—and badly used—Phaidra McTavish pleaded desperately with her girl to reconsider her risky scheme.

"Mom, we've been through this a hundred times," Tessa reiterated slowly, before turning from the mirror. Her rail-thin, anaemic mother looked ten years older than her true age of forty-nine. Tessa's feelings towards her mother were a confusing mixture of pity, anger, ambivalence, disappointment, and loyalty. The daughter had long since given up on reforming her or searching the streets and back alleys when Phaidra hadn't come home. Tessa had come to realize that only a drunk who wants to be helped could be helped. What perplexed Tessa most was how her unemployed mother had a constant supply of booze and somehow arrived home with these expensive outfits.

"Are we supposed to live the rest of our lives in this crummy apartment with hallways that smell like cat pee? Your health insurance is gone. We have no money, and I have huge college debts. I can't keep doing three jobs at once. You know how hard I worked to put myself through the last four years at Humber College to get my Bachelor of Applied Arts in Paralegal Studies. You sat around and drank while I put in eighty-hour weeks."

Phaidra started scratching uncontrollably at her forearm until inklings of blood appeared. She thought of the bottle of Jack Daniels hidden beneath the sink in the bathroom. It was the last of her cache until her Monday appointment. Her tongue instinctively licked at her upper lip, imagining the feel of the brown liquid on her tongue. She anxiously began rubbing the top of her thighs.

"We'll find a way. I'll get a job," she offered, instantly regretting words that were like a red cape in front of a bull.

Tessa reached over and grabbed her mother's hand.

"Get real Mom, you know you can't hold down a job for more than a week, and only God knows how you are getting booze."

Her mother pursed her lips shamefully and longingly looked down the hallway towards the bathroom.

"I'm afraid something will go wrong once you're inside his law firm. He treats Blackmore, Craig and Fanning like his personal harem."

"Mom, I've been planning this for years. We are going to make him pay. Ernest Fanning destroyed your health, your reputation, and your life."

Her mother covered her face with her hands and began rocking to and fro.

"Enough!" Phaidra cried out. "You don't need to tell me what he did to me. I was there. You weren't."

"You're right, I wasn't there," her daughter responded calmly. "No one should have had to go through what happened to you. If he hadn't gotten you fired you might not have gotten pregnant with that creep of a Ukrainian boss you had. But then, maybe I would have had a childhood instead of working two jobs from the time I turned ten. Maybe I would not have had to wear the same clothes day in and day out. Maybe I would have had a house to come home to, and parents who took care of me, and had a meal on the table each night."

Phaidra was only partially listening as her nails went back to her forearm.

"It's not like we've got a lot of options. If you can come up with a better plan than mine, I am all ears."

Tessa walked over to the kitchen table and retrieved her laptop. She withdrew an attractive pen from her suit jacket and unscrewed the bottom half revealing what appeared to be a memory stick. Smiling at her mother, she inserted the pen into one of the three USB ports on the side of her Dell Studio XPS. Momentarily, a box appeared on screen requesting directions. She pressed "Play from the beginning" and motioned for her mother to look at the screen. Instantly, a full colour recording of the beginning of their conversation appeared on the laptop with her mother's warning.

"You don't understand what he is capable of. He's won't think twice about ruining you like he did me. What if this goes wrong?"

Tessa let it run for a few minutes.

"The pen cost me $130 and has four gigabytes and a three-hour battery. It'll record video and sound up to fifteen square meters. As added insurance I got this," Tessa boasted, removing what appeared to be a Bluetooth ear bud for her cell.

"This also records audio and video. It cost eighty-five dollars. It's got four gigabytes and a lithium battery that'll last four hours. It dates and times everything it records and downloads onto my computer just like the pen. Everything I face will be recorded. So, Mom, I've got two devices to capture this bastard."

Phaidra picked up the earpiece and looked at it.

"Where did you get these?"

"Online. Where else?"

Phaidra pushed the end of the pen and was surprised to find that it actually wrote.

"Ernest Fanning is an extremely dangerous person."

The young woman stared intently at her mother.

"So am I. Now stop that goddamned scratching."

Chapter Nine

Great Spirit Moon Lake grew peaceful as that time rolled around when children wondered what was for dinner. The sun was moving lower into the western sky, and the boaters and swimmers appeared to have had enough of the day. Even the dogs were too overwhelmed by the heat to bark and had found a shady place to pass the time.

Charlie Langdon sat comfortably on the porch swing. The breathtaking view from Ingrid's cottage had to be the best on the lake. One could look down the entire length of Great Spirit Moon Lake that had to be six miles long and maybe two miles wide. Most properties along the lake had fifty-foot waterfront footage while Ingrid's frontage had to be at least 250 feet wide with a fifty-foot sandy beach. Up and down the lake houses dotted the shoreline, each different in its own respect in size and construction. Some were white-board bungalows while others were 1960s-ish two-story red brick. There were some newer stone renovations with patios and upper story cedar decks. Docks of cement or treated wood jutted out into the lake making the shoreline appear to have fingers reaching into the water. Beyond those man-made interferences on Great Spirit Moon Lake, a dense forest bordered and reflected along the gleaming surface of the lake.

But Ingrid Petersson's house and property captivated him most with its white birch and oaks that stood majestically overlooking the house and shoreline. Her garden boasted a cavalcade of thickly branched roses, giant bushes of lavender, and patches of seven-foot-tall sunflowers. Charlie walked down the steps and the fragrance was like strolling through the perfume section of a department store. Off the east side of the cottage was a vegetable garden surrounded by a chain link fence. He determined there were approximately 1,200 square feet of clearly defined rows of corn, potatoes, and tomatoes. Overhanging the garden was clear plastic tubing that crisscrossed the rows of vegetables serving as a very ingenious irrigation system. He walked around the west side and discovered more fruit-bearing trees. Under one of the trees a dead chicken hung by a cord. Its throat had been cut. Charlie walked around it and returned to the wrap-around porch with its ornately carved railings and spindles. Bundles of drying lavender hung from various hooks suspended from the ceiling. Hand-painted ceramic pots lined the length of the porch and contained shorter rose shrubs in a rainbow of colours. Wind chimes made of seashells hung at each corner of the veranda.

Having forgotten about the dead chicken hanging from the apple tree, Charlie reached for another cookie and came up empty handed. He'd polished off the whole plate.

"My car," he suddenly remembered, and wiping his mouth on his shirt he set out to find Phil Henderson's property. As he walked around the base of the lake he happened upon the man with the horrible stutter tinkering on the outboard motor of a twenty-foot fibreglass fishing boat.

"Hey Barrett," he called out, and the man with his hands inside the Evinrude motor hopped up and smiled broadly.

"Hey Charlie. Be-bet you're after your c-car. C-come on, I'll w-w-walk with you," Barrett greeted with a welcoming smile, and with a quick wipe of the grease off his hands he led the younger man down a gravel road.

Phil Henderson's place was one of the larger, newer cottage compounds on the lake. It was on about an acre but lacked Ingrid's view and garden. Charlie's 911 was parked in the shade under a giant poplar in the corner of a parking lot overflowing with vehicles and boat trailers. Around his Porsche there was a new midnight black Toyota Sequoia, a white Tahoe, numerous Ford 150s, a brand new hunter green Chevy Avalanche, a silver Buick Enclave, and two Acura MDXs. A KIA Sorento was unloading a motorboat off the back of its boat trailer into the water. A couple of Yamaha dirt bikes were chained to an old cement mixer and a front-end loading Caterpillar stood in a trio of spruces.

"Old Phil has d-done well for his f-family," Barrett bragged, without envy. "He averages ten c-car and truck sales a week at his Ford Dealership, has three service b-bays and rents out b-boat storage sp-space here and at the d-dealership."

"Bet you Phil's not too pleased with all the non-Ford nameplates in his lot. Can't be too good for business," Charlie mused, and then his eye caught several unsightly deposits of tree sap splattered across the front hood of his Porsche. His smile disappeared.

"Some c-car," Barrett offered, coughing up and spitting aside a mouthful of thick phlegm. "I've got j-j-just the thing to t-take off that sap. I'll have it off in a ji-jiffy. You okay to f-find your way b-back?"

"I should be okay Barrett. Thanks," Charlie replied, as Sanford headed towards the back of Phil's cottage. Charlie considered how difficult life must be for a stutterer.

"Hey, I hear Lizzie's m-making you d-dinner," Barrett shouted over his shoulder, his voice trailing off.

Even though it was sheltered from the sun, the leather seats were scorching hot and Charlie carefully took the driver's seat while leaving the door open. His cell was on the floor on the passenger side. Four little bars appeared on the top right of his iPhone confirming service.

"Finally a break," Charlie laughed, as he scanned his contacts for Leslie Ingrams' phone number. Charlie left a voicemail asking that all legal papers be sent to James Clinton's office with a copy e-mailed to him. He added a personal note wishing her good luck with the next few days.

A quick glance at his inbox showed an e-mail from Kyla:

"Couriered papers to Clinton. House closing Thursday. My lawyer will destroy you for falsifying my signature on NovaRose. On his advice I removed possessions from house. I may press charges for spousal abuse."

Charlie took a deep breath and then forwarded his lawyer a clarification e-mail about how he had walked in on Kyla and her lover having sex, how he had never touched Kyla, and that she had assaulted him when he had told her about losing money on NIR.

"Kyla, you cunning bitch," he cursed, before shoving the iPhone into the pocket of his pants.

It was almost six o'clock in the evening. He quickly popped open the front trunk and retrieved a sport bag that contained sneakers, running gear, sweat pants, and a shaving kit. It also contained his iPad and chargers. After locking the Porsche he hustled around the end of the lake. As he approached Ingrid's cottage, the screen door opened and out stepped the black haired woman who had kissed him on his mouth. She had changed her outfit and was now wearing a baby blue A-line dress. Tanned breasts overflowed from the low cut front. He struggled to remember her full name.

"Charles Langdon," she greeted nasally, like her sinuses were clogged. "Hoped I see you."

"Lizzy Grant?" he guessed, and the woman grinned, her brilliantly white teeth accentuated by thick, red lipstick.

"You remembered! Ingrid's a lot better and sitting at the table." Charlie observed that the woman didn't enunciate her consonants, her delivery was a South Carolina drawl: *"Ingrez a lod bedder now an' siddin uppat the table."*

Charlie nodded, struggling to keep his eyes above the woman's cleavage. "That's great to hear. Thanks for making dinner."

Lizzie ran her hands down the side of her dress, tightening the material to better present her figure.

"Honey, can you bring back my casserole dish?"

"Will do, thanks for dinner," Charlie replied formally, and before he could move around her, Ingrid's neighbour stepped into his space and put her right hand on his shoulder. Very slowly she inserted her body so that the two were almost touching. She was so close he could smell her shampoo and was able to distinctly see the seven freckles across the top of her bosom.

"I'm not sure how long you're going to be here," Lizzie whispered, "but maybe we could spend some time together. You are a very physically attractive man. You must get told that a lot."

Charlie imagined that before time and raising children had taken its toll, Lizzie Grant must have been a fetching woman. He also grasped that Mrs. Petersson's neighbour was trying far too hard to avoid looking her age with the help of plastic surgery, Botox, and the application of far too much makeup.

"Why don't we plan to do that?" she conspired in confidence, looking towards the door to ensure Ingrid couldn't hear. "Roy's off golfing for a couple of days and I have the cottage to myself. I can be *very* discreet."

Charlie blushed with the awkwardness of it all.

"Mrs. Grant—" he began.

"Lizzie," she corrected, eyes widening. "No one calls me Mrs. Grant." And then she did that thing women do with their tongue when they clean lipstick off the front of their teeth without opening their mouth. She placed her hand on his chest.

"I can be very discreet," she repeated, shifting closer.

Charlie stepped back and reached for the door handle. "I'll be leaving for Toronto after dinner. It was nice meeting you."

After stepping through the screen door, Charlie felt Lizzie Grant's eyes tracking him like a lynx hunting a rabbit.

Mrs. Petersson was sitting at her table and was such a petite woman that her feet barely touched the linoleum floor. She was dressed comfortably in a long khaki skirt and light blue blouse. Her face looked rested by strained.

"Thought you tried to sneak off with Lizzie," Ingrid greeted, with a wink. "Pull up a chair."

"She's quite the lady," Charlie commented, as he sat down. He glanced through the screen door and saw the porch was empty.

Ingrid clucked her tongue and nodded.

The Last Stonecaster

"Deep down, she has got a good heart and is a good mother to her children. If Roy paid more attention to her she would not chase after married men."

"Did you sleep, ma'am?" he inquired, marvelling at how Ingrid had been diplomatic in calling Lizzie a tramp.

"Like the dead," she responded, and then giggled, "perhaps not the appropriate expression to be using today."

Ingrid handed a plate to her guest. It was so crammed full it spilled over the edges while her own held barely enough to feed a bird.

Two mouthfuls later, Charlie had to admit that Lizzie Grant was one hell of a cook. The roast beef melted in his mouth and the gravy was scrumptious. The scalloped potatoes were done to perfection and topped with a ton of butter, old cheddar, and caramelized onions. Yellow beans and beets were seasoned and grilled to perfection. The meal attacked his taste buds and Ingrid ladled more of everything on his plate when he was barely halfway through.

"I love a man with a good appetite," she observed. "My Henko could eat three plates and then devour an entire pie."

Langdon looked up and continued eating heartily.

"Charles Michael, do you always stare?" Ingrid inquired.

The former Telfer Stuart employee stopped chewing.

"I was staring again? Sorry, but I have the oddest feeling that we've met before. Do you ever get those feelings?"

Ingrid adjusted the silver combs holding her hair in place as she wondered why Odin had sent this particular messenger?

"Sometimes. I look like one of your grandmothers, perhaps?"

Charlie had never met his grandmothers. One of the things he shared with each parent is that they had each been teenagers when they lost their mother.

"No grandmothers," was all he shared.

Ingrid motioned at her guest's hand.

"You wear a wedding band."

"Yes," he responded, looking down at his finger. He considered that Kyla would have removed hers by now.

"Your wife's name?"

"Kyla."

"A good cook, perhaps?"

"Not anymore," he answered curtly. Thinking of Kyla would only spoil this great dinner.

Ingrid considered that one of the disruptions interpreted in the runes was an unhappy marriage. An old expression of her mother's came to mind: "*Det ligger en hund begraven.*" This literally translated into "there's a dog buried there," meaning that there was more to the story than was being told. She moved off topic.

"Apple pie?" Ingrid offered, and she retrieved a spectacular-looking deep-dish pie from the kitchen.

"I could be tempted," Charlie laughed. "It looks incredible."

Ingrid nodded appreciatively and her eyes twinkled.

"I made this. Best baker in the area, or so I am told."

As he finished his second piece, the lake had calmed and grown peaceful. The cicadas had quietened and Langdon couldn't see a motorboat anywhere on the water. There were numerous canoes of various colours floating quietly about carrying fishermen hoping for one last bite before calling it a day.

"Had your fill?" Mrs. Petersson inquired, the way she had asked her husband countless times.

"It was a great dinner," he complemented, placing his cutlery side by side in the middle of his dessert plate. "Now, I'm doing the dishes."

Ingrid didn't argue. "My neighbour cooks and my guest does the dishes. I could get used to being spoiled like this. Lizzie is very particular, so could you carefully wash her dish and take it next door. Make sure it is spotless."

"Spic and span," Charlie promised, presenting his best Boy Scout salute.

"Take in extra blankets and sleep well in the bedroom beside mine. I'll see you in the morning."

Charlie stood up and awkwardly took Ingrid by the shoulders.

"Good night, Ingegard Signalda Holmberg Petersson from Visby on the island of Gotland off the coast of Sweden," he whispered. "Don't let the bed bugs bite."

It pleased the old woman immensely that his mind was so detail-oriented and that he felt they had previously met.

"Good night, Charles Michael Langdon," she answered. "Thank you for coming into my life today."

Ingrid fell instantly into a deep, peaceful sleep recounting the day that had just passed. Odin had answered her prayers and her ancestral runes had spoken true about the stranger.

In her dream she saw herself at mid-day walking down to where her lawn met the edge of the lake. Anyone observing her would have seen an old lady inspecting her flowers along the edge of the water. Breaking with a lifelong custom she did not reach into the bucket of nails. "No steel for you today, Nykkjen," she whispered to the handsome water creature that lurked in the weeds below the surface. "Come fetch me if the Gods allow it. I am no longer afraid of you. Perhaps today is the day you will capture my soul."

All Norse children were taught about the mysterious creature that would lure you into the lake water only to devour you. To avoid this, you would toss a piece of steel into the water and chant, "*Nyk, Nyk Naal i vatn. Jomfru Maria kastat styaal, aek flyt,*" which meant, "Nyk Nyk, needle in the water. The Virgin Mary threw steel in the water. You are sinking. I float."

But there had been no steel or chanting today. In the safety of her bed Ingrid's dream recounted lowering herself into the water. She slowly swam about fifty feet from her dock where the lake was forty feet deep. There, she stopped treading water but did not sink as the air in her yellow rain jacket acted like a life preserver. She had worn the jacket so that if Odin heard her prayers and allowed her to drown, her corpse would float to the surface in a couple of days and she'd be easily seen and not have to face the indignity of being sliced apart by an outboard motor. She squeezed the air from the jacket, sending a stream of bubbles about her. Succumbing to gravity, she emptied her lungs. As she descended, her instinct for survival had told her legs to kick but she refused, awaiting Odin's decision. And then something had grabbed her. Her first thoughts had been of the evil lake creature. But Nykkjen would not have had Odin's face on his shoulder.

Ingrid turned over in her bed and pulled the duvet up around her. Subconsciously, she comforted herself by holding the two medallions around her neck. The man who saved her was the stranger foretold by her rune stones. He had the face of Odin on his shoulder, shared the name of her son who the Gods had vindictively stolen a lifetime ago, and had been alerted by her long-dead daughter.

Charles Michael Langdon was Odin's messenger sent in response to her prayers. So what was the message?

Chapter Ten

The Lear 60XR silently descended towards the private airstrip after a gruelling sixteen-hour transatlantic flight. Its 4,454 kilometre range had mandated refuelling stops in Reykjavik and Istanbul. A third pilot had come aboard in Iceland to ease the last leg of the 11,067 kilometres. The luxury jet was one of eight owned by the CFMT International Investment Bank of Dubai. The fleet ferried their wealthiest banking clients and Fortune 500 executives across North America, Europe, and Asia. On this day, the sixteen million dollar craft was illegally ferrying three Canadians to the United Arab Emirates.

Alexander Fanning's father had strongly recommended Dubai over Croatia, although both would have provided safety from extradition to North America. Ernest Fanning felt the second largest city of the United Arab Emirates would offer a better lifestyle. Located on the southeast corner of the Persian Gulf, the city was rich in tradition and opportunity far beyond its interests in oil, which to the surprise of most westerners only represented 5% of the Emirates' annual revenue. Investors had driven tourism, aviation, real estate, and financial services as the UAE's money machines. Ernest had spent considerable time in Dubai and could boast of friendship with the Maktoum family, the ruling monarchy or Sheikdom since 1833. Mohammed bin Rahid Al Maktoum and the Crown Prince Hamden bin Al Maktoum were two of the most powerful men on the planet. Ernest assured his son that Dubai was a far better choice than the capital city Abu Dhabi and was aptly nicknamed the Las Vegas of the Persian Gulf with a vibrant and exciting nightlife. It was the perfect place to escape to—if you have money and the right connections. Ernest had used his connections to arrange transportation and the purchase of two condos overlooking the Persian Gulf at the Palm Jumeriah, a five-star waterfront condominium complex with twenty restaurants, ten pools, a private mile-long pristine beach, and an exclusive security force for the protection and anonymity of its owners.

A close business associate of Ernest Fanning was CFMT's sixty-seven-year-old Executive Chairman and Chief Executive Officer. Richard Andrew Strickland had been at the helm of CFMT for fifteen years and was a powerful financial force in the UAE. He had arrived as one of the 180,000 British Expats emigrating to the UAE in the late 1960s when it was viewed as a land of untapped oil potential with readily accessible ports on the Persian Gulf. CFMT worked closely with the monarchy and drove construction, the development of the ports, the construction of the Burj Al Arab, the world's most expensive hotel, and Burj Khalifa, the world's tallest building. As international investors flocked into Abu Dhabi and Dubai, Richard Strickland helped shepherd currency flowing like rain onto the thirsty desert. Nothing happened in Dubai without CFMT's participation and its Chairman's wealth knew no limits. The bank manoeuvred without so much as a hiccup through Sharia Law, Sunni and Shi'a religious factions, human rights issues, and a diversely conflicting population consisting of 53% Indian, 17% Emirati, and 13% Pakistani citizens. As exports blew through the roof to India, Switzerland, and Saudi Arabia, CFMT encouraged the monarchy to structure stronger import deals with China and Saudi Arabia. That recommendation generated twice the income for the bank and drove the UAE's GDP skyward. When the global meltdown hit in 2008, the Chairman of

CFMT was called upon by the monarchy to help restore the country's financial surge.

Strickland had agreed to help his Canadian lawyer friend who over the years had provided invaluable and highly confidential advice. The $150 million CFMT had garnered from their "premature" sale of NovaRose International stock certainly warranted a favour, so Strickland didn't hesitate when asked by his friend to help whisk Alexander from certain incarceration. The fact that Alexander Fanning and Jay Datrem would be transporting hundreds of millions of dollars into Dubai was further incentive.

The jet executed a perfect three point landing and taxied towards the convoy of four black Mercedes SUVs. Eight heavily armed men in dark suits stood to the sides of the vehicles. Two of them faced the plane while the others stared off into the desert surrounding the airstrip. Each driver remained in the vehicle with the engine running and a semi-automatic across his lap. It was barely six a.m.

The sun was just peeking above the horizon as the plane jerked to a stop and the starboard side door flipped up. The first to exit was one of the three pilots who calmly greeted the gun-wielding welcoming committee, waving to one he recognized. It was not the first time the plane had illegally transported people to this airstrip. The pilot placed a small wooden block on either side of each wheel then stepped far enough away from the Lear to be able to light a much-needed cigarette.

Next to exit the plane were two well-dressed men, each carrying a black briefcase. Following them was a fetching young woman with multi-coloured hair that spiked outward from her skull. She was wearing painted-on blue jeans, a sleeveless top, and tall heels. Every guard leered at her flagrant display of sexuality. Dress codes in the United Arab Emirates were clearly stated with transgressors punished to the full extent of the law. Women were considered as dressing indecently if they revealed too much skin, such as baring their shoulders or knees.

"Into the first vehicle please," a heavy-set guard donning Ray-Bans directed with perfect diction, and the three Westerners did as told.

"You will need to have your lady dressed more appropriately, or she will be detained by the police. Even foreigners must comply with dress codes."

A jet-lagged and anxious Jay Datrem looked at his wife and spoke sharply under his breath. "Put on your jacket and get in the car. I warned you about the dress code."

"We'll keep our briefcases with us," Fanning stated, knowing that each case contained one hundred and twenty bearer bonds, each valued at one million dollars. The founder of NIR knew that bearer bonds provided untouchable anonymity whereas a bank wire could be traced. However, non-registered bearer bonds were live currency and whoever held them, owned them. It would be easy for these armed gorillas to kill them, bury their corpses in the desert, and take the money. Their very lives depended on the depth of his father's relationship with Richard Strickland.

Masking his fears, Fanning turned to one of the armed men and pointed at the plane. "See to our luggage," he ordered brashly, before climbing into the first SUV as if he didn't have a care in the world.

* * *

Charlie Langdon awoke Sunday morning to the welcoming smells and sounds of breakfast being made. He stretched like an old cat and looked up at the sunrays playing with the dreamcatchers hovering above the bed. Birds sang loudly outside his window and there were hushed voices from the other side of his door. He wondered who would visit at this ungodly hour. The need for a shave gave in to the desperate growls of his stomach and the anticipation of what was being cooked in Ingrid's kitchen. His whiskers would wait until after breakfast. Opening the door, he looked directly at three women. There was his Swedish hostess and a woman he recognized from the day before. She was sitting at the table while a third woman was leaning against the kitchen counter eating a piece of toast. The room reeked of tension and he realized he had walked into a heated argument.

"Should I go back to bed?" he offered, and the three faked smiles.

"Well, you are up," Ingrid called from the kitchen, ignoring it all. "The day is half done."

It was barely seven.

"Come sit down," the pretty, business-like female he recognized from the day before directed. "Ingrid, is his breakfast ready yet?"

Ingrid held up the spatula and her eyes flashed at the audacity of the question.

"I am not one of your employees, Anne-Marie Downey. Do not be chippy. He is my guest, not yours."

Anne-Marie ignored the rebuke and grinned cheerfully revealing a very attractive disposition. "Let me pour you coffee. Don't worry if you don't remember me from all the excitement yesterday, and you didn't meet Cassandra. She was in Toronto and missed all the excitement. Just drove up this morning and she's mad as hell with Ingrid. Their arguing is probably what woke you."

The third woman reacted instantly, and if eyes could have killed, Anne-Marie's head would have exploded in flames.

"I would have driven home immediately if one of you had had the decency to phone me," she stated through clenched teeth. Her bloodshot eyes revealed she had been crying.

"I will phone next time," the elderly woman responded, the hint of playful sarcasm sprinkled over her words. Anne-Marie completely ignored Cassandra's outburst and reached out to shake Charlie's hand.

Anne-Marie was dressed comfortably but expensively in colour-coordinated, cottage-type attire. A Birkin bag rested beside her coffee cup. Two Blackberries peeked out from the purse. In spite of the early hour, her makeup and perfectly coiffed jet-black hair looked like she had just come from a salon. The ostentatious diamond on her wedding finger, and the solid gold Omega watch encrusted with diamonds screamed, "I have or I married money." In an instant Charlie sized up Anne-Marie as a very refined, no-nonsense, keenly intelligent businesswoman struggling to overcome gender discrimination on a playing ground ruled by men. Within moments, she would reveal something about her status in life, be it a job title, membership in a golf club, or a fancy car.

"I work for the Royal Bank," she stated bluntly, "I oversee the banks' branches throughout the Muskokas."

Hiding a knowing smile, Charlie responded, "That job sounds like a lot of responsibility."

The other woman who was staring languidly out the kitchen window wasn't listening. She was still reacting to the Swede's near-death experience and was struggling with her emotions. The woman he had yet to meet was one of those short women who appeared statuesque. He guessed her height at five feet, five inches and her weight around one hundred and ten pounds. Ingrid's friend exuded the quiet confidence and musculature of an athlete. Unlike Kyla's made-over version of Francine, this woman possessed a beauty that didn't need help. Without a touch of makeup, her complexion was flawless, although blotchy from having been crying. Her smile was anxious. Suddenly Charlie realized that as he was staring at her bright cerulean eyes, she was looking directly at him. In a moment, she turned and looked out the window. Her sunny blond hair was pulled loose about her head into a pleated ponytail held by a black ribbon. A man's Timex Triathlon adorned her left wrist but she wore no other jewellery. Like the Swede, the blond woman looked to have Nordic features with sculpted cheekbones, an aquiline nose, and full lips. And then, she took several steps in his direction.

"I'm Cassie. Cassie Turner," she introduced, politely offering her hand. Her voice was soft and melodic when it wasn't being directed with anger at his hostess. Her diction was perfectly crisp like an English teacher. "I am glad to meet you. I'm sorry about my outburst, but this has all been so devastatingly upsetting. I just found out about Ingrid this morning and drove from Toronto like a bat out of hell."

"I'm Charlie Langdon, and you should be upset. If someone hadn't phoned me," he accused, glaring at the others, "I'd be upset too. It's very nice to meet you."

Ingrid flicked the younger woman's shoulder.

"Her name is Cassandra *Ingrid* Turner," the Swedish gardener clarified proudly.

Ingrid motioned for him to sit and, as she brushed past Cassandra, the older woman leaned forward and tenderly ran her hands down the length of the woman's braid, whispering softly, "don't be mad at me, little dove."

Another overfilled plate—this one with scrambled eggs, four pieces of toast slathered in homemade strawberry jam, six links of sausage, six slices of bacon, and fried tomatoes—arrived in front of Charlie. It was enough to choke a horse.

"There is more of everything," Ingrid told him, as if preparing his breakfast was something she had done for years. "Eat up while it is hot. I will tell you about these two troublemakers if Anne-Marie will be quiet and take a breath."

Anne-Marie Downey was married to an accountant named Tom Power and they lived six lots to the east of Ingrid in the two-story stone house with yellow shutters. Ingrid pointed out the window to it with her spatula. Anne-Marie and Tom moved up to Great Spirit Moon Lake from Barrie ten years ago. Anne-Marie worked for RBC for fifteen years before being named one of the youngest female Vice Presidents in the history of Canada's largest financial institution. Tom spent most weekdays in the city. As Charlie swallowed a mouthful of toast he knew his first impression of Anne-Marie had been bang on. He didn't have to hold his breath long before the banker continued to "sell" her success.

"Our house is the big one with the three slip boathouse. You can see Tom's new toy by the dock."

Charlie craned to look down the shoreline towards an inflatable speedboat.

"It's a Zodiac Hurricane," she blurted out. "A twenty-one footer with a rigid hull. Flies across the water like a rocket. Why don't you come over this afternoon and you and my husband can take it out? Tom will be back at four. My guy loves his toys."

Given that he intended to be back in Toronto by 4:00 p.m., Langdon avoided accepting the invitation. More sausages and bacon were added to his plate and while he complained, he didn't put down his fork. If the lake hadn't drowned him yesterday, a cholesterol-induced heart attack might if he kept on eating.

"This beauty is my goddaughter and the grand-daughter of my dearest friend, Meryl Patch," Ingrid told him, reaching over and taking Cassie's hand. "Cassie is the baby of Meryl's eldest son. She got her mom's good looks and her daddy's love of sports and the outdoors."

"She's wickedly smart with an IQ of 175. Cassie scored a perfect 4.0 GPA," Anne-Marie indiscretely announced in that female manner that revealed hidden jealousy. "Got scholarships everywhere, either for her brains or athleticism. She can run a deer into the ground without breaking a sweat."

Ingrid hushed Anne-Marie and told Charlie that after winning national championships in long distance, her goddaughter had chosen not to pursue an Olympic career in track. Cassie's love of writing led her to a highly successful career as a writer. She moved to Toronto to pursue journalism and then returned to Great Spirit Moon Lake for local newspapers and magazines. Meryl Patch's granddaughter's face turned deep crimson.

"Enough. You are both being '*sladdertacka*,'" Cassie spat out at their gossiping. "He's not writing a book about me."

The competitive banker didn't like taking a back seat and began peppering Charlie with questions. Cassie remained silent at the end of the table. As Anne-Marie's interrogation continued, Charlie discreetly glanced at her friend and pegged Cassie in her early thirties. Her clothes were simple yet tasteful, not expensive but not cheap. No fidgeting or unnecessary movements. Not one to divert her eyes when stared at—and this one got stared at a lot, given the sexual magnetism she exuded. Scrapes and bruises on her calves—definitely a cross-country runner.

For her part, Cassandra Turner sat patiently, glancing at the new-comer as discreetly as possible. Before Charlie had woken, Ingrid had told her that the stranger predicted by her runes sported a tattoo of Odin and shared the same name as her long-dead son. The Swede admitted that she had instantly taken to him and found him to be of rich character anchored in bravery and compassion. Cassie knew her Swede to be an incredible judge of character.

As the stranger stole glances, she did the same as discretely as the closeness of the kitchen would permit. She found Langdon ruggedly handsome. His face looked honest and didn't have any smugness about it. He looked weary, which she attributed to yesterday's ordeal. Ingrid's goddaughter felt he looked a little pudgy and unfit, desperately in need of exercise. There were cuts and scrapes across his forearms, which were a reminder of the cattails through which he had run towards the lake. Ingrid's rescuer wore an expensive Omega watch and a plain gold wedding band. According to Ingrid, his marriage was unhappy and he hadn't phoned home the night before. His facial features were appealing even with their cuts and bruises. One eye was blackened and he had a bandage across the top on his forehead . . . all that from jumping in the lake to save Ingrid?

Ingrid brought over the pot of coffee and held up her finger for Anne-Marie to stop the inquisition, but the bank executive had to have the last word.

"Charlie, will you be driving Ingrid to church in your Porsche?" Anne-Marie blurted out one last question.

"Church?" his voice croaked, like he was in mid-puberty.

Ingrid poured coffee and looked directly at her guest.

"We must leave here at 9:30 a.m. to get a decent seat by the windows and any hope of fresh air."

And with that, Charlie realized his return trip to Toronto would have to wait until after church.

By 9:25 a.m. Charlie and Ingrid were sitting in the fifth pew of St. Peter's and, despite every window being open, the church was still hotter than the hell against which their prayers were directed. For the next hour and ten minutes they prayed, sang, knelt, stood, and said "God bless you" to a host of strangers.

As the overheated and sweat-covered parishioners gratefully headed towards the exits and fresh air, Ingrid pinched Charlie's arm.

"I do not believe any of this malarkey. I think the Catholic Church is filled with perverts and the Protestants are just do-gooders trying to be non-Catholic. Both spend most of their time frightening people with centuries-old visions and edicts that no longer make sense in today's world, if they ever did. Their version of Heaven and Hell is a watered-down version of Valhalla," she explained. "They are all pagans regardless of my homeland having turned to Christianity so long ago."

"Then why are we here?" he whispered, sweat gleaming on his face as they walked through the oversized wooden doors at the back of the church.

Ingrid smiled as she looked up into the bright sunshine. "I love a good choir and a decent organist. Catholics have the best music. I view it as a free concert and my Gods don't seem to mind."

They brunched at the Family Inn restaurant across the street and when Charlie pulled out a credit card it was refused. Lunch was free for the celebrity who had pulled Ingrid Petersson from the lake. "Roof down," Ingrid commanded as they got in the 911. As they drove, the elderly Swede gave her chauffeur a running commentary.

"More accidents at these stop lights than anywhere else in Bracebridge. That is Burbidge's Hardware Store, and Barrett says their screw nails are crap and break 50% of the time. Ah, that dark brown awning over there is The King of Chocolate, which is Cassie's favourite place for ice cream with walnuts. My girl has got a huge sweet tooth and eats like a starving horse but there is not an ounce of fat on her. You noticed her fitness, perhaps? I watched you two staring at each other like shy teenagers."

Charlie kept his eyes focused on the road.

"Barry Wilkins owns that candy store and the ice cream parlour down the street. He has been hot to trot for Cassie for years, but she thinks he's as dumb as a plank and only has that store because it belonged to his daddy. She is correct. My chickens are smarter than that man."

The 911 sped past the city limits. Ingrid's diatribe continued and Charlie listened politely as he considered what time he would arrive back in Toronto and which employment recruiters he would phone to help him find a new job.

The Last Stonecaster

"That golf course is not making any money and is infested with fire ants," the elderly Swede revealed. "The owners will be forced to sell by spring. Oh, and that Ford Dealership with the balloons is Phil Henderson's. He has got another repair garage down the road. And he has the boat ramp and parking lot he rents out. His wife Margery is Phil's first cousin, but we never mention that. Barrett Sanford is Margery's older brother."

"Barrett is Phil's brother-in-law?" Charlie confirmed, trying to remember all the connections.

"Yes, and his first cousin," she clarified. "Very sad journey his life has followed, and the Gods set out a destiny for him that, to me, was unfair. Barrett Sanford was an incredibly bright and athletic high school student. Henrik loved Barrett. The Sanford kid followed him around like a shadow always willing to lend a hand with anything Henrik was doing. We paid for Barrett's university at York where he majored in mathematics and sciences."

"Math and sciences at university?" Charlie interjected, and the disapproving look on Ingrid's face revealed that she knew the wrong opinion he had prematurely formed of her friend.

"Yes, math and sciences. Barrett was smart as a whip. I can tell you have misjudged him. In the summer after his first year, Barrett came home. One night he and his younger sister decided to race back from Huntsville. Margery was driving her Ford Ranger and her brother was on his Kawasaki dirt bike. Barrett won the race and pulled up on the side of the road just by Phil's parking lot. Margery misjudged the distance it would take her truck to stop on a gravel road. Her vehicle ploughed into her brother. Barrett barely survived. The accident damaged his brain and Margery had a nervous breakdown. Barrett lost a lot of memory and syntax. The stutter grew worse with time and he was not medically fit to drive any vehicle beyond a golf cart, which he uses to do odd jobs around the lake. Charlie, please be kind to him. Barrett is a gentle soul and you could learn a lot from him. *Inte doma hunden efter haren.* Do not judge a dog by the hair."

Charlie gripped the wheel of the 911, feeling embarrassed for having labelled Barrett a simpleton. As the Porsche twisted its way along the highway, Ingrid removed her silver hair clips freeing her white mane to blow freely in the wind.

"That yellow house in the cove belongs to Peter and Kate MacLean, some of the other 'relics' on the lake. Arrived here in the 1960s and never left," she shouted. "Raised six kids on one salary. Pete drinks and smokes marijuana. He's been in and out of rehab twice."

Charles Langdon was about to ask Ingrid about her own family but ran out of time. Barrett Sanford was waiting at Phil's dock with his fibreglass fishing boat. Langdon looked at him through fresh eyes.

"We were just talking about you," Ingrid announced happily, and the broad-shouldered handyman laughed.

"You ready? I've been waiting all morning," he replied anxiously. Charlie noticed that when Sanford spoke to Ingrid he didn't stutter.

"Let me get my hat and picnic hamper. You got the gear?"

"Yeppers. All set."

Charlie locked the car. "Are you two going fishing?" he inquired, thinking this the perfect time to offer his farewells and head back to Toronto.

Ingrid was already headed down the gravel road towards her house. She moved surprisingly fast for an eighty-five-year-old woman who had almost drowned the day before. "Come on," she shouted over her shoulder. "Time is wasting." Charlie remained stationary by the Porsche and the Swede stopped suddenly and flapped both her arms in obvious frustration. "The fish are not going to wait all day!"

Langdon looked at Barrett who pantomimed for him to get moving. Charlie relented and scurried after the Swede who was already half way to her house.

* * *

The paralegal had looked exceptionally professional on her first day of work at Blackmore, Craig and Fanning LLP. Her resume presented her as Tessa Conner, although her birth certificate read McTavish. Using her real name would have been a dead giveaway to long-term employees and, in particular, Ernest Fanning. She had already successfully completed a two-month internship at the firm and had established herself as a hard working rookie.

Months of long hours and a seven-day workweek made the lawyers in the Corporate Department take notice. She gained a reputation of working tirelessly, having a razor-sharp legal mind, and delivering flawless work against short deadlines. It wasn't long until she was working on files headed by Ernest Fanning. One Tuesday afternoon she found herself in an elevator absent-mindedly standing directly beside Ernest Fanning. He was impeccably dressed in a three-piece Italian suit and looked like one of those handsome movie stars from another era. His shoes were polished so well they reflected the cuff of his pants. Casually, her hand slipped the earpiece in place and she touched the button that would begin recording their first interaction.

Fanning smelled of cologne-masked cigarette smoke and when he turned to introduce himself, her knees involuntarily began to shake. Her mother's nemesis offered his hand and smiled warmly. He looked at her with penetrating eyes.

"You're Conner, right?"

Tessa managed a smile, revealing the cute dimples that framed her smile.

"Yes, Tessa Conner."

"I'm Ernest Fanning. Sorry we haven't met earlier. I hear you're the hardest working employee in this firm," he stated exuberantly, finally releasing her hand. "Keep up the good work."

Before she could engage him in conversation, the doors opened on the fifteenth floor and Ernest Fanning exited. Tessa took a deep breath and leaned back against the mirrored wall of the elevator. She wiped sweaty hands on her skirt and turned off the earpiece.

"Well that was really impressive, Tessa," she said aloud, in the now empty elevator.

* * *

Two days later Tessa's supervising associate, Brian Hopkins, asked her to deliver a file to Mr. Fanning's legal assistant Tara Kirkpatrick. Tessa touched up her lipstick and sprayed Bvlgari across the front of her neck, behind her knees, and on her wrists. She attached the skin-tone coloured earpiece and put the pen in the pocket of her blue blouse, carefully pressing the button of each device to *"voice activate."*

With file in hand, she made her way up the stairs to Fanning's office on the forty-seventh floor. The game was afoot.

"You can do this Tessa" she said aloud, focussing herself. She would say, "You can this Tessa" on every occasion she had to collect her drunken mother and carry her to the bedroom. She would whisper, *"You can do this Tessa"* when she was so beyond exhaustion and bone-weary from working double shifts that she could barely study for exams. Her mantra helped slow her down when the world became too much for her to bear.

Tara Kirkpatrick wasn't at her desk. Boldly, the young and impeccably dressed paralegal poked her head into the senior partner's office. There was no turning back now. Both the waterfront view and luxurious decor of the corner office were spectacular. Two silk-wallpapered walls were lined with floor-to-ceiling windows looking out across Lake Ontario. The floors were covered in three different Oriental carpets and the walls were artfully adorned with A.Y. Jackson and Arthur Lismer. A solitary yet spectacular Picasso hung on the wall facing his desk.

"So you know your art," a gravelly voice commented, as the tall, silver-haired lawyer slipped out from behind a large mahogany bookshelf lined with leather-bound law books and an extremely large flat screen television. A large telescope rested in the corner of the office pointing towards the lake.

Tessa jumped, startled at the sudden appearance of the senior partner.

"Pardon me for entering without knocking. Tara isn't at her desk and Brian said you needed this file immediately," she announced, holding the red file in mid-air. "I didn't think it wise to leave it unattended."

Fanning made no move to take the file. His eyes scanned her from head to toe.

"Set it on my chair. Tell Mr. Hopkins I asked for that file an hour ago. Perhaps he has time to waste but I do not."

Tessa reacted exactly as Fanning had intended.

"Sir, it was given to me ten minutes ago and I ran up the stairs to get here," she clarified defensively, ensuring any blame would be assessed appropriately to her supervisor.

Fanning was constantly amused at how easily manipulated these young girls were. No different from Jeanne in his father's changing room.

"My, aren't we ambitious," he finally remarked, "Tessa, isn't it?"

"Yes sir. Tessa Conner," she replied, her heart beating like a snare drum.

"Brian says you are extremely capable. Are you?"

"That's nice of him to say, and I am," she responded boldly.

Ernest liked this one. She seemed to have a good sense of the "cat and mouse game"—although at the moment he wasn't positive which of them was the predator. That made it even more exciting.

"I like to get to know the people whose paycheques I sign," he stated, stepping forward with his right hand extended. He took off the earpiece and tossed it on the table.

"These make you look like a secretary. At all times, look and act how you want others to see you."

"Yes sir," she acknowledged, hiding the angst she felt at the removal of one of her recording devices.

"What is your goal at Blackmore, Craig and Fanning, and why the interest in Corporate and International Law?" he inquired, leading her by the elbow towards his desk.

Tessa walked beside him.

"Well, I don't like the idea of being stuck in a court room day after day, so that ruled out Criminal, Civil, and Family law. Tax, Patent, Trademark, and Contract law would bore me to death. Immigration and Constitutional law is for someone with a lot more patience than I have. Labour and Employment law seems mundane in a country whose businesses are controlled by parent companies in the States. Frankly, of all the areas of law, Corporate and International, seem to have more wiggle room and a chance to play in a bigger pond of international problems and opportunities."

Fanning couldn't have agreed more but was pleasantly surprised with how someone so inexperienced succinctly summed up her perspective. "You certainly have firm opinions for a junior paralegal. These are usually the comments that Associates are considering."

"Well sir, I'm not going to be a paralegal forever. I've been saving money for law school. I had the top mark in the city on the Paralegal Licensing Examination. I absolutely nailed my LSATs. I just don't have rich parents," she added with a grin.

"Languages?" he inquired, noting that her outfit was far too expensive for a low paid paralegal.

"Trilingual with French and Spanish," she responded.

Ernest Fanning reached down and removed an imaginary fleck of something off her shoulder.

"Paralegals are being replaced by computers and any law school in Canada worth attending is going to be expensive," he commiserated, and already knowing the answer asked, "You have no one who can help financially?"

Tessa shook her head. "I'm on my own. Have been for a long time," she admitted, the words coming effortlessly from years of practice.

Fanning reached across his desk and pushed a button that automatically closed the door to his office. He knew about the school debt and her limited means. Fanning had check-marked her the day she was hired.

"That's a neat trick," she mused.

"Tessa," he began softly, "if you shine at Blackmore, Craig and Fanning, I'll get you into a good Canadian law school on full scholarship."

Phaidra's daughter smiled, hoping her devices were operating.

"Well sir, that sounds incredible. Have you helped others to get into law school?" she inquired, feigning innocence.

Fanning glanced out the window.

"I help employees who are special. Ms. Conner, I'm going to assign some of your time directly to me. It'll mean overtime, but if it's a road to law school then I'm sure you'll take it."

Fanning reached up and swept her dark bangs off her forehead. She didn't shy away and he liked that.

Tessa, you can do this.

"Ambition can be a double-edged sword that can be used against you. You do know what I mean?"

Tessa nodded and parted her lips. Her heart was near to exploding.

"How important is it for you to go to law school?" he inquired slyly, the smell of her perfume, her unbridled ambitions, and the intrigue of the hunt arousing his attention.

The young paralegal took a deep breath. "It is paramount," she responded honestly.

The old man nodded knowingly. "And what are you prepared to do to ensure that future?"

"Anything."

The old man took a step forward into her personal space. When she stood fast Goodwin's son knew he had her. Now was the time to let her ambition heighten her anxiousness and lower her defenses. "That's great to hear," he said, his tone firmer and more professional. "Very good chatting with you. We'll see about getting you on some more interesting files." And with that, Fanning pushed the button to open his office door and loudly called for his assistant to bring in his updated schedule. Tessa's heart was pounding but she accepted the dismissal and left the office. Tara Kirkpatrick motioned for the paralegal to wait. When their boss had returned to his office, Kirkpatrick politely motioned for Tessa to approach her desk. Tara's pleasant expression evaporated and her eyes flared in anger.

"Listen up kid. Don't ever enter that office again without my permission. If you have something to drop off, you leave it with me. My boss hates unexpected visits and now I'm going to catch hell. Pull a stunt like that again and I'll make sure you're assigned to relabeling file boxes in the basement for the next year. Capiche?"

Tessa Conner stood more deflated than when Fanning had abruptly ended their conversation.

"I'm sorry but I thought it was urgent. It won't happen again."

Tara began typing on her computer. "Better not."

Over the next two months, Tessa was assigned to a variety of files, keeping her at the office until after midnight most days. Most nights she fell into bed too exhausted to even take off her clothes or even check to see if her mother was home. One day, a phone call from Tara Kirkpatrick reignited Tessa's resolve that had been severely dampened with exhaustion.

"Mr. Fanning has questions on the Bailey Towers file. He'd normally ask Brian, so don't screw this up. Bring your backup files." The phone clicked dead.

Tessa's heart skipped as she quickly touched up her makeup and sprayed on perfume. She activated her two recording devices and picked up a yellow file folder. Five minutes later, a much friendlier Tara Kirkpatrick led her through Fanning's office door.

"Here she is," Tara announced, before returning to her desk.

"Good morning, sir," Tessa said, but her boss didn't look up from the document he was intently reading. For two minutes she stood wondering what to do. Finally, the senior partner motioned for her to sit. His demeanour was calm and deliberate.

"I want you to communicate to your associate that we need to go deeper on David Lansing and Seymour Bailey. I've heard rumours that they have some offshore debts they haven't disclosed. Tell him I want you to help him to get into their tax returns and don't leave any stone unturned. He is to personally ensure there have been no issues with Sarbanes–Oxley. I don't want this deal going forward to the banks if the buyers can't legally raise their share of the financing. Understood?"

Tessa finished jotting her note and replied affirmatively. "Yes sir. Anything else?"

Fanning closed the file and smiled warmly. He arose from his desk and walked around it.

"That's all. I'll need it first thing tomorrow," he directed as he walked to the southeast corner of his office and looked out the window at the Toronto Island Bishop Airport.

"Have you ever looked at the planes landing on the island airport?" he asked. "From this angle it looks like Dash 8s are ditching into Lake Ontario. It's quite an illusion."

Tessa stood up and joined him at the window. Sure enough when the next Bombardier Q-series descended on its final approach, the turboprop did look like it was disappearing into the water. Conner nodded her head. "You're right. I've never noticed that before."

With years of practise, the lawyer casually slipped behind the young woman and gently placed his hand on her right shoulder. The paralegal didn't flinch or move away. They stood for several minutes as two more planes touched down and taxied across the runway. Fanning was intrigued. He leaned slightly forward and inhaled the delicious smell of her hair and skin.

Tessa stayed her emotions and stood still, not wanting to appear anxious or too willing. Her mother's nemesis whispered into her ear. "Tessa, are you still interested in law school?"

Without turning around she replied that she was.

"And you need my help?"

"Yes."

"And you said you were willing to do anything to get into law school. Do you still feel that way?"

She nodded her head and felt his left hand on her other shoulder, caressing her through the thinness of her blouse.

Tessa, you can do this.

"Anything?" he repeated, as he slowly turned her around so that her face was just below his.

Tessa's insides cringed as she looked upward into the slightly bloodshot eyes of the man who had destroyed her mother and taken away her own childhood and innocence.

Tessa, you can do this.

"Anything," she relented, fully aware of the importance of that one simple word to her future.

Ernest smiled and slowly pulled her towards him in a full embrace. With his right index finger he parted her lips and kissed her deeply. Tessa stood higher on her tiptoes as he began massaging her back. The taste of cigarettes was strong.

Tessa, you can do this.

"Mr. Fanning," she said plaintively, pushing herself harder against him and nestling her face against his chest. "I'm not sure we should be doing this."

"You said anything. Did you mean it or not?" Fanning persisted, as he led her to an armless chair and directed her to sit.

Tessa sat and looked up at him, bit her bottom lip, and nodded her head. "Yes."

Fanning straddled the chair so that Tessa's face was at his waist.

"Show me," he ordered lecherously. "You know what to do."

Tessa, you can do this.

When he finished, Fanning stepped away from the chair, refastened his belt, and returned to his desk. He buzzed his secretary and asked her to connect him with his next scheduled call. Without so much as a goodbye, he unceremoniously turned towards the window and reached for his phone. Tessa stood up awkwardly, gathered herself, and left.

A few minutes later the paralegal exited the forty-seventh floor washroom after vigorously brushing her teeth and reapplying her lipstick. Tessa retrieved her laptop from her desk and rode an elevator to the firm's library on the twenty-seventh floor. Finding a secluded cubicle she took the spy pen from her pocket, unscrewed the base, and stuck it into the USB port. Momentarily, the device connected and she pressed "Play from the beginning."

The screen was blank. She disconnected the device and then reinserted it a second time.

Nothing. There was no audio or video.

Panicking, she withdrew the spy pen device from the USB port and inserted the ear bud steel tip into the USB port. When prompted, she pressed "Play."

Nothing. Not a goddamn thing. Something in Fanning's office had blocked her devices from working. Her mother had been right.

Phaidra McTavish's daughter hissed, angry at her overconfidence and naivety.

"Tessa, you stupid bitch."

Chapter Eleven

An enthusiastic Barrett Sanford brought along the most enormous thermos of tea while Ingrid supplied a Tupperware container of thickly sliced black forest ham and hothouse tomato sandwiches. The local took the boat to a good spot, dropped anchor, and the three began casting. It had been a lifetime since Charlie Langdon had spent an afternoon fishing, and it triggered happy memories of his grandfather. He enjoyed listening to Barrett prattle on with Ingrid about all the local gossip and happenings. There wasn't much going on around Great Spirit Moon Lake that Barrett Sanford hadn't caught wind of. He noticed once again that the handyman didn't stutter when he spoke with Ingrid.

"There is not a thing Barrett cannot fix," Ingrid boasted, and the Hawaiian-shirt-clad handyman grinned widely at the complement and poured the contents of the thermos into three plastic cups. Sandwiches were gobbled up and then Ingrid's thickly iced chocolate walnut brownies disappeared as quickly as they appeared.

When the sun moved to the west Ingrid announced it was time to head in. She had caught three good-sized striped bass. Charlie had pulled in a ten-pound pike and four eatable trout. Their guide had managed to snag a four-inch sunfish. As they moored, Barrett handed a scaling knife butt first to Charlie.

"G-get to it," he ordered, with a wink. "The b-biggest c-catch cleans all the f-fish."

Ingrid grilled dinner in the biggest iron skillet Charlie had ever seen while the two men husked cobs of corn and picked some fresh tomatoes and cucumbers. After eating their fill, Barrett made off with the container of maple fudge Ingrid offered and headed over to Tom Power's place after a frantic phone call came about a clogged toilet.

As they sipped steaming hot cups of peppermint tea in the living room Charlie glanced at his Omega.

"I should be driving back to Toronto," he announced. "I've overstayed my welcome."

Ingrid's chair rocked back and forth. She had considered for many years that Odin was not going to allow her to enter Valhalla until she found some way of carrying on the legacy of her ancestral line of Stonecasters. But now there was hope. Somehow, Odin intended this stranger to be a conduit to her ancestors given that she had no daughters to take her place.

"Let me tell you when you have overstayed your welcome. Besides, you do not seem too anxious about rushing home. Would you like to hear a story perhaps?"

Charlie smiled at his Swedish hostess. It's not like anyone was expecting him.

"I love a good story," he replied, sitting back in his wolf fur-covered chair.

"Good," she responded with a smile. "I think it is important that you hear it from the beginning. First of all, young man, you remember my full name, perhaps?"

Charles Langdon never forgot a name. He never forgot anything he was told.

"Ingegard Signilda Holmberg Petersson," he recounted promptly, noting the proud look on the storyteller's face.

"I was born March 3rd, 1928, in Visby on the Island of Gotland to the south of Stockholm in the Baltic Sea. Visby was the port of our island and we were connected to the mainland by ferries. Centuries ago, a wall had been built around the city for protection from invaders. Many Viking expeditions set sail from Gotland, to the east into Russia, and to the west across the Atlantic to North America, long before Christopher Columbus arrived and took credit not his. But that is another story," Ingrid said, with a shrug of her shoulders. "On holidays Mother would take us to explore places of worship. My mother showed us stone and steel crosses upon which runic glyphs had been carved thousands of years earlier. You know runes, perhaps?"

"Runes are like an alphabet. They were symbols the Vikings used to predict the future. Only certain people could actually use them, and I think they were called Oracles or Shaman. You have paintings of them over there," Charlie responded, pointing to the wall. "Isn't that right?"

"That is a good enough explanation," Ingrid considered, before sharing the story of her life with the messenger from Odin who was her key to entering Valhalla.

> My mother's name was Birgitta Elisbet Ellingson and my Father's name was Lonegrin Magnir Holmberg. Father worked the nets on the trawlers. When the Gods looked favourably upon us there was plenty of food to be divided equally amongst all the families. If the Gods were angry for missed sacrifices or evil deeds, there would not be enough fish for the community and people would go hungry. Fortunately, my family had other means of earning money, so we never went hungry.

> My mother had golden hair that flowed to her waist like a field of late summer wheat. She let me brush her hair and with each stroke Mother would whisper stories of my ancestors, about elves and trolls and the symbols carved on the runes. I loved hearing about the most famous of my ancestors, who to use your words was an Oracle or a Shaman. Vikings also called them Stonecasters, and my ancestor, Sigrid Gustavson, not only interpreted the runes

but had visions of the future. Sigrid was the youngest of five daughters just like me. She lived in the fourteenth century and had five daughters sired by King Valdemar IV of Gotland.

My parents believed I was blessed with Sigrid's ability to see the future and talk with animals. There had been numerous occasions that I dreamt something would happen and it did. My mother admitted she did not have Sigrid's vision of the future, although she was seldom wrong when she interpreted the runes. Mainlanders paid handsomely to sit with Birgitta Holmberg. No one doubted her skill.

My parents ran a rooming house. On the first floor there was a large kitchen, a hand pump for fresh well water, a pantry, and an eating room with six tables that sat thirty paying guests. On the second floor we had six bedrooms. We girls shared one room, my parents their room, and the others we rented to sailors awaiting the ferryboats to Norrkoping, or Stockholm. Each room had two bunk beds that slept six. Our house was spotless, the mattresses were lice-free, and my mother's saffron pancakes and sweet potato pies were famous throughout all of Gotland.

Father was at sea before sun-up and would come home on the late high tide. When the sea was heavy and the nets empty it was the boarding house rent and earnings from Mother's runes kept us fed.

My parents, like all Gutes, believed that a girl was ripe for marriage after her fourteenth winter. Each of my sisters was married before they turned sixteen. By the time I turned ten they were all gone. The girls wasted no time in leaving our boarding house and filling their homes with little screaming yellow-haired Gotlanders. I lost count of all my nieces and nephews but knew that with the departure of each of my siblings, my workload increased.

And then World War II broke out. Ships and sailors overwhelmed our harbour. I slept on a cot in my parents' room and we rented out the girls' room for six more guests. Mother and I ran like crazy chickens from morning to night and there were days I fell asleep as I washed the dishes. Money was pouring into our strong box but Mother was fraught with despair. I overhead her telling Father that when she cast the stones for us our family's future was rife with danger. With every reading, the rune tiles of *Perth* with the tile of *Odin* were selected again and again. Those two symbols meant death.

"Charles Michael, I need to explain how Sweden fit into the World War II," Ingrid reflected, realizing that her country's neutrality was paramount to what unfolded.

Sweden struggled to remain neutral even though Germany had taken over Norway, Finland, and Denmark. Our homeland was in an awkward position with England's sea mines on one side and Germany's sea mines on the other. Even though Sweden was neutral, German soldiers on leave from Norway were given the right to pass through our country. They could use our trains and boats to get home. German soldiers and sailors began billeting at our boarding house with sometimes ten sleeping to a room. Mother passionately despised the Germans because of the way they had abused our people during World War I. She warned Father that they would destroy our family, but he ignored her and was thankful for all the money they paid. Our German borders seemed friendly and always paid properly. Some gave us tins of coffee, bags of sugar, bars of chocolate, and tobacco for Father. My father told my mother we could not turn away the

German sailors without expecting repercussions. Actually, that is how I met my husband.

"Henrik was a German sailor?" Charlie interrupted, and Ingrid's look of disgust made him regret opening his mouth.

"Does the name Henrik Petersson sound Germanic to you?" she rebuked sharply, staring angrily like an eagle about to strike. "Charles Michael Langdon, would I have married a goose-stepping bastard Nazi butcher?"

As Langdon fumbled with an apology, Ingrid dismissed him.

"As I was saying before I was interrupted," she enunciated each word for effect, "that is how I met my husband."

It was late August 1943 and news arrived that Germany had dissolved the government in Denmark. There was much fighting in the Danish streets. The Germans imposed martial law just after they arrested King Christian and the Prime Minister. Swedish sailors brought news that the Danes had scuttled their ships rather than turn them over to the Nazis. We were also told that fifteen Danish patrol ships escaped and found refuge in harbours just south of Stockholm. There was celebration in Gotland when we learned about the Danes' heroism.

It was Saturday supper and our dining room was crammed to the rafters. Mother, Father, and I were running from kitchen to table serving food and drink. There were a few Swedes but mostly Germans that day. One German sailor spoke fluent Swedish learned during summers at his grandparents' farm north of Stockholm. His name was Konrad Wagner and he was a giant with a square jaw and a large nose that looked like it had been broken many times. Wagner was Midshipman First Class on a frigate moored in our harbour and had won a silver medal in wrestling at the 1936 Olympics. He showed us a photo of him with Adolph Hitler and other German champions. Konrad was a handsome boy and I hoped he would notice me. I told him my sixteenth birthday was just a month away, and he winked at me.

Konrad introduced his shipmates beginning with Wilhem Reichman who was his best friend. Wilhem was not half the height of his Olympic pal but had broad shoulders and the look of a happy man who laughed heartily. I remember thinking he needed to take a bath. In the chair beside Wilhem was Karsten Shroder from Munich whose parents ran a pastry shop, and his girth showed he liked sampling their products. Karsten had a very youthful face . . . not old enough to shave let alone be in the navy. He had terrible acne with pockmarks around the back of his neck.

The ugly sailor sitting beside the boy was introduced as Axel Mueller and he had a frightening scar over his left eye and horrible teeth that were yellowed with tobacco. He was from Essen and his father was Gestapo. Mueller smelled badly of liquor and kept making rude motions with his tongue when I met his gaze. Unbelievably, he ignorantly spat a piece of gristle onto Mother's floor. When I bent to pick it up he slipped his hand up between my thighs and groped my buttocks, half-lifting me off my feet. The Olympian knocked his hand away. Mueller chortled with delight and rubbed his hand on the front of his pants. Mother sent me to look to the other tables.

Ingrid raised her glass of water and took a sip, her hand shaking as she continued.

The scarred sailor then took a small bouquet of heather from his tunic and put it on the table. Mother saw the bouquet and her eyes bulged because heather within a house invited *spaecraft*—black magic and death. The Olympian comprehended the superstition, having spent his summers in Sweden. He politely explained the issue to the scar-faced sailor and reached to remove the heather. Axel Mueller stopped him and the two began shouting. Father came from the kitchen to see what was amiss. Mother pointed to the heather and Father rushed over.

And then a brawl erupted in our dining room. When Axel violently shoved Father into another table, my mother slapped him across the face. The coward returned her slap. When I ran to defend Mom I was hoisted in the air and hastily deposited beneath a table.

"Stay little one," a booming deep voice commanded. I watched as a giant Swedish sailor grabbed the scar face by the neck, hammered his head, and effortlessly threw him face first through our wall. I say 'through our wall' because the sailor's head went into the wall. With that, every German attacked the Swede. I had never seen grown men fight, and I must admit it was both terrifying and exhilarating. The other Swedes in the room rushed into the melee to defend their friend. Tables, chairs, glasses, and plates flew about like they had been caught in a maelstrom.

Konrad Wagner snuck up behind my giant with a dagger in his right hand. I could not believe an Olympian would stab a man in the back. I raced across the room and jumped on him. He glared at me confused as to what to do.

"Stop it Konrad!" I shouted defiantly. "You are an Olympian."

"Let go Ingegard," Konrad screamed, but I chomped my teeth on his right ear; he squealed like one of our piglets and began spinning to shake me off. And then Father was upon us, grabbing Konrad's arm while pulling at me to let go. The wrestler kicked Father away and then grabbed my hair. That was when the Swedish sailor crossed the room and thumped the wrestler's jaw with one mighty punch. The Olympian's face caved in like it was made of wet clay.

A loud gunshot exploded and everyone froze like statues. An abnormally tall German officer stood in the hallway pointing his gun at the ceiling. He had the shiniest boots that reached his knees. The officer lowered his aim directly at the Swedish sailor.

"Nein," my mother shouted loudly, blood streaming from her nose. She ran over and stood directly in the line of fire. "Your men attacked my family. Look at my face. Is this how the German Navy conducts itself towards unarmed civilians in a neutral country?" The Luger remained fixed.

Mother then hurried to the front door and retrieved a framed picture of 'Der Fuhrer,' which we hung on the wall by the door whenever Germans boarded.

"Would Herr Hitler approve of this behaviour?" Mother screamed, glaring at the officer as she held up the frame for him to see. "*Bitte*. Enough harm has been done tonight."

Ingrid stopped telling the story, walked into the kitchen, and began organizing dishes on the counter.
"What happened?" Charlie asked impatiently, exasperated that she would stop at such a critical juncture of the story.
"Pardon me?" the storyteller asked innocently, enjoying her listener's greed for more.
"The officer with the gun!"
Ingrid waggled her finger.
"You will have to wait for my story to continue tomorrow night."
Charlie groaned like a ten year old being sent to bed.
"You can't be serious. I have to leave tomorrow," he complained, staring at a Swedish version of Scheherazade.

"Tomorrow night, Charles Michael," was her firm reply. "Now, wash the dishes and put the garbage in the bins by the back door. We'll leave a plate for Tomte on the wicker table."

Chapter Twelve

An exhausted Kyla Langdon arrived at Duane Michaels' house for a quiet Sunday dinner and was surprised to see so many cars in his driveway. There was a cherry red Ferrari, a midnight black Lamborghini Diablo, a black 2014 Fisker, a silver Tesla Sport, and two new brightly-coloured Jaguars. Evangeline's return flight from Houston had been cancelled so when the ex-NFLer called, the real estate agent eagerly assumed it would just be the two of them. She flipped down the visor mirror of her Roadster to check her lipstick and hair.

Kyla's last few days had been hectic but productive. After beating the crap out of Charlie she had driven her Mercedes around the corner and pulled up behind the moving van she had hired. When Charlie drove off in his Porsche, she gave the movers the go-ahead. Four hours later, the contents of the truck were unloaded into the magnificent 3,200 square foot condo she had purchased seven days earlier on the forty-ninth floor of The Four Seasons in Toronto's trendy Yorkville district, with its galleries and excessively expensive stores. It gave her immeasurable satisfaction that she was living at the same address as her life consultant Suzanne Weston.

While formulating her plan to dump Charlie, she considered how Suzanne would go about it. Suzanne Weston's mentorship and guidance had unlocked Kyla's potential, helped her to see the big picture, and, provided her with the tools to secure success beyond her wildest dreams. Meeting Suzanne Weston had been the best thing that had happened to Kyla since arriving in Toronto as that doe-eyed farm girl from Clinton, Ontario. Suzanne had taken a naive Francine and turned her into a star.

Kyla had not been Kyla Langdon when she first arrived in Toronto. Her birth name was Francine Powell, and her first few months in Toronto had been exhilarating with everything and everyone new. But the lustre began to rust when she realized that her after-tax pay barely covered her living expenses. She couldn't possibly afford the fashionable wardrobe or exciting life of her dreams. Looking at all the unattainable expensive shoes, purses, and outfits in store windows incensed her. Seeing an endless parade of highly successful and beautifully presented women embarrassed her. They took taxis but she had to commute on a smelly subway battlefield where men constantly groped her or made suggestive comments.

Loneliness and boredom set in. Working in a dental office was a quiet occupation and most nights she sat alone in her tiny apartment and ate microwaveable dinners in front of the TV. When her solitude became crippling she listened to coworkers' advice to get out and meet men at bars, nightclubs, and gallery openings. Her early shyness quickly eroded when Francine realized how the dating game worked. The men she saw weren't like the farm boys or the guys at college. They wanted sex at the end of the evening. Francine quickly learned that she could have the nightlife she wanted simply by using her God-given attributes. The farm girl's virginity was lost without fanfare.

Francine had several dental clients she enjoyed including the Langdon family. She was saddened with Rose Langdon's death and felt a compunction to help Rose's son keep on track. She kept in touch with him when he left for university and wrote encouraging letters. When Charlie graduated from Queen's, he was a tall strapping young man full of confidence, hope, and potential. Unlike most young men she knew, Charlie Langdon was decent, and they began to form a wonderful friendship. Despite the difference in their ages, they fell in love. After they married, she determined that as Francine Langdon she could achieve her dreams. But with each new inflow of money or new job title, Charlie spent more time away from her. Their sex life waned and she found herself once again eating microwaveable dinners in front of the TV. Loneliness and boredom returned and she felt that her dreams had once again been derailed.

Francine Langdon noticed the attractive woman come into the dentist's office on numerous occasions but had never worked on her teeth. She was fascinated with the tall, slender, magnificently dressed consultant who pulled up to the building in a sexy, black, two-seater Mercedes convertible. All the girls in the office slobbered over Suzanne Weston as if she were a movie star.

And then one day, completely out of the blue, Suzanne Weston walked over to Francine and introduced herself.

"Hi Francine. We've never been properly introduced, but I've admired your look for years. My name is Suzanne Weston. Can I buy you a coffee?"

Her lunch break disappeared into a flurry of questions, as if Suzanne were interviewing her. Francine was captivated with the world traveller who spoke half a dozen languages, owned a two-bedroom condo at the exclusive Four Seasons Residence in Yorkville, and a six-story apartment building in the eighth arrondissement of Paris where the Rue La Boetie intersected Avenue des Champs-Elysees.

"The Penthouse is mine. The other ten apartments are all long-term leases."

"How did you manage to own a building in Paris?" Francine probed unabashedly. Her imagination ran to Suzanne having been the mistress of an extremely wealthy Parisian who had set her up for life.

Suzanne sat back and smiled. It was a story she loved to tell.

"I arrived in Paris in 1998 as an exchange student studying languages. The plan was a yearlong term with equal amounts of time spent in each of Paris, Rome, and Geneva. I was a very young and naïve twenty-one year old."

Francine Langdon did some quick math to determine Suzanne was thirty-eight.

"I fell in love with Paris the first night I arrived. I had never seen anything so magnificent. One afternoon, I was walking along the Avenue des Champs-Elysees when I observed an elderly Parisian lady patiently waiting for the traffic to clear so she could cross the street. I quickly approached and offered assistance. She accepted, and we walked to her absolutely breath-taking apartment on the top floor of a building just off the Avenue. Her name was Genevieve Lancot and she invited me in for espresso with biscuits. We struck up a friendship and within weeks I moved from the school's residence into one of her four bedrooms. Eventually, she told me that she owned the entire building. It had been a gift from the love of her life, a now long-deceased former President of the Republic. After surviving the Nazi occupation in World War II, she met him while he was a high-ranking soldier with a wife and three children. His family had wealth and he bought her the building as a place where they could meet and for her to earn a respectable living as a landlord. He stayed in her life for twenty years until, with great fanfare, he was laid to rest. It was obvious of whom she was speaking but I never pressed nor did she ever reveal or confirm his true identity."

Suzanne Weston's face relaxed as she remembered her friend.

"Madame spent the 1960s, 70s and 80s teaching etiquette, fashion, and foreign languages to the daughters and wives of the upper class and diplomatic core. My new friend beguiled me with her fountain of experience and I realized that I needed to learn everything she knew. After university I remained in Paris for eight years gleaning an unparalleled education from my incredible mentor. In return, Madame Lancot had my full attention, my companionship, and with time, my love. Genevieve died in her sleep and, much to my surprise, left me everything she owned—including the building and the luxurious contents of her apartment. As I thought of my future, I realized that Madame Lancot had created me to be able to teach others.

After much planning, I set up my own consultancy and quickly found worthy clients in Paris and Toronto willing to pay me handsomely to transform their potential into reality. I am fortunate to be wealthy enough to be able to select my clients."

Francine Langdon stared like a ravenous dog looking at a delicious meat-covered bone. Suzanne's life was a story with a fairy-tale ending. Weston was smart, rich, beautiful, and independent.

Suzanne recognized the look. "I can help you with your dream, but it will take a lot of work and money."

"How long and how much?" Francine asked eagerly. "I can't take living like this anymore. I want to be you."

Suzanne Weston smiled indulgently and acknowledged, "Francine, everybody wants to be me. Now, let's meet tonight for dinner and I'll explain in detail how I work. That is, if you are available."

Six hours later in a very posh restaurant that Francine had only read about, Suzanne Weston retrieved a black moleskin book from her purse. Charlie's wife listened intently as her hostess explained her role in successfully transforming high potential women.

"You would be my twenty-fourth client in eight years. Every one of your predecessors completed my transformation with the utmost of success. Not one earns an annual salary of less than $300 thousand. Four of them married Internet billionaires with iron clad prenuptial agreements."

"Can you tell me who any of them are?"

"Confidentiality and discretion are paramount with my clients," she explained truthfully, and then elaborated on her remuneration, which included an upfront payment of $25 thousand cash and a second equal payment at the end of the transformation. Following that, there would be a legally binding 5% of the pre-taxed future earnings of her client in each of the first five years of their "new" career.

"You know that I would give my left arm to do this, but dental hygienists don't earn much."

Suzanne dabbed the side of her lips with the cloth napkin. "Yes, but your husband Charles Langdon does. Last year, Charles earned north of $250 thousand at Telfer Stuart Advertising—or at least that's what he filed on his income tax return. I'm certain, there are other monies he neglected to report. Including the money he inherited from his mother's insurance policy, the two of you currently have two of you currently have $837,562.87 invested across stocks, GICs, RRSPS, and Canadian treasury bills. When the stock market haemorrhaged in 2008, your husband jumped on the gold wagon and invested $50 thousand in gold at $145 per ounce. At today's price, you own $500 thousand in gold certificates. I think you can afford me."

The farm girl from Clinton's face scrunched up in utter amazement. "How do you know all this?"

"Francine, the issue is not how I know this but that you do not. Half of those dollars belong to you. Don't you think you should take better care of your own finances? Why are you so content in letting someone else write your destiny?"

Francine's face turned ghostly pale.

Suzanne Weston leaned forward. "Francine, when I am done with you, you will out-earn your husband and won't think twice about paying me five points on your gross. Make a decision whether you want to become a woman of independent means with a life not unlike my own. Now, you need to make a choice, because I've invested two and a half hours and the clock is ticking."

Francine's apprehension was visible. "What if I'm not smart enough to pull it off?"

Suzanne Weston folded her napkin and placed it on the table. She quickly signed the bill and replaced her credit card in her purse. As she stood, she leaned over Francine and whispered in her ear.

"Do you think I would be talking with you if I hadn't already decided you're a winner? Francine, you are more than smart enough. You are being held back and need me to unlock your potential. I have not achieved my success by taking on losers for clients."

After signing the contract with Suzanne Weston, Francine told Charlie she intended to quit her job and focus on self-improvement. The young adman was heavily invested in a new client pitch and frankly didn't care. The next day Francine resigned from the dental office and withdrew $25 thousand from the bank.

Suzanne outlined the plan that would encompass six months of intensive transformation beginning with speech therapy, professional etiquette, presentation, personal branding, and selling skills. Francine would learn how to walk, sit, stand, eat, laugh, and ask questions. She would glean the skill of listening and eliciting information of importance.

The consultant insisted on improving the basics of her client's knowledge. "You will read two hours every day to be able to discuss anything with anyone. Your reading list will include the *Wall Street Journal*, the *Atlantic Quarterly*, *Vanity Fair*, *Vogue*, *Art Europe*, and the *NY Sunday Times*. You will write down questions that are confusing. I will answer them. You will also keep a dictionary handy. Here is a list of two hundred words I want you to memorize and begin employing in your everyday communications."

Weston was adamant Francine fully comprehended what men enjoyed most. "In the next two months you will know more about professional baseball, basketball, and football than your husband who prides himself a sports aficionado. ESPN.com will become your go-to site."

Langdon's determination steeled as her mind absorbed the lessons like a porous sponge sopping up water.

"Francine," Suzanne purred, stroking the back of Francine's neck. "You must learn that the simple touch of your hand can encourage a man or a woman to buy whatever you are selling without thinking they receive sex in the exchange. The minute you cross that physical line to close a deal you will be lost forever. Don't look so shocked. When I'm done with you, men and women will be captivated by your look, your persona, and your confidence. To illustrate my point, I can tell that you are sexually attracted to me. Everyone is, so don't be embarrassed."

Francine's skin instantly blotched red with embarrassment.

"My dear, we all have imaginations. Now, onto more pressing matters. We need to tackle that unkempt horse's mane you call hair and rid ourselves of those revoltingly hideous caterpillars that top your eyes."

Long wavy brown tresses were shorn to the floor. Her off-the-shoulder length hair was dyed a vibrant, ashen blond hue. Eyebrows were sculpted and an excruciatingly barbaric bikini wax attacked unwanted hair below the waist.

"Your smile needs to be electric and magnetic," Weston announced, and Francine's teeth were straightened and whitened. Four porcelains were added.

Weston emptied Francine's closet and made a sharp pronouncement. "Even I couldn't wear these clothes and make them look good. They have to go. You will have a wardrobe for daytime, late afternoon, and evening. You will learn to adore Ralph Lauren, Alexander McQueen, and Proenza Schouler. I can't wait to see you wearing Christian Louboutin."

"The shoes with the red soles?" Francine asked, bringing a rare smile to her consultant's face.

"Yes, the red lacquered soles and high stiletto heels. You have spectacular legs and dainty feet that permit you to wear his more creative and colourful expressions. You'll spend a fortune on Louboutin, but it will complete the picture."

Over the next week, Francine put more than $62 thousand on Charlie's credit card.

"You have a darling figure," Suzanne complimented, "but you look too soft and too old-fashioned girly. I have someone who will keep the sexiness you exude but cut away your pudginess, firm you up, strengthen your core, and bolster your confidence. She'll also educate you on diet, because you are what you eat."

And so stage two began with five training sessions a week with Suzanne's personal fitness trainer—a former triathlete, a champion body builder, a Fourth Degree Shotakan Black Belt, and a nutritionist named Crystal Garvey. Crystal tackled Francine with the same enthusiasm she employed in her own Spartan-like training. It began with diet. Francine, a meat-eating, dessert-loving girl, became a vegetarian who started the day with a kale and chlorophyll-laced protein shake and cleansing pills that gave her diarrhoea for a month. Her caloric intake was halved. Gone were caffeine, soda, chocolate, nicotine, alcohol, and any form of recreational drug. Five eight-ounce glasses of water flushed her system until her 10:00 p.m. bed curfew.

Crystal Garvey's exercise regimen was physically exhausting, involving endless squats, lifts, stretching, planks, free weights, and push-ups. Three weeks into the program, Garvey introduced Francine to the heavy punching bag, grappling, and floor work designed to arm her with defensive abilities and bolster her self-esteem.

Six months later, Francine Langdon looked, walked, and conducted herself like a new woman, like the slick package she had become, drawing stares from everyone.

"Francine, you have made wonderful progress and I am so very proud of you," Suzanne began. "We are nearing the end of our plan and I've decided on the career that will allow you to achieve your dream. It will be very lucrative with your newly acquired skills, your appearance, and my contacts."

Francine anxiously sat forward.

"You will become a real estate agent–but not just any real estate agent. You will become the agent for the Chinese money flooding from Hong Kong into Canada. One of my clients is the seventh top agent in Hong Kong. The two of you will strike a deal. While other agents are scurrying to sell houses, you will find the houses desired as investments by Chinese clients who won't think twice about spending $5 million. You have the brains, the drive, and the whole physical and mental package to be a success. Your conversational skills have become engaging and intelligent. Over the next month as you secure your real estate licence, a tutor will help you hone your rudimentary Mandarin. Remember, there is no way for you to become fluent, but I want clients to see the effort you are making and that you care about their language and customs. You must always express yourself politely and respectfully to those with money. I will secure your first job in thirty days with a firm whose owners I know well. By the end of the first year, you will be their number one agent. The others in the office will detest you. In two or three years you will quit the company and open your own firm which will allow you to keep the whole commission."

"Alright. I like that," Francine agreed confidently. "What else?"

"Your name has to go."

"Do you have a suggestion?"

"I don't make suggestions. I have always been able to match the perfect name with the person," she added reflectively. "Your name will be Kyla—Kyla Victoria Langdon. Let me hear you say your new name."

Francine looked into Suzanne's sparkling eyes, smiled warmly and held out her right hand.

"How do you do? I'm Kyla Langdon. Kyla Victoria Langdon. And you are?"

One year later, Kyla Victoria Langdon had sold thirty-eight houses and had brought home more net income than Charlie. Twenty-five of those properties were purchased sight unseen by overseas buyers introduced through Suzanne's Hong Kong agent. Kyla became a selling machine, hated by office colleagues for her ruthless aggression and unyielding desire to win the commission. Every year thereafter, her property sales and commissions rocketed, and as Suzanne had predicted, Kyla hung out her own slate. Now she kept twice the commission and paid four employees to do the grunt work. Unlike her husband's leased Porsche, her new company purchased her a 2015 Mercedes SLS AMG GT Roadster. It was the first sold in Canada and, with its gullwing doors, V8, seven-speed transmission, and 583 horsepower, the $312 thousand futuristic vehicle bolstered her already golden image of being a winner. She was named "Uber-agent of Toronto," was photographed for the cover of *Real Estate News*, and named one of "The Top 25 Businesswomen in Toronto to Watch."

Kyla Victoria Langdon stopped thinking about the past and hopped out of her Mercedes. Her body was tingling as she started walking up the granite stones towards the front door, anticipating all the things Duane would do to her. Excessively aggressive rap music from within the house pounded a disturbingly loud beat.

Before she could ring the bell, the front door swung opened and Kyla was confronted by three exquisite-looking women dressed in traditional Chinese garb, hair and makeup done as if they had been just teleported from the sixteenth century to Duane Michaels' twenty-first century foyer. The thick, white foundation facial makeup disguised their ages.

"Good evening, Ms. Langdon," the tallest of the trio said in a crisp British accent. Her hazel eyes sparkled as if they were electric. "I am Ming Lee. The peacock blue dress is Mai Li Chu. Our sister in red with the generous breasts is Kiki Chen. Our master has told us to make you welcome. Please enter."

Kyla stared blankly at Ming Lee who along with the other two, led her gently into the front room.

"Kyla baby," a booming voice shouted at the top of his lungs, and an imposing Barbarian warrior came bounding towards them with a battle-axe in one hand and a spear in the other. The three magnificently dressed "slaves" dropped to the floor in a supplicant position.

"Master," they announced in unison.

"You're late," Michaels cried, and moving past the prone women he tossed aside the axe, picked up Kyla by the waist and lifted her high in the air. He reeked of marijuana.

"Baby, have you met my new slaves? We've just invaded northern China."

Duane half-dropped Kyla to the floor and turned to Ming.

"Come here, Ming baby," he ordered, and when she obeyed, Duane grabbed her up and kissed her deeply, all the while staring at Kyla to gauge her reaction.

"Will you be enjoying us before or after the feast, my master?" Ming asked calmly, as if she were inquiring about a glass of water.

"Conan will feast on you after we eat," he replied, pushing her aside and reaching over to slap the girl in the red kimono on the behind.

"Yes, master."

"Get the princess ready," he commanded, as a group of heavily muscled fur-clad men rushed through the house yelling in mock battle.

"Come, Conan," a warrior shouted, and Duane turned from the women and chased after the warring horde, screaming bloody murder.

Kyla's protests fell on deaf ears as she was forcibly hustled up the stairs and led into one of the guest bedrooms by the girls. There was a broad array of traditional Chinese dresses draped across the bed.

"Let go," she ordered, aggressively pushing the girl in the red dress to the ground. Mai Li Chu quickly wrenched Kyla's left arm and pinned it behind her back. Attempting to break the hold as Crystal Garvey had trained her, Kyla twisted her hips and prepared to deliver a rear "donkey" kick. But before she could, Kiki was back on her feet and punched her in the stomach. Kyla buckled over, gasping for a breath as six hands stripped her naked. The leader of the three hushed everyone and stood face to face with Kyla.

"Kyla, stop struggling. You're making this more difficult than it has to be," Ming Lee spoke, minus the crisp British accent. Langdon didn't exactly relax, but stopped the shoving match. "You're new to Duane's world. Tonight he's Conan the Barbarian and we're the conquered Chinese. Last week he was some Mexican General attacking the Alamo and we were Texas homesteaders' wives. Last month Duane was an astronaut and the three of us were alien princesses on Mars."

The woman pulled off her black wig. "Kyla, I'm not even Chinese. None of us are. My name is Amanda Rousseff and I was born in Brazil. I've been with the Michaels the longest. Kiki over there is Karen Nguyen. She's from Buffalo and her parents were born in Vietnam. Karen has an incredible temper so she's not one to mess with. And Mai Li? Honey, take off your wig." The third of the trio pulled off her black wig revealing the lightest blond hair.

"I'm Eliene Streefkerk. I was born in the Netherlands. I've known Duane for five years."

Kyla stared at the trio as the blond smiled and refastened her wig.

Amanda put her hands together as if in prayer. "This is their game. If you're going to survive with Duane and Evangeline you will have to play along. Tonight, Duane wanted Chinese slaves, so here we are. He assigns us names and we dress up and offer his guests cocaine, other mood-enhancing drugs, and an assortment of colourfully ribbed condoms. When the party reaches a crescendo, he will offer us to his generals. Duane insists on everyone practising safe sex and Heaven help the guest who attempts otherwise. He will keep you for himself. Tomorrow morning he'll pay us each seven grand in cash. When it's only the Michaels present we get one grand a night. But consider that we are never in any danger of physical violence, and we never have to pay a pimp. This is a really sweat deal."

Karen looked over to Kyla and laughed. "Duane told us to tell you that three of his guests want to buy houses in Toronto. So there's a big commission for you—which are his words, not mine."

"You three may be prostitutes, but I'm not," Kyla argued, unable to stop calculating the commission on three houses.

Amanda laughed and the others joined in. "Duane told us you would say exactly that and asked us to remind you that you've already earned a lot of commissions on your back."

That statement embarrassed her and the newcomer looked sheepishly around the room.

"I need to talk with Duane," she stated, defiantly placing her hands on her hips. These three had no idea with whom they were dealing.

Karen Nguyen casually stepped forward and, with a lightning-fast hand, grabbed Kyla's upper lip between her thumb and index finger. Kyla writhed in pain as the girl in the red dress maintained a vice-like grip, rendering Kyla helpless. True to Amanda's warning about her temper, Nguyen's face looked ready to kill.

"None of us get paid tonight if you don't cooperate and play along," Karen hissed. "This is huge money, and I'm not going to let you screw it up."

Kyla gripped her assailant's hand as tears streamed from her eyes. She tried desperately to break the girl's hold, but nothing Garvey had taught her worked. Her tormentor held tight and led her around the room by the lip as if displaying who was queen of the castle.

"Enough," Amanda directed, and Karen reluctantly released her grip.

Kyla stepped away from the three, tenderly touched her mouth, and grimaced.

"Let me try to explain this differently," Eliene stated calmly, holding up a dampened facecloth she had retrieved from the bathroom. She motioned for Kyla to put it on her lip to contain the swelling that was about to ensue. "You're the flavour of the month for the Michaels. Each one of us was that flavour, and now we aren't. In time, someone else will replace you, and then you will replace one of us. That's how Duane's world works. But for now, we all stand to make a lot of money. Last year we each made close to $175 thousand."

"Tax free," Amanda interrupted.

Karen helped the blond fix her wig and added, "We get to take home some drugs, and that's another bonus of Duane's world."

Amanda replaced her own wig and checked it in the vanity mirror. She pursed her lips and wiped lipstick off her front teeth.

"And besides," Amanda continued, "how successful will you be when Duane spreads that you screwed a client to close a sale?"

The noise of the party-battle raging below had reached epic proportions. Kyla remembered a comment from Suzanne Weston. "*When you dance with the devil, he decides when the music stops.*" She considered that the commissions would net two hundred grand.

"So what do I do?" she asked in a defeated tone.

Karen Nguyen picked up a magnificent silk dress. "Good girl. Tonight, you're the Empress. You get the most beautiful dress and jewels. Don't take any drugs during the party. We do that on our own time."

The trio began dressing and spraying Kyla. Eliene held up a wig and winked. "It's okay Kyla, everything will be fine. Just follow our lead, and don't ever do anything to cross Duane Michaels."

* * *

As they trekked along a pathway through her forest, Ingrid pointed out trees where mischievous elves preferred to hide. By a hillside of shale she warned that trolls lived beneath the earth.

"Don't come this way at night," she instructed, as they moved past an area that abutted the lake.

And according to the elderly Swede, not all the evil spirits were of Norse origin. At least half had Ojibwe names and origins.

After an hour of hiking they arrived at a bend in the most southerly of Ingrid's three rivers. For being almost ninety, the Swede set an aggressive pace—especially when the swelling of Charlie's testicles had only just started to ebb.

"This is the Pottawatomi River," she explained. "It was the tiniest of the rivers I showed you on the map of our property. We never trapped this river. The Ojibwe felt it was best for irrigating our farmlands because of its proximity to the fields with the richest loam. They had a rule about using nature's resources for only one thing at a time, so the idea of using a river for both trapping and irrigating was bad medicine."

There was a small wooden table with two chairs by a clearing on the north side of the river. Charlie removed their lunch from the knapsack while Ingrid filled a pitcher with river water. The Swede looked towards a stand of small pines and reached into her pocket. A female deer and her fawn walked unafraid towards her from the undergrowth. When she held up an apple and spoke, the two leaned forward and allowed the elderly woman to hug them like puppies. Momentarily, she whispered in the mother's ear and directed her attention to Charlie. The deer looked at him and walked over. Slowly she nuzzled his chest. This went on for several minutes until the two gentle creatures returned to the pines and quickly disappeared into the camouflage.

Langdon was astonished.

"You know, in the olden days, that little interaction would have gotten both of us burned at the stake."

The elderly gardener smiled. "Lovely, aren't they?"

As they sat at the table, Charlie leaned forward.

"The German naval officer didn't shoot because the giant turned out to be Henrik . . . right?"

Ingrid fastened the cord on a wide-brimmed straw bonnet.

> After being shamed by my mother, the officer holstered his Luger, clicked his heels sharply, and removed his hat.

"If my men are at fault then I am deeply embarrassed," the naval officer apologized in flawless Swedish, as he glared at the throng of men intertwined about the room. He smiled awkwardly and I knew he was one of those deceitful men Father said used a smile to hide their true feelings.

"I am Manfred Richter, Korvettenkapitan of the Frigate Rhineland-Platz," the man with the luger said, introducing himself as if we were at a social gathering. His uniform was impeccable and he wore a tiny thin moustache across the top lip. His sideburns were unusually long and wispy. For being so quick to fire his pistol, I thought that Richter looked like he would be more comfortable working at the tobacconist shop.

My parents stared at him but neither responded. My mother's nose had swollen and her chin was covered in blood. Father was unsteady on his feet from the blow he had sustained.

"These men are under my command," he added, not knowing what else to say. The officer then made a perfunctory bow accompanied by another click of his boot heels.

The shame on his sailors' faces told all. With great difficulty, Konrad Wagner rose to his feet, stumbled sideways, and saluted. His face and tunic were splattered with blood and his nose was pointed sideways.

"First Midshipman, what happened here?" the officer demanded, speaking Swedish.

"A misunderstanding Korvettenkapitan," Wagner replied sheepishly. As he attempted a bloody smile, I could see that his two front teeth were gone. "The lady speaks true. As Senior Midshipman I accept responsibility."

The other German sailors quickly queued up and faced their commander whose stern expression betrayed his displeasure.

The Swede who had come to our aid was bloodied yet defiant. In his right hand he gripped a broken wine bottle and in the other a dazed German who was dangling inches off the floor.

"If you would not mind setting him down?" the officer asked calmly.

"I will when you agree to pay this family for the damages caused by these cowardly animals you call sailors."

The officer nodded through an obviously displeased smile.

Our giant dropped the sailor to the floor, placed his left boot on the rear of his victim and sent him sprawling.

There was a noise coming from the side of our dining room. It was the scar-faced sailor whose head was still lodged into the wall.

"Get him out of there," Richter ordered loudly, and several Germans struggled to pull him loose.

Then Manfred Richter walked over and stood before my father. I noticed he had clever eyes that were very narrow, giving him a more threatening appearance.

"Sir, this behaviour is not representative of the German Navy. My men will be brought before the Kapitan who is a severe disciplinarian. Damages will be compensated immediately."

"Get out of my house," Father commanded. "We do not want your money. Just leave and do not come back."

The officer did not know how to react to such a rebuke made by a Swede in front of his men. The smile that had been plastered on his face disappeared in an instant. He turned away from my father and began barking orders. The sailors jumped to attention, fixing their uniforms and began restoring order to our dining room. One retrieved a broom and began sweeping up broken plates, glass wear, and food.

Despite my father's protests, the Germans queued up and shoved Deutschmarks into my parents' hands. The last to step forward was the instigator. His face was a bleeding pulp yet when he confronted Mother he had the audacity and contempt to laugh. Like the others, he pushed money at her but his Deutschmarks were wrapped around a sprig of heather. Mother pushed his hand away and spat in his face.

The officer bellowed and the sailors filed from the room. And then the house fell quiet and the Swedes boarding with us went to their rooms. My giant threw several logs onto the fire and sat on the floor facing the front door like a guard dog.

"The runes foretold that the Germans would bring harm to our house and you refused to listen," Mother chastised Father, and the two began arguing until Father took her in his arms.

I got a pot of boiling water and a towel to address the damage inflicted on our protector's face and knuckles. His skin was like tanned leather, his face carved granite, his blond beard rough as thistles on the hill behind the barn, and, his eyes as crystal blue as the Baltic on a sunny July afternoon. As I tended the wounds his eyes never left mine. I put my tiny hand on his massive chest.

"My brave Viking warrior," I whispered sincerely, "thank you for our lives."

Despite the hour Mother brought out a plate of meat, bread, and sweets and insisted our sailor remain. As he ate, he politely introduced himself.

His name was Henrik Petersson and he was from a farm on the north mainland. At seventeen he had sought his fortune at sea and had circumvented the globe eight times. His ship was the Swedish Merchant moored beside the German frigate in our harbour, and he was First Mate. The ship was the *Sleipnir*. That was the name of Odin's eight-legged horse.

"Next spring," the First Mate announced, "I will be appointed Captain."

As he ate with a voracious appetite, he boasted the *Sleipnir* was ninety-six metres long and weighed almost five thousand tonnes. When Mother indiscreetly asked, he responded he had never married.

I asked how a Swedish merchant ship was allowed to sail during a war without being attacked by one side or the other. Henrik explained that sea travel was highly restricted because neither side wanted neutral Sweden to transport anything that might help the other. But all shipping could not be stopped or Sweden would not be able to continue to survive as a country. There was something called the Gothenburg Traffic treaty between England and Germany. It allowed six Swedish ships to cross the Atlantic each month to transport items that would allow Sweden to continue to run her factories—with no war materials transported for either side. Because of its tonnage and newer engines, the *Sleipnir* was selected to be one of the six, so it was permitted to travel across the Atlantic to transport oil from Argentina back to Sweden. Anyway, the *Sleipnir* had been forced to put into port when their sonar equipment had malfunctioned. Henrik's Captain had given him permission to come to my mother's boarding house to buy saffron pancakes. Captain Backstrom would understand him not returning for the night, but there would be hell to pay if the First Mate showed up without the pancakes for their breakfast.

While she had been talking, Ingrid repacked their table items into the rucksack and expertly sparked a small fire in a ring of stones along the edge of the river. From the knapsack she withdrew a small kettle and two tea mugs. Charlie noticed that whenever the story involved Henrik, Ingrid's voice mellowed into the tone of a much younger woman.

Ingrid ran her fingers through the length of her hair and then replaced the two silver combs behind her ears.

The repairs to the *Sleipnir* took two days and Henrik visited often, explaining he and the Captain were not rushing to leave Visby. The Captain had a woman down the coast in Roma. Mother doted on the First Mate and it is a miracle his stomach did not explode with the amount of food she fed him. Eventually, he admitted his age of forty years. I whispered to him that I was weeks away from turning sixteen.

When the repairs were completed, I was devastated because it meant Henrik would be going. I may have almost been sixteen but my heart was older. Mother filled a wooden box with his favourite foods and my parents hugged him as they did my sisters' husbands. And then he turned to me.

"I want you to have this," the sailor offered, handing me a heavy silver medallion of Odin's horse. My mother lifted my hair and fastened the chain around my neck. "It belonged to my grandfather's grandfather," he explained solemnly. "You wear it to remember."

I stared like one of my brainless chickens. He kissed me gently on the forehead and any words froze inside my head like winter ice in our harbour.

"I will remember you protecting me," he promised, and then he left.

We stood silently watching him walk along the city wall towards the docks. Mother said that if he turned three times it was a sign of marriage. I held my breath at her prediction as Henrik fully turned and waved. He walked another fifty metres and then turned again. As he reached the wharf he looked back and stared directly at me. My heart melted and my knees buckled causing me to almost topple over.

"It will be a long and happy marriage," Mother pronounced proudly, and then turned to Father. "Husband of mine, before you utter a word about his age, consider your own."

* * *

The loss of their biggest client hammered Telfer Stuart's industry credibility. The news of the firing spread like wildfire among competitors who circled the crippled agency like orcas scenting a wounded seal. Internally, employees huddled behind closed doors, speculating who'd be fired next. With Charlie Langdon gone, no one felt safe.

Leslie Ingrams brought forward the next roster of firings. Beyond Charlie Langdon, and the ten already out the door, twenty more had to be terminated. Leslie, Kevin, and Irv put all subjectivity aside. To the owners, this was a money game, and any vestige of company loyalty vanished as employees' careers were derailed with the tap of a key.

With her HR department and the company lawyer preparing the termination letters, Leslie reached into her top drawer and unwrapped a granola bar. As she took a bite of what would be her dinner she was grateful that her husband's schedule allowed him to pick up their two daughters and prepare their dinner. The lights of the Toronto skyline were twinkling below, and she wondered if she would even see her husband before he went to bed.

Leslie knew that her two bosses would remove the thirty employees without losing sleep. She, on the other hand, would probably be sick to her stomach until the last termination was executed. Leslie wished that Irv and Kevin had put her name on the top of the list. As she reached for her cup of tea she wondered how Charlie had survived telling his obnoxious wife that he'd been fired.

* * *

Phaidra McTavish took one last look in the bathroom mirror, anxious at the new lines that had appeared on her forehead. She practised smiling in such a way to minimize creases. It was just before noon on a Thursday, and Tessa's mother had thirty minutes to bus to K.T.'s Liquor and Smokes on King Street East near Parliament. For two years, she'd gone to K.T.'s every week and returned home with four forty-ounce bottles of Jack Daniels. If only it were Monday she would have been happier. That day took her to Sun Flower Dry Cleaners and its delightful owners. By good fortune, she had befriended a tiny Japanese lady at the market. After several encounters, Katsumi Hatoyama shared a private dilemma. The lady's husband, now in his mid-seventies, had desires. Katsumi implored Phaidra's help. Tessa's mother found Mr. Hatoyama to be a lovely man with the simplest of needs and the bargain was struck. Every Monday afternoon, Phaidra appeared at Sun Flower Dry Cleaners, had tea and a pleasant conversation with Katsumi, and then spent the next hour with Katsumi's husband in their upstairs apartment. Mr. Hatoyama bathed and expertly massaged her body with oil. She waited patiently but Katsumi's husband sat down beside her and held her hands.

"Thank you Phaidra McTavish. That was so pleasing to me," he whispered shyly.

Phaidra smiled. "Would you like to make love to me?"

Mr. Hatoyama stroked her cheek softly.

"Young lady, you have brought me such pleasure. My body no longer functions that way but I still enjoy the touch of a young woman's skin. I would not like my wife to know because she might think less of me. I hope this arrangement will continue and we can see each other again."

After Phaidra showered and dressed, Katsumi would thank her and hand her one hundred dollars, which was immediately spent on three bottles of Jim Beam. For two years, Phaidra had kept Mr. Hatoyama's secret. When Phaidra mentioned Tessa's new job, Katsumi selected clothing items that had not been picked up from their shop in over a year. She compiled ten extremely expensive high-end brand skirt and jacket combinations with labels including Vera Wang, Ann Taylor, and Donna Karan.

And that was why Phaidra McTavich loved Monday and the Hatoyamas.

But today was her dreaded Thursday's appointment with Kipper Tungston. Phaidra cringed as she hopped on the bus, thinking about the next two hours. The K.T.'s Liquor and Smoke's owner had noticed Phaidra on one of her more lucid days. She had found him repulsive with body odour that made her nostrils cringe. His fingernails were caked with dirt and in desperate need of clippers. The owner's breath was heavy with the smell of weed and Kipper was so vulgar he couldn't piece together a sentence without an expletive. She hesitatingly accepted an offer of lunch and after countless free drinks had sex with Kipper in his back storage room. Tungston used her roughly but Phaidra reluctantly agreed to a weekly session and left the store with two bottles of Jack Daniels and twenty-five dollars. It was a disquieting relationship of convenience, given that Kipper Tungston owned a liquor store and she was a drunk.

Chapter Thirteen

Langdon seldom spoke of his mother, but after breakfast with Ingrid Petersson on their sixth day together he suddenly opened up. Sitting with the elderly Swede on chairs amongst her apple and pear trees, he quietly recounted his mother's battle with cancer. Everything flooded out like a burst dam once he began. Charlie spoke about his marital status, his wife's infidelity, and his firing from the agency. It hurt to talk about Alex Fanning more because of the betrayal than the loss of money. He even owned up to the true reasons for the facial cuts and bruises he sported. Charlie spoke for three hours until the morning sun had moved overhead. All the while, a passive Swede didn't ask questions, make comments, or pass judgment. When Langdon stopped talking, a wave of exhaustion overwhelmed him and when he awoke an hour later, Ingrid was beside him holding his hand.

"Let us fix some sandwiches and take your car for a long drive," she suggested, and they did. Ingrid didn't offer a running commentary. Instead, the two listened to the Brandenburg Concertos and enjoyed J.S. Bach, the views of Northern Ontario, and the peace of each other's company. The 911 sped effortlessly along the paved highway and when they returned to Great Spirit Moon Lake, Ingrid put on a sunhat and headed into her garden. Charlie pulled up a wicker chair and watched her putter amongst the six-foot tall stalks of corn.

"Charlie, the next part of my story is disturbing. I have only ever spoken of this to five people, all of whom have passed. I have not told Cassandra because her heart is too tender."

Langdon sat quietly.

"It is important for you to hear this because one day you must be able to recount my story. Time has played with the details of my memory to protect my sanity perhaps. Some nights I relive this as if it were happening to me all over. And then I go for a long time and I cannot accurately remember faces or details at all. You will understand that after I finish, I will not want to discuss this ever again. Promise?"

"Yes Ingegard," Charlie responded, wondering to whom she wanted her story recounted.

Ingrid pulled up a dandelion, held it to her nose, and inhaled deeply.

> Father was gone when we awoke the next morning. Mother and I breakfasted quietly on cinnamon porridge, chocolate, and bread. I was upset and exhausted because I had fought through violent nightmares from the moment I had gone to bed. When I awoke to reality, I could not understand my dreams but felt serious danger for my family. Mother listened intently as I told her that the sailor with the scar on his face had been in my dream. There had been men dancing and shouting. I remembered feeling pain and humiliation. The smell of heather was throughout my dreams and Father had red paint on his face. I saw myself looking out at a vast sea with waves higher than our house. I saw the Nazi spider symbol. My mother told me to collect the eggs and when the dishes were done we would leave the house.
>
> I liked feeding our chickens. Whenever I approached the henhouse, the eight of them would line up and begin clucking in unison. If I raised my hand, they stopped and waited for me like I was the choirmaster. Father warned

me not to be seen talking with my non-human friends, but that was difficult because whenever birds flew overhead and I passed any animals they often spoke to me first. I could not be so rude as to ignore them. As I withdrew the eggs I imagined the *Sleipnir* far out in the Baltic Sea. I wondered if Henrik had finished the saffron pancakes for breakfast and was perhaps thinking about me.

As I was re-entering the kitchen I heard a terrible commotion like vicious wolves had jumped through our windows. I placed the egg basket on our table and ran into the dining room. There were German sailors holding Mother down on the floor. They had stripped away her clothing. I think there were four or five, but there could have been more. One man was at her head pulling her arms taut with his boots rammed up against her shoulders while another held her legs apart. The sailor with the scar was on top of her, rutting like the animals in the fields. She struggled desperately but was not able to scream because heather had been crammed into her mouth.

The young sailor with the pockmarks on his neck looked over and saw me. I turned to run but Karsten grabbed my arm, punched me, and pulled me into the dining room. I was surrounded and groped and hit. The sailors snarled like feral dogs and ripped off my clothes. I kicked but was dragged to the floor. I tried to fight but there were too many and they pinned me like a ragdoll. One slapped me so hard I was dazed. As a sailor began to climb on top of me, I wondered why the Gods had deserted us. I felt so helpless.

The sudden blast of a gun exploded into the frenzied blur of entangled bodies. Axel jumped up and the men holding my legs and arms released me. I crawled across the floor to my mother. She was on her stomach, the heather still in her mouth. Mother's eyes did not blink and I knew she was dead.

Henrik was there, which confused me because he was supposed to be far off into the Baltic aboard his ship. He wielded father's axe like the thunder God smiting enemies with Mjolinir, and I watched in horror as he cleaved the top off Karsten's head. My giant raged in unbridled fury.

Suddenly the room fell silent even though the men continued to fight. A circling glow of light appeared in the corner like the sun peeking up from the horizon early in the morning when the sky is still dark. The light intensified and shone brightly. Within it was a form that took on the shape of a female. The spirit became clearer as if she were truly standing there. Her face was perfect and long blond hair cascaded down to the floor. The vision smiled with gentle eyes and I realized the men in the room could not see her. When the phantom turned towards the maelstrom her face changed when she saw ten or twelve sailors besieging Henrik and one of his shipmates, Mikaeli. The lady screeched like a hawk and the serenity she had exuded turned into bitter contempt. She flew into the midst of the chaotic brawl, touching the transgressors with the tip of her hand. One by one the brutal sailors dropped like stones and were corpses by the time they met the floor. My lady shouted encouragement at Henrik and Mikaeli who battled ferociously like the sons of Thor. A befuddled and bloodied Axel Mueller attempted to skulk from the room unable to understand what carnage had befallen his comrades. Laughing, the lady froze the scar-faced sailor where he stood. Slowly she approached and put her ten fingers close to, but not actually touching, his chest. The coward's eyes bulged and looked like they would pop from his head as she spoke at him in his own language. With an ear-piercing cry the lady flung her hands apart eviscerating the sailor's ribs like they were twigs on a branch. Mueller's guts and entrails spilled outwards as his body collapsed.

The lady inside the orb of light walked—or rather, floated—towards me.

"You are Freyja," I said quietly, as if no mere mortal could ever speak with the Goddess of peace and tranquility. Her hands stroked the entire length of my body.

"Time will heal you, my Ingegard of the mountain. These evil souls will burn. Odin is giving you Sigrid's gift of sight. Now, awaken and leave this place with your champion and never return."

I faded back to reality sickened by all I felt and saw. It was oddly quiet with the only sound being the ticking of our wall clock, and the whimpering of the wounded sailors. In the periphery of my vision was my father slumped in the corner with a bloody red hole in the middle of his forehead.

When Henrik looked at me, he sobbed so hard that his shoulders shook. The axe fell from his hands. and he grabbed up a table cloth and covered me.

"Do not cry my warrior," I whispered, trying to calm him. "Freyja will watch over you and me."

"Be still little dove," his deep voice resonated quietly as he wiped his nose on his sleeve. "I swear before Odin that no more harm will befall you."

His mate Mikaeli called that my parents were dead. In my delirium, I told him, "Freyja is beautiful like Mother," but Mikaeli was not in the mood to listen. His face was covered in blood and he was shaking uncontrollably. Henrik directed Mikaeli to kneel and block my vision. I heard guttural cries of pain from the sailors that yet lived and knew that Henrik was avenging us. Through half-closed eyes, I saw that he was slitting throats and cutting off their genitals.

"Stop watching!" Mikaeli shouted, and he pulled my face into his chest. When Henrik returned to my side, Mikaeli released me to his care.

"Ingegard," he spoke scarcely above a whisper, "more Germans will come and you will not be safe here. We have a good doctor on the ship. Will you let me take you there?"

It was then that I saw a knife with a red Nazi spider on the butt of the leather hilt. It was lodged deep in my Viking's shoulder.

"Henko, there is a knife stuck in you. Does it not hurt?" My head was spinning and I had called him "Henko." That became his name to me from that day forward.

"Just a scratch," he lied, with a gentle laugh. "Now, my little dove, we must leave. Mikaeli, cover her mother's body."

Ingrid leaned forward, hugging her arms around the front of her knees in resigned silence.

"Charlie, I must stop now. Let us move over there. Elves won't go near oaks so we will be safe."

When they had repositioned their chairs, Ingrid closed her eyes and instantly fell into a deep sleep. Charles Langdon felt despondent as he sat there looking at her silhouette. He lowered his eyes and began to quietly weep as he had the day his mother had died.

Chapter Fourteen

Duane Michaels knew very little about his wife's family history. He knew she had come from a good, hard-working, middle-class family who lived in Cambridge. He had met her parents and siblings and found them pleasant enough. Duane knew that Evangeline's father Eddie Martinez worked for the post office and her mother Carole worked at Wal-Mart. Eddie had come from Mexico as a kid and Carole was an African-American from whom his wife got her beauty. Michaels also knew that before Evangeline worked for American Airlines that she had been married, but got divorced when her husband was sent to prison. Duane Michaels knew all he cared to know, but he might have been interested to know that there was a secret to Evangeline's family that began with her father.

Eddie Martinez was not Eddie Martinez. He had been born Bueno Espinoza in the back-end slums of Juarez, a Mexican city infested with corruption, crime, and the ongoing battles between the *Federales* and the drug lords of the *Criminales*. The life expectancy of a boy was seventeen. To overcome that statistic, his poverty-stricken parents hired a coyote to whisk their fourteen-year-old through a sixty-seven yard tunnel into the USA.

For three years, Bueno Espinoza worked below the radar of US Immigration in New Mexico and Arizona. He painted, gardened, washed dishes, and stole his way northward into Canada. At eighteen, he was working illegally in Leamington, Ontario, picking tobacco when he met a Mexican-born Canadian from Kitchener. The teenager was Eddie Martinez, a boy who as a baby had been adopted by Canadian parents and granted citizenship. When his adopted parents emigrated to England, Eddie refused to accompany them, preferring the more ethnically integrated country in which he lived.

Bueno Espinoza grasped the God-given opportunity placed at his feet. When the last leaf of tobacco season had been hung to dry, the two teens hitchhiked to Toronto to find work. Bueno encouraged them to save money by passing up on the comfort of a motel and sleeping on the side of the road. One night while Eddie slept, Bueno took a hammer to the boy's head, beating his brains to a pulp and his face to an unrecognizable blob. He slipped a photograph of his own family into Eddie's jean pocket. On the back of the photograph were the words "Bueno Espinoza."

Without the slightest hint of remorse, Bueno lugged the corpse to a landfill site and unceremoniously dumped it. Hastening away, Espinoza clutched Eddie's summer wages, a drivers' license, an Ontario Health Card, and, most importantly, a Canadian passport. Bueno Espinoza was no more.

The new Eddie Martinez who took up residence in Cambridge was taken on as a full-time postal deliverer. After a number of years Eddie met and married Carole Johnston. Three children later, Eddie and Carole Martinez lived in four-bedroom house in a pleasant family-centric neighbourhood. They had two good-paying jobs, money in the bank, a twenty-year mortgage, and the future prospect of Eddie's government pension. Their biggest worry was their eldest daughter. Evangeline had her first period at ten and by twelve had the body of a full-grown woman and her mother's incredibly good looks. The girl detested school and spent a great deal of time fending off the unwanted attention of every male student with whom she came into contact.

"School won't matter," her father stated. "With our girl's looks, she's going to marry a wealthy man and give us a hundred grandchildren." Eddie's constant reassurance drove his daughter's confidence and worried his wife.

Evangeline Martinez was excited for the visit of her mother's relatives from Detroit and was instantly captivated by her American cousin Sophia's unbridled confidence and maturity. Eddie and Carole's daughter began imitating everything about her older cousin's hair, makeup, lipstick, clothing, and attitude. The more sexually-aware Sofia took Evangeline under her wing and they spent the next two summer months hidden away in a small room above the garage. For Sofia, her cousin was a willing participant caught up in the intrigue of a naughty secret. For Evangeline Martinez, it was unbridled love.

One warm summer afternoon when she was hanging laundry on the back line, Carole Martinez heard sounds coming from the room in the garage above her husband's Buick. Half-suspecting she would find her philandering husband with another woman, Carole burst through the door. Instead of finding a guilty-faced postal worker she found something worse.

Sofia Johnston was on the first bus back to Detroit and Evangeline was beaten with her father's belt for having sinned against the bible. With Sofia exiled, Evangeline moped around the house for the next two years as if someone had shot her dog. Eddie insisted his daughter spend time with the son of a co-worker at the post office. The boy's name was Terrance Greene and he was an ace student and an outstanding athlete. The only issue in the Greene family was Terrance's younger brother Tres who was a bad apple and had been arrested numerous times.

To appease her parents, and to be released from her permanent grounding, Evangeline agreed to see him. The Greene boy was a decent guy and the relationship went sexual. While Evangeline ached for the carnal excitement and satisfaction that Sofia had provided, she had no option but to settle for a heterosexual partner, or face the wrath of her parents.

Terrance graduated high school and took a job on the assembly line of the Toyota plant. Aiming for a management position he outworked every other man on the production line and received outstanding performance reviews. With her appearance and love of makeup, Angie got a full-time job behind the perfume and makeup counter at a local drug store chain. They married and the first seven years of marriage flew by.

It took an event on the opposite side of the planet to change the course of their lives forever. What began as a seasonal storm over the Pacific morphed into a devastating typhoon, which relentlessly hammered the Pacific Rim. The Japanese economy took a severe beating and its auto parts industry was paralyzed. Orders were issued to cut parts supply to its North American production facilities. Production slowdowns and cutbacks were scheduled across the United States and Canada, including a shutdown of the Corolla line in Cambridge. Entire shifts of employees, including Terrance Greene, were laid off. The plant closure that was supposed to last a month dragged on and the union payment barely covered the weekly food bill. Greene eagerly accepted any job that came up and worked twice the hours for half the pay of his job at Toyota. Evangeline took on additional shifts and started babysitting to help offset mounting bills.

Terrance was cleaning the garage one August afternoon when his younger brother Tres showed up asking for lunch. He would never have done that if Angie had been home. Evangeline despised her brother-in-law and considered him a drug-using convict, which was not far from the truth. Tres Greene had dealt weed through high school and spent two hard years in Juvenile Detention. Those two years drained him of whatever decency he had been born with. Tres arrived home a hardened man looking for trouble and taking to the streets.

Terrance's decision to open that door to his younger brother would prove the undoing of his life.

After watching a Jason Statham movie and eating grilled cheese sandwiches the Greene brothers had a couple of beers. Tres won a ten-dollar bet pumping out a hundred push-ups and then pulled out a bag of weed to celebrate. Terrance reluctantly took the joint offered to him. The two boys drank and smoked through another action movie. The beer and marijuana wouldn't have been a problem. For kicks, Tres slipped two Amytal into his brother's Budweiser. He thought it would be fun to see how much trouble his older brother would catch when Evangeline got home and found her straight-laced husband stoned out of his head. For once, Tres wouldn't be the only screw-up in the family.

"Chilling out, big bro?" Tres asked, but Terrance was anything but relaxed as he paced about the room shaking his head from side to side.

Inside Evangeline's husband's nervous system, the Amytal mixing with weed and beer was like an intense hit of LSD, shifting him in and out of reality. From enjoying a beer with his brother, Terrance found himself unexplainably grasping a Glock 31. Itching at his face, he realized he was wearing a balaclava. Someone was screaming. He looked over and saw his younger brother pointing their father's 870 Remington shotgun at customers scrambling to lie down on the floor. He was at the local bank branch. When had they gone to their parents' house? How did they get the key to unlock his dad's gun cabinet? Terrance stared at the black Glock and slowly lowered it. Higher than a kite, he removed the balaclava and walked to Tres. Neither was aware that the silent alarm had already been tripped.

"What are we doing?" he slurred. Through a stream of giggles, Tres continued to rant like his head was going to explode. Customers and bank employees quivered in fear, their faces filled with terror.

Fred Jenkins was the oldest employee at the bank and was retiring in December after thirty years. Fred and his wife Marsha had just put a down payment on a new Concorde "Class C" Motorhome. The two intended to drive to Arizona for the winter. While sitting in the end stall of the bathroom, Fred had been flipping through Concorde's brochure thinking of the cherry wood cabinetry, the satellite dish, and the skylight above the shower. He'd gone through the brochure so many times every page was dog-eared. Marsha Jenkins' husband of forty years innocently stepped out of the washroom unaware of the robbery in progress until he saw people lying on the floor and heard shouting.

"Jesus H. Christ!" he blurted out, unknowingly raising his rolled-up magazine.

Tres Greene turned and mistook the rolled brochure for a weapon. He instantly opened fire with his father's 870 Express Tactical Magpul, one of the most dependable weapons on earth. Even completely stoned, Tres could not miss from such short range. Fred Jenkins' 165-pound body was thumped twice in the chest. The impact propelled his dead body five feet backwards into the bathroom door.

"Fuck man, did you see that?" Tres Greene screamed hysterically, laughing like a mad man. "That was incredible. It was insane."

Terrance gasped when he saw the old man hit the floor and tried to say something, but his brother continued discharging the weapon, obviously enjoying the reaction to its power. Two shots to the ceiling and brought down a shower of shattered plaster and broken light bulbs. And then Tres turned the gun towards the people lying on the floor. One bank customer, a woman in her mid-thirties, saw the gun pointed in her direction and panicked. Holding up her hands she crawled up to her knees.

"Please don't shoot. Please. I have children. Please—"

The unforgiving blast from the Magpul hit and mangled her body.

Terrance dropped the Glock and tore across the bank and body-checked his brother. The Remington flew from Tres' grip and skittered across the marble floor. The brothers began wrestling until bank employees picked up the weapons, bringing the melee to a halt.

Three months after the jury trial began, the Greene brothers faced a grim verdict. At their later sentencing, Tres Greene, who had been found guilty on twenty-six charges, received four consecutive life sentences without chance for parole. His older brother had been found guilty on sixteen charges. Given a clean police record and efforts to restrain his brother from killing again, Terrance Greene was sentenced to fifty years with parole no sooner than twenty. In the courtroom Evangeline Greene sat stone-faced and humiliated.

Barely six weeks after their arrival at Milhaven Federal Penitentiary, Tres Greene was found hanging from the door of his jail cell. Terrance was not afforded permission to attend the funeral, but that was the least of his concerns. From the day of his incarceration, Terrance's 245-pound, Serbian-born cellmate had used him like a woman and beat him black and blue just to pass the time.

Evangeline's life was shattered. For the next two years she dutifully visited Milhaven, trying to make small talk and avoid staring at her husband's badly bruised face. Weekly Sunday visits became monthly visits, and then bimonthly. After some time, her father Eddie sat her down and spoke his mind.

"Honey, Terrance was a good boy but he has destroyed his life and will take you down with him. You can't waste the best years of your life waiting on a convict. Your looks are the key to your future and with every wasted year those looks will leave you. Angie, this is your life—it's not a dress rehearsal. Get on with it and tell him goodbye."

Evangeline stopped visiting Terrance, writing letters, sending e-mails, or even taking his phone calls. Leaving Cambridge, she stayed with friends in Toronto and secured a job as a flight attendant with American Airlines. Her cousin Sofia arrived within two weeks and the two shared an apartment and a bed. A year after arriving from Detroit, Sofia took off with an older woman, leaving Evangeline to fend for herself. She met Duane Michaels in La Guardia's American Airlines lounge when her flight was delayed. Angie knew nothing about football and didn't fawn over the superstar like everyone else. Duane was smitten and put forward his best behaviour. Evangeline Martinez found Duane entertaining, and for the first time in her life, discovered a man who physically turned her on and sexually satisfied her. The two were married inside of four months.

When Angie cut all contact and filed for divorce, Terrance Greene lost all sense of who he was. Minutes behind bars dragged out as if they were days, playing on his sanity. Thinking of his wife had allowed him to block out all of the unspeakable and degrading acts of physical and sexual abuse he was forced to endure. There was no help for him and no one to whom he could turn for protection. Prayers to God went unanswered and all seemed hopeless. When he could take no more, Terrance wrapped a sheet through the frame of the top bunk and slipped it around his neck. His suicide would have been successful had not his Serbian-born cellmate awoken and intervened. Angry for having had his sleep disturbed, he beat Terrance so badly he spent the next two months eating his food through a straw in the infirmary.

Chapter Fifteen

Life was peaceful on Great Spirit Moon Lake. Eight-hour sleeps, good food, and comforting companionship had brought Charlie Langdon back to the land of the living. The debilitating anxiety he had carried on his shoulders from Toronto had all but melted away. Each night he fell into bed unable to stay awake. Each morning, he woke ravenous and anxious to see what the day would bring. Langdon was disgusted with how out of shape he had gotten and decided to remedy that with yoga and running. The first week on the trails had been brutal with unused muscles and lungs that refused to co-operate. After several weeks of aches and pains, old muscles reappeared where fat had invaded.

With Ingrid's concern that he might get lost in the forest, Charlie agreed to run with Cassie Turner, although he was a little reluctant to publically display what a slug he had become. Cassandra acquiesced to her godmother's request and the two set out around the lake. Charlie was overwhelmed with the ease with which Cassandra bounded effortlessly through the forest like a deer. He would run like a blind man through the unmarked woods until he'd see her far ahead, leaning up against a pine or stretching out against a bolder.

"Come on, you can do better than that," the gazelle would encourage. "My grandmother can run faster than you, and she's dead."

*   *   *

One morning after being put through his paces with Cassandra, Charlie dropped over to Phil Henderson's Ford Dealership to use the Internet.

After ignoring most of his e-mails he went onto CNN. There was no update on NovaRose International or the whereabouts of its fugitive CEO and CFO. He was about to log off when he Googled his running partner. Cassie Turner had sixteen pages devoted to her track success during university, the success of her book on the Ojibwe nation, her celebrated marriage, and her husband's obituary.

Twenty pages came up when he typed in the name of his Swedish friend. There were numerous photographs and articles about Ingrid and Henrik donating money to the hospital, the high school, the library, the marina, and the park. There was a monument in Bracebridge dedicated to Henrik Petersson. Then, he came across a lovely thirty-year-old photo of the Peterssons at the opening of the new high school.

Charlie had come to accept that there was a lot more to Ingegard Petersson than was beyond his realm of understanding. It was not just that she believed in her world of runes, Norse Gods, and spirits. Her influence on him was leading him to question everything he believed. Her life story was so beyond believable that he found himself being convinced it might be true. Upon hearing each segment of her life history it was impossible to think that she had made it all up.

Langdon thanked Phil and headed back around the lake. He found Barrett Sanford was mowing the lawn on his sister's property. The rest of the morning and afternoon was spent loafing around. Charlie fished off shore and caught three rock bass and a small perch. He wandered into the vegetable garden and pulled a couple of weeds and then chopped kindling for the fireplace. He husked corn, picked tomatoes, and checked the apple trees. The whole time his mind was free of any negative thoughts of Kyla, Alex, NovaRose, Duane, or Telfer Stuart Advertising.

Late that evening as he was settling down for the night his bedroom door opened and Ingrid entered carrying a candle. Without any sense of unease, she crawled up beside him on the bed.

"I know you had a busy day, but I must carry on with my story. Cover me up."

Charlie spread the duvet over her and awkwardly crawled under his covers.

> Henrik lifted me, more concerned about causing me discomfort than the pain from the knife stuck in his shoulder.
>
> "I am such an oaf," he apologized, because with every step my head exploded in pain. I pulled his beard and pointed to the kitchen.
>
> "Lift that floor board," I ordered, and pointed to a place beside the wood stove where my parents hid our strongbox. Henrik took from the box my mother's runes, my great grandmother's books of interpretation, a heavy pouch of money, her silver hair clips, and our medallions honouring the Gods.
>
> "Bring my chickens," I asked, but my request was ignored.

"You know Charlie," Ingrid commented, as an aside, "I obeyed Freyja and we never returned to Visby, so I never saw that house again. Even if we had returned it would not have been there for me to see. The Germans burned it to the ground that very day and shot nine of our neighbours in retaliation for the killing of the nine sailors."

> Henrik and Mikaeli hustled towards the dock. Half a dozen German sailors were flirting with one of the local girls and did not notice us climbing into a small skiff that had been pulled up on the shore. Two sailors from the *Sleipnir* were attending it, and neither asked the First

Mate and Mikaeli about their wounds, or the young battered girl being lowered into the boat.

"Lie still Ingegard," Henrik commanded, and I had no energy to do otherwise. The sailors took to the oars and the rhythm of their strokes and the lapping waves felt soothing. The skiff made quick time across the bay to the *Sleipnir*. I looked up and saw her name in large white letters on the side of the black ship. I had lived my life beside the harbour but this was the nearest I had come to a ship. She was enormous but I felt no fear.

Henrik carried me up a long flight of wooden stairs that was suspended over the side of the boat. On the deck there was a gathering. An old man in a raggedy blue pea jacket and wrinkled grey cap approached us. He had a long white curly beard and one bushy eyebrow that crossed both eyes.

"First Mate, what is this?" he voice boomed, and the others fell silent.

"Alexius, we must raise anchor immediately," Henrik responded urgently.

The white beard who I realized was Henrik's Captain peered at the bloody knife protruding from his First Mate's shoulder. He then examined Mikaeli's face.

"Mother of Thor," he exclaimed, "Mikaeli, your nose is carved off."

Captain Backstrom then inched forward and saw the blood coming out of my ear and the severe bruising across my face.

"How hurt is she?" the Captain probed cautiously, and his meaning was clear. What a spectacle I must have been.

The First Mate spoke for all to hear. "Nine sailors from the German frigate attacked the girl and her mother. Both parents were killed."

There was a rumbling from the crew.

"And the nine?" the white beard inquired.

"They will not bother her again," Henrik answered sternly. "Captain Backstrom, we have no time to waste. Set sail or put us ashore."

The older man looked around the deck. He stomped his feet like he was getting snow off his boots.

"Anyone witness you kill the Germans or board this ship?"

"No," Mikaeli responded quickly.

The pain in my stomach overtook me and I began to whimper.

"Alexius, decide, damn you," my protector cursed anxiously.

Captain Backstrom nodded, looked up to the heavens, and then began barking commands at the crew.

"Henko," I muttered deliriously, as we descended stairs, "Did you bring my chickens?"

My giant carried me through darkly-lit corridors until we entered a well-lit room where a man of six decades greeted us.

"Christ, you look a fine mess," the stranger shouted gruffly. "Who do we have here?"

The doctor sported a full head of thick red hair and was clean-shaven except for the biggest bush of sideburns. Mother always told us that a man's eyes revealed his soul.

Wire-rimmed glasses framed wrinkled eyes that had seen too much for one lifetime.

"Lay her on my examining table, and be gentle," he directed calmly. The doctor folded a pillow twice and placed it under my head. The pressure from the pillow hurt like my head had just been hit with a piece of wood. I tried to push him away. The doctor motioned for me to lie still then looked at the others.

"Mikaeli, take off First Mate's coat and tear off the shirt so I can get directly at the wound. Leave the knife where it is. How long ago were you stabbed?"

"I do not know," Henrik answered slowly, the loss of blood taking its toll. He was dreadfully pale, just like the ghostly spirit of Freyja in our dining room.

"An hour," Mikaeli jumped in. "About the same time I had my nose cut off."

"The girl?" he whispered quietly. "Was she . . . bothered?"

Mikaeli shrugged his shoulders. "We don't know."

The red-haired man looked at me as Mikaeli began fussing with Henrik's clothing.

"What is your name, girl?"

I told him.

"That is a lovely name. I have two daughters—Linnea and Emelie. The crew call me Dr. Bjorkman but to you I am Magnus. Ingegard, may I take a look at you? I promise not to hurt you."

Dr. Bjorkman draped a blanket from the ceiling for privacy and while he inspected my wounds he spoke about his two girls. My left ear pained viciously and was ringing loudly as he swabbed out the blood. He made my face presentable, which was not an easy task given the severe bruising and black swollen eyes that made me look haggish.

"Ingegard, has your mother told you about babies?"

I sheepishly nodded yes.

"I know it is a difficult question," Magnus said quietly, "but I must ask and you must be truthful. Did those brutes rape you? Did they put anything inside you?"

I shook my head. "No. One was about to when Father, Henrik, and Mikaeli saved me."

"You are certain? There is no shame in this."

Again I told him no. "They beat me and took off my clothes but they did not do to me what they did to my mother."

The doctor held my gaze and then accepted what I said.

"Alright then."

"What about my left ear?" I asked, seeing the doctor staring at it. "There is ringing in it."

"The loss of hearing may be temporary or permanent. It will ring for a while and your balance will be off so take care when you stand."

I mercifully slipped away into a coma-like sleep the moment the needle of morphine pricked my shoulder. When I stirred we were far at sea and the ship rolled and swayed with the waves. The doctor fed me broth with crusts of bread in it. I travelled in and out of reality for days with my body and mind mixed up with the pain, anxiety, and drugs. I felt such a sinking sense of gloom.

My soul was racked with guilt that I had survived but my parents had not. The aroma of heather continued to fill my nostrils even though there was none on the ship. Magnus reassured me that my feelings were normal and that they would become less raw in time but never truly go away.

Henrik appeared twice daily but would never come past the threshold of the door. I realized he was trying to make himself smaller, which was impossible for a man of six and one half feet and one hundred and forty kilos. Mikaeli's face was bandaged from below his eyes to the top of his upper lip. He came to my room with stories about his escapades with the First Mate. I learned that Henrik was a champion bareknuckle fighter and the crew made more money gambling on his boxing prowess than crewing the *Sleipnir*. Henko had won over a hundred bouts.

My Henrik Petersson was an even greater warrior than I had thought.

* * *

"He still runs like an old woman and I say that with no disrespect to any old woman I know," Cassie mocked as she and Ingrid rolled out dough to make piecrusts. "Running with Charlie is like babysitting. You should be paying me. He sweats like a pig and puffs so hard that I'm afraid he's going to have a heart attack."

Ingrid sprinkled flour across the wooden sideboard and reached for the rolling pin.

"Well if he does, then you will not have to run with him anymore, will you? Pay attention to what you are doing. By the Gods, girl, you are putting far too much dough into the pie plate. Are you trying to make crust or glue?"

* * *

No one on Great Spirit Moon Lake expressed any curiosity as to why Charles Langdon was living with Ingrid. Saving her life had given him a carte blanche of acceptance. His daily routine began with stretching, push-ups, calisthenics, and an excruciatingly exhausting trail run with Cassandra Turner. Over the first few weeks, Charlie was drenched and could not get his second breath while his partner loped along like she was enjoying a walk in the park. But now a month into it, his legs didn't ache, his lungs no longer burned, and he was at least able to keep Ingrid's goddaughter in sight. In another month, he intended to give the blond-haired rabbit a run for her money.

Over lunch, Charlie asked his housemate about the girl next door. Ingrid smiled as if she had been waiting for this.

"Cassie is a very private person and the dearest soul I know," Ingrid began. "I will share some information, but only what I would say if she were sitting here with us." And what the Swede said intrigued him.

When Meryl's granddaughter had been a journalism student at the University of Toronto she was assigned to interview Dr. Phillip Turner, a renowned psychiatrist who had written many books. Cassie became enamoured with the older, successful man, being taken in by his reputation and lifestyle. They married and moved into a big house in the city. Her novel on the Ojibwe of Great Spirit Moon Lake was published and, for a number of years, the two looked like the perfect couple to the outside world—but looks can be deceiving. She continued to write and her husband's practice flourished until he was diagnosed with cancer. After he passed, Cassandra travelled overseas for almost a year. Upon returning, she sold their Rosedale home, almost all of their possessions, and retreated to Great Spirit Moon Lake. Now, she lived comfortably off the proceeds of the house and contents sale, Phillip's insurance, and the ongoing royalties from her book sales. She kept to herself, never dated, and had no interest in writing a second book.

Ingrid stopped abruptly and looked sharply at Charlie. "Cassandra means the world to me, Charles Michael Langdon, so do not ever take her lightly."

* * *

At the onset of his second month of his physical rejuvenation, Charlie came across Cassie Turner waiting for him at the fork in the road that led up a crevice-riddled trail to the end of Ingrid's property boundary she called Thor's Hammer. He saw her stretching up against the giant maple and his heart skipped a beat. Seeing her had become the highlight of every day even though they seldom spoke. After pleasantries, Ingrid's friend told him they were going to run up Chippewa Creek, which was the local name for the river. Cassie noticed and appreciated his improvement as they ran off-trail and took to the side of the fifteen-foot wide river.

After thirty minutes Cassandra stopped abruptly and motioned for him to do the same.

"Be quiet," she ordered, as her eyes locked on something across the river.

Charlie saw nothing except water, trees, and the side of the escarpment. The sound of river was all he heard. He was about to ask her why they had stopped when two bear cubs came running from a stand of evergreens, playfully bouncing off each other as they raced towards the water. The twins couldn't have been more than four months old. Charlie smiled but Cassie's stern expression told him to be quiet. Then, with a crashing sound of breaking tree branches, an enormous black bear revealed herself from within the trees. The mother lumbered down to where her cubs were frolicking in the shallow water and stood poised to scent danger. Cassie and Charlie remained transfixed as the massive bear stared intently up and down the river. Fortunately the two runners were downwind and the six hundred pound bear could only make a visual determination of any threat. It seemed like an eternity before the mother released her stare and shepherded her offspring to the safety of the forest.

"Back away slowly and don't talk," his running partner whispered calmly, and she reached over and took Charlie's hand. They backtracked about twenty feet from the river's edge when Cassie realized they were holding hands. She recalled Ingrid's vision of her standing hand in hand with Charlie facing a serious obstacle. Cassie let go and scampered up atop a boulder searching for any movement across the river.

"We're fine," she announced quietly. "We can run back now."

"That was incredible," Charlie spat out excitedly, after they had run about fifty feet. "How did you know they were there?"

Cassie glanced over without easing her pace.

"My father made his living as a nature photographer. Over the years, his photos appeared in magazines including *The National Geographic*. Dad used to take me with him on his canoe and camping trips and taught me to observe and feel the elements of nature. As we approached the bend in the river, I happened to see a large number of birds taking flight and heard the forest go quiet. That typically announces the presence of a carnivore. When we stopped, I was able to smell animal fur and knew we were downwind."

"Well, if I'd been alone I might have been her breakfast," Charlie quipped, and that got a rise out of Cassie.

"No, you would have been okay. Bears get the fat they need from gorging on salmon, not by eating out-of-shape advertising hucksters."

Ingrid's goddaughter burst out laughing and he joined in, realizing this was the longest conversation they had ever shared.

"Catch me if you can," Cassie challenged, and after shoving him sideways into a bush she bolted down the gravel road. When he finally arrived at her driveway, Cassie was unlacing her Sauconys.

"I'm going for a swim. See you later?" she asked, and the two exchanged a warm smile, but there was no forthcoming invitation to join her in the lake. When he had run forty feet down the road towards Ingrid's house, he glanced over his shoulder. Meryl Patch's granddaughter hadn't moved. She was still at the end of her driveway looking at him. After they exchanged waves, Cassie took off towards her dock and dove into the lake.

Ingrid was scrambling eggs when his feet hit the porch. Like radar, she had an uncanny ability to know the exact minute he'd arrive home. This morning he was almost giddy with news to share.

"Breakfast will be on your plate in two minutes so shower fast," she said smiling. "Good run?"

"Outstanding. Saw a bear and two cubs."

A look of concern appeared. Finally, something had happened that Ingrid hadn't known.

"I would have run right into them if Cassie hadn't warned me."

Ingrid pretended not to be worried and pointed towards the bathroom. "Do not linger or you will ruin your breakfast."

Over breakfast Charlie broke the silence with an announcement. "I have to get back into the city. I need to find a place to live and get a job. I figure the smartest thing to do is return my Porsche to the dealership."

Ingrid was thickly spreading her homemade boysenberry jam on toast. She didn't look up and seemed intent on covering every inch like she was painting the background scene on an oil painting.

"I have friends in other agencies so it shouldn't take long to find a new job. I'll see my lawyer and make sure all the divorce papers are in order."

The Swede took a bite of her toast and washed it down with a sip of her coffee. He could smell the rubber burning inside that brain of hers. With Ingrid, silence was not acquiescence or agreement.

"I've already banked my severance from Telfer Stuart. That will keep me afloat for a while. The money from the Porsche will cover a lot of rent and I'll put Kyla behind me so I can get on with my life."

Ingrid picked up the coffee pot and refilled Charlie's cup. He realized that she hadn't uttered a word. He suddenly stopped talking and looked directly at her. Ingrid continued chewing her toast.

"What?" she inquired, as if she hadn't been listening.

"Did you hear what I said?"

"Ja," she replied, biting into her toast.

He looked at her curiously. What was going on in that little Viking mind of hers?

"Well, what do you think?"

"Honestly, this is the best boysenberry jam I have ever made. Here, put some on your toast."

Langdon knew when he was being played.

"Great jam? Now what do you think about me going to Toronto?"

Ingrid swallowed her toast and exhaled.

"Charles Michael Langdon. It seems you have already made up your mind. You intend to get back on the same road, doing the same thing that ruined your life. So keep rambling. I am surprised, because I thought you were a much smarter man."

For a moment, Charlie sat dumbfounded.

"Well I can't stay here forever," he blurted out.

"Why not?" she returned. "Are you so unhappy here that you have to get away from me, perhaps?"

He shook his head.

"Let me ask a question," she stated, as she pushed her plate to the side. "Why were you so happy visiting your grandfather during the summer?"

Charlie knew. "He made me feel like I counted. Grandpa let me help with everything he did. There wasn't a thing he couldn't fix and I enjoyed getting my hands dirty helping him."

Ingrid smiled coyly. "And so, you deserted all of that just to rot at a desk with people who worked you to death, contributed to the failure of your marriage, damaged your health, and then fired you? And now, you want to work with them again? But what do I know? I am just an old, half-deaf woman who talks to spirits."

Charlie drained his cup and walked over to the kitchen window. A sky full of cumulus clouds had crept in, blocking the morning sun that had accompanied his run with Cassie. He stuck his hands in his pocket and looked back at his white-haired hostess.

"Ingrid, I can't keep living off you. I have to do something to earn my way."

The elderly woman walked into the kitchen and put her hand on his chest. "Are you happy here?"

Charlie laughed. "I can't remember being happier in my entire life."

The old woman leaned hard on her hand. "Were you happy in Toronto?"

"No. I was miserable even before I lost everything and got canned."

"Well, at least you know the difference between your life in the big city and your life here on the lake. You will do something for me, perhaps?"

Charlie shrugged his shoulders just as Barrett Sanford might. "Of course."

"Charlie, I want you to drive to Toronto and sell your car. Go to your lawyer and confirm that your wife is still committed to this divorce and that there is no hope of reconciliation. Collect whatever belongings you need. Learn what you can about your friend who made off with your money."

It dawned on Charlie that Ingrid had been waiting for him to announce his departure. He stood idly and patiently let her continue.

"You will need a couple of days?" she asked innocently. "When you are finished, return by bus and bring your belongings. Now, I have an idea that makes me think of your grandfather and the happy summers you spent. Barrett Sanford told me he is overwhelmed with work and bad headaches. It is difficult for him to get around the lake in the fall and winter driving his golf cart. He needs help and you need a job. So, the two of you will help each other and you will pay me room and board. You both will need a vehicle to get around during the fall and winter so I will let you use my old Ford F150, which Phil Henderson will have ready the day you get back."

Charlie threw back his head and laughed.

"You want me to be a handyman?"

Ingrid sharply poked him in the arm and, despite being a little person weighing less than his gym bag, she rocked him on his feet.

"You are a snob. It is honest work that will allow you to stay where you are happy and healthy. Give this idea one hundred days. If you are miserable after that, then return to Toronto. Think of working here as a sabbatical."

The two stared like poker players not wanting to blink first.

"Fifty days," he bargained, but the girl from Gotland shook her head.

"One hundred days," she restated through gritted teeth. Before he could say "seventy-five" she held out her hand to seal the deal. He paused.

"Out of curiosity, is this something you've seen in your runes?" he inquired. "Did you consult them?"

Ingrid's face revealed she had.

"And they said this was my path?"

"One hundred days," she responded firmly, extending her right hand.

"Alright then, I'll agree to one hundred days, but I need to hear from Barrett that he wants this."

They shook hands and Ingrid patted his chest. "By the Gods, you are a hard negotiator. Barrett is waiting on his dock to discuss the partnership. And just so you know, the more time you spend together and become friends, the less he will stutter."

Ingrid quickly reached into the pocket of her apron and withdrew an envelope.

"Here is your one-way bus ticket from Toronto. Phil will pick you up at the depot on Friday night and bring you to bingo. Barrett will drive us home."

Charlie opened the envelope. "Barrett's waiting, you've already bought my bus ticket from Toronto, and have Phil lined up to pick me up? And I am the good negotiator?"

Ingrid began flittering about the kitchen putting the dishes in the sink. The sunbeams had found their way through the wall of clouds and were flickering playfully through the prisms dangling from the window in front of her.

"I phoned Cassie and told her you were leaving for Toronto after breakfast. She agrees with the one hundred day plan. Your travel bag is packed and sitting on the front porch. I made you a lunch and a thermos of coffee for the drive. Eat carefully and do not spill it on your car seats."

Charlie kissed her goodbye and walked slowly to the screen door. As it closed behind him he could here the old lady cackling away like one of her chickens.

Chapter Sixteen

"Is he improving?" Ingrid asked, yet again, of Charlie's running, as she and Cassandra cut back the tall stalks of corn in her garden. It was an annual tradition for Ingrid and her goddaughter to cull back the garden and prepare it for the colder weather.
Cassandra gathered up an armful of corn stalks and carried them to a wheelbarrow.

"Sure, he doesn't run like an old woman with a peg leg anymore," she laughed, glancing at her partner wielding the axe like an old pro. "Charlie is getting better."

The elderly gardener smiled at her young friend's jab. "Have you noticed that Charlie has lost a lot of weight with all this exercise? He certainly looks healthier than when he arrived into our lives."

Cassie picked up another pile of stalks.

"I really don't know why he's still here. You've got a total stranger living in your house. He seems pretty decent, but don't you think it's time he goes back to Toronto?"

Ingrid walked across the corn patch and motioned for her helper to follow. The two walked to the back porch and Ingrid withdrew her charm pouch from her apron. "Sit."

Cassie did as told and watched as seven runes were placed before her.

"The stranger is here for a purpose that involves both you and I. Our destinies are intermingled and the two of you will share your lives together."

"Read them again," the younger woman insisted politely, and without protest, her grandmother's best friend replaced the well-worn white tiles into the charm pouch.

"Fine. You select five tiles and lay them here," Ingrid directed, pointing her index finger to a point on the yellow plastic tablecloth. As her ancestors had done for a millennium she interpreted them, smiling like the Cheshire cat. Cassie knew that look well.

"Same?"

Ingrid nodded.

"So let me get this straight. My destiny is with a yet-divorced man who is jobless and doesn't have two nickels to rub together? We will marry and supposedly have children, and a life of happiness and wealth. That about it, you crazy old woman?"

"Yes. You will both have long lives if you approach your journeys together. I see great fortune and a fulfilling marriage. You will have many children and write another book."

Cassandra sat back.

"Your runes can't be that specific. Show me which stone tells you I'm going to have a bunch of kids and write another book. You're adding what you hope will happen, aren't you?"

The cat stood up and stretched. His mistress flicked over a square piece of cheese and he greedily pounced on it like it was a mouse. As he chewed hungrily the cat plopped back down on the porch stoop and flicked his tail in gratitude.

"I only tell what I see, although my visions are not what they were in my younger days."

"Have you told any of this fabrication you've concocted to Charlie?"

The Swede shook her head. "Not a word."

Cassie sat quietly watching the cat lick his front paw. "And you believe this is the man your runes foretold when I was sixteen?"

Ingrid Petersson, like her mother and her grandmother, did not make it a practice to read the runes of young people. With so much of their lives ahead of them, any misreading of the runes could set a believer down a path upon which they were not intended to travel. Cassandra's eyes had lit up when Ingrid cast the runes and saw a life of happiness with a very special man with whom she would raise a houseful of children. The runes told of wealth and a joyful journey through life.

But then Cassie had made a mistake of youth and her journey took a bizarre detour. When she brought her new husband to meet her family, Ingrid knew instantly that Phillip Turner was not the man of which the runes had spoken. The Swede felt falseness about him and questioned his motives for wanting to marry her goddaughter. He, in turn, thought Cassandra's godmother was certifiably crazy.

But most interestingly, Miigwaans Cardinal blatantly told Cassie that her new husband had an evil spirit that would be used against her. When the Ojibwe woman touched Phillip's hand she felt a sharp pain in her right side and took Cassie aside. "Make certain his health insurance payments are up to date," were the Native Canadian's words before adding, "Niigaanii says your man talks like he is touched in the head."

Ingrid collected the runes and placed them in the charm pouch. A big fat blue jay squawked somewhere amongst the trees and the cat discretely rose up and disappeared into the shrubs.

"Cassandra, it is time to close the book on Phillip. Believe me, I know about closing books on people. Put away the photographs and any memories of your marriage. Understand that not all men are like the man you married. Only the Gods know how he misused you in the time you spent together, but he was not part of your destiny. Something special is going to unfold on Great Spirit Moon Lake, and, it involves you and Charles Langdon. If you have faith in me and know that I look upon you as my own child, then heed my words."

Cassie nodded her head.

There was rustling in the bushes by the orchard followed by the appearance of Ingrid's cat clutching the blue jay in his mouth. The bird was still struggling yet the hunter made no effort to end its life. He proudly meandered up the steps, walked across the back porch, and looked up at his mistress. With a flick of his head he dispatched the bird before dropping it at Ingrid's feet.

"Disgusting," Cassandra scolded, "I hate when he does that."

Ingrid patted the cat realizing she had told him not to touch the red bird but had not mentioned the jay. With that acknowledgement, the bird's body was back in the cat's mouth and the infinitely proud feline disappeared down the steps. As the two women watched him, Ingrid smelled the air.

"Lizzie is here," she warned, knowing that her neighbour was customarily prickly towards Cassandra. "That perfume of hers could choke a horse."

"How to ruin a good visit," Cassie replied, disappointment evident in her tone. She quickly hopped up and kissed Ingrid's forehead. "I'll see you later. I appreciate our talk and I promise I'll keep an open mind. Love you, old woman."

As pre-announced, a sparkling Lizzie Grant rounded the corner of the house. She was wearing a soft pink sundress with thin yellow vertical stripes, low-slung heels, and, a light cashmere sweater. Her smile dissolved when she saw Cassie standing there.

"Oh, hi," she said, in a sickeningly sweet voice. "I didn't know Ingrid had company. Don't leave on my account." With no effort to conceal it, her jealous eyes scanned the younger woman from head to toe. It incensed her that Cassandra Turner could look so breathtakingly beautiful without a stitch of makeup and without having given a second thought to what she was wearing. Lizzie recalled vividly that Cassie Patch had come onto her radar when the girl had turned sixteen. From then on, Cassandra had turned the head of every male on the lake. With each passing year, the girl continued to blossom and her athletic prowess and happy disposition was salt in an open wound. Cassie's departure for university and subsequent marriage and move to Toronto was nirvana to Lizzie. "Good riddance to bad rubbish," she had told Roy, ecstatic to have her nemesis gone. And then to Lizzie's dismay, and in her words, "the fucking shrink croaked and the girl returned to the lake like a bad yeast infection." Having Cassie Turner living on Great Spirit Moon Lake was a constant reminder to Lizzie of how cruel time had been to her own appearance.

"Hi Lizzie," Cassie responded politely, feeling the hostility directed her way. "Sorry I can't stay, but I've got a ton of stuff to get done. Have a good visit."

"See you," Lizzie purred, as she watched Cassie head down the gravel road. The Grant woman was carrying a square tin that no doubt contained something she had made for Ingrid's guest. Given the Swede's unrivalled baking ability, it was akin to bringing coals to Newcastle.

I brought these for Charlie," she stated, as she deposited the colourful square tin on a side table. "I know you can out-bake me on your worst day, but I am just trying to be neighbourly."

"Coffee or tea," Ingrid offered politely, but the woman with the deep-seated jealousy shook her head.

"Cassie's getting wrinkles around her eyes," she opined. "Have you noticed?

Ingrid didn't rise to the bait and threw back her own question.

"Roy coming home soon?" she inquired, knowing Lizzie's husband was on a hunting trip. "It must be lonely without him."

And so it went for the next twenty minutes. Like the old tabby playing with his near-dead blue jay, Lizzie tried to get a rise from Ingrid. Finally, Lizzie stood up and took her leave.

"You seem to have really taken to this Toronto man. Are you feeling indebted to him for having saved your life?" Roy's wife asked when she reached the bottom of the porch steps. "He sure doesn't seem to be in any rush to get home. Phillie told me Charlie and his wife are splitting."

As Ingrid picked up Lizzie's tin of baked treats she glanced over her cat and discretely whispered something. His eyes opened wide and he instantly stood, walked between Lizzie's legs and dropped his bird at her feet. When he licked the inside of her right calf, Lizzie looked down and her eyes registered the bloody, half-eviscerated bird lying on her left shoe. Shrieking in disgust she recoiled and fell squarely on her rump with an uncomfortable thud.

"Jesus Christ!" she screamed, as she scampered back to her feet and kicked off the shoe. Not bothering to pick it up or even say her farewells, she hobbled one-shoed around the corner of the house, cursing with every step.

Ingrid covered a laugh that erupted from her mouth and smacked her lips at the fat tabby that nodded in acceptance before playfully tossing the bloody corpse of the bluejay onto the shoe.

"Good job, old friend."

*   *   *

Charlie Langdon's return to Toronto was less strained than his trip north. During his forty-eight-hour sojourn, the Porsche dealership relinquished his lease without question, two recruiters each assured a job offer within a week, and his lawyer bought him lunch and turned over a box of items autographed by Duane Michaels. Two days later he boarded the Greyhound bus carrying two suitcases. An anxious Phil Henderson was waiting at the depot when the bus pulled in.

"She knew you'd come back, eh," Henderson announced. "Marge and I love the idea of you and Barrett partnering up. It'll be a good thing for everybody."

When Phil and Charlie walked into the church hall there was a chorus of "hellos and how-are-ya's" and the bingo caller stopped the game to add his hello over the microphone hanging around his neck. The friendliness of the community was novel to him and Charlie smiled awkwardly. Ingrid Petersson waved for him to hurry.

"You are late. Charles Michael. We have already played two games and I am not doing well," she chirped, unable to mask the elation she felt when he walked through the door.

"Yes, ma'am," he replied to Ingrid, looking at the others sitting nearby and adding facetiously, "Oh, thank you for asking . . . I did have a good trip, and it's really nice to see you too." The group at the table burst out laughing and Ingrid blushed.

"I brought you a half a pie and a thermos of milk," she offered, as she thrust four small cardboard squares at him. "Here, spread out these cards. Now pay attention."

Ingrid poked his arm and pointed at a Tupperware container by her feet.

"Be discreet, or you will have to share your treats with all these vultures," Ingrid warned, as the caller shouted out I-19 for the third time.

More people dropped by the table as the game progressed. The former adman stopped feeling self-conscious and realized how wonderful it felt to be noticed for something other than what people expected to get from you.

"Everything okay?" Ingrid asked, as she marked I-19 on her card and pointed to the same number on one of Charlie's three cards.

"Everything is fine. It's nice to be back. Actually, I couldn't wait to get out of that city, but I figure you already knew that, didn't you?" he said, picking up the fork and biting into the healthy-sized piece of pie.

Ingrid smiled and patted his arm. "My runes do not lie."

Someone in the far corner of the church hall yelled "*bingo*" to a chorus of groans from disgruntled losers—not the least of which was an eighty-five-year-old woman from Visby.

Charles Langdon's one hundred day contract began the next morning after his plate of eggs, pancakes, roasted potatoes, and sausages. He and his new partner sat and wrote out a work schedule. Charlie structured their week into a logical priority flow of tasks, assigning units of time and approximate cost estimates of parts and labour. They both agreed to put in seven-hour days from Monday to Friday.

As the autumn unfolded, the trees around the lake blossomed into magnificent yellows, oranges, and reds. By November, that phenomenal kaleidoscope of colours left the forest as the daylight waned earlier and the mornings started in the darkness. It wasn't long until a chill filled the air and flakes of snow began blowing across the water. Within weeks, the flakes were accompanied with heavy snow.

With the onset of the winter, Barrett and Charlie's work list intensified. There were cottage roofs that needed to be cleared of snow, eaves to be cleared of ice, driveways to be ploughed, roads to be salted, failed furnaces to repair, and broken tree branches to be cut into firewood. The two got more done in a day than Barrett Sanford had previously completed in a month. Charlie handled all the billings and took it upon himself to analyze his partner's personal banking accounts ensuring an optimal yet secure rate of return.

Ingrid felt renewed watching everything unfold. She was happier than she had been in twenty-five years despite the daily deterioration of her health and the aches and pains that would not leave her in peace. She was thrilled that her goddaughter was coming out of her shell like a butterfly from its cocoon. Her girl now made up excuses to "drop by" and visit after Charlie got home from work. Cassie's eyes were sparkling and there was a renewed confidence about her that Phillip had done his best to destroy. Her messenger from Odin was a new man who looked healthier and years younger. He was thriving in the partnership with Barrett. Having escaped an unhappy marriage and debilitating job had been a blessing from the Gods.

Charlie Langdon would have agreed with everything his housemate was thinking and feeling. He loved the routine of running with Cassie, breakfasting with Ingrid, working with Barrett, and then hearing his housemate's story. His life was wonderful except for Ingrid's deteriorating health. Every morning the bags under her eyes showed a lack of sleep, and a nagging cough constantly plagued her day. Her sight and hearing were both failing rapidly. He felt that as their destinies had been intertwined it had come with a dangerous price. As his health and spirit grew stronger, his friend's grew weaker.

Chapter Seventeen

After having to quietly endure her mother's caustic reaction to her failed encounter with Ernest Fanning, Phaidra's daughter determined that she needed help. An online search presented a mid-town store called Stealth Spy Shop. The tiny first-floor store was long and narrow with a glass display case, behind which stood a very handsome but nerdy-looking employee with short hair, dark hazel eyes, and a cheerful smile. He was twenty-something and wore a blue Toronto Maple Leafs hoodie, jeans, and high top Nikes. His eyes lit up the moment she walked in.

"Welcome to my shop," he greeted, his enunciation crisp behind a slight Indian accent. "I don't believe you have been here before."

Tessa took in the store. Posters of cameras, weapons, Matt Damon's Jason Bourne, and the 1960s *Star Trek* posters lined the walls. Inside the locked display case were spy cameras hidden in smoke detectors, alarm clocks, keychain fobs, books, baby sound monitors, and picture frames.

"This is my first time," Tessa replied truthfully, "and you've got some pretty cool stuff. Your online reviews are great."

"Thank you very much. We try very hard to serve our customers. What is it you need?"

"Fool-proof recording devices that aren't noticeable and not too expensive."

The man behind the counter nodded knowingly.

"Alright. It would help me to serve your needs better if I knew the exact nature of what you are trying to do," Manpreet Sachdeva suggested. Most of his customers were middle-aged men wanting to spy on women or people trying to catch their spouses having an affair. He was in business to make money. It was a treat to have a pretty female customer, especially one not wearing a wedding ring and smelling like freshly cut flowers.

Tessa Conner revealed little as she continued to scan the display cabinet.

"My boss is harassing me," she began, and she withdrew her two recording devices from her purse and placed them on the counter. "I need proof before I go to our Human Resources department and file a complaint, or it will be his word against mine. You know how that always plays out for the woman. I bought these to record him."

"And you are here because your devices failed to perform?" he inquired.

"I tested them both before and after the incident and they recorded perfectly. But nothing from his office."

Sachdeva listened attentively as he picked up the pen and then the earpiece.

"By the way, my name is Manpreet. You can call me Manny if you like."

The girl smiled but didn't offer a name so he continued.

"I have questions to which I'll need answers. First, do your encounters always occur in the same place? If so, what is the exact size of that location?"

"We were in his corner office that faces to the west and south. It's about twenty square feet and has two walls of floor-to-ceiling windows. There is a big wooden desk, paintings on both non-window walls, and a floor-to-ceiling bookshelf."

Sachdeva ignored his cell phone that rang to the tune of *Star Wars*. "On the bookshelf?"

"Rows of legal books, a flat screen TV, CD player, and framed photographs."

The spy techie reached beneath the counter and held up a black box about the size of a pack of cigarettes. Three two-inch rubber antennas protruded from the top. It was no thicker than a pack of playing cards.

"Did you see anything that resembles this?"

Tessa thought back to Fanning's office and her mind replayed the view, the paintings, the carpets, his desk, a bookshelf with the widescreen TV, and yes, there had been an odd-shaped device with four or five antennas. She had believed that to be the router for Internet.

"Yes, but it was bigger and with more antennae. It was directly beside the television."

Manpreet selected a larger version about the size of a hardcover book. "This?"

Tessa nodded.

"This is the CS-808 Five Band Z-RO Jammer. It's very sophisticated and expensive. Operates on 6600 megahertz and jams any wireless signal within sixty feet. It blocks cell phones, video recorders, and the two items you tried to use."

Tessa listened attentively. "But you know how to get around the CS-808, don't you, Manpreet?"

"It might be possible," Manny replied coyly. "When next will you be with him?"

"In two days on Monday afternoon," she replied.

"Are you truly trying to protect your job, or to put yourself in a position for financial gain? I have a lot of people here with the latter objective."

Tessa was impressed. Sachdeva was a kindred spirit.

"I want to protect my job, but if this presented other opportunities then I wouldn't turn my back on them."

Sachdeva smiled as he walked over and locked the door. He flipped the square, red "OPEN" sign to "CLOSED" and returned to the counter.

"Brilliant. How much are you willing to pay me to provide you with a fool-proof solution to your problem?"

Tessa looked into the brown eyes fixed on her own.

"You can get around his jammer?"

"Absolutely. How much will you pay me to make sure this is foolproof?"

"Two grand."

Without blinking, the assistant manager of Spy Sleuth Store countered.

"Two grand for the equipment and my assistance plus 5% of whatever you get."

"Be serious. 5% is ridiculous."

"Monday is just around the corner," he countered, hyping his Indian accent for effect.

Tessa Conner knew that Manpreet had her by the shorts.

"Alright, but you'll get 5% only if this works. Otherwise you return my two grand."

Sachdeva nodded his acceptance.

"Good, but first, introductions please. And you must call me Manny."

Chapter Eighteen

A light snow flickered through the air when Ingrid and Charlie set out on a walk through the northern forest of her property. The deciduous trees had shed most of their leaves and the groundcover wasn't sure what colour it intended to be. The pace was slow and Ingrid walked along prodding with her walking stick. Charlie kept close, fearing she might fall.

Ingrid picked up a stone and threw it at a spruce tree. An eruption of coughs interrupted her cursing at some evil spirit. After several more stone tosses she turned to her young friend and picked up her story where they had left off.

> Every afternoon, Captain Backstrom would place a cup of thick tea in my hand. Beneath the unkempt, bristly white beard and stern expression was the soul of a kindly grandfather. The Captain had sailed with Henrik for twenty years and there was great affection between them. Alexius despised the Germans and thought the world was a better place with nine fewer of them. He regaled me with stories of hurricanes and typhoons so vicious

that his beloved *Sleipnir* did everything but sink to the bottom of the ocean.

The Captain tried to distract me from my injuries and parents' deaths, but it was Dr. Bjorkman who had the greatest impact on my improvement. Magnus spoke in words I could understand about the psychological trauma I was experiencing with sleeplessness, nightmares, flashbacks, and feelings of guilt. I was happy to stay hidden in the cabin but the doctor insisted I get fresh air on deck. So outside I went twice a day, accompanied by Henrik or Mikaeli. The crew always had a friendly word.

"It is a good day for a walk young miss," each would repeat, and I would smile.

One day Captain Backstrom inquired if I had my mother's gift with runes. When I cast the stones for Alexius a vision immediately appeared before me that showed great danger for the Captain. My vision showed Alexius riding Odin's horse being attacked by two long black snakes. Valifrid Gustavson saw the Black Plague represented as black snakes. It was no coincidence that our ship was called the *Sleipnir*. The horse was in deep water and thrashed about as the Captain shouted out to his men. There was a great feeling of dread that filled my heart. In no time at all the Captain and Odin's horse slipped beneath the water and all was still. I closed my eyes and was once again staring across the tiny table at Henko's friend. Alexius smiled and looked at me with great anticipation. I knew that the destiny of the ship was pre-determined by the Gods and nothing I said could change that. I looked at the Captain and told a happy story of him growing old surrounded by those he loved. He laughed and clapped his hands on his knees and pressed a coin into my hand. It was my first payment as a Stonecaster—a lying one at that.

One Sunday morning our ship was fighting against a stubborn northern Atlantic gale. All hands were called on deck and the doctor arrived to my cabin with strong whiskey to calm my nerves. We sat for a long time until he casually mentioned it was the anniversary of his marriage. As the doctor spoke in soothing tones, I relaxed and forgot about the tempest raging about us.

Before shipping aboard the *Sleipnir*, Magnus worked in a medical clinic in Stockholm. It was 1917 and while Sweden had declared neutrality in World War I, the government was openly supplying Germans with armaments and volunteers. At the same time, other Swedish political powers supported the Russian Tsar and supplied volunteers for his White Army. The populace of our country was caught in a political web because some held a deep hatred for both Germany and Russia while others did not. The country fell into civil war. Protesters fighting in the streets were imprisoned without trial.

Then riots escalated when corrupt politicians allowed German soldiers to openly occupy homes in Stockholm. Swedish troops shot and killed unarmed Swedish protestors. In retaliation, their comrades struck back by planting dynamite in the sewers beneath three government buildings including the one in which Magnus' clinic was located. The buildings exploded into a mass of flying bricks and steel. Over one hundred and twenty-five Swedish government officials were slaughtered, including Magnus' wife and daughters Linnea and Emelia who had just arrived at his clinic to surprise him. He lost all hope, fell into a bottle and wandered the streets hoping to be shot. His cousin found him in a back alley and took him to sea. Until that moment, I had not known that he was related to the captain. When Magnus finished his story he looked over at me and shrugged his shoulders.

"Just my destiny," he muttered, resigning himself to the tragedy. "Just destiny."

I remember staring at Magnus. I had been raised to understand that the Gods write our destinies. I wondered why they had to write such horrors into a destiny like the bombing of a building or the killing of parents and attack on an innocent girl. Was it a test for us to maintain our faith regardless of how the Gods wanted to unfold our destinies? I could see why people lost faith. I was still angry with Odin for having let Mom and Dad die. It was all so confusing. Accepting your faith meant accepting that your destiny might include some horrible things that you cannot change. I thought a lot about that then and for the years to come.

The next day the seas were calm and the sky clear. You would never have known that only the day before the *Sleipnir* had been bounced around the ocean like a toy boat. As Henrik and I strolled past the crew I turned and took his arm.

"We are not going to Venezuela," I shared. "You and I are going to Nova Scotia. I have seen our new life in a very clear vision that came to me last night. We live in a house that looks out onto the ocean and then we will travel inland and have a stone house with oak trees, a garden, rivers, and a lake."

Henrik looked at me like my brain had collapsed and repeated that the *Sleipnir* was forbidden to set ashore.

"The *Sleipnir* will not take us to shore. We arrive in one of the lifeboats. Please convince Captain Backstrom to give us one."

"Ingegard my dove, even if Alexius agreed, we might not make it to shore in a lifeboat," he replied truthfully, explaining that the currents might not be in our favour.

"Ask. I am certain of it," I directed.

The Captain of the *Sleipnir* said he could not make that decision without consulting the men since giving up a lifeboat was dangerous business. He called a meeting and explained our wish. To a man, the twenty-nine sailors agreed to let us take one of the three lifeboats. Since each lifeboat carried ten men I realized that they were placing themselves in danger before they would be able to refit in Venezuela.

"There is something else to discuss," Henrik said quietly, to me after the men agreed. "If we attempt to make shore then we must do it properly. Understand?"

I did not but nodded.

"Good, then it is settled. I am sorry for you that we will not have all the correct bridal clothing and celebrations."

I looked up into his face as the realization of his words struck home. Tears filled my eyes.

He reacted nervously when he saw my eyes.

"But then perhaps you do not want to wed me because I am old."

How could he not know what was in my heart?

"Oh Henko, you could not be more wrong. I will love you at my final breath," I promised, and he wrapped me in his arms. The sailors on the deck cheered.

"She said yes," they cried out, and the *Sleipnir* knew great joy that day.

Being at sea in international waters the Captain had the legal ability to perform a wedding and he proudly offered to conduct the ceremony. It was an unusual wedding and unlike any I had attended. I did not wear Mother's wedding dress or my great-grandmother's wild flower tiara, there was no dowry, and my parents were not with me but I knew they were watching from Valhalla.

Our crew went to great efforts to make my day special as Captain Backstrom pronounced us husband and wife. Each man punched Henrik on the shoulder as a warning to look after me. Some punches made him wince.

Alexius called for silence and handed a small wooden box to my husband. The lid was beautifully crafted with seashells with our names carved upon it. It was filled with coins and paper money.

"First Mate Henrik Petersson," the Captain shouted formally, "today we represent this bride's family and offer you the dowry of Ingegard Signilda Holmberg. As her brothers, we warn you before the Gods to never dishonour her family."

My heart caught in my throat. None of my sisters had ever had a brother at their wedding and I had thirty who had all contributed to my dowry. I cried unashamedly such tears of pride.

Neils Boorman, our cook, played an accordion and another sailor plucked an old violin missing a string. The men danced and sang and we had a feast. At nine o'clock, Captain Backstrom sent the men away to continue in their reverie. He offered his cabin for our wedding night.

And my husband most gently and wonderfully took me in his arms and I knew no fear. My heart sang with joy to Freyja. Her promise had come true and I was fulfilling my destiny.

* * *

Charles Langdon was sitting uncomfortably on an unpadded high wooden stool at Cassie's kitchen island. Charlie mused that his running partner had the most incredible state-of-the-art kitchen on the planet but could barely boil water without burning it. Cassandra readily admitted that the professional kitchen had not been her idea, and if she never saw the inside of a kitchen it would be too soon. Her husband had considered himself a gourmet chef. Having a deep bank account had afforded Phillip to acquire whatever he fancied and having a kitchen that Gordon Ramsay would have envied. The first time Charlie had come into Cassie's kitchen his mouth dropped. He had never seen a six-foot wide stove.

"Does that thing fly?" he had mocked at first sight, and Cassie had dutifully explained.

"None of this was my idea. Phillip was into cooking and spending money like water. This little beauty is called La Cornue Grand Palais Range and it's constructed of cast iron, solid brass, and this part is porcelain enamel. It's got both a gas and electric oven, and count 'em . . . six cook top ranges. Just what any normal person would need."

"How much?"

"Well that's completely tactless," she rebuked.

"You're right. Sorry. How rude of me. So how much?" he repeated, and they both laughed.

"Installed, it was forty-five grand," she blurted out. "Can you believe that? The coffee maker over there with the brass eagle on top," she said, pointing to the Hammacher Double Espresso Machine, "can make either one cup or forty. I don't know forty people I want to be making coffee for. It cost Phillip about ten grand. I told him it was lunacy."

"But you just made our coffee with the Keurig single cup?" Charlie questioned, pointing to a second coffee maker on the counter.

"Are you complaining?"

"No."

She pulled open a door beside the sink. It wasn't full of the pots and pans he expected to see.

"Here we have the Wolf warming drawer to keep things toasty for your guests," she mocked, "or, the Wolf Sub-Zero freezer drawers to keep things chilly. I've never used either of these."

Charlie sat attentively. It didn't take a rocket scientist or even a psychiatrist to understand that there was a lot going on behind this rant. Cassandra was working herself into a real tizzy. "Okay, so he spent money like a drunken sailor."

Cassie raised her index finger and motioned for him to follow her. When they walked to the lower level she opened a door and turned on the light to her wine cellar.

"Know anything about wine?" Cassandra asked.

Charlie entered and stared at the spacious glass enclosed wine refrigerator that all but filled the room. Inside were motorized shelf racks upon which sat endless bottles of wine. There were perhaps twenty unopened cases piled in the corner. He knew enough to recognize several of the labels.

"Henri Jayer Cros Parantoux, Vosne-Romanee Premier Cru, Cote de Nuits," read one label. He looked down at another of five unopened boxes of "Screaming Eagle Cabernet Sauvignon, Napa Valley."

"Cassie, do you know how much these bottles are worth?" he inquired, scanning the labels and quantities of the obscenely priced wines. Kevin Stuart fancied himself a wine connoisseur and cluttered his coffee table with magazines about the best wines on the planet.

"Phillip enjoyed entertaining and showing off his knowledge of great wines. I remember him bragging that the Henri Jayer was worth about eight grand a bottle. That box of Screaming Eagle is about twenty-five grand."

Langdon scanned the room and took a quick inventory. "You've got about four hundred bottles in here."

"No, 662. And to save that little advertising brain of yours trying to do the math, these wines are worth over $390 thousand," she replied casually. "Isn't that utterly foolish?"

Cassie shut off the light and closed the door. They walked back upstairs to a door leading to the side of the house.

"I know you like cars," she commented, as she unlocked the door between the kitchen and the garage. There were two vehicles protected beneath plasticized car covers. She removed one cover and then the other. Charlie Langdon's eyes bulged at the pair of original Shelby Mustangs. If the mileage was limited and all the parts original, the two would bring well over a million dollars.

"Jesus," he uttered, rushing over and staring inside the windows at the odometers. "They're real. Do you know what these are?"

Meryl Patch's granddaughter nodded, somewhat dismayed that her running partner could get so excited about an automobile.

"Yes, the royal blue is a Carroll Shelby 1962 Cobra with a classic aluminum roadster body and a 260 cubic inch V8 that cranked out 260 horsepower. Only seventy-five of these were built. The white one is a 1965 Shelby with a 427 cubic inch side-oiler V8 which put out 510 horsepower."

The ex-adman stared at Cassie. "I guess you heard Phillip describing these gems once or twice."

"Every day. When I got rid of our house in Toronto I sold five other Cobras just like these two," she admitted as they replaced the car covers. "Phillip collected expensive, rare things and loved bragging about them. Made him feel better about himself and more superior to others. You would have thought that as a psychiatrist he might have clued in to all that. In the early days of our marriage, I realized he had collected me just as he had his cars, paintings, cases of wines, and everything else. Not a very nice feeling."

Langdon watched her face sadden.

"You know these vehicles shouldn't be stored unattended here," Charlie warned, as they clipped the 1965's car cover in place. "None of this should be here. If the wrong people found out about the cars and your wine collection, you could get robbed and hurt."

Cassie led the way back into the kitchen.

"Ingrid says I should sell the cars and the wine and get on with it. Even her runes have told her that I have to extricate myself from the past," Cassandra declared. "I know she's right but I just haven't gotten around to it."

She caught the look that appeared on his face.

"Charlie, don't think that I dwell on Phillip or his death. My time with him was not something that made me happy. He shattered my confidence. I shouldn't be speaking ill of the dead but most days Phillip treated me like a trophy on display to everyone."

Langdon wasn't certain how to reply.

Cassie looked at the page on his computer screen and saw the headline about Telfer Stuart. The ad shop was in the news again with another backlash. Two additional clients had called for a review. Industry speculation was that they'd be closing up shop within the next business quarter.

Ingrid's goddaughter decided they had talked enough about her life wondering if she had said too much. Looking at the computer she changed topics.

"What are the odds of an agency keeping clients who put them on notice?" she inquired.

"Snowball's hope in hell," he responded truthfully, as Cassandra put his cup into the microwave. He was glad to be leaving the topic of her husband.

"I read online that you were a star at pitching clients. You led the pitch that won the Chicago firm. Wouldn't it be smart for your agency to hire you back to save the clients you won in the first place?"

Charlie walked over to the microwave and pulled out the hot cup. It felt good to know that she had checked him out on Google. "Of course it would, but even if they contact me I'm not sure I'd want to work for them."

Cassie brought out two apples from the fridge and placed one in front of him before taking a bite of her own. "Any chance your Chicago client would want to re-hire your agency?"

Charlie Langdon wondered what motive was lurking behind the questions. Was Cassie trying to get him to leave?

"No, it doesn't work that way. They hired a new marketing chief who gunned us to make room for his friends."

"And he's the boss?"

"He reports to the CEO, who's actually a pretty decent person."

"Well your on-line reputation does not portray you as a guy who takes one on the chin and goes down for the count," Cassie commented, her mouth half-full of apple. "It seems to me that you need to grab the bull by the horns and make some phone calls. The longer you procrastinate, the harder it will be for you to get back in the saddle. Or then, maybe you've decided to languish up here?"

This last unexpected comment struck home like Kyla's elbow across his jaw. He recoiled instantly.

"I'm not hiding," he exclaimed defensively, too off-balance to ask if this was the kettle calling the pot black.

"Then, Mr. Langdon, in all of your profound wisdom, what exactly is it you are doing?" Cassandra Turner countered pointedly, and when Charlie's mouth opened to speak, nothing came out.

* * *

Tessa Conner's cell rang Sunday evening just before seven. A hushed voice from a private number requested she dress nicely for a late dinner and would be picked up at 8:30 p.m.

The young paralegal selected a short, teal-coloured off-the-shoulder dress with a respectably low cut front. She wore higher than normal heels and a light cashmere sweater. At 8:25 p.m. she checked the contents of her purse and got into the back seat of a limo chauffeured by a Jamaican driver complete with dreads.

"Miss Conner," he confirmed, and she nodded. "Good evening. We're going to a restaurant in the east end. Your uncle will meet you there."

"Is it Flaubert on McCown Drive?" she asked, quietly noting that Fanning was her uncle.

"No, it's Le Vrai Normand, on Dupont Boulevard by the park," the driver corrected, and his passenger smiled.

"Le Vrai Normand on Dupont is a favourite of mine," she lied, clearly repeating the name.

Upon arriving Tessa was led through an almost empty restaurant to a candle-lit table in a quiet corner. The headwaiter had a white handlebar moustache and wore his tuxedo like he had been born into it.

"Something to drink, Mademoiselle?" he asked, and was surprised to be declined since Monsieur Fanning's Sunday evening "nieces" tended to imbibe liberally and giggle a lot.

Tessa studied the room and casually positioned Manpreet's audio and video recording amulet hanging on her neck facing forward. Placing her purse beneath the table she removed a square plastic-encased box the size of a paperback book by John Grisham. The adhesive strip peeled off and she pressed Manny's device upwards so that it adhered firmly to the base of the tabletop. Sachdeva explained that it was virtually impossible to anti-jam the device her boss was employing. What was not impossible, he had explained, was to "temporarily numb" the lithium ion battery that powered it, thus preventing the jamming device from stopping wireless signals. His device had been proven totally reliable, and Tessa was in possession of a perfect recording of the events of their Monday meeting.

Sitting back she took a small mirror and reapplied her lipstick.

"Two times," she directed quietly. Outside the restaurant a car honked twice.

Her silver-haired boss approached from a side door and quickly sat directly beside her so that his only chance of being observed was from someone entering through the backdoor. Fanning was wearing a three-piece Armani along with that obnoxious, superior attitude that projected he owned the world. Manpreet had predicted Fanning would bring a mobile jamming device and Tessa had no doubt it was in the briefcase, which Fanning carried in and placed at the foot of his chair.

For a moment Ernest allowed his eyes to wander over her body and the memory of their Monday encounter came flooding back. Tessa had been a very enthusiastic partner. He looked forward to their next time in the back of his limo after they finished dessert.

"You should wear that colour more often. It brings out your eyes," he admired, motioning to the waiter.

"I'm glad you approve," she smiled coyly. "You have such lovely taste."

"I've ordered for us. I trust you like salmon?"

As they began their salad niçoise, Phaidra's daughter leaned provocatively forward.

"Mr. Fanning, may I tell you something?"

The lawyer took a sip of the Domaine Leflaive Montrachet Grand Cru the restaurant kept stocked in special reserve for their wealthier patrons. Appreciating the rich mouth-feel of the French wine from the Côte de Beaune, he nodded.

"Yes, but only if you call me Ernest, when we are alone."

She shifted and watched her host's eyes follow the movement of her bosom.

"Ernest, I feel awkward about this."

Outside, a car horn honked twice for a second time, reassuring Tessa that Manny's device stuck under the table was effectively "numbing" the lithium ion battery powering the mobile jamming device in Fanning's briefcase.

"Tessa, there's nothing to feel awkward about. Let's just enjoy ourselves."

The lawyer picked up and bit into a piece of pesto-covered tomato, sliding his free hand onto her thigh.

"But I feel like I'm prostituting myself," she whispered. "What we've been doing in your office isn't exactly written in my job description."

"Don't be naive or vulgar," he chastised, immediately withdrawing his hand from her leg. "It's very unbecoming. I can help you, and based on what I've seen so far, you can certainly help me," he added, with a quiet grin.

Tessa sipped her wine and dabbed her lips with the napkin. Two couples entered the restaurant and were seated by the window. Fanning stole a quick glance and then ignored them. He returned his hand to her thigh.

"How often will I have to 'visit your office' before you get me into law school?"

"Tessa, I admire your directness."

"Please don't think me rude but your law firm has repeatedly taught me that you need a contract to keep everybody honest. Ernest, how can I be certain that you'll take care of me if I take care of you?"

The lawyer signalled for more wine as a silent alarm went off in his head. He studied his dinner date carefully and then looked around. Was he being baited or was she just so young that speaking this plainly was part of her makeup? If this were an attempt at entrapment, the portable jammer in his briefcase would block any devices that might be used to record him.

"Tessa, let's agree that you will be available three times a week," he responded quietly. "I have a place we can use. I insist that you be sexually exclusive to me and I'd like a complete blood test before our next rendezvous. And it goes without saying that our arrangement be discrete and is not for any locker-room girl chatter. Will that work for you?"

"I understand Ernest," she responded. "Sex three times a week, exclusivity, and, of course discretion. In return, you guarantee me law school. Shall we say six months from today?"

Ernest took another sip and squeezed his hand.

"One year from today and you'll understand if we don't put this in writing," he laughed openly.

"Just to clarify, you aren't into anything kinky? Just what we've been doing?

"I'm not into kinky but I do hope you have an adventurous imagination."

Tessa smiled teasingly and bit her upper lip.

"And you promise you will put me through law school?"

"Yes. Let's make a toast to our deal."

"Three times," she requested, and outside the restaurant, Manpreet obliged by honking three times.

"Pardon me," Fanning asked confusedly, lowering his hand. "Three times what?"

Phaidra McTavish's daughter reached into her purse and removed the rebuilt iPad that Sachdeva had bought on Kijiji. "Put the ear buds in and watch," she ordered.

"What is this all about?" the confused lawyer asked, removing his hand and sitting back.

"Ernest, just put in the ear buds and press that little blue chevron pointing to the right. Consider this foreplay."

Within seconds of the screen coming to life the blood drained from her dinner companion's face. As his eyes followed the images he realized that Tessa had positioned a recording device pointing directly at the sofa in his office. Their entire sexual interaction on Monday had been captured. She had deployed a second device closed to the sofa because in the inset it showed them from a different angle with her saying "no" at least three times and looking plaintively in the direction of the camera. Incredibly, Tessa Conner had gotten around his jamming device. Momentarily, the image of his office was replaced with him from the time he walked into the restaurant and sat down at the table. This video had him on screen communicating his sexual demands and clearly stated what she would receive in return. Looking at her he realized her amulet was a camera and it was still recording. His stomach churned for having been played so expertly by a novice.

The recording ended and Fanning withdrew the ear buds and immediately placed the iPad beside his briefcase. She'd gotten around the mobile jammer as well.

"Yes, it's all coming clear to you. The device in your briefcase isn't working either. Just like the one in your office. By the way, you can keep that iPad. It's a throwaway and untraceable. There's nothing on it except the video you saw."

Fanning realized that the tables had been turned on him.

"You're wondering how I got these recordings past your jammer? Well, my techie is apparently smarter than yours. Did you know you can temporarily neutralize the lithium battery inside your device which prevents it from jamming?'

Fanning ceased talking, aware that he was still being recorded.

Phaidra's daughter took a sip of her wine before continuing.

"Nothing to say? Didn't think so. I'll do the talking. I want you to pay for law school. You want my recordings. Here are typed instructions for my bank," she stated, pushing a folded slip of paper across the table. "By Wednesday at noon wire two hundred thousand dollars into that account. When I've got a confirmation I will personally bring the recordings to your office. Naturally, my partners will keep one recording as my insurance policy."

Fanning picked up the pink napkin and wiped his moustache. As he spoke he held the serviette in front of his lips.

"Blackmailers always return for more."

Tessa Conner shook her head. "No sir, I won't. I just want to go to law school. And if anything should happen to me—like I get hit by a car, disappear, or get a hangnail—copies of these recordings will be sent to your Board of Directors and the RCMP. You get the picture? Unlike your thief of a son, there won't be a rock for you to hide under."

Outside in the parking lot an exuberant Manpreet Sachdeva sat high-fiving himself. What a liar she'd been. She was going to milk this sucker for $200 thousand. He'd take his 5% and at least another $25 thousand. After all, he was in possession of all recordings. If Tessa didn't play ball, he could cut her out, keep the recordings, and go directly at her boss.

"We're finished," she concluded, raising her eyebrows. "Nod if you agree."

The lawyer begrudgingly nodded his head and motioned with a dismissive wave of his hand for her to leave. The irony of the entire blackmailing episode was not lost on him. Goodwin Fanning would be rolling over in his grave about now.

As Tessa got up to leave she found herself unable to resist the temptation.

"By the way Mr. Fanning, my name is not Conner. It's Tessa McTavish," she admitted fool-heartedly. "My mother is Phaidra McTavish. Do you remember what you did to her?"

The look of recognition in Fanning's eyes revealed that he knew of whom Tessa spoke.

He remembered Phaidra McTavish as an exceptionally attractive and vivacious secretary who had been built like a Playboy bunny. He met her just after getting married to Bettina. The woman had traipsed into his office and ambushed him like the Senators assassinating

Caesar in 44 BCE. She had been relentless in bedding him to the point that one night when he opened the door to his car Phaidra was sitting in the passenger seat wearing nothing but a bottle of Dom Perignon and two champagne flutes. Her voluptuous body and uninhibited spirit had been impossible to resist. That night began a torrid, sexual affair, the likes of which Ernest Fanning had never experienced. McTavish was so carnally voracious that he felt he'd finally met his match.

But about six months into their affair Phaidra showed up with a vial of cocaine. She told Ernest it would heighten their sex. Ernest Fanning had few scruples in life but was firmly opposed to drug use. He'd watched friends lose everything over drugs and booze. The young lawyer summarily ended the affair, and knowing he couldn't have a jilted lover hanging about the office, arranged for Phaidra McTavish's termination from Blackmore and Craig.

"Phaidra's daughter?" he questioned curiously, looking into Tessa's all too confident eyes. Was there a resemblance?

Tessa felt a great vindication as she left the restaurant. It could not have gone any better.

After settling the bill, Ernest Fanning strode to his limo against which his driver was enjoying a smoke. As his passenger approached, the fifty-two-year-old, heavyset man opened the pack of cigarettes and offered one.

"No guest tonight?" David Fowler asked rhetorically, as his boss accepted the cigarette and lit it.

"Things turned a little dicey," Fanning responded casually, as he drew the tobacco smoke deep into his lungs and held it there. "David, I need you to take care of a few things."

The chauffeur flicked his cigarette to the pavement and pulled out a pen and pad. The pen looked like a toothpick in his meat cleaver-sized hand.

"The young lady with whom I had dinner is an employee at our firm. Her name is Tessa Conner but she was born McTavish. Her address is 112 Wharncliffe Drive. Her mother's name is Phaidra McTavish and she was an employee of mine from about twenty-five years ago. Retrieve their information from our company files. You've got the passcodes. Get Tessa's banking and credit card information. Phone Vito Carbrese and have him pick up Phaidra and Tessa in the next twenty-four hours."

David Fowler repeated the names and address.

"Alive?" the younger man inquired, as if he was asking if a customer wanted fries with their burger.

"Unharmed."

"Vito's not cheap."

Fanning tapped the ash off the end of the cigarette and looked up at the stars. It was a crystal clear night and Orion's nebula was shining brightly.

"Pay him, but he's got twenty-four hours and the clock's ticking."

"Yes sir," Fowler acknowledged. "What else?"

"Tessa recorded both tonight's dinner and a sexual encounter we had last Monday."

"She recorded you despite the jammer?" Fowler repeated. "You saw it with your own eyes?"

The lawyer nodded his head.

"Blackmail?"

"Yes. Somehow she got around my supposedly infallible jamming device by neutralizing the battery. That make sense to you?"

"No."

"Well, she's got me dead to rights on video and I'm fucked three times sideways if we don't recover it. There is at least one accomplice who was somewhere out here parked in a car. He responded to her cue by honking his horn. You notice any vehicles that honked?

The former Detective smiled broadly puffing out his barrel chest and stretching his thickly muscled arms. "Brown Honda Prelude parked across the street in the donut shop. The driver was a slight-figured dark-skinned man in his mid-twenties, possibly East Indian. And he acted very nervous."

Ernest appreciated his driver of five years. David Fowler had been on the force for twenty-five years, ten of which had been spent as a Detective First Class with the Toronto Vice Squad. The policeman had a list of citations as long as his arm, as well as an ability to make problems or problem people disappear—even if it meant stepping a considerable distance outside the law. But a love for the ponies had rung up too many gambling debts, forcing him from retirement. He came to Fanning's attention through a colleague who had highly recommended Fowler as a talented fixer, bodyguard, and driver. The ex-cop had proven his reputation time and again.

David E. Fowler stood six feet, two inches and tipped the scales at just over 240 pounds. Despite being in his fifties and having "army short" white hair, Fowler was a formidable-looking man who knew how to take care of himself. Always armed with a Sig Sauer in a holster under his left shoulder, he never left home without the blackjack he carried in his back trouser pocket and a well-used set of brass knuckles. He owned two pairs of black shoes and two pairs of brown shoes, both of which were fitted with steel toes for destructive kicking power. A titanium high-impact telescope police baton was attached with Velcro to the inside of his jacket for easy access. His less-than-passive approach to his police career hadn't been without personal damage. He'd suffered a broken nose, a cracked and wired jaw, two gunshot wounds, and four broken ribs. But David was more than just an undiscerning brutal weapon. He had a real cop's brain with that inexplicable way of observing everything, just as he had tonight in identifying Tessa's accomplice.

Ernest Fanning looked at his driver. "You didn't happen to get a license number?"

"No need," the ex-Detective responded, pointing across the lot. "There are two outdoor cameras at the gas station beside the donut shop. Give me a few minutes and I'll get the plate number."

Fanning motioned for another cigarette.

"Have Vito pick him up tonight. I want every electronic device he owns. Have Vito find out who else is in on this."

David lit his boss' Marlboro, handed him the rest of the pack, and trudged across the street. Ten minutes later the big man returned holding a piece of paper upon which was scribbled "BBMR 245."

Before he pulled up into Fanning's driveway his phone pinged with a text from a pal in Division 52.

"We've got a name and address," Fowler confirmed, and Fanning got out of the car without responding or returning his driver's pack of cigarettes.

*　　*　　*

"So how's the running going with Charlie?" Ingrid asked, for the umpteenth time, as Cassie turned off the TV. She folded up the afghan under which they had kept toasty while watching *The Treasure of Sierra Madre*.

"Really well," came the reply. "He's almost keeping up. Cassie stopped short of admitting she had discovered that he was smart, a great conversationalist, self-deprecating, and rich in family values. She didn't mention that she viewed Charles Langdon as one of the nicest people she had ever met.

"Still positive he's not the one?" Ingrid queried, as she pulled on her Canada goose jacket and opened the front door. There was a whisking of snow across the porch. "Put down your sweater, little dove, you do not need to walk me home. You can watch from the window and I'll flick the lights on and off to tell you I am safe. Now answer my question before I go."

"I just don't know. It's all so confusing. Charlie's life is screwed up and he's still married. I'm just as much a basket case after the job Phillip did on me."

Ingrid reached up and tickled her friend's chin.

"Well, that is a step in the right direction. It tells me that you have been thinking about it. Soon you will realize I am right. Just give yourself time to discover what I already know. Your destiny lies with Charles Langdon."

Days after Cassandra had shown him the Shelbys and the wine cellar Charlie was still pondering her question about him hiding from his problems when Ingrid got back from visiting the Hendersons. Margery Henderson was ill, and Ingrid had taken over medicinal herbs with which she made tea and a chest plaster. The morning brought with it a definite chill and the smell of another snowfall was hanging in the air. The Swede removed her coat and asked Charlie to light a fire. As he arranged the kindling, Ingrid began coughing a deep "bark" that sounded like the worst kind of bronchitis.

"Are you alright?" he asked, but his friend either ignored or didn't hear the question. He and Cassie had come to realize that Ingrid's hearing was shot and she only pretended to catch conversations.

"Ingrid, are you okay?" he repeated louder, and the white-haired lady looked over and gave him a dirty look.

"It's just a cold," she responded, before walking slowly over to the mantel and staring at the objects. She did her best to suppress another coughing spell as memories surrounding the mantel objects flooded her mind. Her body ached in places she didn't know could hurt. When she had collected herself she turned and continued her story.

> By the next midnight the *Sleipnir* was within ten miles of the Canadian coast. We could just make out shore lights off Nova Scotia. Our crew looked anxious as we climbed into the twenty-foot longboat because the barometer was high and foretold a gale. I told them that in my vision we had arrived on land so there was nothing to worry about. Captain Backstrom kept reassuring me that our boat was unsinkable and would self-upright if waves got the better of us. Alexius said it was made of balsa wood, as if that would make me feel better. Mikaeli told us there was food and fresh water for a week but that made me more nervous since our race to shore was supposed to take six hours. I knew we were supposed to make it, but my visions had never shown how long it might take. I had never even considered that and should have because visions can be deceptive that way. We had a compass, life jackets, a lantern, warm clothing, and rain slickers. A canvas tarp covered most of the opening to keep out the sea that was rolling heavy and pitching us about like a cork. Alexius fastened a rope around my waist to the

gunnels and then put his hand on his First Mate's shoulder. Together they prayed to Thor.

"The current will make the ten miles seem like twenty," Alexius calculated. "You have to get to within five miles by four o'clock to meet the incoming tide." Captain Backstrom looked up at the sky. "There is weather coming and you will lose the stars and shore lights within hours. Are you certain about this? Venezuela is a lovely place to sit out the war."

"I am sure, my friend. Ingegard has seen this in her dreams. If Odin is kind, one day you will sit in front of our fire with our children upon your knee. We will laugh about this night and the war."

The *Sleipnir* was massive up against our tiny lifeboat made of balsa. The crew sang to us as we drifted away and Henrik pulled the oars like a madman. I found myself praying to Freyja for physical strength and of course to the mighty Thor to calm the seas and winds. My offer to help row brought roars of laughter from my Viking.

"Each oar weighs more than you, my wife."

It was not long before we could no longer see the *Sleipnir*, and as the hours passed the shore lights did not seem to be getting closer. Clouds hid the stars and the howling winds brought relentless driving rain that stung our faces and bare hands.

"Thor, why have you deserted us?" Henrik screamed angrily, and I told him that there was no need to worry, but he was focussed on his oars and keeping us upright.

Waves rolled up from all directions. We lost sight of the coastal lights and the stars and soon neither sea nor sky could be separated. I held onto Henrik's leg for comfort and I am not ashamed to admit that I was afraid.

"Take the compass and the torch," my husband ordered, handing me a small leather case and a flashlight. "Keep us pointed due west."

Mountains of water relentlessly crashed on our sanctuary and the compass was ripped from my grasp. I would have gone overboard had I not been lashed to the gunnels. Ice-cold water filled our craft and I bailed but to no end. My husband, exhausted and losing the battle, lifted the oars and tossed a sea anchor over the side to provide us stability in the waves. With all the remaining strength he could muster, Henrik fastened the tarpaulin across the top of our balsa wood boat, sheltering us from the numbing sea and biting, hail-filled winds.

"Ingegard, you did say this lifeboat was how we got to Canada? Perhaps you can convince your beloved Freyja that we are ready to step onto dry land," Henrik called out above the roaring winds.

Ingrid suddenly stopped telling her story when she realized that her guest was fidgeting and only half-listening.

"Something is bothering you, perhaps? It is important for you to pay attention so you do not forget anything. What has upset you?"

Charlie picked up the poker and stabbed at one of the logs sending sparks flying in all directions.

"Ingrid, I've been thinking."

"About?" his white-haired hostess inquired, as she moved the fire screen back to its rightful place.

"Well, our one hundred day contract is almost through. I still have unfinished business in Toronto."

Ingrid avoided eye contact.

"We have a deal and you still owe me twenty-five days. Are you not happy here, perhaps?"

The Last Stonecaster

"It's not that I'm not happy. Cassie says I'm hiding."

Ingrid chuckled and grinned.

"That is my darling girl. No beating around the bush with that one."

Charlie nodded his agreement and was about to say something about Cassie when Ingrid walked over to him and took his face in her hands.

"Charles Michael, everything happens for a reason and with time you will learn that the loss of your wife, your house, your job, and your money means nothing. And my darling Cassandra is only partially right because you are recharging your batteries and if that means hiding out for a while then so be it. And in twenty-five days, if you have determined that you must leave here and face your Toronto demons, then go face them."

"Doesn't it seem unusual that you've got a complete freeloading stranger living in your house?"

Ingrid shook her head.

"Well, first of all, you are paying room and board so you are not freeloading. Second, the Gods brought us together when we most needed each other. You must feel our connection far beyond the image of the Viking on your shoulder. And third, the runes tell me that you are supposed to be here in this place at this time."

"The runes told you all that?"

"Yes. You are here for a reason and your destiny is interwoven with mine, and Cassandra's. I know that as surely as Freyja is watching over us right now."

*   *   *

After finishing some jobs with Barrett Sanford, Charlie went for a drive. He pulled the F150 into the McDonald's drive-through in Bracebridge and ordered a Big Mac and a Coke Zero. As he munched into the burger he thought of Cassandra's questions about Telfer Stuart and his former Chicago client. He had no doubt that his old agency would likely close their doors by February. More people would be on the street.

By the time he drove home, Ingrid was sound asleep on the sofa by the fireplace. His dinner was one the table. He gently carried the Swede to her bed and deposited the tiny mystic beneath the heavy duvet. Putting his plate into the fridge, he crawled onto his own bed, looked up at the dreamcatchers hovering above his bed, and instantly fell into world of Norse Gods, Ingrid's balsa lifeboat, and Cassandra Turner.

He awoke wearing yesterday's clothes and heard Ingrid at the stove preparing breakfast. After exchanging "good mornings" Charlie told her he had some things to do.

"Ingrid, I'm going to phone Barrett and tell him I need today off. I have to drive into Bracebridge and use the library's computers to print off and sign some things," Charlie announced, as a plate was set in front of him. It had taken almost three months but Kyla's lawyer finally had sent the final decree papers for their divorce. Once signed, the Langdons' uncontested divorce would finalize nine months hence.

Ingrid brought more pancakes before he had taken his first bite.

"I need Cassie to pick up some things in town and I'll be too busy today to go. Would you mind if she tags along?" Ingrid asked, before erupting in spasms of coughs. It rattled her tiny frame so roughly that she had to grasp the counter for balance.

Langdon looked concernedly at his friend but said nothing. Ingrid had given him hell for continually asking about the cough and told him he was acting like an old maid.

"Not a problem," he replied, through bites of the pancakes, given that she was already on the phone. He wondered if Cassie was picking up medication for the damned cough.

Ingrid's goddaughter sat quietly as they drove along the provincial highway into Bracebridge. Cassie had already completed her run and didn't ask why he hadn't shown up, figuring he was ticked after her obnoxious statement about him hiding at the lake.

"I was surprised Ingrid said you wanted me to go into town with you," she stated sheepishly, taking off her ski jacket when the F150's heater finally kicked out a stream of warm air. "I didn't know if you'd still be mad at the things I said yesterday."

"I'm glad you're coming along," he stated truthfully, not correcting her perception of who had invited whom. "I am not mad in the least. I needed someone to say what you did."

Cassandra smiled and her shoulders relaxed. "Good, I thought you were mad."

For the remainder of the ride into Bracebridge neither spoke but the silence was far from being uncomfortable. The two shared a pleasurable drive just being together without forcing any rules of social etiquette.

After dropping Cassie at the hardware store Charlie entered the library to find it virtually empty except for a woman sorting books. He settled down behind one of the two computers and logged in. The Internet was surprisingly fast and he momentarily downloaded and printed off Kyla's divorce papers, which were accompanied by his own lawyer's cover note directing him to sign where outlined and then return-fax the document:

"BTW Charlie, have someone witness your signatures. Legally, the separation is a one year period, but we can justifiably claim you've already been out of the house for three months meaning that in nine months you'll be free." J. C.

The settlement gave Kyla all proceeds from the sale of the house and its contents. Kyla kept her Mercedes, RRSPs, and all stocks, including NIR proceeds that amounted to a little under $300 thousand. Kyla's real estate operation was off the table and would remain in her sole possession. For his part, Charlie was permitted to keep the six-month severance and any money coming out of the cancellation of his Porsche lease.

Kyla was taking it all but Charlie Langdon no longer gave a damn. If this was the payment to be free of her then it was worth every penny.

Charlie looked at the librarian. She had a pleasant enough face with that kind of thin, dark brown hair that looked greasy even after having just been washed. Thick eyeglasses perched on the tip of her nose making the librarian look intelligently bookish but mousy. The woman was mid-height and paper-thin.

The librarian introduced herself as Miriam Walker and gladly offered to witness and then re-fax his papers.

"They've been received," she confirmed, in the most pleasant voice. "Here are the originals. The printing cost for the fifteen pages is seventy-five cents."

"Thanks," Charlie responded, reaching into his pocket.

"Couldn't help but notice," she whispered confidentially, "you're getting a divorce. That's rough."

Charlie was uncertain how to respond.

"I'm sorry, that was tactless," the thin girl added quickly, her freckled cheeks blushing beneath her tortoiseshell-rimmed glasses. "My mother always tells me that I never know the right thing to say. No one will know what I faxed, Mr. Langdon."

"Don't worry. I appreciate your discretion," Charlie replied calmly, as he fixed the clasp of his briefcase.

The librarian stood there as if she had something else to say.

"You're the man who saved Ingrid," Miriam blurted, her eyes squinting. Everyone was still talking about the hero of Great Spirit Moon Lake.

He nodded.

"Well, chivalry is far from dead."

"Do you know Ingrid?" he inquired politely, as they shook hands.

Miriam laughed, revealing beautiful teeth and a lovely smile. Charlie's Mom had always insisted that every person had an appealing physical trait. Miriam's smile was hers.

"Everyone knows Ingrid. Grandma and Ingrid started up the bakery across the street in the seventies. They were best friends until Gram died in 2002."

"Your grandmother?"

"Meryl Hatch. Ingrid sold Mom her share of the bakery in '88 when Henrik died."

"Ingrid is a remarkable woman," Langdon offered.

"You don't know the half of it," Miriam boasted. "Ingrid paid the university tuitions for me, my two brothers, and all of our cousins, except Cassandra. She got scholarships everywhere."

The Last Stonecaster

Charlie's brain clicked that Miriam and Cassie Turner were first cousins.

"Anyway, I teach night school, volunteer here at the library three mornings a week, and the rest of the time I'm at the bakery. Go over and try our chocolate chip cookies."

Miriam was distracted as a man in his mid-forties approached the counter asking for books on Chinese dynasties as well as information on the Kuomintang and Chiang Kai Shek. By heart, Miriam knowledgeably rattled off the titles of five books and their exact location. Charlie leaned on the oak counter and was impressed with her wealth of knowledge.

"Did Ingrid and Henrik have children?" he asked curiously, and the librarian leaned forward as if discussing a conspiracy.

"This is a sensitive topic. Don't raise it with her."

"Okay," Charlie promised, and the two brought their faces closer like co-conspirators. Meryl's granddaughter had a pleasant enough face but none of her cousins' natural beauty.

"An epidemic of Scarlett Fever swept through here and Georgian Bay in the fall of 1962 and killed hundreds of people, mainly young children and a disproportionate number of the Ojibwe. Thirty-five children and twelve adults tragically died in our community. Ingrid and Henrik lost their son and daughter."

More people entered the library and Miriam motioned that she had to go. "You know Ingrid is really special. She is a Norse mystic from a bloodline that dates back to the 1200s. They were called Stonecasters and somehow they managed to survive a Christian society that tried desperately to wipe out the old Viking beliefs of multiple Gods. I guess that makes her the last Stonecaster. I wonder if it bothers her that she didn't have a daughter to take over for her?"

Charlie had often wondered the same thing.

"My Grandma started writing down Ingrid's visions in a red journal when she realized her mystical friend could truly see the future. Grandma would date something Ingrid had seen in a vision and then record the date when it actually happened. One day when I was ten, I was staying overnight at Grandma Meryl's house, and found the journal. My eyes almost popped out of my head with what I read. It was incredible what Mrs. Petersson had seen before it happened."

Langdon waited patiently to ask, "Give me some examples."

Miriam cleared her throat. "Grandma made me promise to never reveal what I had read because she thought Ingrid might get into trouble."

Charlie leaned forward and smiled warmly. "Do you think I would do something to hurt our friend?"

"No, of course not," the librarian replied, anxiously looking over at the people milling by the front counter. "There were hundreds of predictions. For example, on September 22, 1959, Ingrid had a dream about a very young president of the United States and his wife being covered in blood and being smothered by a flag with one star. That's the way she saw the assassination of Kennedy exactly four years to the day before it happened in Dallas, Texas. And in 1961, Grandma wrote about Ingrid seeing a 'strong-armed' man dressed in white walking across a white desert covered in the blackest of nights. She described the moon's surface exactly how we have now come to know it. That 'strong-armed' man in her dream was Neil Armstrong. I never had a chance to finish the whole journal because Grandma caught me and gave me a spanking. I had never seen her so angry."

"Where's the journal now?"

"No one knows what happened to it."

Langdon smiled and touched her hand. "Well, I promise your secret is safe with me and I won't mention it."

Miriam exhaled a sigh of relief and looked behind her as a mother and three children entered the library. "I've got to go."

"I appreciate talking with you, Miriam."

An hour or so later when he crossed the street and entered the bakery, Langdon immediately saw Miriam's cousin sitting up at the counter. Cassandra was enjoying an espresso and savouring the icing atop an oversized chocolate doughnut that could have easily served four people. He couldn't get over how much the girl could put away and not have an ounce of fat on her to show for it.

"Hi, you hungry?" she asked.

"Yes."

"This is Miriam's mom, Helen," Cassie mumbled, with her mouth crammed with chocolate. "Aunt Helen, this is Charlie Langdon."

The lady working the counter brought over a cup of hot chocolate and four oversized cookies laden with chunks of dark chocolate and slivers of walnuts. Helen Walker looked like an older version of her daughter if Miriam put on eighty pounds, dyed her hair silver, and lost the tortoiseshell-rimmed glasses.

"Miriam phoned you wanted to try the chocolate chip cookies," Helen opened. "Did my girl yap your ears off? She does that a lot. She said you were about the most handsome man who ever walked into the library. Thought you looked somewhere between a younger Harrison Ford and Ryan Reynolds. What do you think, Cass? Harrison or Ryan?"

Cassie chortled and took another bite, enjoying watching Charlie squirm. A thoroughly embarrassed Charlie Langdon could see from whom Miriam got that gift of gab.

"Miriam was delightful and very helpful," he said politely, "and didn't 'yap my ears off.'"

The librarian's mother's face beamed as she topped up his coffee.

"She's not married, you know."

After window-shopping the length of Main Street, Charlie and Cassie drove slowly back to the lake. There was a slight uneasiness to the ensuing silence as both seemed to have something they wanted to share. Ingrid's goddaughter began first.

"Charlie, you know I've been a widow for four years?"

"Yes, Phillip died of cancer."

She nodded. "I've told you it wasn't much of a marriage?"

"Yes, you felt he thought of you as one of his possessions and treated you like you didn't count."

Cassie crossed her legs impressed with such a succinct explanation. "You've probably gathered that I retreated up here and have been living like a hermit. I think you also know that I'm not hurting for money."

Charlie looked over but didn't reply. After several moments, Cassie continued.

"Well, our Swedish friend has told me that it is our destiny to share our futures. All of which is very bizarre since you're married and I haven't had a date since becoming a widow. Has Ingrid shared that little tidbit with you?"

Langdon expressed a sigh of relief with Cassie's directness. He hated people who pussyfooted around the bush.

"Yes and I don't know whether it's her runes or her own desires to see you meet someone new. She thinks the world of you."

Cassandra smiled. "Well, Ingrid certainly believes the sun rises and sets on you," she replied.

"Since we're laying our cards on the table, you know that I am getting a divorce and that there is absolutely no chance at reconciliation."

"Uh-huh."

"My soon-to-be ex-wife is taking me for everything we own, so unlike you, I don't have a ton of dough sitting around."

"Okay."

Charlie slowed as they approached a county truck salting the road. "We've already discussed that I'm jobless, but there's more I need you to know about me."

"Alright."

He began slowly after carefully passing the truck and returning to the inside lane. "I was in a seven-year marriage with a woman named Kyla. It went sour, which was as much my fault as hers; maybe even more my fault because I spent too much time at work and not enough paying attention to her. My absence sparked her to change from a delightful young woman to an aggressively driven person. She has been in a relationship with someone for awhile."

Cassie sat quietly and kept her eyes focused on the road.

"The day before I arrived here, I discovered my best friend had embezzled from his company, taking all of my investment with him. He's now a felon on the run."

"Alexander Fanning and NIR?" she asked. Everyone had read about NovaRose.

"Yes."

"I met him about five years ago at a cocktail party. He was your best friend?"

"Yes, and he hung me out to dry along with all the other investors. I would never have imagined that in a million years. He was like my brother."

Cassandra cleared her throat and placed her left hand on the driver's shoulder. "Charlie, no wonder you looked so beaten up when we first met. What a horrid time you've been put through. I am so truly sorry that you had to face all of that, but I am glad you shared it with me."

Langdon glanced over at her. Cassandra was such a wonderfully decent person he couldn't understand her husband not having appreciated her more.

"Your comment the other day about me hiding up here is probably right. I made a deal with Ingrid to stay one hundred days to see if I could make a life here. She thinks returning to Toronto is wrong since I was so miserable there. Having Ingrid come into my life has been like being given a second chance with a new mother. I feel like we've known each other forever. Working with Barrett has been one of the best jobs I've ever had. He's one of the nicest and smartest people I know, and it thrills me that he doesn't stutter when we are together because that means he views me as a friend."

They approached the city limit and Charlie slowed down a little. The sun was peeking in and out of clouds. Charlie exhaled and took a leap of faith.

"And at the risk of making an utter fool of myself, getting to spend time with you has been like winning the lottery. Regardless of our Swedish friend, I feel some sort of a connection with you that's hard to explain."

As the Ford pulled into Henderson's lot, the cab of the F150 grew silent again with both occupants hesitant at where the conversation was headed.

"Charlie, if you are happy here then keep doing what is making you happy," Cassie suggested, "but that doesn't preclude you from making some phone calls to Toronto or Chicago. Does it?"

"No, it doesn't."

"There's always more than one way to skin a cat. I don't think it's written in stone that you have to do one thing or the other. Come up with a new solution."

With that, Cassie opened the door and stepped out. She leaned in before closing the door. "And I feel a connection to you, too."

The truck door slammed shut and she headed off down the road. At that exact moment, Charlie remembered Ingrid's mother commenting that if Henrik looked back three times he and their daughter would marry. Cassie turned and waved. After twenty or thirty steps she looked over her shoulder and wondered why he was still sitting behind the wheel. Her face showed a puzzled expression and she raised her hands as if to ask, "what?" When she reached the bend of the road that lead to her house she fully stopped and turned towards the truck. Charlie hopped out and raised his hand. Cassandra waved a third time and walked down her lane.

"Three times," Charlie said aloud. "Birgitta was right."

The moment Charlie walked in and took off his coat, Ingrid smiled, and motioned for him to sit.

"I hear you caused quite a stir at the library and bakery. Lovely women but either can talk the eyes off a spider. I don't know who Ryan Reynolds is, but I remember Indiana Jones and you do look a little like him when you are not scowling. I've always thought you looked like the actor William Holden. Did you and Cassie have some time to talk?"

"Yes, but you need to let us figure out what you've already got inside that warped Viking head of yours."

The elderly gardener laughed and put on the kettle for tea. She looked fatigued and her skin colour was off. Charlie could hear a steady wheeze coming from her lungs but was reluctant to make any comment on her health. Ingrid turned and stared right at him as if she were reading his mind.

"I think I stopped my story in the balsa wood lifeboat. Shall I go on?"

> It was a terrifying night on the open Atlantic. At times our sanctuary was flipped upside down but would correct herself like Alexius had promised. The wind screamed like Havsra, the evil sea-wife. I vomited until there was nothing left inside me and yet I kept retching. I began questioning my dreams and wondered if the Gods had been toying with me. My husband held me tightly in his arms. Eventually, I heard his voice calling me from afar. I opened my eyes and looked up into the sun. There was a flock of cawing seagulls circling above.
>
> "Ingegard!" Henrik shouted.
>
> My husband was not in the boat and I feared he had been washed overboard. But then I saw him standing on a boulder on the craggy shore.
>
> "Wife, your dreams were right," he conceded, with a grin that stretched clear across his face. "Thor brought on the storm to drive us west. Come set foot on Canadian soil. Your skin matches your eyes."
>
> My legs wobbled as I stepped from the boat. The coastline reminded me of Gotland with its many inlets. The late August grasses along the hills were a wheat-coloured brown, and the trees met us with their leaves dancing in the sea air.
>
> Henko held my arm and we walked inland until we met people. We learned that we had landed near a small fishing village about 250 kilometers south of Halifax.

"They seem happy to see us," I told my husband, "But I can see suspicion behind their smiles. Maybe they think we are enemies."

"Ingrid, you might be right and I have been thinking," he began as the Canadians ran towards us. "You should tell them you are nineteen years of age and we shouldn't talk about our Gods. You get my meaning?"

I did. You can never tell how foreigners will react to strangers and their customs.

The Nova Scotians led us into the village. Henrik explained in his limited English that we were neutral Swedes looking for asylum. We were the biggest news to hit Barrington since the Halifax explosion. Everyone in the village turned out including a wiry old Swedish sailor named Ellingsen. Being able to speak Swedish with him was a gift from the Gods. He checked Henrik's sea papers and confirmed to everyone that we were who we claimed to be. They accepted our explanation of having been set adrift in order to come to Canada. Through our interpreter, I explained that we had been married at sea on my nineteenth birthday and the women giggled and hugged me. We were fed sheep stew and shown where we would stay. Henrik and I had the sleep of the dead in our first on-land bed.

The next morning after a delicious breakfast of chicory coffee, eggs, and charred fish, the county constable announced that we needed to be taken to Halifax to meet the authorities at the Canadian Navy and Army building. The journey by truck would take five uncomfortable hours over very bumpy terrain along the coast. Henrik made a present of our lifeboat to the villagers.

We arrived exhausted, nauseous, and hungry. They hustled us into an enclosure surrounded with a barbed wire fence and armed soldiers. Several uniformed men brought out maps of Sweden, Norway, and Denmark. Henrik brazenly informed them that their maps were out-dated and rubbish. He picked up a pencil and began correcting their coastlines, water depths, and currents. The officers were overwhelmed by his knowledge and saw how much he could help. As such, we were whisked from the fenced detention compound and provided temporary papers that afforded us freedom.

Accommodation in Halifax was restricted given the influx of soldiers disembarking for Europe. We were to live by the Halifax Public Garden in the middle of the city, which was a five-minute walk from the most beautiful bay that had been in my earlier vision. Our room had a tiny kitchen with running water and a hotplate. A wall separated another room that would serve as our bedroom, sitting room, and dining room. We shared a bathroom with five other apartments.

And so our new life began. Henrik worked in the Halifax citadel with cartographers, remapping and charting intimate details of the Baltic Sea towards Russia. His knowledge of the northern coastlines and ocean depths was unequalled except by Captain Backstrom. I got a job collecting tickets at The Halifax Gaiety Theatre. Until our arrival in Halifax, I had never seen a motion picture. After I collected the tickets, I worked in the concession booth selling beer and popcorn. I got to see every film fifty times and read all the movie magazines and flyers. I fell in love with Bogart in *The Maltese Falcon* and *The African Queen*. Henrik called him a pipsqueak with a funny way of talking. I wanted to be Joan Fontaine every time they played *Rebecca*. Working at the Gaiety dramatically improved my English and showed me a world that I had never known existed.

One evening my husband arrived home with a heavy heart. The *Sleipnir* had been torpedoed off the coast of France and had gone down with all hands. No one could confirm whether the torpedo had been British, American, or German. We cried for Alexius, Magnus, Mikaeli, and the crew. I never admitted to my husband that I had read Alexius and Mikaeli's runes. I never told him I had lied about the danger I saw. Would it have made a difference? After all, destiny is destiny.

Chapter Nineteen

Charlie and Barrett were putting storm windows on Bryan Dempsey's cottage in preparation for the blizzard due later that week. Climbing up and down a slippery aluminum ladder with a temperature hovering around zero was not a lot of fun. When they stopped to warm up, Charlie excused himself and pulled out his iPhone to text his assistant Kathy Graham.

"Still in contact with your pals at Daily Planet Foods in Chicago?"

Moments later a response pinged.

"Yes. Why haven't you called? My time is running out and I can't find a job."

"Any chance you can forward an e-mail to your pals and ask them to get a hard copy to Jack Reeseborough?" Getting Daily Planet Foods CEO's attention was the only play Langdon had, and frankly, he had nothing to lose.

Upon receiving her one word affirmative response he forwarded the message he had composed the night before:

Dear Jack,

Thanks for reading this.

As a result of Telfer Stuart's firing by Daily Planet Foods, thirty-one employees (including me) were terminated and now two additional clients have been spooked by the press and have put the agency on notice. TS will be out of business in the next six months.

Our dismissal by DPF reflects my naivety and your CMO's duplicity, not agency incompetence. This note is not a complaint. It's about doing the right thing. Jack, your reputation is one of fair play and professionalism. Standing on the sidelines while Tom Potter distorts truth is inconsistent with that reputation. Replacing a successful agency from your most profitable products with a "CMO-friendly" agency will hurt your company's performance, and ultimately you. The current agency pitch process is a front for Tom to bring in pals who won't disagree with him. The entire industry is aware of this. His approach will damage the great work already underway for your brands. The calibre of the strategic and creative product will slide quickly and your sales' results will suffer. The duplicity of your CMO will come home to roost on your company's performance, your shareholders, and your reputation.

There is still a time to rectify this dangerous course. Please think on this. Respectfully, Charles Langdon.

* * *

Alexander Fanning's concerns of being robbed, murdered, and dumped in the desert didn't materialize. Richard Strickland had delivered on his promise. The three were "deposited" at the Palm Jumeriah where they immediately locked the doors and breathed a sigh of relief.

The Datrems collapsed into their bed and Alex took a look on-line. The SEC had offered a reward of $125 thousand for information on their whereabouts. Sightings had been reported in Vancouver, Montreal, and Houston, Texas. Videos were floating on-line showing the authorities carting boxes of files out of NovaRose's head office. Alex wondered about the reward and his father's warning about international bounty hunters trying to cash in. He slowly closed the cover on the laptop and lowered his head onto his folded arms. How had all of this gotten away from him so quickly?

Alexander recalled receiving the incredibly positive Phase One results on the prototype cancer cream that had exceeded the expectations of his medical research scientists. Four thousand test results over a two-year period had proven that his gambit with Dermmexx5 had paid off, putting his firm ahead of the pack to be first to market a skin cream with an 80% and higher proven success record in diminishing and countering the growth of four strains of melanomas. NIR's share price had skyrocketed.

And then Phase Two human clinical results showed that the cancer-retarding effects of Dermmexx5 only temporarily stalled the cancer's growth and then acted like a reversed catalyst, causing the original melanoma to reinvigorate itself at an even faster growth rate. Dermmexx5 was an unmitigated disaster.

It was his fiduciary responsibility to inform the NIR board of directors and investors. But instead, Alex dismissed the Phase Two results, citing an inferior research procedure. He ordered a confirmation of every result needing the 120 days of re-testing to buy time. The Board applauded their CEO's thoroughness and encouraged due diligence.

Alex realized he needed the help of his Chief Financial Officer if there was going to be any hope of escaping the inevitable meltdown of the company. Jay Datrem listened and without any reserve agreed that in order to secure their wealth they had to bolt.

"We have one, maybe four months before the shit hits the fan," Jay confirmed. "We need to start shifting NIR's funds, delay all account payables, and hold off on any new salaries or hiring." It took the CFO fifteen minutes to calculate the numbers.

"Lex, if we start today and slash and burn we will be able to pull out at least two hundred million dollars before the retesting is complete. We'll need to escape to a country that doesn't have an extradition treaty with either Canada or the United States," Datrem stated. "I only know of five."

"Will you take your wife?" Fanning asked cautiously. He knew that Jay's marriage had been rocky for over a year.

"What kind of a question is that? Of course I'll be taking Linda. Why wouldn't I?"

"No reason. Do we put our Toronto houses on the market?" Alex asked, and Jay shook his head.

"Absolutely not! We can't draw any attention to ourselves. This has to be executed in one fell swoop," Datrem stated, as if he was organizing a company board meeting. "We'll transfer the funds in the form of treasury or bearer bonds. Any offshore banking records can be traced. We will keep the money with us until we're safely out of the country. We split all monies fifty-fifty?"

"Agreed. I'll need to talk to my father. He's got connections everywhere and we'll need him to orchestrate transportation and living arrangements. He can do everything third party so no red flags will be raised."

"Okay," Jay replied, knowing the powerful names his partner's father kept in his vest pocket.

Alex exhaled deeply, clearly exasperated. "I'd like to tell Charlie Langdon."

Datrem motioned his arms like an umpire signalling "out" on a stolen base attempt.

"No way. You tell one person and he tells one person and two minutes later we're standing in handcuffs. We are only going to tell your father because we need his help."

Reluctantly, the youngest Fanning nodded his head.

Jay patted his shoulder. "I know he invested heavy and will take a huge hit. When we are basking in the sun you can send him as much money as you like."

Fanning realized Jay was right. He would make it up to Charlie and pay him five times whatever he had lost in NovaRose.

Chapter Twenty

Cassie picked up Ingrid for their mani-pedi appointment. The two would eat at Cassie's parents' house and be back to Great Spirit Moon Lake by 8:00 p.m. Ingrid pulled Charlie alongside her as they walked along the snow-covered path.

"Do not wait up. We will be late."

"But you'll be back around eight."

Ingrid looked up at him and patted his cheek with her mitt-covered hand. "That is late."

A light dusting of snow was on the windshield and Charlie quickly swept it off. He waved as the two drove off.

* * *

Cassie and Ingrid returned at 8:15 p.m. Charlie greeted them happily. It was always good to have people you care about safely home on dark wintry nights. As Langdon took her coat Ingrid looked about the room as if sensing she knew not what.

"How was the drive? Were the roads clear? Did you have fun?" he asked, throwing out questions.

"We always do," Cassie responded. "I'll see you tomorrow for our run. Dress warmly and wear two pairs of socks. It's going to be very cold," Cassie said, as she waved goodnight, stepped onto the porch and quickly closed the front door to keep out the frigid night air. "Night old woman, see you tomorrow."

Ingrid inhaled deeply and held her fingers up as if she was feeling the air. Charlie knew that her damned paranormal senses were picking up something. Suddenly she turned. "Cassie gone?"

"She said goodnight. You were daydreaming."

Ingrid crossed her arms and tilted her head.

"So what were you up to tonight?" she inquired, in that uncomfortable tone mothers employ when they suspect something.

"Oh, not much," he responded, masking the lie, "just a quiet evening. What was for dinner?"

"Cornish hens, mashed potatoes, carrots, and a half-good attempt at a chocolate layer cake."

"Good conversation?" he inquired, as the white-haired Swede eyed him.

"Yes. So, Charles Michael Langdon, any visitors tonight, perhaps?"

God Almighty. Nothing eluded her. "Lizzie Grant dropped over," he replied.

Ingrid straightened out the pillows on the sofa. "She remained long, perhaps?"

"Not especially long. I told her that you and Cassie were in town and she said she would visit tomorrow."

Ingrid smiled.

Charlie walked out to the kitchen for a glass of water. He slowly sipped the water anticipating the story to come.

Lizzie had indeed arrived after Ingrid and Cassie had driven off. After kissing him, she pushed past, dropped her winter coat on the floor and kicked off her boots. She was wearing a long flowing sheer caftan that left little to the imagination. The smell of wine was strong on her breath.

"We need drinks. You got any wine here?"

"No. Where's Roy tonight?"

Lizzie stood up and walked to the front door. She flipped the double-lock.

"Charlie, I didn't come here to talk about my family. This is the first chance we've had to be alone together."

"Lizzie, you'd better go," he told her. "Right now."

"Charlie, you've been fantasizing about me since the day you arrived and now we have the whole evening," Lizzie blurted out unabashedly.

"You're a great-looking woman and I'm flattered you want—"

"Don't patronize me," she rebuked sharply, the wide smile narrowing beneath a sharp glance. "I know what you want."

Charlie was flabbergasted. "Just go. We'll pretend like this never happened."

Rejection was a hard pill to swallow. Lizzie stood awkwardly and her mouth opened like she wanted to say something. Finally, a name shot out from between those dark red lips.

"Cassie. It's all about Cassie, isn't? Have you been screwing her?" she accused venomously.

Langdon walked over to the door and opened it. "Get out."

Ingrid's neighbour glared as she strode past him. "You'll regret this." The door slammed like a shotgun had been fired across the lake.

Charlie was about to lock the door when it suddenly re-opened and a snow-covered Lizzie Grant pushed her way past him. Without saying a word, but shivering badly, she gathered up her coat and boots.

"Asshole," she spat out, as the door slammed for a second time.

* * *

That had been three hours earlier, and now Ingrid Petersson, wearing a thick plaid dressing gown, was fussing about the room, straightening out wolf pelts like an old hen.

"Bet you wish Cassie had stayed," Ingrid suggested, through a sharp cough, and Charlie's mind was ripped away from his bizarre evening encounter with Lizzie.

"Are you too worn out to tell a little of your story?" he inquired, wanting to forget everything about Lizzie Grant.

Ingrid sat in the rocking chair and pulled a wolf pelt around her legs. Charlie's face perked up when Ingrid motioned for him to sit beside her.

We remained in Halifax two years after the war ended. Henrik got a job working the docks. We received news that my sisters and their families had survived the war. I continued to work at the theatre and made extra money reading my runes for those who asked.

One night my husband returned home filled with excitement. He had met a gambler who owed money to bad men who had broken his arm and beaten him severely. The thugs had threatened to kill him if he failed to repay the loan within twenty-four hours. Henrik showed me a deed for one hundred acres of land in Ontario. The desperate man had inherited the land and was willing to sell it to cover the debt. I was sceptical and thought the gambler was trying to fool Henrik, but my husband assured me that a land agent in Halifax had confirmed its validity. My husband reminded me of the vision I had seen aboard the *Sleipnir*.

"You had a vision of us living by rivers and a lake. I think this is the property. Please consult your runes. Is this part of our journey that Freyja spoke of?"

I retrieved my charm pouch and told my giant to withdraw two tiles while I would select five. I cast the stones and at first glance everything seemed to fit. *Ehwaz*, the horse told of a journey and new people to meet. *Berkana*, the sign of fertility and family was well placed if we honoured the Gods. I looked for deeper meanings in the symbols because runes seldom tell you only good or bad things. There is always a little—or a lot—of each.

"Is this our journey?" my husband pressed impatiently. "Should we buy this deed?"

"*Kano* is reversed and that bothers me," I answered cautiously, looking at the rune of seriousness and potential emptiness. "I think that if we are unwise our family may be exposed to health concerns, physical pain, and potentially great sorrow."

"What sorrow?" he inquired, worry crossing his brow.

"I do not know," I told him. "You said the deed includes rivers and a lake? I imagine the forest will be the home of elves, dwarves, and lake spirits."

"You are probably right. The surveyors' drawings of the one hundred acres clearly show three rivers with one the exact shape of Thor's hammer, and there are oaks along the lake and in the forest. You know how much Thor loves oaks."

I smiled at such a good omen. "Is there a house?"

"A stone-built house apparently with a cold cellar," Henko responded, scanning the document. "It is built amongst the oaks and is on a lake seven miles long and two wide."

It all sounded too fantastical. My husband saw the apprehension in my face.

"My dove, we must be more certain. If we buy this farm we will have to work like animals but we will have property, a roof over our heads, a fireplace to cook in, five milking cows, six sows, a hog, a roost of chickens you can teach to sing, three rivers to trap, a forest to log and a huge lake to fish. Can you not see anything beyond the runes? Can you not bring on a vision that will tell us what to do?"

I walked from our house and prayed to Freyja. A sharp cold January rain drenched me as I looked into the Heavens and slowed my breathing. I stood there a long time before a vision came to me as clearly as life itself. I was far from Halifax, walking through a forest of evergreens that completely surrounded a beautiful clear blue lake. It was sunny and warm and I could hear forest animals about me. My senses were overwhelmed with the aroma of pine trees and the sounds of birds singing overhead. Off amongst a bush of low cedars a white-tailed deer crouched. I said hello and the buck approached unafraid. He told me to follow the trail to the water. Then I found myself standing in a wide, shallow river that was cool to the touch of my bare legs. Two children sat on the opposite side of the riverbank playing with sprigs of lavender. Through gales of laughter the boy shouted to me.

"Mother, we are waiting for you."

The little girl beside him stood and waved for me to come across. She had long blond hair like Sigrid's. I saw a stone house in front of which were people dressed in Native clothing—an Indian man, woman, and several children. The woman's face was so familiar to me and I was certain I had seen her in a vision. The moment she spoke I recognized her voice.

"Ingegard from across the big water, this is your home. Come to us, my sister."

But then my vision grew cloudy and I was no longer standing in the water. I was cold and afraid. The forest was now snow covered and I felt the horror of being back in the dining room with the German sailors. There were dark shadows surrounding me and my body was crippled with cold and fear. Henrik was not able to help me. But then, the Indian man from the stone house appeared and I was no longer afraid.

In the spring of 1947 we packed our belongings into an old red Ford truck and left Halifax in search of the farm we had just purchased in the province of Ontario, to the west. We journeyed westward through Montreal, Kingston, Toronto, and then northward. Henrik fashioned a canvas tent across the back bed of the truck under which we slept. Some cold mornings the tarp would be frozen with ice when we awoke, but we did not care. Our destiny had revealed itself.

Chapter Twenty-One

An elated Tessa Conner did not return to her apartment after the Sunday dinner escapade with Ernest Fanning. Adrenaline was pumping through her veins like she had just sprinted a sub-four-minute mile. Realizing that Fanning was not the kind of man to take for granted, she determined to get out of town and not leave anything that might betray her location. She left her cellphone, credit cards, debit cards, laptop, and anything else that Fanning might be able to use to track them. A friend agreed to the loan of a car for three days at which time Fanning would have wired the money and Tessa could return home. Phaidra was disoriented, slightly hung over and in need of a shower as the two drove north of Toronto to a dirt-cheap motel called the SeaQuest. Its name was comical given that the motel wasn't within sixty miles of any body of water other than its half-empty swimming pool. Tessa paid cash for three nights and requested a room without a view.

Manpreet Sachdeva saw no reason to leave Toronto and after driving home, picked up some KFC and parked in front of his computer console to play *Game of War: Fire Age*. He'd grown tired of the cartoonish look of *Clash of Clans* and preferred the more realistic graphics of *Game of War*. And when Kate Upton appeared in the Super Bowl television commercial as a Greek Goddess promoting players to participate in *Game of War* he was hooked. Manny was deep into the game constructing his defenses against players in France, Germany, and Japan. The money he had invested in *Game of War* had moved him into an elite players' circle which increased the skill set required and cut away the long wait times that plagued the everyday player.

Sachdeva's focus was split between the stone barricade he was reconstructing and the amount of money he would demand from Tessa. "No less than $30 thousand or I'll have to cut her out and go at this on my own," Manpreet said aloud, as her reached over and took a swig of a diet Pepsi.

The player from Tokyo suddenly launched his attack, forcing Manpreet to re-divert troops to support his outer defenses.

"$50 thousand," he reassessed. "Maybe even $75 thousand. That's a better sounding number, and much more equitable."

A gentle tapping on his apartment door interrupted Manny's thought-process. His watch showed 1:07 a.m. On the other side of the peephole stood an extremely attractive, smartly dressed woman. Manpreet's heart skipped a beat and he forgot all about the attack his castle was facing from the Japanese player on the other side of the planet.

"Hi," she greeted, her voice muffled through the door. "I'm locked out and my stupid cell is dead. May I use your phone to call my sister to bring the spare key?" Her smile was scintillating.

Without hesitation, he flipped the chain-lock and undid the deadbolt.

"Of course," he replied, opening the door, surprised to see that she was not alone. There was a man with her pointing a weapon directly at his chest. Most people would have assumed it was a pistol. But Manpreet Sachdeva recognized the X2P Smart Weapon, which was the most powerful and digitally smart Taser on the planet. The X2P was illegal in Canada, used only by the RCMP. Unlike previous renditions of the weapon, this one connected through your clothing into your body fluids and adjusted its voltage accordingly. It delivered

1,200 volts to incapacitate the target's neurological system. It was digitally enhanced to provide a computer download of what it had done. Sachdeva was such a nerd that he even knew that "Taser" was short for Tom A. Swift who was a fictional character in sci-fi books written by Victor Appleton. He had several copies at the store.

And all that in the split second before Manny received a firsthand lesson of the X2P.

As the prong with the double wires lodged into his shirt at heart level, the Taser free-flowed its precisely measured voltage. Instantly, Sachdeva's body was incapacitated with uncontrollable spasms that crumpled him to the floor. His neurological system lapsed into complete shutdown like he was experiencing a massive stroke.

The woman and her partner quickly stepped into the apartment and quietly closed the door.

"I need to confirm his ID," she commented, and the X2P's voltage was cut. The female knelt, removed his wallet, and looked at the Driver's License. She then put two fingers to the side of his throat and checked his pulse.

"His heart's beating like a jack rabbit. Pick him up but be careful. The idiot pissed himself."

*   *   *

"The first package has been delivered by Vito," David Fowler spoke into his cell. "We'll know everything in two hours."

Ernest Fanning thanked him and sat back in the wing-backed chair of his home office. Tessa's accomplice was in for an extremely unpleasant night with the Italian and his cohorts.

Vito Carbrese did not fit the mould of the usual Tony Soprano mobster. Vito was fair-skinned, and didn't look Italian, or even Greek, which was his mother's side of the family. He presented himself like your average guy who might live in the house next door.

Vito stood six feet tall and was slender in what some might feel an effeminate way. Clean-shaven, he looked much younger than his forty-three years and dressed stylishly like a businessman who sold Ferraris or Rolexes. Nothing about his appearance or mannerisms would reveal that he had spent six years in a federal penitentiary, or that he had zero compunction about exterminating someone. He was unreservedly loyal to his friends and family. Every Sunday he attended mass with his beloved mother whose bills he paid without fail.

Carbrese had been raised in Little Italy in west end Toronto. One of three brothers he learned early how easy it was to get money. Starting in the schoolyard, Vito was that kid who stole other students' lunch money behind the threat of a punch in the nose. That led to petty crimes including shoplifting, minor break and enters, and offering "protection" to small storeowners. He employed other kids and, despite being "known by the Police," and arrested numerous times, was never charged. Carbrese was too cunning to be found in possession of anything stolen and his robberies were always below $5 thousand with goods easily sold for twenty cents on the dollar. Vito took special pleasure in torching businesses that refused to pay for his protection, and that's how he got arrested on his twentieth birthday—torching a restaurant. An old lady in the one bedroom apartment across the street was sitting at her window and spotted Carbrese leaving the burning building. She phoned the police and identified him in a line-up.

After serving six years, Vito got out and was contacted by the cop who had made the collar. It turned out that Detective First Class David Fowler personally employed ex-cons when he needed to step beyond the confines of the law. Fowler found Vito Carbrese a place to live and put cash in his pocket. He helped Vito's mother move into a better apartment with a decent landlord, good heat in the winter, and a view of a park. Carbrese was grateful. If a store needed to be shut down then Vito would torch it. If a drug dealer needed to disappear then Vito would dispose of him. Carbrese delivered and Fowler paid. Even after the cop retired from the force, the two kept in contact. At least once a month, David had a standing invitation for Sunday dinner at Vito's mother's apartment.

It was three in the morning and Vito Carbrese was eating a ham and cheese sandwich in the basement of an abandoned storage facility in the west end of Toronto. He had fastidiously layered paper napkins down his shirt to avoid mustard spillage. Two rough-looking associates sat nearby playing cards and arguing over who was cheating the most. The attractive woman who had baited Manpreet Sachdeva to open his door was dismantling the firewalls the techie had installed on devices that had been retrieved from his apartment, the spy store and his Prelude. Her hair was pulled back and she had changed into jeans and a sweatshirt. Thick glasses replaced her contacts and her concentration was intense.

"You making any progress?" Vito asked his brother's daughter, who didn't raise her eyes but held a thumbs up.

A completely disoriented Spy Sleuth Shop manager opened his eyes to the darkened room. His head throbbed and his throat was dry. He mumbled, "where am I," and the three males in the room approached. Efforts to move were wasted and Manpreet realized through a heavy fogginess that his wrists and ankles were duct-taped to a steel framed chair. He had soiled his pants, and despite the circumstances in which he found himself, felt embarrassed.

"What have I done? You've got the wrong guy," he exclaimed, the words sounding slurred inside his own head.

Vito motioned for him to look at the table off to the left. Upon it were laptops, cell phones, and cardboard boxes of what appeared to be belongings from his Honda, apartment, and work office at the Spy Sleuth Shop. Carbrese offered a bottle of water.

"Here, this will help. It is just water. Drink."

The cool refreshing liquid felt good on his parched throat.

One of the other two stepped forward and showed him a phone book. As Manny was wondering why he needed to see a phone book, the man lifted the tome and brought it crashing down on his head. Three more hits were delivered. An already throbbing head screamed with pain.

"Who else is helping Tessa Conner?" a voice quietly asked.

"Tessa? This is about Tessa?"

His questions were answered with three more rapid whacks with the book.

"I ask and you answer," the slightest built of the three tormentors clarified. "Who else is helping?"

Manpreet couldn't help himself from whimpering and blurted out everything he knew.

"Don't hit me again. Please. I'll tell you whatever you want to know."

"Good boy. Just respond to my question. Who else is helping Tessa?"

Manpreet began sobbing.

"I think it's just me. Tessa Conner came into my shop ten days ago for assistance to record her boss sexually assaulting her. She hired me to get around his jamming equipment. I recorded them having sex last Monday as well as him initiating and agreeing to a paid sexual arrangement. She's going to blackmail him. Is that what this is about?"

"Who else is helping Tessa Conner?" the voice repeated, more urgently.

Manpreet stared helplessly at the three.

"I told you. I think it's just me."

The thin man looked disappointed and sat down. The other two effortlessly picked up the chair to which Manpreet was shackled and carried it to an over-sized drum. Effortlessly flipping the man and chair they submerged their victim's head in freezing cold water. Experience told the two when to let him breathe. Gasping, Manpreet repeated his answer and yet the dunking process was repeated until everything went black. He awoke lying sideways on the concrete floor.

"Get up," a voice order harshly, and Manpreet rolled over realizing that he was no longer attached to the chair. His clothes were drenched and he was freezing. Crawling up onto his knees he found himself facing the table upon which his belongings were laid out.

"Show me everything that has to do with the recordings you made for Tessa Conner. You can still come out of this alive, if you convince me that everything is on this table."

Shivering uncontrollably, Manpreet wiped his face.

"I need glasses," he asked sheepishly. "Please may I have my glasses?"

Manpreet carefully began arranging the devices by size. It was all there, even the memory sticks of the recordings he had hidden in the back room closet of the store. What they didn't have was what he had stored in the Cloud and transferred under dummy files to his parents' home computer.

Vito walked over and placed his hand on Manpreet's shoulder.

"Mr. Sachdeva, do you know anyone at 57 Park Lane Road? Does that address ring any bells?"

Manpreet's eyes opened widely.

"Ah, I see it does," Vito acknowledged calmly. "It's your parents' house. Your little sister Fatima still lives at home. That's sweet. Fatima is such a pretty girl and her Facebook page says she plans to study archaeology and loves Adele. Who doesn't?"

Manny began crying openly, his head rocking from shoulder to shoulder.

"I think you get the picture," Carbrese said firmly. "If I think you are lying, then a couple of things are going to happen. First, my psychotically sadistic friends are going to clip a set of jumper cables to your nuts. It will make the X2P Taser feel like a mosquito bite, and it's always very entertaining to watch. Second, we will collect your parents and Fatima. These two bad boys have already decided who gets your sister first and who has to settle for sloppy seconds. Do you want that?"

"No sir, I will tell everything. I promise. Please don't hurt my family."

"Good, you've already met my IT expert. Maria is annoyingly brilliant but what my little cousin can do with a computer is sheer genius. As smart as you think you are, Maria is smarter."

Through tear-filled eyes, Manpreet watched as Vito's cousin approached the table. She removed her glasses and smiled as if greeting a new acquaintance for the first time. The woman was dressed casually and wore a pullover emblazoned with a picture of Freddie Mercury in his un-moustached days of long hair. Her smile was no longer scintillating but looked sad.

"Manpreet, I'm so sorry about last night, but blackmail is very naughty. While you've been playing with my boys, I've had a busy night searching through your disgustingly filthy apartment, your shit-box of a Prelude and your little spy shop. *"I am exhausted and underpaid,"* she whined, and Vito laughed at the performance.

"Anyway," the girl continued, "I collected everything I could on my own, but you and I both know there's more. My handsome cousin wearing that smashing suit and Versace tie needs to know we have all of your recordings. When I tell him I'm convinced, then your parents won't be hurt, your little sister won't have her cherry broken, and you might still walk out of here with your manhood attached." Maria leaned very close to his ear. "Manpreet, I don't want them to hear me, but those two big guys are sick. They take immense pleasure in hurting women. If you love your mom and Fatima, then don't hide anything from me." She leaned back and spoke louder. "So what is it going to be Manny?"

"I swear I'll tell you the truth," he cried out, staring into her eyes. "Please don't let them hurt my family. I'll tell you everything."

Vito's cousin ran her fingers through his still-wet hair and leaned so close that the two were almost touching noses. "I noticed that you have exceptionally brown eyes, Manny. May I call you Manny?" The woman stole a sideways glance over at Vito who covered his eyes.

His cousin Maria Carbrese was beautiful, insolent, precocious, and smart as a whip. At the age of five she had won a speed contest unlocking a Rubik's Cube in less than thirty seconds. At ten she was expelled for hacking the school's computers to improve the grades of her three best friends. Now at nineteen, her life evolved around anything technical, including writing programming on a freelance basis. Vito employed Maria whenever her expertise was required.

"I know you will," Maria Carbrese said sweetly, picking up her iPad. "Now, let's have every password for what you stored in the Cloud, or on any Clickfree-type automatic backup device, or memory stick that's not on this table. I'll also need what you remotely sent in code to your parents' home computer, Fatima's laptop, or on any of Tessa Conner's home or office devices. And when we are done with all of this you and I are going to have a serious debate."

"A debate?" Manpreet asked, completely confused.

"Yes. I want you to explain to me why you would be wasting your time and money on *Game of War* when you could be playing *Clash of Clans*. Manny, you didn't get sucked in by the TV commercials featuring Kate Upton's ginormous breasts, did you?"

* * *

Charles Langdon relaxed into the chair and stretched his arms over his shoulders. It was well after midnight and Ingrid was puttering around without the slightest regard for the late hour. She seemed preoccupied with no interest in sleep. He looked around the room.

"The original house that the gambler's family built wasn't this one?" he asked for clarification, "it's the burnt-out foundation by the river, right?"

Charlie had run there for the first time the previous morning. The snow-covered remains of a fireplace amongst the overgrowth had caught his attention. Looking across the river he had seen three gravestones peeking out from the woods. Upon closer inspection he discovered the final resting place of Henrik Petersson and their two children.

"That is right," Ingrid answered, her throat hoarse from coughing. "Henko and I built this house. The burned down house was our first home. You saw the tombstones, perhaps?"

Charlie answered tentatively, "I did."

"And the names?" Ingrid asked timidly, not wanting to discuss her children—not yet.

"Yes."

Ingrid pulled the blanket around her tiny frame. Even in the dim light it appeared that Ingrid's face was flushed and her eyes clouded over.

"Now you understand my surprise when you introduced yourself as Charles Michael?"

Charlie nodded. The name on her son's marker was "Mikaeli Charles Petersson."

"Can we not talk about my children yet?" Ingrid inquired respectfully, and without awaiting the answer, and despite the late hour, took up where she had left off.

> The stone house of the deed was built in a stand of oaks. Thor favoured oak trees since they once gave him shelter during a dangerous storm, which is why today we place acorns on our window ledges. Well, when we first approached the house we made sacrifices to appease the Gods.
>
> The next day Henrik threw a ten-pound iron rod into the lake to warn Nykkjen the Water Spirit we would not be tempted by his spells or foolishness. That first night, I had a vision of walking through fields of barley, wheat, hay, and corn all surrounded with stones. So Henrik cleared close to four acres of stones that only a Viking of his strength could have moved. Those stones became our fences, cordoning off sections of the farm. We rented a Massey-Ferguson tractor to plough our fields and immediately planted barley and wheat so we could harvest our first crops by late summer. We cut down over fifty trees and used the tractor to pull up the roots. Henrik sold forty-five of the trees to a logging company laying roads and the rest was winter fuel.
>
> Our property was blessed with an abundance of wild berries, leaks, rhubarb, apple trees, and mushrooms. I put up over eight hundred canning jars and stored them in the cold cellar beneath the floor of our kitchen. We smoked or salted bass, salmon, pike, and trout for the winter. I was responsible for laying the trapping line across two of our rivers.

"You had a trapping line?" Charlie interrupted.
Ingrid smiled proudly, even though interruptions annoyed her.

"Do you remember that in my vision of our farm I saw my two children and an Indian family by the house? They were Niigaanii and Miigwaans Cardinal. When Miigwaans and I first set eyes on each other we embraced like long lost sisters.

"I know you," I shouted in glee. "You have been in my dreams."

"I know you too," she cried out. "I have seen you since we were children. You lived by a shore with boats that fished in the big sea. "You have many sisters and know how to talk to animals. I have tried to reach you in our visions and now you are here."

"The Cardinals were of the Ojibwe nation and they became our greatest friends. Without their help we would not have survived the first winter. Niigaanii showed us where to lay our traps for beavers, foxes, wolves, otters, and minks. Because of him we had enough meat from our traps to last us through the winter and enough furs to make a healthy profit."

The Swede coughed deeply and took a sip of water before continuing. Her coughs sounded painful and slowly she continued.

> Niigaanii Cardinal was a powerful man with hair as black as a raven's wing. His face had sharp features and his eyes were as brown as the soil and locked on you like a wild cat about to pounce. Niigaanii's name meant "leader" and he and Henrik became best friends. Niigaanii Cardinal was the only man I had known who could arm wrestle my giant and almost win.
>
> Miigwaans Cardinal was an incredible woman. She was a highly intelligent beauty with black eyes that were windows to happiness. Her hair fell like ribbons of ebony to her waist and she was without doubt the most beautiful woman I had ever seen. Miigwaans shared that she had been a spiritual leader in a tribe in North Dakota. In a vision, Miigwaans saw the Chief of the tribe was selling land for personal gain. When she confronted the elders it became evident the entire council was corrupt. They expelled Niigaanii and Miigwaans with only the clothes

on their back. The two travelled north and settled here able to survive on what money Niigaanii could earn with his traps and as a guide to hunters and fishermen from the big city. They raised three children.

My sister and I would walk through our forests sharing our visions and the history of our ancestors. I told her of our Norse Gods and she shared Ojibwe beliefs. Her Odin was Kitchi-Manitou who created the world in a way that all living things would find harmony and balance within nature. Her Freyja was Mussu-Kummik Quae, or the Sky Woman they called Mother, creator of the Anishinabeg: humans. Norse beliefs have seven powerful Gods; Miigwaans told me of the Seven Grandfathers who brought seven gifts to the Anishinabeg. The gifts were wisdom, love, respect, bravery, honesty, humility, and truth. Aside from the gift of humility, which is not something a Viking would see as a gift, our Norse history taught the same. There were an infinite number of similarities and I wondered how that could possibly have happened with so many miles between our homelands. Miigwaans shared that there were stories of giant-size invaders from across the great sea who might have been my adventurous ancestors.

That first winter arrived with a vengeance but our house stood warm, our animals survived, our traps were seldom empty, and the Goddess of Fertility put a child in my womb that was born on the 22nd day of May, 1952. That was my mother's birthday. Henrik howled at the moon and announced his son's name: Mikaeli Charles Henrik Petersson. Charles was his Henko's father, and of course you remember Mikaeli from the *Sleipnir*.

Our neighbours honoured our son with a bounty of presents. They brought ten chickens, a most useful papoose, leather moccasins, eight new traps, a long-handled shovel, a sturdy fishing net, and a she-goat for milk. Niigaanii's gift was a .22 gauge breech-loading hunting rifle for Mikaeli. It had a beautifully beaded shoulder-strap meticulously crafted by Miigwaans.

Our second summer was a scorcher but our crops were abundant. We cleared more fields and took our harvest into the local town markets. Mikaeli was either in his papoose or on his father's knee. With flour made by Miigwaans, I began cooking meat pies and baking fruit pies, tarts, and cakes. My sister and I sold them to the logging camps. Those men were homesick and starving. They paid handsomely and treated us with respect. I earned extra by reading my runes and the men would line up for hours.

My beloved Goddess of Fertility finally heard my prayers and I gave birth to Birgitta Adriana Holmberg Petersson to honour our mothers. Our child was born on April 25, 1954 with a full head of blond hair. Miigwaans told me that Muzzu-Kummik-Quae had put the seed inside me just as she had recreated the earth. My Ojibwe sister chanted beside Birgitta's crib for most of the first week and crafted her dreamcatcher. The Gods were clearly favouring us with prosperity and health.

And then the winter of 1962 arrived. Freyja once again blessed me with fertility. I was two months pregnant when the biggest snowstorm in fifty years besieged our community. Henrik almost died and made a discovery that fulfilled what the runes had earlier foretold about our journey.

Ingrid's voice was raspy. Charlie could see that despite her desire to avoid going to bed she had finally run out of steam.

"Ingrid, it is time for us to go to bed. It has been a long time since I've been awake this late without working on a new business pitch," he said softly, helping her from her chair. "I am going to brew you some honey tea for your throat. I will dream of your Ojibwe friends and the farm."

The elderly Swede did not protest and looked at him from the corners of her tired eyes. "I am happy you threw Lizzie out. She is no better than Huldra the Troll," she added, referring to the chameleon-like troll who takes on the personage of a beautiful temptress to seduce human men before eating their bones.

* * *

That same night, just as Cassie Turner was settling into a deep sleep, a tremendous crashing sound erupted from downstairs. Her first thought was that a tree branch had broken off the giant old poplar and had rocketed through the twelve-foot wide bay window in her front room. She ran down the stairs, dreading the mess she'd find.

Cassandra hesitated at the bottom of the stairs. The middle section of the front window had been shattered and but there was no tree branch jutting through the empty window frame. Rather, there was a medium-sized, red-handled sledgehammer lying on the floor in the middle of the room. Ingrid's goddaughter bravely unlocked the front door and walked out onto the porch, but the person who had thrown the hammer was long gone. Snow was blowing through the broken window and flittering across her front room and down the hallway. Any tracks were now covered in white.

"Good God," she exclaimed. She thought of phoning Charlie but then Ingrid would awaken, which was the last thing Cassie wanted. After securing all the doors and first floor windows she took an hour to clean up the glass. Remembering there were sheets of plywood in the garage she carried in two and hammered them into the frame. Thoroughly spent, she crawled into bed.

* * *

The next morning Barrett Sanford arrived at Ingrid's house as Charlie was sitting down for breakfast. Barrett tapped on the door and walked in.

"Morning everyone. Coffee hot?" Barrett inquired, as he pulled off his winter coat and stepped out of his high snow boots. Ingrid pointed at the chair opposite Charlie who had just sat down for breakfast.

"Have you eaten properly?" his hostess inquired, knowing the answer.

"I had an apple and toast at six."

"You are a full grown man, Barrett Sanford. How many times have I told you that you have to eat a good breakfast?" Ingrid chastised, and Barrett winked at Charlie.

"That's why I'm here," he laughed, as he shovelled the food into his mouth at a furious pace, seemingly swallowing without chewing. Charlie pulled out their workbook and rattled off the jobs facing them that day. It would begin with the installation of a new Lennox furnace that had just arrived from Barrie.

Ingrid followed up the porridge with a heaping plate of eggs, bacon, and toast which she set down in front of Great Spirit Moon Lake's handyman. He grinned broadly and reached for a fork. Charlie wondered if Barrett ever ate a decent meal that Ingrid didn't prepare.

The phone rang and Ingrid's smiling face dissolved immediately from a smile to one of concern. Both men stopped chewing to listen.

"Are you hurt in any way? Why did you not call me, or the police?"

Another hesitation on the phone as Ingrid listened.

"Of course he is here, and so is Barrett. I will send them right over. You will stay with me for a couple of days and I will not be arguing about it."

Ingrid replaced the receiver. "Go to Cassie's immediately."

"Is she alright?" Charlie asked anxiously, already grabbing his coat and boots.

Ingrid took Barrett's plate from in front of him even though he was only half done. He quickly reached up and grabbed a handful of bacon that he stuffed into his shirt pocket.

"Someone threw a hammer through her window last night. Scared the daylights out of her and made a huge mess. See to it right away. Charlie, do not come back here without her."

The door slammed behind Charlie before Ingrid finished her sentence. Barrett threw on his boots and shouted thanks. The elderly Swede turned and looked out the window over her kitchen sink. She raised her hand and clenched her arthritic fingers into a fist.

"Lizzie Grant, you are crossing paths with the wrong Viking."

Chapter Twenty-two

The SeaQuest motel was passably clean and Tessa and Phaidra ate their meals watching the television. Even though it was against her better judgment, Tessa brought along two bottles of Jack Daniels and told her mother to make them last until the bank confirmed Ernest Fanning had wired the money into her account. Phaidra expressed her gratitude but knew two bottles wouldn't last until Wednesday.

Monday was uneventful and the two remained in the room with Phaidra all but climbing the walls. They watched TV, napped, took long baths, and kept asking the other for the time. On Tuesday evening they were eating Swiss Chalet when the motel door burst open and three men rushed in. It happened so quickly that neither had time to react or even scream. Both women were gagged, hooded, bound, and whisked into the windowless white GMC cargo van parked outside their room.

"Ladies, Ernest Fanning sends his regards," Vito Carbrese stated cheerfully, as the unmarked van sped off. "Cooperate and you won't be hurt."

* * *

In the expansive dining room of their Rosedale mansion, Ernest and Bettina Fanning were having dinner at the eighteen-seat table when the lawyer's cell vibrated in his pocket. Three rapid buzzes followed by two signalled a call from David Fowler. Excusing himself, Ernest made his way down the hallway into his office and closed the door. Bettina continued eating a stalk of asparagus only half-aware that her husband had left the room. Her thoughts were of a patient who had unexpectedly died the day before.

"Our Italian friend has two lovely dates for tonight. The horn honker works alone and has been co-operative," Fowler shared, cautiously selecting his words over a cell.

"Great," the silver-haired lawyer responded, and an annoying weight lifted off his chest. "Ensure no surprises will be forthcoming. I'll leave it to you to orchestrate the going away party."

The former cop hung up without responding. Lighting a cigarette, David inhaled slowly thinking how fortunate they had been to find Tessa and Phaidra. Ten minutes after Tessa's credit card was swiped through the terminal at a liquor store, he received the police alert. It cost him five grand but it was worth it. Two hours later, Vito Carbrese and his team were on site. Fowler had no doubt that the mother had stolen her daughter's card, slipped down the street, and bought the booze. Addicts could become such idiots in their uncontrollable desperation for a drink or fix.

* * *

After they insulated and re-boarded Cassie's window, Charlie and Barrett escorted her across the snow-covered pathway to Ingrid's house.

"We'll phone into B-B-Bracebridge and have new windows c-c-cut. This will k-k-keep out the c-c-cold until they are delivered later t-t-today. I'll c-come back and make sure they are installed right."

"Thanks Barrett," she said politely, before turning towards Charlie. "I can walk there without an escort. I'm not a child," Cassandra exclaimed, disgruntled from lack of sleep.

Charlie was carrying her overnight bag and tried to poke some fun to lighten up her mood. "Who would put a sledgehammer through your window? Have you got a disgruntled boyfriend?'

Cassie exhaled and shook her head.

"Don't be a moron. You know I haven't even had a date since Phillip died."

Charlie and Barrett remained quiet for the rest of the walk until they saw Ingrid impatiently awaiting them on her front porch. She was bundled up and stamping her feet to keep warm.

"I think I can make it the rest of the way without being molested," Cassie stated, and before her running partner could object she yanked her bag from his hand and headed up the steps pointing at her godmother. "Old woman, you are sick. You shouldn't be outside in this cold, and I'm too old for you to boss around."

Having safely deposited their charge, the two headed over to tackle the Thompkins' new furnace. Dissembling and removing the old furnace piece by piece up the old rickety basement staircase was a royal pain. Installing the Thompkins' family's new "Dual heated 1750 XP" took just as much time and effort, but Sanford was a cheerful coworker who did his best to educate his apprentice along the way. By the time they wrapped up, the city boy was filthy and brimming with a sense of accomplishment.

Growling stomachs had to be addressed so the two ate lunch around two o'clock.

"Ingrid t-talk about her k-kids?" Great Spirit Moon Lake's handyman asked timidly, as they sat emptying Ingrid's food hamper. "It's a really sensitive t-topic."

Charlie Langdon withdrew two thermoses, handing one to Barrett. They discovered steaming hot homemade vegetable soup. A large Tupperware container was crammed with ham and cheese sandwiches, six hard-boiled eggs, and four large carrots. A second smaller container held date squares.

"How sad that fever killing all those people," Charlie responded, twisting truth as to who had told him what.

Barrett smelled the soup and reached for a spoon.

"Buddy, you're really asking about her son's name being like mine," Charlie clarified, and Barrett stopped slurping his soup.

"Pretty weird coincidence, eh?" Sanford mused quietly. "Of us lake f-folks, only Cassie, Phil, Margery, and I know about the n-name thing."

Charlie drank the soup directly from the second thermos. Barrett looked like he was done talking for a while so the younger worker picked up a sandwich and took a bite.

"So Barrett, do you know Miriam Walker, the girl who works at the library?"

Sanford's eyes widened and he shrugged his shoulders. "Yes, why?"

Langdon carried slowly. "So what do you think of her?"

"I dunno. She's a p-pr-pretty d-d-decent p-person. Good family. Smart as a whip. Works hard and d-d-donates a lot of time to helping others. P-pr-pretty f-face. What's it t-t-to you?"

Charlie chewed on his sandwich and drank some more soup. Out of the corner of his eye he watched as his partner began squirming uncomfortably. He found it interesting that Barrett saw the plain-looking girl as being "pretty."

"No reason. Just making conversation. I thought she was a nice person. I just can't believe someone hasn't come along and married her yet."

Barrett stood up and started rearranging the tools on the top shelf of his toolbox. He lifted out a wrench and pointed it at his younger co-worker.

"I get it. I'm not slow, you know. You're trying to be a matchmaker because Miriam and I are both alone. You should keep your nose out of other people's business. You don't hear me talking about you and Cassie, do you?"

Charlie stared at the older man. He hadn't stuttered once.

"Besides," he continued, "I'm forty-eight and she's only thirty-four. That's a b-b-big—a big gap."

"Henrik was twenty-five years older than Ingrid," Charlie hastened to point out. "They did just fine together."

Sanford closed the toolbox and pulled out his cigarettes. He seldom smoked in front of Charlie and never in someone else's house. He lit one and exhaled.

"Ingrid p-put you up to this?"

"Nope, it just crossed my mind, that's all. Don't get your pantyhose in a knot. You love reading books and she works at a library. You've both lived here your whole lives and know the same people. But what would be the big deal about asking her out?"

Barrett shook his head and motioned for Charlie to pack up their lunch gear. His face flushed and filled with consternation. "Charlie, not everyone has your c-c-confidence or looks. Some p-people around here think I'm a ret-retard since the accid-d-dent. Miriam's really s-s-s-smart. I can b-b-barely remember what I ate for b-b-breakfast. Even if I g-g-got the g-g-guts to t-talk with her I'd p-p-prob-b-b-ly m-m-make a f-f-fool of myself."

Langdon watched the meltdown he had incited and felt horrible. What had been a good intention had rendered his friend into a stuttering mess. There were powerful inner demons Barrett Sanford still fought.

"I'm sorry, Barrett. I should have minded my own business. It was totally wrong of me."

The two walked out to the truck and Barrett tossed his toolbox onto the flatbed. They drove into Bracebridge to pick up a case of 60-watt light bulbs for Phil Henderson's dealership. Not a word passed between them, and the silence damn near killed Charlie.

"Stop at the b-bakery for coffee and a crueller," Barrett directed. Charlie turned down the main street. When he pulled up to the curb Barrett sat staring across the street from the bakery, at the library.

"You go to the bakery," Barrett stated, "I've got something to do. If she laughs in my f-f-face I'm going to k-k-kick your t-teeth in."

As Charlie entered the bakery he glanced across the street and watched as his friend entered the front door of the city library. After paying Miriam's mother and prising himself away from Helen's incessant chatter, he anxiously left the bakery carrying the coffee and doughnuts. An exuberant-looking Barrett Sanford was leaning contentedly against the driver's door of the Ford wearing a grin so wide it almost reached from ear to ear. He grabbed Charlie by the shoulder and shook him so hard Langdon dropped both cups.

"Miriam didn't laugh at me. She said yes. I have a date."

Chapter Twenty-three

Evangeline Michaels' flight from Charles De Gaulle arrived at Pearson twenty minutes late. It was 11:20 p.m. and being Wednesday night, Duane would be entertaining his girls. It had been a brutal flight with four inebriated Texans disrupting First Class and making her life a misery. Sexual innuendos were part of the turf, but the "accidental" touches of her backside had been too much and she had been forced to ask the Captain to pay the Texans a visit. Now as the airport limo drove towards home she could only think about taking a hot bath and crawling into bed . . . alone.

After signing the chit she inched carefully to the front door, trying not to slip. Despite the driveway having been recently shovelled and salted, the cold made the cobblestones treacherous. The driver dutifully rolled her suitcase and overnight bag. He looked up at the glare of the lights shining through every window facing the street. The sound of the music pounded into the driveway.

"Sounds like quite a party," he observed, as he deposited the cases by the front door.

Evangeline unlocked the front door and smiled as she stepped into the warmth of the spacious foyer.

As the driver walked back to his car he didn't notice a man standing in the shadows by the fifteen-foot arborvitae hedge lining the driveway, in front of the equally tall fence. Even the two cameras located above the front doors wouldn't pick up the half-frozen trespasser hidden there. The intruder remained long after his Evangeline entered the mansion. The ex-con could tell from her poor posture and slumped shoulders that the return flight from Paris had been exhausting. Angie had been working far too hard lately with overseas flights. At least that was his impression since he started tracking her movements. Somewhere deep in Terrance Greene's imagination, he fantasized that the attractive flight attendant would happily run into his arms, beg his forgiveness, and plead to be taken back. They would move home, he would get his job back at Toyota, and Evangeline would get pregnant. It was that dream that had shielded his sanity from the years of unimaginable torment and degradation he had experienced behind bars.

There was laughter and screaming inside the three-story brick house. A naked woman with huge breasts and short black hair ran past an un-curtained window on the first floor. He saw the giant football player carrying a blond woman across his shoulders through a second floor window. A dizzy spell overwhelmed Terrance, forcing him to slump against the fence.

"Oh Christ," he exclaimed, and he quickly pulled open his winter coat and unfastened his pants as his bowels exploded onto the snow-covered ground below. Grimacing through the searing pain of his defunct anal tract he tried unsuccessfully to steady himself and toppled to the ground. After several minutes, the dizziness subsided and he sat up. The nurse at the clinic informed him that most AIDS patients at his stage of the illness found solace and comfort in palliative care. She had been so kind and didn't treat him like a pariah. Her eyes were sympathetic and Terrance wondered if working with the "walking dead" depressed her and kept her from sleeping at night.

Terrance struggled to his feet and walked hastily down the street. It wouldn't go over well if the police or a private security car came along and saw a black ex-con dying with AIDS hovering about in such an affluent neighbourhood. Stumbling through the ravine, he exited a short walk from a bus stop where he caught a ride downtown to the halfway house where he had a room.

"We'll have a little girl," Terrance said aloud. "I wonder what we should name her?"

* * *

Cassandra was spending the evening with Anne-Marie Downey at a banking function in town. She was sitting in for Tom who was in Montreal. A week had passed since the "hammer incident" and Ingrid had finally permitted her goddaughter to return home. Charlie had a roaring fire underway and settled into the sofa as his housemate sipped on a cup of camomile tea.

> It snowed almost every day in that disastrous winter of 1962 and the low temperatures set records. We only ventured to the barn to feed the livestock. The children were miserable and bored since most days the buses could not operate and they were stuck at home. Henko announced that he had to check the trap lines.
>
> "What is a little weather to a Viking?" he asked, ignoring my request to stay put. "I remember storms in the North Sea with great swaths of cold salt water rushing into our holds. By Thor, I remember seeing the war-like arms of the Kraken reach up to try to pull us to our deaths. But here I am as Odin is my witness. If my old friends Mikaeli and Alexius were here they would scoff at you for calling this little bit of cold weather a storm."
>
> Henko said he would trek to the farthest end of the first trapping line along the eastern escarpment that bordered our property. That meant snowshoeing close to ten miles through drifts that were over fifteen feet deep. Henrik would be pulling a sled carrying gear, tools, and whatever pelts he would find frozen solid in heavy blocks of ice.

I warned my husband he could not cover twenty miles with the snow and thick brush. Each trap took twenty minutes to dig up, empty, and reset. There were twenty traps. I told him it would be impossible for him to make it back in the daylight.

"Ingegard, have you had a vision about this?" he asked, and I told him I had not. "Have you not had other visions of me as an old man? I am certain you have."

I truthfully told him I had seen the two of us as elderly people.

"Then what is your worry? Are you acting foolish because you are with child? Do you not believe your own visions?"

I reminded him of my terrifying vision of being alone in the snow surrounded by menacing dark shadows.

"Little dove, I have told you time and again that you are rethinking that horrible day with those German bastards."

And with that, my stubborn Viking told me to keep a light on in the upper window and to stay inside the house. As I struggled to shut the front door, the blast of icy wind from the north told me the day would worsen. My Ojibwe sister Miigwaans told me time and again to smell the wind and listen to the animals. I could hear the livestock in our barn crying for help. They were freezing and rampaging with that unbridled fear that comes before death.

By noon, monstrous, bluish-grey clouds turned the day into night and unleashed snows with a vengeance. I could not see the end of our porch. Just before the phone lines went down, Meryl Patch phoned that she had taken my son and daughter from the school and would keep them safely with her. By mid-afternoon, the north wind was so violent I feared it would snatch up our roof. The thermometer was showing thirty-five degrees below Fahrenheit. Our animals would be dead by morning. I lit every lantern and put them in our attic window. When I was not stoking the fire I sat by that attic window staring out into abyss. I struggled to stay awake because I knew that if the snow covered our chimney I would freeze to death too. But I fell asleep and the evil night spirit "Marerjdt" appeared. She sat on my chest and held me fast. I was filled with terror.

"Ingegard of the mountain, your foolish husband lives with the trolls and dwarves," she squealed, with a voice that sounded like fingernails on a chalkboard. "The draugs are walking over his bearded head listening for his last breath. I see broken bones and hear him crying out to you in the dark, but here you hide like a coward while your Viking prepares himself to ride beside Odin to the final battle of Ragnorok. And do not think your Gods will protect your offspring. They will die soon enough."

I was cursing at Marerjdt when I awoke shivering from fright and the cold of the attic. I rushed downstairs and threw wood on the dying embers in the fireplace. It was morning but the house was eerily dark except for the light coming from my fire and our lanterns. I sat casting my runes but they revealed nothing, and with each passing minute my despair became overwhelming. I took a knife and cut my forearm, gathering the blood in a dish as an offering to Freyja. I desperately called on Thor who rules the wind, thunder, and the skies and asked him why he had forsaken us. I begged and pled to Odin to send me a vision so I would know what to do.

The weight of the snow suddenly collapsed the porch and overhang surrounding our house, breaking along with it all the front windows. Snow poured into our house.

I frantically piled furniture, rugs, mattresses, and what wood I could spare to block the openings and the deadly chill. I stopped to vomit and grew frantically concerned that my unborn child was in stress with my heavy lifting. I am ashamed to admit I was so filled with despair that I cried for my mother.

I knelt in front of the fire and stared at the flames. I could feel life ebbing from Henrik's body and his soul preparing to enter Valhalla. For the first time in my life I felt anger for my Gods and found myself cursing them.

* * *

When Lizzie Grant drove back from Bracebridge she was pleasantly surprised to find her husband's truck parked in the driveway. Roy was supposed to be north of Sudbury hunting deer. She retrieved the two grocery bags from the backseat and walked up the back porch and through the kitchen door. Roy was sitting at the table with a half-drunk Budweiser before him on the table. It was just before noon. Instantly, she knew there was a problem. Roy seldom drank, and never before noon. She pulled off her ski jacket and stepped out of her Kodiaks.

"Hey, this is a nice surprise. Did you call off the hunting trip?"

"No."

"Little early for a beer, isn't it?"

Roy took a swig without looking at her.

"Sit down, Elizabeth Jane," he directed, firmly yet politely. Roy was not a big talker so whenever they did talk it was usually about the kids. Whenever he used her full name it meant there was something serious going on.

"Is something wrong? Is it the kids?"

"No, the kids are fine."

"Then what's going on?"

"Did you hear someone threw a sledgehammer through Cassie Turner's front window?"

Lizzie started removing the items from her shopping bags.

"I've got to get these things away or they'll spoil," she responded, dismissing his question as she carried the milk towards the fridge and opened the Westinghouse door. Without warning, her husband leapt up and slammed it shut.

"Roy!" she screamed, and the glare of his eyes frightened her.

"Sit down Elizabeth," he ordered, and silently, she went to the table and sat.

"I asked you a question," he repeated sternly, like he was addressing a child. "What do you know about it?"

His wife looked out the window and then back.

"Everyone on the lake has heard about it. You weren't here, Roy. I didn't bother mentioning it on the phone because it didn't seem like that big of a deal. The police figure some teenagers wanted to stir things up. There was no harm done except some broken glass."

Roy pulled another Budweiser from the fridge. Lizzie waited for her husband to take the lead.

"No one saw any boys in the area. No man living on the lake would have reason to do it. There are only one or two women with the girth to be able to throw that old hammer. One is Louise Templeton and she was in Fort Lauderdale. The other one is you, and I figure you put the hammer through the girl's window."

Lizzie shook her head and screwed up her mouth.

"Roy what are you talking about. Why in the world—"

"I'm not through!" Roy interrupted sharply as his flat hand came down hard on the kitchen table, causing his wife to jump in her seat. In twenty-five years of marriage, Roy Grant had only lost his temper twice—each time over his wife's extramarital activities.

"In fact, I don't figure it was you. I *know* it was you," he clarified, his voice much sterner. "You've been jealous of the Patch girl from the time she sprouted tits and started turning heads. She's what you were before you lost your looks."

His wife's eyes widened. Roy had never been so hurtful.

"So you put the hammer through her window out of jealousy. Charlie Langdon is the only new face on the lake, and maybe he's having sex with Cassie and that's what set you off. Or you wish he were screwing you. Maybe he already has, and then passed you over for her—"

"Roy!"

"Shut up," Roy growled. "Just shut up. I've had enough of your screwing around. Do you think I don't know about Phil and Tom? At least those bastards kept their traps shut about it. No matter how hard I tried, you were never happy. But now you pull a stunt like this where someone could have been hurt. What's next? Are you going to hire someone to beat her up?"

Lizzie had trouble meeting her husband's relentless stare and was frightened at the intense anger of his face.

"Alright, I did it," she relented, knowing she had to think quickly.

Roy sat back in his chair and waited. His teeth were gritted and lines of strain crisscrossed his forehead.

"I was afraid to tell you what happened," she stated, her eyes widening as she clutched her hands together. Exhaling deeply, she bit her lip. "It's not what you think. Charlie Langdon and I did have sex, but it wasn't consensual. I went to visit Ingrid but she and Cassie had driven to Bracebridge. Charlie invited me in and before I could resist he pulled me into the bedroom and forced himself on me, and—"

"Stop it. You're so full of shit. You've always been so full of shit. Okay, so why didn't you scream? Everyone would have heard you. Where are the cuts and bruises? Why didn't you phone me or call 9-1-1?

"I was too afraid and humiliated to say anything," she cried out, trying desperately to force a tear. "He threatened to hurt me."

"Jesus Christ. Go look in the mirror. Who in their right mind would want to do that to you? Maybe twenty years ago, but not now, and not a man like Charlie Langdon."

The blood drained from Lizzie's face.

"For once in our marriage tell the goddamned truth. Langdon didn't attack you, did he?"

"No," she conceded truthfully.

"You offered him sex but he turned you down. That's more likely what happened, right?"

"Yes," his wife whispered sheepishly, as a lone tear finally appeared and ran down her cheek.

"So you blamed Cassie and broke the girl's window."

"Yes."

Roy stood up and the look of anger in his face made Lizzie think for the first time in their marriage he was going to hit her.

"Well, I actually got you to tell me straight," a disheartened Roy Grant declared, as he walked slowly to their back door. He put his hands in his pockets and cleared his throat.

"Part of me wants to walk out of here and never come back. Part of me wants to fetch my hunting rifle and put a bullet in your conniving head."

Lizzie's face had turned a ghostly shade of pale.

"I'm going to stay with you for the sake of our children and grandchildren. But if I get one wind of you near Cassie Turner or anything to do with her, I'll turn you into the police. You don't talk with Charlie Langdon or go to Ingrid's when he's there. And if I so much as get an inkling you're fooling around with another man I'll walk out and not come back. And I'll tell our children and grandchildren why I left you. Do I make myself perfectly clear?"

Roy glared at his wife until, like a puppy caught peeing on the carpet, she lowered her head.

"Yes, Roy."

* * *

Charles Langdon awoke, made coffee, and tapped on the bedroom door. It was shortly after six o'clock. Without waiting for a reply he nudged open the door and walked in. Ingrid stirred slightly and a wisp of white hair appeared from beneath the mountain of duvet. The buds of her iPod were still in her ears and she pulled them out.

"What? What is it, Henko? Are the children okay?" she asked, half into a dream of years gone by.

Charlie hesitated and then approached the bed with the coffee cup extended towards her.

"It's Charlie. It's time to get up."

Ingrid rubbed at her eyes and strained to look through the window. "The sun is not over the pines. It's not six o'clock. What's wrong?"

"Nothing. I made coffee."

"Did you wake Cassie up?" Cassandra had now taken to spending every second night at Ingrid's house given her godmother's deteriorating health. Between her and Charlie there was never a moment Ingrid was left on her own.

"No, I was quiet as a mouse."

Ingrid propped herself up with the pillows and rested the iPod on her night table. She motioned for Charlie to be quiet and listened for any stirring in the third bedroom. The white-haired head poking out from the duvet accepted the cup and looked up at her young friend.

"Charles Michael, you are like a little boy on Christmas morning. You awoke me from my first sound sleep in months to have me continue telling my story?"

Pursing his lips Charlie Langdon nodded, realizing how foolish it was to awaken her when she was so exhausted. He immediately regretted what he had done. Nonetheless, the next words out of his mouth were, "Come on Ingrid. We're at a critical part. If you continue, I'll go to church with you this Sunday without complaining."

"Bingo as well?"

Charlie winced.

"Bingo too," he agreed reluctantly.

Ingrid smiled. "Okay, but I feel peckish, so please make toast and if Cassie awakens you get no story."

Along with the four slices of rye toast, Charlie hurriedly grabbed two apples and a banana. Ingrid wore her dressing gown as she exited the bathroom and returned to her bed.

> I was half frozen with the harshness of the cold pushing through the barricaded windows and at my wits end with Marerjdt's stinging words ringing cruelly through my ears.

> "Your foolish husband lives with the trolls and dwarves. The draugs are walking over his bearded head listening for his last breath."

Her words echoed savagely as I cast the runes and stared at their symbols but nothing was revealed to me. I cast them over and over and my anger and frustration grew.

"Tell me something!" I shouted impatiently of them. "I am the fifth daughter of a Viking Stonecaster of Gotland. I am a direct descendent of Sigrid Gustavson. Damn you, I demand the sight of the future. I need to see."

But nothing happened as I sat there listening to the tempest pounding our crippled home and the cold air seeped through my makeshift barricade. I felt betrayed by Odin and Freyja. Delirious with rage at the inaction of my Gods I picked up my runes and charm pouch and threw them at the flames.

"Damn you all," I screamed in blasphemy, watching my ancestral runes fall amongst the burning logs and embers. The pouch erupted in fire and the runes sparked and hissed angrily.

I continued cursing until a bright light flared across the room and from within it a familiar spectre appeared. Freyja stood within the light. She glanced about the room and slowly floated to the fireplace. When she held out her hands the runes and my pouch flew from the flames onto my lap. They were undamaged and unburned.

"Ingegard, you have been foolish and have offended the Gods with your words. Odin allowed me to help despite being angry with you for believing you are more than a mere mortal. You are a speck in time to the Gods and must never forget that. The God of Gods may withdraw Sigrid's sight for your transgression. There is much at stake for you and now is not the time for despair. It is the time for trust and faith." Freyja's face calmed, and the howling winds fell silent. "Close your eyes and breathe."

I slowed my breathing and closed my eyes, trying to shut out my fears for Henko and Freyja's threat of Sigrid's vision being taken. I listened to the crackle of the wood as it burned. I felt the warmth on my face. I smelled the scent of the maple wood being consumed by the flame. I eased my soul and thought of my chickens and our children playing in the river. I found myself back in Visby on a warm summer day. I felt Henko's very first kiss on my forehead. The wonderful smell of Mother's saffron cakes filled the room. Father's hair cologne touched my nose. My sisters were teasing me about my green eyes. I was collecting eggs and singing with my chickens. And then I was chained to a post covered in blood. And then on a Viking longship amongst giants pulling at the oars. I was surrounded with warriors watching as I gave birth to a fifth child. They cheered for their king. Lights flashed about me and my head swooned as I walked with my children along the river. And then I was in a dark cold place that smelled damp and musty. I was chilled to the bone. Somewhere nearby I felt my husband's pain and heard his voice calling out to the Gods.

"My warrior," I said aloud, "do not fear the trolls and dwarves. It is time for me to fetch you home."

But then I saw myself struggling in deep snow and near death. There were bewitched beasts surrounding me as if Loki the trickster had cast a spell across the forest creatures. I was terribly frightened. And then I was an old lady and my Ojibwe sister was walking from me into the cold snow waving good-bye and telling me not to follow. Suddenly the vision flashed and flared and I was back in a cave. The sight became clearer than any I had ever had.

My husband's bones were broken and he was freezing to death in a dark cave. The evil Marerjdt had said he was with the trolls and dwarves and her words told me he was under the ground, possibly in one of the crevices along Thor's Hammer where the escarpment reached down to the side of the river bed. Marerjdt had mentioned the draugs walking over his head. Draugs were living dead who walked the earth. I could not see them in my vision because of the blinding snow. I saw my husband crashing through the snow downwards into a crevice. I heard him cry out when his bones broke on the jagged rocks.

When I opened my eyes I was scrunched in a ball on the floor in front of the fire. There was no glowing light and no Freyja. I jumped up and ran to our maps. I considered that by noon yesterday, the storm would have overwhelmed him and he would have needed to construct a shelter. The map outlined a half of a mile stretch where three dangerous crevices snaked along the river through a stand of birch trees. It was four kilometres from our house but would seem like thirty, with me being pregnant, and the weather so brutally unforgiving.

I considered making my way around the lake to Niigaanii and Miigwaans' cabin. But they were as far from me as was my husband. I wrote a note explaining where I suspected my husband was trapped in hopes that if someone came to our house they would be able to track me and provide help.

Onto our second sled, I packed our medical kit, rope, a hurricane lantern, splints, a hatchet, a thermos of steaming hot coffee, candles, chocolate, and dry clothes. The snow was so deep it had cocooned our house and I was forced to leave out an upstairs' window. I strapped a compass and flashlight by a leather strap around my neck. With snowshoes on my feet and goggles covering my eyes I began my trek. It was barely afternoon and yet the sky was as black as midnight.

I cut through the forest rather than follow the curve of the river knowing that I was increasing the risk of encountering the un-dead draugs but I held to the belief that they too would have sought shelter from the tempest. The depth of the blinding snow and unforgiving winds slowed me like a snail crawling through the mud. It took four excruciating hours to reach the first stand of birch trees along the escarpment. Sliding down the hill I found the river and located the boulder beside which we set a trap. The frozen corpse of a male fox was still clutched in its steal jaws, which told me Henrik had not made it this far. I continued along the river to find the next trap. I saw what Henrik called the "married couple"—two beautiful poplars whose upper branches intertwined like they were holding hands. My husband had a way of naming things would help the children remember their way home if ever they got lost or disoriented. The next trap was by the river to the side of the trees. It was empty and reset, which told me Henko had made been here.

In her cruelty Marerjdt had unwittingly revealed too much. I searched the area knowing Henrik was close by. He had determined he could not make it home and needed to build an emergency shelter and start a fire.

Ingrid stopped as a half-asleep Cassie Turner stumbled down the hallway towards the bathroom.

"Morning," the girl muttered groggily, before closing the bathroom door.

"We will stop now," Ingrid said.

It was the first time Langdon hadn't been happy to see Cassie.

* * *

Kyla Langdon laughed heartily when she dropped the king of diamonds for two points and jumped her red peg into the final hole.

"Damn it," Evangeline swore, as she tossed her last card onto the table. "I don't like cribbage. I haven't won a game yet."

Kyla gathered up the cards and put them away.

"You're just a beginner. As kids we played every day. Dad always said it would help us with our math."

"Do you mind if I get some Perrier?"

"No, make yourself at home."

Evangeline Michaels hopped up from the living room sofa and walked across the plush carpet of Kyla's condo. It was a calm and serene escape from the unrelenting noise of her home.

"So, Duane's back Thursday?" Kyla confirmed.

Angie nodded and curled her bare feet beneath her bottom as she sat on the sofa.

Over the past four months, the two had become friends and intimate lovers. Having a woman like Kyla Langdon around might not have gone over with a less confident female, but Duane's wife was far from the jealous kind. The two women had a lot in common. Each had married too young and divorced but still managed to dramatically upgrade their stations in life. They each had money and a taste for both men and women.

Angie confided, "I think someone is stalking me. Do you think Duane is having me followed?"

Kyla shook her head. "Why would he do that? It sounds out of character even for Duane, doesn't it?"

Evangeline stood and walked over to the floor-to-ceiling windows. The thirty-eighth floor view of Toronto's night skyline was breathtaking. She counted the lights of six planes circling above the city, awaiting clearance to land. The flight attendants would be enjoying a momentary reprieve as the illuminated seat belt sign forced passengers to stay put.

"I don't know how much longer I'm going to continue to work for American Airlines," she considered aloud. "I'm thinking of getting Duane to back me in a shop that sells high end fashion. Being a flight attendant is no longer working for me and I'd like to sleep in my own bed every night."

Kyla's mind raced a mile a minute considering that Angie's presence would disrupt the equilibrium of the Michaels' relationship that Kyla enjoyed. It was something she couldn't let happen. The real estate agent drew upon Suzanne Weston's lessons of guile and joined her friend by the window.

"I think being followed is a bigger issue than whether or not you should give up your day job. Let's focus on that first. One option is to simply ask Duane—but he could lie through his teeth and you'd never know. He's told me how much he adores you. I'd be surprised if he's having you followed."

Evangeline now counted eight planes flying overhead in various stages of descent or holding patterns. The view from the condo of Toronto's lakefront night skyline was an unparalleled sight. Kyla's last comment was bothersome and she wondered just how close was Kyla getting to her husband? What else were they discussing in her absence?

Kyla moved up behind her friend and slipped her arms around Evangeline's waist. She let her hands wander in an effort to derail the conversation. Slowly she began nuzzling Angie's neck.

"What if it is a stalker?" the flight attendant inquired, as her concentration fluttered.

They stood for a moment until Kyla whispered, "We hire someone to shadow you and determine if someone is stalking. That's what we'll do."

Evangeline Michaels' mind was off the stalker and she anxiously turned around and pulled Kyla to the carpeted floor.

Chapter Twenty-four

Cassie was glad for a quiet lunch with her friend. She reached for the container of honey mustard and squirted a liberal amount on both pieces of bread.

"You and our Mr. Langdon seem to be getting along," Ingrid opined as she sliced a chicken breast for sandwiches.

"Ingrid, stop being such a matchmaker. I don't think either of us is in a position to be rushing into anything. The last thing I want is to be in a rebound relationship with a man not even divorced. How many times have you told me you can't rush your heart?"

The Swede smiled at hearing her own mother's expression come out of her godchild's mouth as she toyed with her sandwich. Her appetite had long since left her and the thought of food turned her stomach. Ingrid could see anxiousness seeping from Cassie. "Something else on your mind, perhaps?"

Cassandra finished chewing and swallowed. "You are not feeling well and it's getting worse every day. Is there anything I should know?"

Ingrid looked up. "I'm fine," she lied. "There's nothing you should know. Eat up."

Her younger friend sat rigidly.

"I can tell when you are lying. What are you not telling me? What's the medication you keep having me pick up at the pharmacy? Why aren't you eating properly anymore? Why are you coughing so much, and what did that doctor in Toronto tell you two years ago?"

Ingrid's face revealed nothing as she spoke. "That's a lot of questions."

"I'm not kidding. What haven't you told me?"

Ingrid pushed her plate to the middle of the table. She looked into her friend's eyes. She had looked into those a thousand times and it was hard to withhold the truth but there was no gain in having her goddaughter worry—or worse, argue—for hospital care. Death was inevitable for everyone. The Swede considered carefully what to say.

"Cassandra, I am an old woman and have outlived myself. You are too young to understand that people reach a point in life when the Gods no longer 'give' but 'take'. As to my health, the pharmacist is giving me painkillers for my aches, and to help me sleep. Just like your grandmother as she got older, I am having more trouble hearing and my vision is weakening. You cannot worry about what cannot be undone—unless you know some way to make me twenty years younger, perhaps?"

Cassie realized her godmother was not going to come clean.

"Okay, but when you want to tell me what's really going on, I'll be there day or night," she countered, before picking up the remainder of her sandwich and taking a large bite. "But you are not telling me everything."

The Stonecaster stretched her neck from side to side, hating that she was being untruthful.

"I know you do not accept the spiritual beliefs. My health is of no consequence. This body is simply an earthly body. When I die, I will go to where I will be with my husband, my children, my parents, and the Gods to whom I have prayed since I was a child. So let us play a game. You will stop asking me about my health, and I will not make you feel that I am not being truthful."

Her goddaughter stiffened her spine but held her tongue. An uncomfortable smile slowly appeared on her face.

"Alright, I'll play your game old woman."

*   *   *

Charlie was whipped when he arrived home for dinner. He and Barrett had completed six jobs including towing two boats to a winter storage facility. And his workday had been on top of a gruelling ten-mile morning run along a snow-covered trail.

As Ingrid served their meal she had a twinkle in her eye.

"How be we start the story during dinner?" she proposed. "I think it might wake you up and I do not seem to be coughing much tonight."

And as Charlie dug in, Ingrid looked off into space and began.

> Henrik would not have been unable to erect a proper lean-to with the intensity of the wind so he would have found a wide-branched fir tree under which he would dig out a retreat. The branches would serve as his roof and walls and he would be able to start a fire for warmth. On the side of the hill I saw a large spruce, which would have suited his needs. I retrieved rope from the sled and tied it around my waist and attached the other end around a boulder. With my hatchet I cut down a branch from the first tree to probe for safe footing. When I got to the spruce I was exhilarated to see the runner of Henrik's sled. But then my heart sank when he was not sheltered beneath the tree. I knew from my vision that he had fallen down the crevice within feet of where I stood.

> I prayed to Jord, the Goddess of the Earth, to guide me to the opening of the crevice without allowing me to fall in myself. My body was shaking uncontrollably and my goggles were iced over. I could no longer feel my fingers or feet as I probed the branch in and out of the deep snow. Suddenly, a wide tract of snow collapsed revealing the hidden crevice. I lit and lowered my lantern by rope into the dark abyss. It settled four metres below. Realizing I would need to build a fire to warm my husband I chopped

down three small trees, dragged them to the crevice, and after withdrawing my lantern let them fall down the hole. I struggled to drag a five-metre branch, which I dropped through the crevice opening. It would serve as my ladder. Then I lowered food, blankets and supplies, and, carefully holding my lantern, scurried down my makeshift ladder.

Holding the lantern high above my head, I removed my goggles and peered into the dark. It was still frightfully cold and I had no doubt that this was the musty-smelling cave of my vision. I shouted out Henrik's name and it echoed.

"Get away Tallemaja!" a voice called out, believing me to be the troll who disguises herself into a beautiful enchantress to entrap and feast upon Vikings. "By the Gods, let me die in peace, you witch."

"Henko, it is Ingrid. It is Ingegard," I screamed out.

My giant was delirious from the pain he had suffered in the fall. As my vision had shown, he had broken his right arm and his left leg bone was sticking through his trousers. We hugged and cried and I chopped up the logs and immediately started a fire. The warmth was painful and after I had put a splint on the leg we ate hungrily. He shivered uncontrollably with the cold but moaned with delight with each morsel of chocolate or hot drink he consumed from the thermos. The light from the lantern and our fire illuminated the cave, creating shadows across the rocky crags, stalagmites, and stalactites.

"I should have listened to you. My arrogance has put you and our child in danger," he whimpered. "Forgive me, Ingegard."

The storm howled through the night but we were sheltered and warm in the trolls' cave. At one point, I was forced to climb to the surface for more firewood. I do not know how it happened but I split the handle of my axe, rendering it useless. I searched Henrik's sled but could not find a spare. I realized that when the last of this fuel was gone, we would freeze to death if we remained in the cave. Without the rope to guide me, I would never have found my way back to the opening of our crevice.

When I re-entered the cave and approached the fire, Henko was holding up our lantern staring at the wall just behind him.

"Look Ingrid, look at the stones," he exclaimed, and despite the immense pain of his broken bones, he stumbled over to the wall and withdrew his knife. Hacking furiously, he carved out a chunk about the size of my hand.

"Here, hold up the lantern," he asked, and when I approached, the wall became illuminated in hundreds of bright yellow reflections. My husband held up the stone to the lantern and scraped at it with his knife.

"It's gold. All those yellow reflections are gold."

I had to forcibly pull him back to the fire as he screamed that we were richer than all the Viking kings. His yells echoed throughout the cave and would awaken any sleeping troll.

"Be quiet Henrik, and stop being so foolish. This is not our cave and that gold belongs to the trolls. We have more urgent concerns, like what to do when the last of our fuel is gone. When that fire dies so will we if we are still in the cave." That was when I told him about the split axe handle, but he did not react. He looked at the tree that had only partially fallen down the crevice.

"Not to worry," he said assuredly. "After we make foot loops in your rope you will climb to the surface and tie the rope to the nearest tree. I will use that tree branch and the rope loops as a ladder. You will have to help me when I reach the top. But hear this, my little dove—that gold is on our land and it belongs to me."

In the morning, as the last embers of our fire died away, we made ready to exit the cave and find our way home. I called upon Freyja to protect us. My Henrik pulled and yanked on the rope as he climbed up the tree branch ladder. I watched from above as he moved upward, inch by inch, cursing in pain all the way. Finally, his hand reached up to me and despite being a third of his size I somehow pulled him out of the hole.

I attached snowshoes to his feet and removed my rifle from the sled. If we pushed hard we might get home in four hours. Henrik was in agony dragging his broken leg through the drifts of snow. I had to struggle to keep my alertness as we trudged through a dreamlike forest of white. I felt painful cramping and worried for my baby. As we moved along, everything took on a familiar look. It was the snow place of my frightening vision with the dark shadows.

And then we heard the faint sound like someone singing our names. We took off our goggles and searched with strained eyes. It was not singing. It was howling.

"Your vision of the shadows was not the Germans I killed," Henrik stated. "It was wolves. My darling bride, remind me that you have had visions of the two of us as old Vikings. That is right, is it not?"

Through glimpses of the falling snow we saw a pack of six wolves racing towards us along the riverbed. More of them would be coming at us from the sides. Leading the attack was a huge black alpha. His canine instincts told him we were injured prey ready to be killed and feasted upon. I called out to the wolf leader that we were friends and needed his help but my words did not touch him. I believed he was bewitched by the forest elves or perhaps even Loki. I remembered from our Ojibwe friends that the wolf pack surrounded their quarry to stir panic and exhaust them. The alpha would patiently look for an opening and then charge ruthlessly, shouldering the victim to the ground. Before the prey could regain footing, the next two would leap forward and pin it to the ground. The remaining wolves would rush at the neck for the kill.

Henrik was delirious in pain and his broken arm made it impossible for him to hold and aim the rifle. I put a hunting knife in his good hand and quickly unslung the rifle knowing it would be up to me to kill the alpha. I prayed to the Gods and raised the rifle.

But then another massive wolf suddenly catapulted from the bushes to our left and came leaping at us.

Chapter Twenty-Five

Evangeline Michaels' driver wheeled her suitcase to the front door and muttered goodnight as she stepped inside. He noticed that the customary booming music was missing. Evangeline locked the door and took a deep breath. What an unexpected pleasure to return home to find peace and quiet. Duane had flown to New York for a series of interviews on his entry onto the World Wrestling Federation circuit.

As she kicked off her boots there was a commotion just outside the front door. Momentarily, her cell beeped alerting a call from Dimitri Trechikoff, the security guard Kyla had hired to shadow her.

"Ms. Michaels, it's Trechikoff. I've got a scruffy-looking intruder who says he's your husband."

"Duane?" she exclaimed.

"No ma'am."

"Ask his name."

When the Russian repeated the name she exhaled loudly and directed her guard to bring him to the garage. When she stepped through the back door Evangeline was visibly shocked with what she saw. Standing before her was a thin, old man with dull-yellowy skin who looked like a seventy year old. Terrance's eyes looked dead with short, dullish grey hair that had receded four or five inches. His face was lined with wrinkles or scars. The bridge of his nose was off-centre.

"Terrance?"

Greene relaxed and his demeanour softened.

"Angie," he greeted softly. "It's been a long time. Tell this goon to let me go, I'm not here to hurt you." Dimitri Trechikoff kept his Beretta 92F stuck deeply into the interloper's left side.

"Then why are you here? Money?"

"Money? No, I don't want money. Why didn't you return the messages I left with your folks?"

His ex-wife took a step closer. Staring at the sickly representation of the man to whom she had been married was upsetting. Terrance looked like he was dead.

"Have you been stalking me?"

"Stalking you? No, I come around here to make sure you get safely into the house after your flights."

"That's called stalking and you can't do that. We're divorced and I'm re-married. You and I are no more. Do you hear me? We are no more!" she repeated emphatically.

Terrance took a deep breath bringing on spasms of coughs. It took a moment for him to continue.

"Evangeline, I made a mistake. I paid for that mistake in ways you can never imagine. You were right to leave me when I was behind bars. But now I'm out. You're still my wife. I've never stopped loving you."

Evangeline's stone-like expression took on a look Terrance didn't recognize.

"What rock have you crawled out from under?" her voice growled, "Are you crazy? I'm not your wife. Now, stay away or I'll have you put back in jail. I don't ever want to see you again."

"Angie, you don't mean—"

"Dimitri, get this thing out of my house. I don't ever want to see him again."

Angie spun around, re-entered the house, and slammed the back door.

Terrance's mouth opened to protest but nothing came out. Trechikoff twisted Greene around and kneed him viciously in the lower stomach. As Terrance buckled over, his wife's guard grabbed his right ear and violently pulled him to the rear of the dark blue Cadillac Escalade parked in the back driveway. Evangeline's security guard flipped the smaller man into the vehicle through the hatch. The car ride lasted an hour and then abruptly stopped. The Russian opening the back hatch and effortlessly lifted, and deposited, a completely incapacitated Terrance Greene on the snow-covered ground. The skyline of the city was some distance away to the west and by the mounds of trash surrounding them he determined they were in a garbage dump somewhere in Pickering.

"Ms. Michaels doesn't want to see you again," the hulk stated, as he slowly withdrew the Beretta from his shoulder holster. Then from a second holster at the base of his back he presented another handgun. He held them up in front of Terrance's face, displaying them with great pride.

"This is my Beretta 92F and it packs a ton of firepower," he boasted proudly, and without hesitation raised it quickly, pointed across the yard at a large steel barrel and fired three times. The sound was explosive and crushed into Terrance's eardrum like he had been punched.

"Yes, loud and brutal. Tear apart a man's chest like spaghetti," he stated, "but the barrel heats up far too quickly." The Russian ground the tip of the hot barrel to Greene's cheek, searing a dime-shaped circle through four layers of skin. Terrance cried out and pulled away.

"See what I mean? Now, this baby," he said, lifting a Colt .45 Gold Cup, "is more subtle. Is *subtle* the correct English word to use for a gun?"

Terrance nodded, still smarting from the burn. He noticed his nose had begun bleeding.

"Good, thank you. This lovely piece is more accurate and what I prefer for killing." Dimitri took aim and shot out the driver mirror on a car wreck thirty feet to their right. "Deadly accurate."

Without warning, Trechikoff kneed Terrance, sending him sprawling. He lurched forward and pinned Greene to the ground with his right boot on the man's neck.

"My boss pays well. The next time you see my face will be the last time. Understand?"

Terrance croaked out an affirmative answer.

"Alright then," Dimitri Trechikoff responded, holstering both weapons before unleashing a torrent of well-directed kicks. Terrance curled up into a ball, instinctively covering his head. It had been a while since he had submit to kicking. They'd been a regular occurrence in prison until the medical staff became concerned with the severe flu symptoms and complete fatigue that constantly plagued Terrance. After a series of blood tests diagnosed him HIV-positive he was quickly withdrawn from general circulation and placed in quarantine. The Penitentiary Administration acted swiftly to avoid risk of excessive medical costs. They orchestrated Terrance Green's probation and shipped him back to Toronto.

The Russian security guard walked over to the Escalade, punched in the four digit keyless entry, and got in. He stared at Greene before raising his finger and pantomiming slitting his throat. Terrance rolled over and spat the blood from his mouth wondering why his wife had forsaken him.

* * *

Ernest Fanning arrived at Blackmore, Craig and Fanning just before eleven o'clock in the morning on Wednesday. As he strode nonchalantly past Tara Kirkpatrick he thought about the previous night's phone call from David Fowler. Fanning had re-entered the dining room an exhilarated man. After a glass of Port he had looked across the table at his disinterested wife. Bettina was still a fetching woman even though the fiery red hair had softened and her figure had filled out over the years. He walked to her end of the table and stared momentarily before leaning over and kissing her. Bettina was taken aback as he slowly pushed back her chair and pulled her into his arms. Her momentary hesitation eased and when she kissed him enthusiastically, he took her by the hand and led her upstairs. Two hours later they fell asleep totally exhausted in each other's arms.

Alex Fanning's father smiled at that pleasant memory as he sat down at his desk. It was going to be a deadly day for three people because of Tessa Conner's foolishness and greed.

Manpreet Sachdeva would be the first to go. Vito Carbrese's had been successful in securing every recording. Sachdeva was a loose end that needed to disappear.

Around midnight, Phaidra McTavish's lifeless body would be found in the stall of a public washroom along the waterfront. Police would have no reason to suspect foul play and the coroner would determine cause of death as an accidental overdose. Fanning felt a tinge of remorse. What would have happened if Phaidra had not shown up with the cocaine? How much longer would their affair have continued? Would she have gone down the slippery road of becoming a drunk and drug addict?

And Tessa would cease to exist one day after police discovered her mother. Carbrese would orchestrate an email sent from Tessa's home computer to her boss' computer at the law firm. It would offer her immediate resignation with the explanation of her need to get away given the horrific news of her mother's death. Like Sachdeva, the girl's body would never again be seen.

"You have the meeting with the 'Ethics and Conflict Committee' at 11:30 a.m., Mr. Fanning," Tara Kirkpatrick interrupted, surprised that her lecherous boss had not offered any inappropriate comments about how her outfit accentuated her figure.

"Dennis issue an agenda?" he inquired in a perfunctory tone as he picked up his copy of the Wall Street Journal. Dennis Patterson was the National Partner in Charge, acting very much as the firm's Chief Executive Officer. On top of that accountability he was a powerful billings generator in the firm's Business and Regulatory practice. Fanning and Patterson had grown up together in the firm but it was Fanning's name that had been added to the letterhead.

"No sir. I do know that the entire committee will be in attendance."

Ernest quickly scanned the newspaper headlines. "Anything about NovaRose or Alex?"

"No sir, nor in any of the major newspapers or online."

Fanning looked at Tara as he tossed the newspaper haphazardly on his desk.

"What's the word on the grapevine? Who is the committee fucking over today?" Fanning asked, as his gaze dropped to her chest.

Tara Kirkpatrick shook her head. "Everyone's extremely tight-lipped, but something big is up. I heard they asked for security to be on hand after the meeting."

Ernest Fanning nodded and returned several phone calls. At 11:20 a.m. he went into his private bathroom, brushed his teeth, gargled, and combed his hair and moustache. The committee was always after someone and after forty years it had grown tiresome hearing the same complaints.

Just as he was walking out of his office his cell rang and the caller ID showed David Fowler.

"Is it done?" he asked anxiously.

The ex-cop hesitated and then spoke slowly. "Our technical support is completely resolved."

"Good, I'm in a rush. When will your other two presents be wrapped?"

Tara Kirkpatrick stuck her head through door and pointed at her watch. Fanning nodded.

"Well, there's something that surprised us," Fowler admitted, making his boss instantly nervous and more attentive.

"What surprise?" the lawyer inquired apprehensively, since nothing ever surprised his fixer.

"There is a healthy chance that the younger present belongs to you."

Fanning's eye twitched as he struggled to understand the meaning. "Come again?"

"The older is swearing that the younger was a present you gave her twenty-five years ago. The younger is unaware of this."

There was deafening silence on the line and Fowler could only imagine what his boss was thinking.

"Do you think there is any validity, or is it a gambit to buy time?"

"If I were a betting man—which we both know I am—she's telling the truth, but there are tests which will irrefutably confirm it."

"Don't do anything without absolute proof. Call me at three," Fanning directed, as he ended the call and pocketed his cell. The one time he had gone bareback with Phaidra McTavish had occurred two nights before she had shown up with cocaine. It was the only time as an adult he had broken one of his father's cardinal rules. If it was true, then why hadn't she come to him for help or sued for child support? And then as he hustled down the corridor to the meeting, Fanning stopped as the abject horror of this revelation struck home. If what Phaidra claimed was true, then he had had sex with his own child. Something in the pit of his stomach turned and he felt like vomiting. But there was no time and he forced his thoughts back to the upcoming meeting and made his way to the Algonquin boardroom on the sixty-second floor. Upon entering, twelve familiar faces looked at him as he took his chair by Dennis Patterson's right hand.

"I've got a ridiculous schedule today," Ernest announced arrogantly. "Let's cut the pleasantries and move through this quickly."

Dennis Patterson half-smiled, and asked that the minutes be recorded by George Decker, the lawyer acting as the committee secretary. George headed up the firm's Patent department.

"Ladies and Gentlemen, thank you for attending on such short notice. I've reviewed with each of you the purpose of today's gathering and will dispense with the review of our last meeting's minutes. Let's get to it." Patterson gathered himself before commencing in a very deliberate and officious manner.

"In 'vicarious liability,' a firm is held legally and financially accountable for the actions of its employees while involved with company business. When the firm is made aware of a legal transgression, such as an act of sexual harassment, it is imperative that the firm act swiftly and judiciously, not only for the welfare of the abused employee, but to address the risk of civil action being lobbied against the firm."

Ernest was thinking about Tessa being his daughter when he suddenly realized Dennis hadn't reviewed anything with him. He raised a finger to interrupt.

"Sorry old man, I think you missed briefing me."

Patterson angled his chair to face Fanning.

"Ernest, this committee is in session to discuss *your* conduct at Blackmore, Craig and Fanning, specifically allegations against you of sexual harassment. You of all people understand that the policy of this firm is a zero tolerance of harassment of any kind. Our actions and response are documented in our Code of Ethical Behavioural. I would ask that you listen to the complaints and then the committee will hear what you have to say. I realize that you've participated in enough of these discussions to understand that everything said today will be recorded in order to protect you and all of the employees involved in this matter."

Ernest Fanning felt sideswiped but sat perfectly still and remained silent.

Dennis opened a red file and removed several pages.

"Ernest, no less than three female employees have accused you of sexual harassment. We have carefully investigated their complaints and have given them our assurance that their complaints will be addressed to the full extent of the law. For the record, I want to state that Ernest Fanning is directed not to have contact of any manner with any of these three employees inside or outside of these premises. Do you understand, Ernest?"

"Yes."

"Please note that Mr. Fanning understands the 'contact' directive."

Ernest looked around the table but not one lawyer would make eye contact.

"The names of those involved are not to be raised in order to protect the individuals from repercussions. But for the record, each of the three accusers has boldly waived this right. The three are Theresa McCreavy, Puna Rajan, and Victoria Betteridge."

The silver-haired lawyer casually looked up and, despite a solid effort to not betray any emotions, his face reddened. Quickly, he reached into his jacket pocket and withdrew his cigarette case and lighter. Ignoring the "No Smoking" legislation he drew deeply and exhaled through his nose. Theresa and Puna were articling students. Victoria Betteridge had been with the firm seven years and had been admitted into the partnership the previous Christmas.

Dennis continued, "Theresa McCreavy was hired last June as an articling student. Last week, she registered a complaint to our Head of Personnel and Hiring, Tom Chapin alleging verbal and physical sexual harassment. Instead of bringing this forward through the proper channels, Mr. Chapin took it upon himself to speak with Mr. Fanning. Following that conversation, Mr. Chapin took great pains to coerce the articling student into resigning. Ms. McCreavy refused and took her complaint to the Law Society of Upper Canada. By nine o'clock, I personally interviewed Ms. McCreavy who confirmed her complaint. She also directed me to contact one of our new paralegals she believes is being harassed by Mr. Fanning. We have been unable to reach Tessa Conner who has been absent since Friday. For the record, we are including Ms. McCreavy's sworn affidavits, a sworn affidavit of her conversation with Tom Chapin, and a copy of her complaint as submitted to the Law Society."

Patterson took a drink of water from a tall cut crystal glass. Fanning noticed his hands were trembling. Several lawyers shifted uncomfortably as if the leather seats of their chairs had shocked their behinds. Every lawyer in the boardroom knew Fanning was a star when they were so young they were worrying about acne.

"In a recorded interview, Ms. McCreavy stated that Puna Rajan had a similar experience and was willing to come forward. At noon yesterday, I interviewed Ms. Rajan and her sworn affidavit has been admitted to the record. Puna joined our firm as an articling student in May of last year. Ms. Rajan showed incredible poise, prudence, and professionalism in documenting the times and places that she was coerced by Ernest Fanning. Ms. Rajan admitted she had been the victim of a previous sexual assault while a law student. That experience psychologically traumatized her. As a result, she succumbed to having a sexual relationship with Ernest Fanning for a period of three months."

Ernest's focus was losing its mettle as his mind flipped to images of his wife and son.

"At three p.m. yesterday, I was approached by Victoria Betteridge. Ms. Betteridge confided that she had been forced into a six-month sexual relationship with Mr. Fanning. Ms. Betteridge stated that she had remained silent out of embarrassment and fear that coming forward would destroy any hope of being admitted into partnership."

There was an uncomfortable stirring around the table. Victoria was one of the most popular lawyers in the firm. Fanning's eyes remained locked on a tiny scratch in the table just in front of him. He realized there were no ashtrays and he flicked the cigarette ash into his half empty cup of coffee, wondering how deeply their witch-hunt had reached.

"Finally for the record, we interviewed Tom Chapin last night and have his sworn affidavit confirming Theresa McCreavy's complaint and his breach of accountability. Mr. Chapin verified that Mr. Fanning placed undue pressure on his position being aware that Tom had falsified certain aspects of his CV when we originally hired him into the firm. Mr. Chapin was terminated with cause last evening at eleven and advised to seek legal representation."

At this point the National Managing Partner abruptly stopped and the deep tension lines on Dennis' face showed how emotionally exhausting the last few days had been. His ulcer was burning like a branding iron searing into his chest. Why had Fanning been so careless? For years they had turned a blind eye to his philandering, but now action had to be taken. It would hurt the firm badly because Ernest's name was synonymous with Blackmore, Craig and Fanning.

"Roger," Patterson stated, turning the meeting over to Roger Walters, the co-chair of the committee.

The well-dressed lawyer spoke clearly, enunciating every consonant perfectly as if he were speaking to a room of grade eight students. Walters had one of those faces with oversized eyes like a Margaret

Keane painting. Ernest had taken him aside as a junior and told him to take speech lessons and buy a decent wardrobe.

"At this point, I am required to clarify that in the case of an accusation of sexual harassment the firm must show firstly that the accused partner engaged in the misconduct, and secondly, that the employment relationship between the accused and the company has been irreparably damaged. Once these two factors have been clearly and contextually presented, the subsequent action or punishment must fit the crime. Fortunately, we have irrefutable evidence which confirms the alleged misconduct."

"What evidence?" Ernest interrupted, as he tossed the remainder of his cigarette into the cup.

"We are not obliged to discuss the specifics in this meeting," Walters responded, "but since we will be turning over the evidence to the RCMP within the hour, I can't see that it would hurt. Dennis?"

"Go ahead Roger," Patterson directed, as he leaned back in his chair.

Roger Walters shifted a few papers and selected one.

"Ernest, these allegations were raised coincident with our decision to sweep the executive offices and boardrooms for any illegal recording equipment on the premises. You are aware that the firm does that every year to ensure confidentiality for our clients. Your assistant Tara Kirkpatrick confirmed your office has never been swept . . . so that's where we began."

Fanning's heart leapt into his chest.

"The 'sweep' uncovered evidence in your office in a hidden panel behind your bookshelf. There was audio/video recording equipment and a box containing videos and DVDs clearly documenting illegal and amoral actions you conducted in your office. Those recordings conducted on our premises, found in a legal search, are a breach of professional conduct and will be used to support your dismissal as well as being turned over to the authorities."

Ernest took a drink of water.

"At this point I am required to ask if you would you like to state anything for the record?"

The silver-haired lawyer was blankly looking out the window, stroking his moustache. It was not hard to imagine the headlines in the newspapers just above his photograph with the word "disbarred" printed below. Charges would be laid and with the evidence they held he'd be convicted and sent to jail. Bettina would be shattered. Whatever he was going to do would have to be done today. He thought about his advice to Alexander to get out while he still had time.

"Ernest, would you like to state anything for the record?" Roger repeated.

He shook his head. Any comment could be used against him in a court of law.

"For the record, Mr. Fanning has declined to comment. At this point, the firm's dictated course of action is the suspension with pay of the partner against whom claims of sexual harassment have been made. However, given the enormity of this breach of professional conduct we wish to show the three accusers that we whole-heartedly support them and are acting swiftly, effectively, and judiciously. Our course of action will also serve as notice for all female partners and employees who you abused to come forward. You can always file a suit for wrongful dismissal."

"Dennis, can we talk alone?" Ernest implored, under his breath. Dennis looked away.

"The termination of one partner technically requires a majority vote of the partnership. However, in a case such as this repugnant, amoral, and clearly documented breach of our Code of Ethics and Professional Conduct, this committee, with the support of the Governing Committee, is technically able to negate the need for such a vote. This morning at nine o'clock the Governing Committee of Blackmore, Craig and Fanning voted unanimously for immediate termination without the majority vote of the partnership."

Rogers faced the lawyer he had idolized.

"Ernest, security will accompany you from the building. They will require you to turn over all company property including your office keys, office pass cards, desk keys, your cell, your iPad, your Dictaphone, and all credit cards. Your computers are company property and were confiscated during this meeting for a forensic analysis. You can keep your home computer. We remotely downloaded all of its files during the night. A press release will be issued at one o'clock announcing your termination. When this meeting is adjourned, you are forbidden by contract to contact any clients, employees, or the press. Dennis and I will be contacting your clients as soon as the press release is issued. We are required to suggest you seek legal representation immediately and must inform you that our recommendation to the authorities is that you be immediately arrested, charged, and held without bail. I'm certain they will consider you a high flight risk given the recent conduct of your son Alexander."

Ernest Fanning felt trapped. The recordings they discovered in the wall behind his bookshelf would send him to hell for eternity. Slowly he turned to the National Partner in Charge.

"Dennis, there's no way around this? I've helped build this firm for forty years. Allow me to resign for health reasons."

Patterson glared at Fanning and spoke infinitely quietly.

"You disgust me, you arrogant bastard."

Dennis then faced the committee. "An all-partnership meeting is scheduled in this room for 1:15 p.m. this afternoon. This meeting is adjourned."

Roger Walters walked to the double doors and rapped twice. Two security officers stepped through and escorted a thoroughly deflated Ernest Fanning from the room. His eyes never left the floor.

"I'm allowed to stop at my office and get my coat and briefcase," Fanning stated quietly and the security officers agreed. As the trio walked down the corridors, Ernest immediately gathered himself and took a deep breath. From that moment, the silver-haired lawyer conducted himself as if he were on the way to lunch. His trademark smile found its way back to his face as he greeted those he knew by name.

The confused look on Tara Kirkpatrick's face told him his assistant was unaware of the ambush.

"What's going on sir? They've taken stuff from your office," a disoriented Kirkpatrick asked quickly, as Fanning and the two guards passed her and walked towards his office.

"Just peachy, Tara," her boss answered in a hoarse voice, and before the two security guards could react, the lawyer rushed into his office and locked the red mahogany door.

Knowing Tara had a spare office key he hurried to his desk, opened the bottom right drawer, and withdrew an expensively crafted wooden box about the size of a Ken Follett novel. After opening it, Ernest stared at the loaded Sig Sauer that David Fowler had insisted be kept in the event of an emergency. Hearing Tara's key being inserted into the door he raised the Sig to his mouth. For a brief moment, he stared at the framed picture of Bettina on his desk.

The tip of the barrel tasted slightly oily as Ernest Fanning slipped off the safety and squeezed the trigger.

Chapter Twenty-six

After helping Barrett dismantle a garage-full of old machine parts in one of Phil Henderson's rental units Charlie headed over to Cassandra's house.

"Have you noticed any deterioration to Ingrid's health?" Charlie inquired as he accepted the cup of peppermint tea.

"She's old, sick, and won't talk about it. That cough of hers has been getting worse and I think her visit to the doctor in Toronto told her bad news she's kept to herself. Has she told you something?"

"Me?" Charlie expelled. "Why would she tell me something she wouldn't have already told you?"

Cassandra Turner sipped her camomile and smiled awkwardly.

"Oh, Charles Michael," she teased playfully, imitating her Swedish friend's accent, "for being smart you can be really thick. Haven't you figured out that you are her surrogate son and a messenger from the Gods? Of course she might tell you something. I'll bet she already has. I know she's telling you the story of her life. She's never done that for me, no matter how many times over the years I've asked."

Charlie picked up his teacup and joined Cassandra on her sofa. "Well, she hasn't told me anything about her health," he said quietly, "except to stop asking her about it."

It had been a long time since Cassie had spent so much time with a man. Phillip had always had the unswerving need to control the conversation, decisions, arguments, and foolish things, like what kind of stone counter to have in the kitchen. In complete contrast, Charlie Langdon listened, asked questions, and genuinely gave a damn about what she thought. He didn't try to control or make her feel small. Quite the contrary, he had an uncanny way of bringing her out and making her feel wonderful.

Similarly, Charlie Langdon hadn't spent much time with a woman since before Francine had transformed into Kyla. Being with Cassie was a new lease on life. She was an utterly fabulous person but the most attractive aspect was that her real beauty lay within.

Three hours later, the two were still talking and laughing.

* * *

That night Ingrid appeared especially weary. Her coughing had deteriorated into more of a dry, painfully sore growl. It hurt to hear it. There were dark half moons under each eye that no longer contained any white. Her skin tone was off and she had lost so much weight that she looked like a tiny elf with white hair. Charlie's nagging fear of the inevitable was overwhelming, but as requested, he kept his counsel and pretended that everything was fine. As soon as Langdon began clearing the dishes he suggested she get to bed early but Ingrid refused, fearing that each night might be her last. It was crucial she finish her story.

> The black wolf continued his deliberate charge and his pack encircled us. The other rogue wolf that had appeared did not attack us but instead placed himself facing the attackers. A gunshot exploded but I had not yet been able to make my finger pull the trigger. More gunshots shattered the air. I raised my rifle and began pulling the

trigger but nothing happened. The safety was frozen stiff and would not release. A wolf jumped at Henrik and he clutched the wolf's throat and stabbed repeatedly at its neck. More shots filled the air. And then the rogue wolf turned and ran directly at me. Using the rifle as a club I cracked it across the skull, but it regained its balance and yanked the rifle from my grip. I pulled my knife from its sheath and slashed wildly.

"Odin," I screamed, as my knife struck home but the wolf was too powerful and thumped me backwards to the ground. I bit and kicked defiantly.

"Gaawin," the wolf screamed, in Ojibwe. "Gaawin!"

I continued to struggle, fighting for the life of the child within me.

"Niigaanii," the wolf shouted repeatedly. "It is Niigaanii. Ingrid, stop."

I was breathless and convulsing uncontrollably as I stared through cloudy eyes.

"Niigaanii?" I sobbed, and buried my face in his fur coat. I cried with uninhibited joy and relief as he began rubbing my arms and legs to get my circulation flowing. Henrik lay unconscious beside two bloody wolves he had slain with his knife. When my Ojibwe friend raised me I saw the dead bodies of nine wolves, including the mammoth black alpha.

"Aaniin ehi-zyaayan?" he asked urgently.

"*Ningiikaj*," I replied, telling him I was fine but my teeth were chattering so hard I thought they might break.

Niigaanii reloaded his rifle and retrieved mine, forcing the safety lever to operate.

"With great effort he manoeuvred his sled under my crippled husband and then gently lifted me onto it. Taking off his wolf coat he wrapped me from head to foot. Our Ojibwe sang to the spirits of his ancestors to give him strength. Niigaanii drove forward with the strength of ten Viking warriors, never resting despite the headwind and snow that slashed at his face. How would he ever find his way home?

"Guide him, Freyja," I prayed weakly, and the crying wind roared as if to drown out my pleas for help.

And then my Ojibwe sister and her eldest son Ma'iingan were carrying me into the house. Miigwaans chanted as she stripped off my frozen clothes. I screamed as the warmth from the room painfully stabbed like a thousand rose thorns sticking into my body. I fell into delirium and the evil Marerjdt was once again on my chest, telling me I would lose the child within me and that my other children were going to die a terrible death because Henrik had plundered the trolls' gold. Marerjdt slapped me and mocked that a red man was cutting off my thieving husband's fingers and toes. I heard Henrik screaming and cursing. Miigwaans ran over and began cursing at Marerjdt and calling to her spirit world.

As Marerjdt laughed I saw something suddenly appear beside my sister. It was an Ojibwe spirit dressed in deerskin with black hair that swung wildly about. She stared at me with eyes that shone like burning embers. The two non-mortals looked at each other and began exchanging curses and vicious threats. Marerjdt shrieked and ran at Miigwaans' Shaman, but Miigwaans's Iron Woman Spirit clawed and strangled her with talons, picked up the evil Norse spirit, and threw her across the room into our fireplace. An explosion of flames engulfed Marerjdt and she disappeared from sight.

"Help me, Shaman," I pled, desperation filling my soul. "Save my husband and my children."

"That one will trouble you no more," she promised. "Your husband will be by your side for many summers."

"My children?" I asked, my heart pounding. "Will my baby live?"

The warrior Shaman touched my cheek.

"*Giga-waabamin menawaa*," the spirit's Ojibwe softly spoken words told me I would be fine, but avoided my question. "You must sleep now. Do not lose faith."

When I awoke the room was hot and I ached everywhere. My head pounded like there was a drummer inside. My eyes suffered snow-blindness and could see only blurs.

"*Aaniin ezhi-ayaayan?*" Miigwaans asked, her voice trembling. "How are you?"

"Nimbakade," I replied slowly. "I am hungry. Where is Henrik?"

"Henrik is recovering beside you," Meryl Patch's voice answered, and I felt her take my hand. "Mikaeli and Birgitta are asleep in the other room. You've been unconscious and Niigaanii says the death spirit has been at your door for three days." Meryl leaned over and kissed my forehead. I could tell she has been crying. "Ingrid, you lost your baby. The strain to your body was too much for the little one to bear."

A piece of my heart slowly died inside my heaving chest. "It was a girl?"

Miigwaans nodded sadly. "It was a daughter."

Meryl stroked my hand and told me that Niigaanii had reset and re-splinted Henrik's broken bones. The Ojibwe had removed two frostbitten fingers and three toes. Miigwaans told me not to worry about Niigaanii's wound where I had stabbed him. I had almost killed our friend thinking him a wolf.

We three remained silent for a long time and then when I was able, I shared with my Ojibwe sister that her Shaman had protected me and defeated Marerjdt.

Miigwaans whispered knowingly, "My green-eyed sister from across the big water, you are not the only one with powerful spirits and visions."

That storm of 1962 claimed thirty-five lives in Ontario and Quebec. Meryl Patch stayed with us through February. She fed us, cleaned, and saw to the children. My Ojibwe sister and her husband returned with the pelts of our attackers, including the alpha wolf that hangs on my wall. For months, Niigaanii took over the trap lines. My eyesight returned but my hair turned snowy white. I do not know what we would have done without our friends.

My husband's stubbornness had cost us our animals, almost killed the two of us, and put dear Niigaanii's life in peril. It had lost us our unborn daughter. Henrik was humiliated and distraught at his rash behaviour. Losing a limb is a horrible thing for a Viking unless it has been lost in battle. Being the reason for the death of a child is an even greater cross to bear. I know that when he stared at his missing fingers and toes he always thought on the sorrow and heartache he had brought upon us.

I shared with him the night spirit's warning about plundering gold from the draugs and trolls and Marerjdt's warning about the risk to our children. He heard me but did not show fear. Instead, he began praying nightly to Thor to allow him, as a Viking, to rightfully retrieve the treasure he had found. It was the way of the Norsemen to never shy away from a fight, run from a battle, or succumb to fears brought on by spirits.

By May, our household and farm looked like any other year. The fields were ready for planting and my family was laughing again. Henrik was eating when he shared his intentions. I almost fell off my chair with what my ears were hearing.

"Ingrid, I returned to the cave and took nuggets to an assayer in Barrie. His tests showed our gold is nearly 100% pure. I intend to mine that gold. I have purchased steel containers from a dairy farmer that he uses to transport milk to the market. They seal perfectly and will allow for the easy transportation and storage of my gold."

I vigorously reminded him again of Marerjdt's warnings but he would not be deterred. I asked if he had learned nothing and poked at his missing fingers to make my point. Anger flashed in his eyes and he told me to consult my stones. I got my charm pouch and withdrew seven runes. The symbols of *Dagaz* followed by the blank tile of *Odin* were unmistakeable portends of death. Henko's face turned white.

"Husband, I see by your expression that you understand the message. You told me to consult my runes and we have. The message is clear—if you mine this gold, it will bring death to our family."

Henrik insisted I use Sigrid's vision but I could not. Since the ordeal with the wolves and the battle of the spirits I had not been able to summon a vision, let alone a normal nightly dream. I did not know if I was being punished for having interacted with the Ojibwe spirit world, or because I cursed the Gods and lost faith in my greatest hour of need. Freyja had told me Odin was angry.

We had reached an impasse. My husband angrily pushed the runes off the table and told me that without visions I was just another rune reader. It was the first time he had ever hurt my feelings. It was the lure of greed that was eating at his soul.

He promised, "I will make sacrifices every day as a tribute to the trolls."

"Henko, before Odin I tell you that we will suffer dearly if you take that gold. We have already lost one child. I almost killed our friend. I have lost Sigrid's vision. What further harm do you want to bring upon us?"

Henrik stormed out the house.

While workers ploughed and sewed our fields Henko brought out every ounce of gold from the trolls' cave. After, we knelt and prayed to Odin to appease the trolls and thank them for their generosity. Waiting for nightfall, Henrik loaded his treasure in forty-five three-foot tall aluminum dairy cans and transported them to the cold cellar beneath our kitchen floor.

Charlie leaned forward. "Ingrid, how much gold did Henrik remove?"

"Henrik calculated $3 million. In the 1960s that was a lot of money."

Charlie whistled. "That would be close to $70 million at today's price. If you had all that money, then why are you still living here?"

Ingrid raised her brow and her eyes stared right through Charlie's skull. "Ah, you are wondering if the old lady is as crazy as they say? You think I exaggerate, perhaps. I realized how hard it is for you to accept the truth of the story I am telling you. Everything you have been taught works against you accepting my words and the spirit world. I know that part of you wants to believe, and someday you will."

Charlie didn't know how to respond. No matter how convincingly Ingrid told her story it was hard for him to believe in Norse Gods, elves, and spectres that appeared inside bright lights. It was fantastical like a fairy tale.

"No matter, my doubting Thomas, it was all for naught and the warnings of the runes came to pass. The vindictive trolls continued to extract their revenge from the day Henrik pillaged their gold. A drought that summer crippled the region. Our rivers slowed to a trickle and we could not irrigate our fields. With everything so dry, brush fire burnt out one third of our farm. Our cattle got diseased and died. The chickens stopped laying eggs. The whole community was in distress because of the gold. And I lost Sigrid's vision."

Ingrid's face was strained with anger, still plaguing her after all these years.

"I only had to look in his direction and my giant would turn away in shame."

Chapter Twenty-seven

Charlie seldom thought about his life in Toronto. His days and evenings were happily filled with Ingrid, Cassie Turner, and Barrett Sanford. Langdon could not remember a happier time. When he happened to glance in a mirror he liked that he saw a youthful, unstrained face atop a healthy and fit body. His skin no longer looked pale and drawn and his eyes were no longer bloodshot. Great Spirit Moon Lake had brought him from what he had once perceived as the depths of despair. But now, his eyes had been opened to what really mattered in life.

Charlie and Barrett were hanging out at Phil's Ford Dealership drinking coffee when a text from Kathy Graham pinged on Charlie's iPhone.

Phone Irv immediately.

Excusing himself, he slipped into one of Phil's empty offices and dialled Telfer. Irv's assistant, Heather Stickel, picked up and her overly cheerful greeting told him something was up.

"We've all missed you, Charlie," Heather gushed. "It's been hell around here."

After exchanging pleasantries, her boss' insipid voice came on the line.

"Charlie, how the hell are you?" Irv inquired, in a smarmy tone typically reserved for clients or the press.

"Fine, and you?" Charlie responded, in a dismissive tone typically reserved for people he loathed.

"Well, actually, pretty terrific. Why didn't you tell us you had reached out to Jack Reeseborough? Your e-mail sparked him to take a closer interest in the agency review that Tom Potter was conducting. He interviewed a number of people in Tom's marketing department and personally met with the CEOs of the agencies that Potter was recommending they shift their business to. It turned into a pissing match with Reeseborough ordering his CMO to 'un-fire' us. Tom refused and demanded that his boss let him conduct the pitch or get a new guy. Potter should have known that you never toss out an empty threat when the other guy is holding the gun. Reeseborough fired him yesterday afternoon. I just got the call from Jack apologizing and asking us if we would work with them again."

Charlie had to smile. It was proof of the Cherokee adage that "if you stand on the banks of the river long enough you will watch the dead bodies of your enemies float by." Tom Potter's dead body was floating.

"I'm happy for you," Charlie stated honestly. "Now you can hire back those people you gunned to protect your own wallet."

There was an awkward silence on the phone.

"You're absolutely right, and you're the first person Kevin and I want back. I feel awful for having pulled the trigger on you. I was irate about you not showing up in Chicago, but I should have given you the benefit of the doubt. I'll admit that even I'm not impervious to making bad decisions. Charlie, please come back."

Irv was breathing hard on the other end of the line. How this conversation must be irking the bastard to have to eat crow. In the momentary silence Charlie hoped Cassie would drop over to visit when he was done work.

"Charlie, you still there?"

"Yup," he answered, mid-swallow. "You get all the assignments back?"

"To a dollar. I promised Jack we'd have the team in place in one month. We've got fifteen television commercials to get produced and on the air by next March. Think we can pull it off?"

Charlie Langdon did not jump at the bait of the difficult challenge.

"Help me understand this. Telfer Stuart gets the Daily Planet Foods business back because of my e-mail, my leadership, and the integrity of a decent client CEO. The firm will look incredible in the press and that will stabilize all the other clients and get new business walking in. You and Kevin are back in the black and pulling in a ton of dough. The agency will be on track to being acquired by a multinational holding company setting you and Kevin for life. That about it?"

Telfer bit his lip at the last comment. "Absolutely, this is all about you. I will tell the world that. Just get back to Toronto so we can light this rocket and show what our agency can do," Telfer responded, bullshit seeping from his mouth.

Langdon stood up and walked over to a window that overlooked Phil's inventory of Ford Vehicles. As he looked out, a hawk with a wingspan of about ten feet soared high above. The hawks had been known to hunt anything that moved, so cottagers knew better than to let tiny pets roam freely about their property. On a warm Sunday last July, a disheartened Anne-Marie Downey had watched helplessly as a red-tipped hawk had snatched up her yelping Lakeland Terrier puppy clutched in its talons. Charlie followed the arcing path as the hawk headed towards the lake.

"Well, how about it? When can you get here?" Irv asked tentatively.

"Irv, what's in it for me?" Charlie inquired bluntly.

"Well, first of all an apology for having fired you. I think it's important we set that record straight and be perfectly clear to the entire industry that we got this client back because of you. Next, bring back your whole team as you see fit. I think only four or five have got new jobs so they should be receptive if they know it's to work for you."

Charlie winced to think of all those unemployed people who had been unable to secure jobs.

"And a couple of more things need to be rectified," Telfer suggested. "Kevin and I want to extend a partnership to you. You'll get ten percent non-voting equity and, in a year, if everything is going well with Daily Planet Foods, we'll add your name to the door. That equity position will double what you were earning."

The hawk was now just a speck in the sky. Barrett waved at Charlie and pointed at the clipboard he was holding. They still had four jobs to complete before dinner. He nodded and held up his fingers for two more minutes.

"Well, partner, what do you think?" Telfer inquired smugly, believing Charlie would chomp at the bit to get his name on the door of their agency.

"I don't know Irv," Langdon answered truthfully, thinking his former employer obtuse. "I'm thrilled you've got the client back and will be rehiring the team. And I think your offer of the partnership and equity is worth mulling over. But to be crystal clear, Jack wants me running the assignment or there's no deal."

Kevin Stuart spoke up on the speakerphone. "That's right. No Charlie means no Jack and no rehiring of all the people we had to let go. Their jobs depend on you."

Charlie had to laugh out loud.

"Hi Kevin. I thought you might be there. So, just to clarify, the guilt card won't fly with me. Beyond that, I'm going to need time to think about your offer."

"What's there to think about?" Kevin interrupted nervously. "We're giving you everything you've been working for. Is there another offer on your table? Is another agency offering equity and your name on the door?"

Charlie stood up and stretched, yawning audibly.

"I'll phone at noon tomorrow. By the way, Kathy Graham was the one who got my e-mail to Jack. I want her un-fired and given a five-year contract. Bump her severance condition to one year. Her family is in a bad way, so award her a twenty-five thousand dollar spot bonus and raise her salary 25%, effective immediately. Ask Kathy to confirm it with me when it's done. This is the first thing I want done or we can call it a day."

Kevin Stuart didn't consult with Irv before readily agreeing as Charlie hung up without saying goodbye.

Barrett stood off to the side and stared. He had never seen such an aggressive Charlie Langdon. From what he had caught on the phone he realized that his partner might soon be leaving Great Spirit Moon Lake. And that was a horrible thought.

Chapter Twenty-eight

"I'm glad you invited me out," Miriam Walker admitted shyly, as she and Barrett walked from her house into the early vestiges of a star-filled night. The weeklong cold snap had let up and the mercury in the thermometer was hovering just above freezing.

Days earlier, the librarian had been sorting the book return pile when Barrett Sanford burst through the library door and made a beeline in her direction and slowly asked if she would go to a movie the upcoming Friday night. Miriam replied yes. Barrett smiled, and bolted from the library.

"Well, I am g-glad you said y-yes," he replied, and he thoughtfully took her elbow looking down at the unsalted sidewalk. "It's slippery here."

Given his inability to drive, Barrett had faced great embarrassment asking Charlie to drop him off at Miriam's house and then drive him home after the movie. It was like he was fifteen again asking his father for a lift.

"My mother says you were an incredible football player. Your teams won the provincial championship twice. That must have been pretty stellar, being so popular."

Sanford nodded but did not reply. He couldn't remember the last time he had spoken about high school. It was a different time that was hard to believe had actually occurred.

"I really like the *Hobbit* series," Miriam offered, trying to spark a conversation. She had seen Barrett reading Tolkien's books in the library. "I recently began re-reading *The Lord of the Rings*, and didn't think the movies would be able to match my imagination, but they have. Did you read the whole series?"

"Yes," came the one word reply.

And so it went until they reached the theatre and bought tickets. Miriam tried to ignite a conversation while Barrett struggled with one- or two-word answers. The two sat eating popcorn and M&M's until the movie ran its course and it was time to leave.

"Barrett?" she whispered quietly, as they walked up the aisle of the theatre towards the side exit. "It's okay if we don't talk a lot. That's fine with me. I'm a pretty quiet person myself, just like your typical librarian. But I want you to know that I don't care about how you say your words. I do care to hear everything you've got to say, and I'll wait as long as it takes you to get it out. I know lots of people who can talk perfectly but have nothing worth saying. I'd rather hear everything on your mind, no matter how much you stutter, because I think you've got a lot to say. I hope you don't mind me being so forward and I'm sure not trying to embarrass you. But then again, my mother says I can talk the eyes off a snake and don't know when to shut up. That's usually when I get nervous. I guess hearing my own voice settles me down. I'm a little nervous right now, but I'm sure you know that."

Sanford smiled inside and out. "I am nervous too."

"So, phone Mr. Langdon and tell him you are coming to my house for coffee and cheesecake, apple pie, brownies, or date squares. I've got a variety from the bakery because I know you like them all but I don't know your favourite."

"I'll eat anyth-thing."

"Good. And you can also tell him that I will drive you home."

"You sure?" he asked.

"Yes, I'm sure. And I thought that while we're having some dessert, we could discuss what we want to do on our second date. That is if you think you might want a second date?"

Barrett reached for his cell, and as Charlie's number rang, Miriam slipped her arm through his and they walked along the sidewalk towards her house.

* * *

Charles Langdon awoke to a very dark 5:00 a.m. to the sounds of Ingrid puttering about the kitchen. He stretched and tried to work out a kink in his neck. It had been a bad night. Ingrid had endured countless coughing spells and Charlie had passed a sleepless night thinking about his upcoming conversation with Irv and Kevin.

"Good morning," he muttered groggily, and Ingrid turned with a start. She was ashen white and holding her left side.

"Oh, you frightened me," she said quickly, "I did not mean to disturb you."

"I guess we both had trouble sleeping. Cassie and I are going to run to the upper top of your property this morning, so I needed to eat extra early anyway."

Ingrid ladled porridge into a bowl before sprinkling a generous quantity of brown sugar on top. Her movement seemed restricted and strained.

"Ingrid, please don't get mad at me, but I think we should see the doctor today."

"Why, are you sick?"

"No, but you are."

"It is just that too many sleepless nights are wearing me down. I also upset myself last night talking about Henrik and the trolls' gold. It was such an awful time for us," Ingrid deflected, as she brought milk for Charlie's coffee.

Her housemate looked out the bay window. A full moon was hanging brightly but low in the sky and their neighbours on Great Spirit Moon Lake were still warmly in their beds sound asleep.

Ingrid took his hand and immediately launched into her story.

In October of the same horrible year, our children got the measles. Mikaeli was ten and Birgitta eight. The children were happy to stay home. I was in the kitchen when I felt a chilling sensation of a spirit running up my spine. I quickly spat three times and ran to the door, clutching my amulets. When I stepped onto the porch there was something standing at the base of our steps leaning heavily on a long staff topped with the horns of an elk, the skull of a rabbit, eagle feathers, and bear claws. Her gray hair was intertwined with feathers and beads and fell to the back of her knees. Her face looked hundreds of years old and what teeth she had were brown and pointed like picks on a saw blade.

Miigwaans had told me of a legendary medicine woman who had travelled across North America from the time of the great Civil War. The Ojibwe no longer knew if the ancient was of this earth but all knew that her arrival at your house was a bad omen. She was called the Mashkikiiwinini and her words had to be obeyed. Wearing traditional Ojibwe skins and leathers she pointed at me.

The medicine spirit woman hoisted her staff, threw back her head, and shrieked like a hawk. "*Ah-shah-way-gee-go-qua.*"

That was the Ojibwe name of honour Miigwaans conferred on me after we fought the wolves. It meant "woman warrior guide."

The Mashkikiiwinini took several steps forward. Her eyes were small white orbs and had no colour. They gave her an appearance of being blind.

"*Ah-shah-way-gee-go-qua.* Your children are dying of the red fire. Take them from here but do not touch them or you will die. Get them white medicine to ease their pain. Burn your house to the soil. Prepare yourself to face the death spirits of the night. Your Gods have turned away in anger at your blasphemy and for not heeding their warnings."

She turned and faded into the forest like a wisp of wind. Without hesitation, I bundled up the children and drove to the Huntsville hospital. The Emergency entrance was overflowing with parents carrying ill children. Nurses and doctors all wore facemasks and gloves. People were shouting and panicking. It was complete mayhem. Two attendants took Mikaeli and Birgitta. Parents were forbidden to enter. That was the last time I saw my babies.

Ingrid sat down at the table closed her eyes. Her hands were clenched tightly and one of her knuckles cracked under the strain. Charlie quietly pulled up a chair and wrapped his arms about her.

"I do not talk of this," she whispered, choking back tears. "Henrik and I were guilty for the deaths of our own children and all those other innocents because we ignored the warnings told by my runes and visions. I had lost my faith and cursed the Gods for not helping me. Odin punished me by taking back Sigrid's vision. Freyja did not bless me with fertility so that I would become the last Stonecaster of my ancestry. I have had to live with this shame and guilt for too long now."

Charlie watched as Ingrid's breathing calmed. Carefully selecting his words Charlie said, "It was Scarlett Fever and there was no medicine to counter it. No one was to blame, least of all you or your husband. That epidemic struck this region of Ontario and was a horrible coincidence with Henrik's gold. You lost the unborn child because of extreme physical exertion at a critical point in your pregnancy. No woman could have hoped to keep her baby alive with all that you went through trying to save Henrik. These things are not punishments from the Gods. Odin did not write such an incredible destiny for you only to treat you so unfairly. Freyja has helped you throughout your life. It is time for you to put away all these horrible feelings of guilt. Didn't you tell me something about having to leave things behind before you could truly move on?"

The white-haired lady from Gotland cleared her throat and wiped at her tear-filled eyes.

"There may be truth in what you say," she responded slowly. "And thank you for your kind words. Now, let us talk about another matter. I feel that something has happened to cause you grief."

"My old boss offered me a partnership and a lot of money if I return," he stated.

Ingrid looked past him. "Have you spoken with Cassie?"

"No."

"You should."

"I know. Ingrid, can your runes help me?"

Ingrid nodded. "I have cast your runes many times. You are fulfilling your destiny in the way it has been set out. Your journey through life, wherever it is, involves Cassandra. From the time she was sixteen her runes told me of a troubled stranger who would arrive into her life, making her whole. Everything I know tells me that you are that person. The runes I have cast for you and Cassie show a full life with great happiness. Of that, I am more certain than anything I have ever known."

Charlie looked perplexed. "That's why all of this is so confusing."

"Good. Then go talk with Cassandra before you make your decision," Ingrid directed.

Chapter Twenty-nine

After learning about Fanning's suicide, a thoroughly disgruntled and frustrated David Fowler drove like a maniac to the warehouse in which Vito Carbrese was holding Phaidra McTavish and Tessa Conner. Over the years, he and Fanning had developed what he considered more of a friendship than a working relationship. And of all things, the lawyer had been a gravy train of money that wouldn't be stopping at his station anymore. He worried about that. His love of the ponies hadn't diminished, and sooner or later he'd find himself owing money that his cop's pension wouldn't cover. His mind had raced through the alternatives until it finally dawned on him how to turn Fanning's untimely demise to an advantage.

One of Carbrese's men unlocked the door. Fowler hoped he never had to tangle with this goon with a 22" neck and a muscled body that dwarfed his own. The man smiled and grunted, "Ciao."

Vito was on his cell. The third man in the room offered the newcomer a drink or something to eat. The ex-cop pointed at the cola.

"Everything is like you asked," the well-dressed Italian stated, as he pocketed his iPhone and walked over to the table. "I hope you're certain about all this, or we're all fucked."

David anxiously asked, "Did she find it?"

Vito smiled. "There's nothing my little cousin can't do with that computer. It took some doing." The Italian handed his friend a document containing ten double-sided pages.

The ex-cop pulled out a pair of cheater glasses from his pocket and stood beneath a light flipping through the pages. After reading, he shouted an expletive and gave a fist pump. "Fanning wasn't lying. It's all here in black and white."

Carbrese clapped his hands. "So this can work?"

"Yes, we will make it work. It will be the biggest payoff of our lives."

"I can't believe your boss offed himself," Vito commented, quickly making the sign of the cross.

Fowler folded the pages and put them in his jacket pocket. He then recounted what he had learned from a contact at Fanning's firm.

"I guess he didn't have the guts to face it," Vito pronounced. "At least his son had the brainpower to have an escape plan with tons of dough. For all of his smarts and experience, Fanning buckled and took the easy way out." Carbrese looked at his shoes. "So David, what if we can't pull this off?"

"Let's face that if it happens," David responded. "If the mother is lying about having Fanning's child or her daughter won't play along, then we dispose of them. No loose ends." He drained the cola, crushed the can, and sent a two-pointer through the air into the garbage can. Maria Carbrese was sitting in the corner engrossed in Sachdeva's files. She jumped at the unexpected noise and looked up.

"Do you mind?" the thoroughly exhausted IT expert rebuked sharply. "Some of us are working here."

David raised his hands in apology, remembering that Vito's younger cousin didn't take crap off anyone. Heaven help the man who married her. "Sorry."

"Maria, are you just about ready?" her cousin inquired impatiently, and she momentarily nodded. "Good girl. Give us the okay when you've got what we need."

Phaidra and Tessa were led into the room and told to sit. Neither had slept and both looked strained and anxious. The older woman was obviously suffering in desperate need of a drink. Her shoulders were hunched over and her hair was a mess.

David Fowler stared, hoping to God that Phaidra was telling the truth. He hated the thought of having to kill women.

"Ladies, my name is David Fowler and I used to work for Ernest Fanning as his 'fixer.' In the next half hour or so, my colleagues and I are going to either let you go, or kill you. I am going to bring you up to speed with what has happened since you've been our guests. Tessa, we have everything you and your ex-pal Manpreet Sachdeva recorded. His body parts are currently dissolving in a vat of hydrofluoric acid." Fowler stopped to allow the full effect of his words to set in. It was important that the two women understand their abductors had no qualms about killing.

The cold expression transfixed on the younger woman's face revealed nothing. Tessa had already determined that Manpreet was going to be collateral damage. The younger woman casually asked, "May we have a cola please?"

When the women were handed drinks, David continued. "Ernest Fanning is also dead." Unlike the Sachdeva news, this one got the reaction he wanted. Phaidra's mouth drooped open, and Tessa choked on the cola.

"You killed Fanning?" Tessa inquired.

"No, Fanning committed suicide after his firm kicked him out for sexually harassing three female employees. Seems like some other women beat you to the punch. They had irrefutable evidence including boxes of explicit video recordings. Ernest swallowed a gun."

Phaidra set down her can of cola and covered her face.

Carbrese caught Fowler's eye and Vito delivered his rehearsed line. "Where does that leave us?"

"In an awkward situation," Tessa Conner interjected. "You're wondering what to do with us. You obviously have no compunction about murdering people, but I don't think you'd be wasting time talking with us unless you had something in mind."

David admired the girl's poise and walked over to the mother. Not having a drink in over twenty-four hours was obviously agony for her. Fowler turned his eyes towards the daughter when he asked the question.

"Phaidra, I'm going to ask you just once. And remember that I will have the results of a DNA test by the end of the day. Did Ernest Fanning father Tessa?"

"What?" Tessa exclaimed loudly. In that moment of complete shock, David saw her lack of complicity. "Mom, what did you say to them? What is this?"

Phaidra McTavish turned towards her only child. "Honey, I was so ashamed and didn't know how to tell you. By the time you were old enough to understand, you were mad at the world. I thought of getting a lawyer and going at Ernest with a paternity suit, but I didn't have two cents to rub together, and was working two jobs and then I started losing my fight with the bottle. And then you came up with this blackmailing scheme, and I saw how I could keep my secret."

Tessa jumped up and grabbed her mother by the shoulders. She began violently shaking her.

"What are you saying? Ernest Fanning is my father? You told me it was one of the Ukrainian bastards you worked for. Fanning is my father? How could you not tell me? Oh Christ, you let me have sex with him. How could you?"

"Tessa settle down," Fowler ordered, as Vito pulled the girl off her mother. "The DNA tests will show whether this is true or your mother is just buying time. Get over what you did."

The young woman's disgust was so intense she could hardly focus. David walked over and sat her down on a chair. "If the DNA tests prove paternity, you and your mother can leave here alive, and we will all be stinking rich. Now, do you want to listen?"

Phaidra defiantly faced their abductors.

"I swear it's true. And no matter what happens, don't hurt my child. She's just an innocent victim in all this."

Vito Carbrese walked over and gently put his hand on her shoulder. "Phaidra, you look very tired. Why don't you rest in the other room for a few minutes?" he politely suggested, and he motioned for his men to take her. "Boys, get the lady something to eat and some coffee."

David Fowler glared at Carbrese like he had two heads.

"It's horrible what your mother hid from you. Everyone gets it, but the fact that we know this little tidbit of information opens up a Plan B. We prove with DNA evidence that you are a child of Ernest Fanning and you become one of the legal heirs to his fortune." David stopped, and withdrew the document from his jacket. Slowly he unfolded it and smiled. "One night Ernest told me some of the lessons his father had taught him. That's what made him the guy he was and why we're all here today."

Tessa sat up and exhaled deeply. "Is this going somewhere?"

"Shut up and listen," Vito Carbrese directed sharply, and the paralegal leaned back in her chair.

"Thank you, Vito," Fowler said politely, before continuing. "One of those lessons that Fanning took to heart from his father Goodwin was to craft a will that did not have your wife as the key beneficiary. As such, when Ernest wrote up his will, he left everything to his 'then unborn' children, and not one cent to his wife. Now, as luck would have it, Bettina, like her husband, was an only child of extremely wealthy parents, so she didn't blink an eye. In fact, she completed her will exactly the same way. Now, that's where this all gets really interesting, especially because of the inclusion of one simple two-letter word."

"Which word?," Vita asked.

"'My,'" David answered, with a grin.

"In Fanning's will, it states that he leaves everything to 'my' children/issue. Nowhere does it state, 'our' children/issue, referring to those created by Ernest and Bettina. As such, Fanning's future progeny might have been produced in a womb other than Bettina's. And the icing on the cake for us is that he included a section within his will that was signed by Bettina, acknowledging she fully understood all elements and conditions of his will, accepted his wishes, and would never do anything to try to counter those wishes."

Ernest Fanning's daughter's insides began to quiver with anticipation at where this was heading. Fowler shook the pages in his hands.

"What I am holding is a copy of Ernest Fanning's Last Will and Testament. It is the only will he ever completed and signed. His child,

Alexander, can legally benefit from any inheritance when he returns home and manages to survive jail time. But if DNA testing proves Ms. McTavish's claim, there will be a second beneficiary to the Fanning estate, regardless of the maternal partner. And what makes this even better is that there are no other living relatives to contest this will except for Bettina, who tragically will not survive the end of this week. With her out of the picture and your stepbrother on the run, we have a legal pathway towards at least 50% of what Fanning owns."

David walked over to the table and poured a cup of coffee. Begrudgingly, he sprinkled cheap-tasting powdered creamer atop the black liquid. He lit a cigarette and could smell the rubber burning in Tessa's brain.

"And why will Bettina Fanning tragically not survive the week?" she inquired.

Vito Carbrese slowly walked over. "Think about it. Her son is on the run. Her husband has committed suicide after sexually assaulting countless employees. Bettina Fanning will be overwhelmed by the paparazzi and all the malicious shit that will overwhelm and assault her without mercy. Her reaction will be to withdraw and not leave the house. By week's end she will decide she can't face it anymore."

Fowler handed Tessa the will and she immediately began reading the pages.

Momentarily David Fowler continued, "Bettina Fanning will be found dead with bottles of sleeping pills scattered on the floor. No one will doubt her demise as the ultimate act of desperation."

Tessa looked at them both. The plan was scathingly brilliant if she was Fanning's illegitimate child and the will was enforceable.

"Alright, I can buy that," she concurred, "So what's the deal?"

"Three way split, but I need to know that you totally agree that Bettina Fanning has to be disposed of. We don't want her muddying up the water regardless of what the wills say. There can be no going back on that action or we're all just wasting our time."

Tessa stared from one man to the other, wondering how to be set free and then cut them out of the game. She saw no need to share the money.

"I've never met Bettina Fanning," she stated clearly. "It's public record that my father is—or was—worth hundreds of millions of dollars. I can only imagine what they'll find hidden offshore with a thorough investigation. If Bettina Fanning is standing between us being rich then she's got to go. I don't intend to go through all of this and have her contest the will in court. But I don't want to know anything about it. That's something you'll have to take care of."

The former detective glanced over at Maria Carbrese and she nodded. Tessa followed his gaze into the shadows, and for the first time saw the young woman sitting behind a makeshift desk.

"Tessa, you are one cold lady. I know that your brain is racing like a rabbit wondering how you can get out of this building, have us do the dirty work, and then discard us so you can keep all the money yourself."

Vito laughed and walked over beside Phaidra's daughter.

"That's why we like you," the Italian admitted. "We'd all be thinking the same thing."

A wry smile appeared on Tessa's mouth but she remained silent.

Fowler motioned with his hand for Maria to join them. She handed an iPad to Tessa Conner and pushed the tiny arrow on the screen revealing her partners' insurance policy.

"I've never met Bettina Fanning. It's public record that my father is—or was—worth hundreds of millions of dollars. I can only imagine what they'll find hidden offshore with a thorough investigation. If Bettina Fanning is standing between us being rich then she's got to go. I don't intend to go through all this and have her contest the will in court. But I don't want to know anything about it. That's something you'll have to take care of."

Maria took the iPad from Tessa and returned to the shadows. "I've got everything recorded since you walked into the room. And for the record, Tessa, I think you are a total bitch for not even blinking an eye when you heard about Manpreet. He was a decent guy."

Everyone looked at Maria Carbrese who in turn looked at Vito. Her cousin nodded his agreement.

"I have a lot to learn from you, Mr. Fowler," Tessa admitted, realizing that only days before she had handed Ernest Fanning a different iPad and watched him react. They had cornered her. "So, what's the deal?"

"Like I said before. It's a three-way split. We don't contact each other, we don't see each other, we don't talk on the phone, and, we don't think about each other. You deal with your mother, but if she interferes or becomes a problem then we will remove her. You will not return to the law firm. You will wait for two or three days before coming forward. I'll give you the name of a lawyer who will script you, dress you, train you, and act as our go-between. You must come out of this appearing innocent, naive, and the victim. We may not have to release the recordings of you and Ernest."

"I hope we won't have to do that," she responded modestly.

"Only if it will help us," the ex-cop answered.

Ernest Fanning's daughter was no dullard. They had her to rights. "What stops you from murdering me the minute we get the money?"

Vito Carbrese tilted his head as if someone had slapped him.

"Why would we do that? We're partners. You don't go around killing your partners. What kind of people do you think we are?"

David took another tack when he saw Tessa's bewildered expression at his friend's outburst.

"No benefit in removing you with each of us getting well over a hundred million. You're the sacred cow, and we want to keep you safe at all costs. At a future date, there might be an additional play for your half-brother's share of the estate."

"But it's not something partners would do," Carbrese repeated sharply, his tone betraying his reaction to the insult. "That was an obnoxious thing to say."

Tessa Conner realized that instead of fleeing her mother's antagonist for a meagre university tuition, she was now facing the possibility of being wealthier than she had ever dreamt.

"Alright, I'm in," she agreed firmly. "I'll need money to live on and buy new clothes."

Fowler and Vito looked at each other and then the older of the two spoke.

"We'll float you upfront money through the lawyer and then deduct it from your share. Deal?"

Ernest Fanning's daughter stuck out her right hand to her two new partners. "Deal."

Chapter Thirty

It was two minutes past noon when Irv Telfer's phone rang. He anxiously answered, clicking it on speakerphone so his partner could listen.

"It's Charlie Langdon."

"Charlie, glad you called," Irv responded, looking at his partner Kevin Stuart who was nervously biting his baby nail. Unlike his more anally retentive partner, Kevin knew that Charlie would come back. Langdon's reputation meant everything to him and winning back Daily Planet Foods would be a vindication of the damage Irv had inflicted on him. Kevin also knew that Charlie would have some healthy demands.

"Gentlemen, I'm not coming back to Telfer Stuart. It's just not where I want to be anymore," Charlie stated from the cab of Ingrid's F150, which was parked along a gravel side-road into Bracebridge. There was a light snow falling and three deer were crossing the road up ahead without a care in the world.

"What?" Irv blurted. "You can't be serious. This is exactly what you're cut out to do. If it's the money, we can talk about it. I can up the equity another five points."

Earlier that morning, after having spoken with Ingrid, Charlie threw on a coat and had walked down to Cassie's. When she opened the door, Cassie looked like she had just crawled out of bed. "I'm sorry for just showing up, but can we talk?" he asked, and his running partner yawned loudly and offered coffee.

"Take off your coat off and sit," she directed sleepily, pulling another cup from the cupboard.

"I took your advice and contacted the President of Daily Planet Foods who fired Telfer Stuart. He wants TS back and they have offered me a partnership with equity, my name on the door, and a whack of dough," Charlie explained in a steady stream of words, studying her face for any change in expression. "You were 100% right. Everything happened exactly how you said."

As she poured, Cassie hesitated. "Well, congratulations. What are you going to do?"

"That depends on a lot of things."

Cassandra Turner sat down and pulled her dressing gown tighter around her waist. "Have you spoken with Ingrid?"

"We've spoken."

She began nervously tapping the rim of her cup with the nail of her index finger before reaching for the sugar.

"You're talking with me because Ingrid told you to?"

"No. I'm asking your opinion because it matters."

Snow began to fall across the lake and, for a moment, the two sat at the kitchen table looking out the living room bay window. Charlie's departure would break Ingrid's heart, pushing her to her grave. Meryl Patch's granddaughter picked up her cup and took a sip.

"You aren't asking my opinion about the job. You're really asking how I feel about you. If I tell you to grab at this opportunity, then that would say I don't see us having a future."

Charlie didn't interrupt.

"And telling you not to take the job and stay here means that I see a future that involves you."

Charlie gently took Cassie by the hands.

"That's what I'm asking," he responded, with a smile, "because I am hoping that you feel for me the way I feel about you. Setting aside our Swedish friend and her runes, we have to decide for ourselves what we feel and what we want."

They sat quietly holding hands. As Cassandra stared out the window at the falling snow Charlie continued.

"I would understand if you were reluctant because I blew my first marriage and am not even legally divorced yet. No one wants to be in a rebound relationship."

Someone was cross-country skiing along the lake's edge. Ingrid's goddaughter took Charlie's fingers in her own and gathered her words.

"When Phillip died I realized, with his absence, how totally he had subjugated me and emptied me of confidence. My world here has been my escape and, thanks to Ingrid, my salvation and resurgence. It's taken me years to find myself and the idea of entering a relationship mid-divorce is not something I am prepared to do."

Charlie waited, hoping there was more.

Cassandra stood up and walked across the room. The snow was now coming down heavily and the skier disappeared into a cloud of white. If they had gone for their run they would have had a miserable time slogging through this weather.

"Ingrid told me there would come a day when you and I would be faced with a decision. We can't allow you being mid-divorced or being offered some job offer to force us into making a decision before we're ready to commit to each other. We need to let time unfold. So let's for a moment remove both the issues of your divorce and job offer. If you were not married and living here, I would hope that we could spend a lot of time together. Can I see a future for us? I think so, and I feel you do too. When I'm with you I'm happy and feel alive. But Charlie, the reality is that you are married and you do have to consider your career. And don't ever think I'm concerned that you're broke or currently working as a handyman around our lake. Money is the last thing I care about."

Langdon leaned forward and slowly took her in his arms. She brought her face forward and for the first time they kissed. It felt natural and unrushed and, after several minutes, she lowered her head to his chest and the two melded into each other. Charlie whispered into her ear.

"I feel exactly the same way. You make me feel happy and like there is nothing I can't do. Every morning my first thought is about you. Runes or not, I want us to see if we're meant to spend our lives together."

Cassie leaned back and looked up into his face. "So what are you going to tell your agency?"

"Well, I've got an idea that might work. Will you let me practise my answers to them with you before I make the call at noon?"

That conversation with Cassie had been hours ago. A gasoline truck sped by the Ford as Charlie's former boss tried to counter his refusal to return.

"Let's work through this one step at a time," Telfer reasoned, fully aware that the life of his agency depended on Langdon's return. "We'll raise the equity offer to 20%, announce an immediate partnership, and put your name on the door today. We want this to work."

Langdon knew that Irv would be pacing back and forth and Kevin would be biting his nails. It was exactly how he and Cassie had practised. He took a deep breath and took over the conversation.

"Gentlemen, let's put all our cards on the table. We know Jack Reeseborough's offer depends on me running his business. No Charlie, no Daily Planet Foods. Right?"

"Yes," both partners replied in stereo.

"And Telfer Stuart will likely be forced to close its doors if you don't get Daily Planet Foods back and settle down your other clients. Right?"

Phil Henderson's Durango slowed when he saw Charlie's Ford parked on the side of the road. Thinking his neighbour might need assistance, he pulled to a stop until Charlie motioned that he was on his cell and all was okay. Phil waved and drove on.

"Gentlemen, if I were to come back to TS it would be under these non-negotiable conditions that are on the table until the end of this phone call. If you don't agree with my demands then you can phone Jack and tell him I said no."

"Go ahead," Kevin responded, and he picked up a pen.

"First, immediate partnership with 25% equity retroactive to January 1st of this year."

"Yes," Kevin replied without hesitation.

"Second, the day I walk back into the office, I want to see my name on the door. Then, I want to be handed a cheque for $250 thousand. My salary will be raised to be equal to each of yours, including any stock grants or options."

A red-faced Irv Telfer raised a finger to negotiate but his partner ignored him and pressed forward.

"Yes," Kevin replied, "but could we please split that payment across two fiscals? It would help our balance sheet."

"All in writing, of course."

"Of course. Is there more?"

The three deer appeared roadside and retraced their steps across the road. The buck kept a vigilant eye on the truck parked on the side of the road.

"I keep my severance for the embarrassment you caused me. And going forward I want my severance condition extended to eighteen months."

"Yes."

"I want Irv's south facing corner office and his parking spot beside the elevator."

"Yes," Kevin answered, and an irate Telfer picked up a pen and sent it flying across the office.

"I want a new five-year contract that requires me to work only four ten-hour days each week, including the one day I would be spending with our client in Chicago, two days a week I would come into the Toronto office, and, one day a week I would work from my house on Great Spirit Moon Lake. Further, you will furnish my home office with the best video conferencing equipment on the planet. I will have 100% control over all strategies and creative concepts pertaining to Daily Planet Foods, and neither of you will attend a meeting with any of this client's employees. You will never reach out to Jack or even send him a Christmas card. When Daily Planet Foods makes the announcement that they are reinstating us, you will acknowledge in a press release that I, personally, re-won this client for Telfer Stuart. And the press release will come from Kevin. I'll want to approve the paperwork before it is issued."

Irv Telfer's face was scrunched up in unison with his sphincter muscle.

"I'd like the company to lease me a new 911 Turbo S and cover 100% of my costs including any taxable benefit. Are we agreed?"

"Hang on a minute," Irv protested. "Don't you think you are getting a little carried away?"

Kevin stepped up to the plate. "Shut up, Irv. Charlie, we're agreed but I'm at my limit. I trust we've shown you that we get it. In the next thirty minutes I'll e-mail you everything in a letter of intent. After you check to make sure I haven't missed anything, I'll have it formalized into a contract by close of business. Hopefully within twenty-four hours you can sign it."

"Thanks, Kevin. Can you please forward a copy to my lawyer, James Clinton? Kathy has his contact information. If the contract is complete, I'll be in the office Tuesday morning."

"Can I call Jack and tell him we're good to go?" Irv inquired anxiously.

"No. Remember Irv, no contact with anyone in Chicago," Kevin Stuart confirmed. "Charlie, you'll phone Jack the minute the paperwork is signed?"

"Yes," Charles Langdon replied officiously. He was shaking with excitement and couldn't wait to get home to tell Ingrid and Cassie what he had pulled off.

* * *

"Alex, you'd better take a look at this," Jay Datrem shouted, as he stared intently at his computer screen. Linda looked up from the sofa where she and Alexander Fanning were watching *Avatar* for the tenth time.

The ex-CEO quipped, "Where are we today, in Timbuktu?"

"No, it's worse than that. It's all over the Internet that your father is dead," Datrem relayed awkwardly. "I'm really sorry, Alex."

Alexander pulled up a chair and began calling up other sites. His shock was heightened with confusion over the allegations of sexual harassment and rape.

"I've got to talk with Mom," he blurted out, his face staring blankly.

Linda approached the two of them and read over her husband's shoulder.

"Jesus, your dad shot himself?" As she continued to read her eyes widened as the story highlighted the details of the sexual harassment. "This will kill your mother."

Jay was more pragmatic about the whole thing. "Alex, I'm sorry, but we've got bigger fish to fry. Without your dad, why should Richard Strickland care what happens to us?"

Alexander's mind was exploding. The scandalous circumstances surrounding his father's suicide would make his mother a pariah and laughing stock.

"Alex, get with it," Datrem stated firmly, accentuating his words with a shoulder shove.

Bettina's son exhaled and sat back. "Strickland can't betray us. He arranged for our asylum. We flew here on his plane and scores of people have seen us. He can't make them all go away, can he? We've made him rich. If he turns us in, his name is the first one we'll offer up."

Linda Datrem pulled up a third chair. Today her hair was bright orange and gelled upward in spikes. Her shorts barely covered her bottom. It was a wonder she could maintain her balance atop the five-inch heels she wore.

"Without your dad, we are nothing but an unnecessary risk to the banker. Why wouldn't he just kill us and steal what we left in his bank? He's so powerful he could wipe us off the face of the earth and no one would know."

Neither of the men across the table had a reply.

Forty-eight hours later, Alex read online that yet another female employee at his father's firm had come forward with DNA-backed allegations that Ernest Fanning had fathered her while having an affair with an employee of the firm.

"Jesus fucking Christ," Alex cried out. "Now I have a sister. How much weirder can this get?"

At that exact moment, Richard Strickland was scanning the CNN paternity story aimed at his deceased friend. The unflappable Chairman of CFMT was seated comfortably at his desk when a tall, wiry, impeccably-groomed man with inscrutable facial features entered the room like a panther stealthily crossing the jungle floor. Aashiq Amirmoez had spent most of his life in the army and through a razor-sharp intellect, unwavering persistence, and unfathomable cruelty he had risen to the rank of Colonel. As CFMT's head of security, Amirmoez and Strickland had cemented a mutually rewarding relationship that had spanned fifteen years.

"Please sit down, Colonel," Richard directed politely. "Would you like anything?"

"No sir."

"How is your daughter? I heard she had a rough time delivering your grandson."

"Thank you for asking, sir. My daughter is improving daily. My grandson enjoys hearing himself cry and fortunately has powerful lungs that allow him to fulfil his wish."

"Oh yes, the pleasures of newborns. Please give your daughter my best, and if there is anything she needs you simply have to ask. Are you up to speed on the Fanning situation?"

"Of course, sir."

Aashiq Amirmoez straightened out his shirt cuffs and rubbed one of the 18-karat gold cufflinks monogrammed with the bank's initials. "All records of any financial transactions or e-mails between CFMT and Ernest Fanning have been erased. All phone records have been deleted. His holdings have been transferred to accounts in Geneva where they'll remain untraceable until you give me further direction."

"How much did Ernest have with us?"

Aashiq answered proficiently, without referring to any notes. "$25,478,223 in American currency, and 32,559,257 in Euros."

"Good. Let's leave it for a year just to be safe. How are you progressing on the issue of his son and the two others?"

"Everything is underway. The bearer certificates that Alexander Fanning and his partner brought have been removed from our vault. All paperwork relating to the purchase and ownership of their condos has been 'adjusted' to replace their names. All security tapes at the Jumeriah have been confiscated and erased. The manager of the complex is my cousin so we will have no issue there. The cleaning staff and any employees who might have seen them have been dealt with. I've had our computer experts monitoring their laptops and all communications. There is nothing that reveals their location nor anything that could be tied back to us." Aashiq checked his watch. "In the next two hours there will be no physical trace that Ernest's son, his CFO, or the amoral female ever entered Dubai or even heard of CFMT."

Strickland nodded approvingly. "The three pilots who flew them here?"

"Are no more."

"The agents who met their flight and drove them here?"

"Are no more."

Richard Strickland felt relieved as Aashiq confirmed the death of eleven people. "And the disposal of the Canadians?"

The disciplined Colonel replied assuredly, "I must leave now to supervise that myself."

The CEO appreciated the effectiveness of the man who bowed and walked towards the door. However much of Fanning's money had been "detoured" into the Colonel's personal accounts in Switzerland was less than he deserved.

Chapter Thirty-One

Days and nights were no longer distinguishable to the elderly Swede as her earthly body struggled to survive. Her sight and hearing were all but gone, and she was faced with the embarrassment of adult diapers. Nothing gave her relief except being with Charlie and Cassie. She could not longer reject their offers of help and sat idly while they took over her house. She did not need her runes or any visions to tell her that she would soon be reunited with her husband and children.

Charlie was on the phone and smiled happily when Ingrid appeared at her bedroom door.

"*God etermiddag*," he greeted, wishing her a good afternoon even though it was barely ten. "I thought you were going to sleep the day away." The Swede chuckled at the same sarcastic greeting she used on him.

"*God etermiddag*," she replied, walking slowly to the kitchen table. She waved away Charlie's offer of breakfast and asked for a glass of water. Without any hesitation she launched into her story with an urgency that alarmed her housemate.

> As the Mashkikiiwinini had directed, we burned down the house and barn by the river. The death of our Mikaeli

and Birgitta threw a shadow over our lives and the flame between us never burned as bright. I never again was blessed with a child and could not move beyond the deaths of our three children. I realized I would be the last of my line of Stonecasters.

Henko and I finally agreed to put the trolls' gold to good use. My husband exchanged for cash some of the gold, removed our farm debt, and bought a new Massey Ferguson tractor. We paid for Meryl's children and grandchildren to go to university, built a properly insulated house for Miigwaans and Niigaanii, and encouraged their son Ma'iingan to go to the University of Toronto. Ma'iingan became a lawyer, got married, and was eventually elected Chief of the twelve Nations of the Chippewa. We donated anytime the community needed funding.

By the 1970s Henrik was in his 80s and crippled with arthritis. As his health failed, it accentuated the difference in our ages. I was a very young fifty-five year old and in strong health, whereas my husband had become a housebound old man. He encouraged me to get out so I walked the forests and canoed every non-winter day. I continued to cast my runes but stopped praying to Odin for the return of Sigrid's vision. I knew that was a lost cause.

Our beloved friend and neighbour Niigaanii, who was six years older that Henko, died peacefully in his sleep on the night of a brilliant hunter's moon. After Niigaanii's passing, my sister Miigwaans came to live with us. She and I cooked, sewed, painted, gardened, and talked until our throats were raw. Henko called us old cackling hens but the three of us were a good family.

Sadly my Viking warrior lost his memory. Today it is called dementia or Alzheimer disease but then we had no fancy name for it. Henko would tell me I was a nice girl and ask me if I was married. I would tell him I was married to the most wonderful man in the whole world who had saved my life. I told him that once my husband had done something horribly wrong but I no longer blamed him. One snowy Christmas day we discovered Henrik had foolishly left the house to chop kindling for the fire. He dropped dead with his axe gripped firmly in his hand—fitting for a Viking to die with a weapon at the ready. Hundreds of the community helped me bury my beloved friend beside the children. My grief was so deep that I would have crumbled to dust and blown away in the wind without my Canadian sisters' compassion.

After Henrik's passing, Meryl and I started a bakery. My neighbours on Great Spirit Moon Lake made certain I was never lonely. Barrett Sanford and Phil Henderson were there in an instant when we needed "menfolk" help. It was a good life on the lake and my garden flourished as the community blossomed. But then death struck again. Meryl Patch passed away just after we celebrated her seventy-fifth birthday. And then, four winters ago, Miigwaans told me the spirit of death had called upon her. She handed me her best dreamcatcher with the owl feather and Niigaanii's hunting knife. And then, without any delay, my Ojibwe sister sang me a sorrowful song, kissed my forehead, and trekked off northeast through the snow. When I tried to follow she told me to honour her wishes and allow her to enter "her" Valhalla. Forest Rangers found Miigwaans' frozen body two months later some twenty miles into the interior of Algonquin Park.

The years passed with emptiness and my optimistic Viking spirit waned and I began questioning my destiny and faith. As I aged, I felt such guilt that I had outlived all those I loved. My destiny had taken such an unfortunate turn and I was filled with sorrow and such grief that I had failed my ancestors by becoming the last Stonecaster. And then one day I learned that Cassie's husband had died. May the Gods forgive me, but I screamed with joy with his demise. His was an evil spirit that was drawing the very life from my godchild. Cassie's return to Great Spirit Moon Lake was like a strong gale had filled the sail of my ship. Having her near helped me to find a peace that I had not known for a long time. And then one day I was suddenly eighty-five years old. My health was leaving me and my earthly days were numbered. I prayed to the Gods for guidance and they heard me. Odin allowed me to live long enough to share this story with his messenger. I cannot believe he has gone to all this trouble without having a greater scheme for my destiny. Is it perhaps to help me enter Valhalla without the disgrace of being the last Stonecaster of my ancestry?

Ingrid slumped back and her eyes filled with tears. She looked up and took a deep breath. The Gods had allowed her to complete her story. "My young friend, do no forget what I have told you."

Charlie helped Ingrid to her feet and held her limp body in his arms.

"Ingrid, thank you for sharing your life story with me. I will forget nothing you have told me and I have a feeling that you have a role for me that we haven't discussed. Whatever that is, I'll do it for you."

All of a sudden Charlie's body went rigid and he quickly lowered Ingrid into her chair and stepped backwards. Looking deeply into Ingrid's eyes, Charlie's face stilled, and almost trancelike he began to speak. With a voice both deep and loud, he commanded, "Look into my face, Ingegard Signalda Holmberg Petersson. You must hear the words I have been instructed to say. Do you believe me to be a messenger from the Gods?

Ingrid stared at Charlie's face unsure of what was happening. The look in his eyes frightened her.

"Answer me!" he shouted loudly, causing her to jump in her seat.

"Yes."

"Then accept what this mortal says, fifth daughter of Birgitta and Lonegrin Holmberg. You have been living under an onerous misperception. The Gods had nothing to do with the deaths of your children and you must no longer blame them. Freyja did not remove her blessing of fertility from you having further children. Your husband was sickened by the Red Fever and lost his ability to sire children. I removed Sigrid's vision as punishment for you losing your faith when you needed it most. You are fulfilling your destiny. Ingegard, I hold you dearly and will welcome you in Valhalla. Your family awaits you."

Ingrid's eyes were wider than saucers and her mouth agape as she held onto every word. She watched as Charlie's stiff body relaxed. He appeared woozy and swayed from one foot to another before he broke into a wild laugh and began talking in his normal voice.

"So then, Barrett dropped his sunglasses down the septic tank and we both burst out laughing."

The Swede stared intently at Charlie with suspicion clouding her mind.

"His sunglasses went into the septic tank," he repeated, waiting for a bigger response. "Can you believe it?"

"Charlie?" she asked.

"Yes, don't you get it?"

Ingrid wasn't certain what had just happened. Was he toying with her? Was it a ruse? She focused intently on him trying to find deceit, but the innocence of his eyes betrayed nothing. A joyful feeling of elation seeped into her soul. Odin had finally spoken to her through his messenger. After all these years, she now knew that the Gods were no longer angry with her. She would enter Valhalla.

"Nothing son. That's a funny story. You will have to buy him new glasses."

The first vestiges of the morning sunshine played on the prisms and shells dangling by the window. The wind from the north was causing the tops of the trees to sway. Ingrid stood and walked towards the bedroom. She paused at the door and took one last look at her housemate. He smiled politely and reached for his coffee. When her bathroom door closed, Charlie sat back and breathed deeply. It had been a difficult performance but one done out of love. For too many decades, his Swede had been carrying a crippling, painful burden that was not hers to carry.

* * *

The 2012 hunter green Chevy Eldorado drove south en route to Toronto. The four-lane road had been recently ploughed and salted. As the kilometres passed and Ontario's capital city drew nearer, the ploughed fields showed patches of green. Roy Grant considered there'd be no snow at all by the time they reached Highway 401

"How old is Kelly turning today?" he inquired, and Lizzie looked over. She had been off in her imagination. Her husband seldom uttered a word to her since their confrontation.

"Kelly? She's turning nine. We got her a fifty dollar iTunes gift card and two movie passes." The Grants had seven grandchildren and Kelly was the eldest. They tried never to miss a birthday, a big event at school, or any sporting activity.

True to his word, Roy had stopped travelling so much and spent most nights at the lake. However, he seldom talked with his wife and had taken to sleeping in another bedroom. True to her word, Lizzie cleaned up her act and cut out the extramarital games. She began acting, dressing, and conducting herself with a decorum befitting of a married woman and grandmother.

Roy had noticed the difference in his wife's behaviour, but years of betrayal and deception were hard to erase. He might never have faced his wife about her transgressions if Ingrid had not set him straight.

"Your wife threw a sledgehammer through Cassandra's front window. These actions stop now before Cassie gets hurt," his elderly neighbour demanded, as she placed Niigaanii's fourteen-inch blade on the table pointing towards him. "Look in my eyes, Roy Grant. A Viking never makes an idle threat once a weapon is pointed at another. If your wife harms one hair on my godchild's head, I swear before Odin, I will kill her. Now go home and set your house in order. We will not talk of this again."

Grant was thinking back on that conversation and threat when he became aware his wife was looking at him.

"Roy, I don't know if you've thought about it but we'll have to share a bedroom at Joan's house," she stated, "unless we want to own up that we're sleeping apart."

Her husband nodded but remained silent.

"Will that be a problem?" she asked shyly.

"No."

They drove another ten minutes until Lizzie exhaled deeply. "Roy?"

"What?"

Lizzie was facing the passenger window as a twenty-two wheeler barrelled by and sprayed a disgusting amount of blackish slush across her window. She jumped back and then settled down. "Are you going to be mad at me forever?"

Roy glanced over but his wife continued to stare the other direction.

"I've been really trying hard," she continued, "but your silent treatment isn't helping and it's gone on long enough. Won't you at least meet me half way?"

The Eldorado signalled a lane change as Roy negotiated the ramp onto Highway 401 East. After clearing his throat he shared his thoughts.

"You hurt me Elizabeth. You made me look like a fool. The kids have been hurt too. You embarrassed and made us the laughing stock of the community. I can't walk into a room without catching sideways glances or smirks. When I'm talking with a man, I never know if he's slept with you." Roy's eyes clouded with tears and he wiped at his face with his shirtsleeve. "I see the effort you're making and I'm sticking around home like I promised. We're going to need some time and honestly I don't know if I can ever forgive you."

Lizzie shifted and turned her body towards him. He was too busy negotiating the traffic to see that her eyes were brimming with tears.

"Roy, I'm sorry, but I can only apologize so many times. I'm trying as hard as I can and you can't keep shunning me and making me feel small. You have to decide if you want to forgive me. If you can't, then maybe we're just wasting our time. So make up your mind whether you want to forgive me or divorce me because I don't want to be in this marriage to keep up appearances. I screwed up big time and I hurt you and the kids. It won't ever happen again. But even Jesus Christ had a last supper."

Roy realized she was right and that their marriage might as well be over if he didn't at least try to meet her halfway. He reached over and took his wife's hand in his own.

"Alright then," was Roy Grant's succinct reply, but those two words were all Lizzie needed to hear, and a solitary tear ran down her cheek.

* * *

With the World Expo being held in Dubai in 2020, the ruling family of the United Arab Emirates had made it clear that the city was to put on the greatest show on earth. Extensive teams were already working on upgrading telecommunications, security, traffic congestion, and accommodation availability. Companies had already commenced new construction and expansion of convention centres, hospitals, corporate head offices, hotels, and sporting facilities. The Expo was the catalyst for the rejuvenation of Dubai following the hammering its economy had taken with 2008's global financial meltdown.

So it was not difficult for Colonel Aashiq Amirmoez to select the final resting place for the trio of Canadians. He stood at the entrance of each condo at the Jumeriah as his squad of four assassins unlocked the doors, quietly entered and unceremoniously murdered Alexander Fanning, Jay Datrem, and the woman. Aashiq was interested in how people faced inescapable death. Of the three, Fanning's son with the movie star looks had bravely charged the intruders. The other portly man whimpered. His slut of a wife had stood defiant. The three corpses, now in thick, black, plastic body bags, were in the trunk of the Escalade driving just ahead of his car. The convoy of vehicles drove into the rear driveway of the Burj Khalifa complex, the world's tallest building. As one of Dubai's focal attractions, the building's owners were expanding its underground parkway and improving security with anti-tank barriers in the event of terrorist suicide bombers. Construction was well underway and Amirmoez's vehicles pulled up to a section where eight tonnes of concrete were about to be poured into a trench bordered with twenty steel girders. The workers in the area were directed to leave as the black vehicles spirited their passengers to the east side of the platform. Colonel Amirmoez watched from behind tinted windows as the three body bags were dropped into the structured framework. With a signal from one of his men, an oozing river of wet cement poured forth from eight trucks, laying a concrete tomb for Ernest Fanning's son and his accomplices.

Aashiq sat long after the trucks had delivered their payloads. He would remain until the cement hardened, no matter how long that took.

Chapter Thirty-two

"Sit down a moment," Ingrid directed quietly. Charlie's face looked apprehensive like he had been called into the principal's office for breaking up a fight Alexander had instigated.

"What's up? Is something wrong?" he inquired concernedly, wondering if Ingrid was unhappy with his new working arrangement in Toronto. Two weeks had passed since he walked onto the floor of his office and saw "Telfer, Stuart and Langdon" emblazoned on the wall. Teflon Irv greeted him like a long-lost relative and then disappeared into the woodwork. Kevin Stuart delivered on every aspect of Langdon's new contract. Admittedly there was a lot of travel to and from Toronto and the flight to Chicago certainly added to the strain, but the four days each week on Great Spirit Moon Lake balanced it all. He continued working with Barrett, although the scheduling and time organizing had been taken over by Miriam Walker.

The elderly gardener squeezed his hand. "Charles Michael, everything is fine but I need a few quiet words with you about the arrangements concerning my passing."

Langdon straightened his spine and breathed deeply. "Don't be morbid," he protested, remembering a similar talk with his mother. "That's a long way off."

"We both know that I have few earthly days left. Please do not make this more difficult than it has to be." Ingrid withdrew a thick white envelope from her apron and placed it on his lap.

Charlie looked at the patterns on the wall being created by the sun filtering through the prisms. Slowly he looked down at the envelope upon which his name was typed in bold letters.

"This explains everything. All the arrangements have been made and paid for. My lawyer's name and number are written on the first page. I have known Peter Byrne since the seventies and paid for his law degree. He's a good boy from a caring family and will do everything I have requested. I've asked him to arrive this afternoon so you two can meet." Ingrid breathed slowly to calm herself. "First of all, you know that as a Viking, my death is only a beginning and I must enter the next world with my most important possessions, which includes my medallions, Niigaanii's knife, Miigwaans' owl dreamcatcher, my compass, our children's moccasins, and twenty fist-sized gold nuggets in my safety deposit box in the Bracebridge bank."

Charlie noticed her runes and book of interpretation were absent from the list.

"All of my land property," she continued, "excluding the two acres around this cottage and five acres around our original homestead and cemetery, is being donated to the county to be developed into a park. The contracts were drawn up by Peter and the city has already legally committed to my wishes."

Charlie nodded but kept both eyes fixed on the sun patterns.

"I have investments of over five million dollars earned from the gold. I've bequeathed two million to the families of my four deceased sisters." The last of Ingrid's surviving sisters, Tindra, had died five years earlier. "Two million has been bequeathed to the Six Nations of the Ojibwe to be used to promote the history of the tribe throughout North America and provide scholarships for education. All of the Ojibwe artefacts in this house will be housed in the Bracebridge library for Miriam Walker to oversee. The final million will be set up in trust for Barrett Sanford in the form of a yearly pension that will be distributed to him over the period of his life."

With that comment Charlie finally looked up. "I like that idea," he confirmed, and the Swede smiled warmly.

"I thought you would. Now, listen carefully, and for once do not interrupt. I am leaving you this house, the two acres upon which it sits, and the five acres of our original homestead. I ask that you never sell and that my property stays in your family. I request that you personally maintain my gardens and the upkeep of the cemetery in which I will be buried with my family. My heartfelt hope is that in the far off future, you and Cassie will be buried beside me. Everything else I have not donated and everything I own in this house or on my property is yours."

"What?" Charlie blurted out.

"Be quiet," she ordered civilly, before repeating herself. "Everything not being donated to the community, the library, Barrett, my sisters' families, or to the Six Nations is yours."

Charlie abruptly shifted uncomfortably in his seat. "Shouldn't everything go to Cassie, or Meryl's family?"

Ingrid's face calmed but exhaustion made each word an effort. "Cassie became wealthy the day she became a widow and would not want me to leave her anything. I have given a great deal to Meryl's relatives. Mikaeli Charles, the day you saved my life you became my family. You are now the only living person who knows the journey of my life. I will implore Freyja to allow your child to become an extension of my ancestry. In that way, I will not have failed Sigrid by being the last Stonecaster. This is why our destinies were brought together. You must accept this so that my legacy will not die with me. *Jag alskar dig.*"

"But Ingrid—" he began, not noticing she had used her son's name as she gently placed her trembling fingers on his lips.

"*Jag alskar dig,*" she repeated softly, professing her love for him.

"*Jag alskar dig,*" he echoed, and his heart fluttered with the thought of her no longer being in his life.

Ingrid's eyes closed and she struggled to remain upright. "There are three things you must promise me. On the anniversary of the day we met I want you personally to repair my dock. No one can be with you. It has to be done solely by you."

"The dock? Are you serious?" he laughed. "We should just buy some dynamite and blow it up."

Ingrid grinned. "Yes, that would be an easy solution. The approved building permits from the Lake Association are in the envelope. It is important for you to understand that the property line of this house actually extends into the lake twenty feet past the end of the dock. Ours is the only property on Great Spirit Moon Lake that has this distinction. It is all outlined on the original deed and survey. Do not forget that."

"Alright."

"Now, the first thing is to check the base footings. Remember, you do it completely alone."

"I have no idea how to build a dock," he admitted.

"Remember to throw steel in the water."

"For Nyykjen," he stated.

"For Nyk," she confirmed. Ingrid picked up her glass of water and drank.

"The second thing requires that you help me honour a thousand years of my ancestors. I am leaving you my runes with my family's books of interpretation. I implore you to study these and share your learning and my life story with your daughter. Freyja will reveal which child."

Charlie Langdon understood the depth of her request and responded solemnly, "Ingrid, I promise to learn and teach my daughter. You will not be the last Stonecaster and your ancestry will live on through me and my child."

Ingrid saw complete truth in his eyes and a heavy stone and years of guilt were lifted from her heart.

"Thank you, my son. The final promise is that I want Cassandra to write a book about my life. It is time that she fully returns to the land of the living, and being with you and writing this book will do the trick. You do remember everything I told you?"

"Every name and place. I'll tell her exactly the way you told me."

The eighty-five year old rose onto wobbly legs and gripped the back of the chair. "I know that you are struggling in accepting the truth of my life story. It is hard for you to believe in Gods and spirits and accept my beliefs. Do not fret, Charlie. It is good that you have these doubts. One day you will come to believe that everything I have told you is true. Be patient for that day."

Charlie Langdon looked at his friend and slowly nodded.

"We are done. Meet with Peter Byrne today. Open that envelope the day after this body dies. I will hold you to your promises."

Chapter Thirty-three

"Baby, Duane wasn't asking you a question," the behemoth behind the desk responded absent-mindedly as he picked up the black Sharpie and continued autographing photos of himself. A rejuvenated Duane Michaels was revelling in his re-found fame. Since agreeing to the six-month contract with the WWF, he'd won two fights in the cage and a chunk of the football fan base he'd lost when he retired from the NFL.

Kyla Langdon was sitting cross-legged in the brown leather armchair facing his desk. Her lips were tightly clenched and her eyes were glistening with confusion mixed with anger. Evangeline was on a cross-Atlantic flight from Rome and wouldn't arrive home until after midnight. The rest of the mansion was empty except for the cleaning staff.

"All I said was that Duane wants to start having sex with you, Evangeline, and the girls," he repeated, hating these talks. Kyla had held her exclusivity twice as long as any of her predecessors. "It's not that big of a deal."

"I don't know how you can say it's not a big deal. It is a big deal. I don't get it. Everything seems so wonderful with the three of us. Now you want me to have sex with your trio of whores. How long before you pass me around to your party pals?"

Duane put the cap lid back on the Sharpie, stood up and put his knuckles on the desk. Kyla had seen Duane go ballistic with less provocation. He rolled his head on his shoulders, cracking his neck. Michaels' steel-strong muscles seemed to inflate as he stood there. But instead of losing it, he smiled and spoke quietly.

"Kyla, you are here because Duane wants you here. Evangeline and Duane found you exciting because everything was so new to you. You were hot and innocent and willing to do whatever we wanted. But now, we know your moves and it's grown stale. Frankly, the novelty has worn thin."

"Worn thin?" Kyla repeated, her nostrils flaring at the insult.

Michaels trundled around the desk and clasped his fingers together.

"How can I put it so you'll understand? Think of it like this. Duane drafted you onto the team as a starter and you were really good. But a lot of the season has passed and Evangeline and I feel your best game is behind you. I don't want to trade you away. Duane wants to put you on special teams and see what happens. All the girls get moved off the starting line-up. Some of them make it on the special teams. Some don't. Look at this as a second chance to prove yourself."

Kyla Langdon uncrossed her well-tanned legs and shifted in her seat. Who was he to tell her she had to "prove herself?"

"I'm sure Evangeline won't agree," the real estate agent argued, pulling out her ace. "She won't stand for this."

The exasperated ex-NFLer smiled awkwardly. "Well baby, I hate to burst your bubble, but this was Evangeline's idea. You can ask her when she gets home."

That hit like an unexpected slap. Kyla stood and walked around behind the wing chair, wincing at the betrayal.

"What if I don't want to be downgraded onto your special teams?"

Michaels returned to his chair and sat. He picked up the Sharpie and started autographing photos. There wasn't much time before he had to meet his publicist for a photo shoot.

"Kyla, stop taking this so personally. You're starting to piss Duane off, and I'm on a tight schedule to get out of here."

"Well, it is personal, Duane. It's my body and I decide who I'm with."

Duane looked up and smacked his meat-cleaver of a hand on the desk.

"That's where you're wrong! Duane can make your career disappear overnight. Imagine the headlines when people hear that one of Toronto's top real estate agents fucks clients to close deals. Get ready to read online how much you like snorting cocaine, and that you've hidden money away during a divorce proceeding. Yes, you told Angie about that and she told me. You won't be able to sell a two-story gold-shingled doghouse to the SPCA. You'll be finished." He grinned about the doghouse comment but then stopped when he saw the hurt expression on her face.

"Come on, Kyla baby, we've had a lot of kicks. You've made a fortune in commission just being with me and Evangeline."

Kyla was trapped. Michaels had her to rights. If she walked out, her career was over. If she stayed, the money would keep flowing in but she'd be nothing more than a whore. There was no choice but to play along until she had stockpiled enough money commissions to extricate herself.

"Only with the girls?"

Duane stood up, walked around the desk and took her in his arms. He kissed her very tenderly on the mouth and began running his fingers through her hair. Evangeline had predicted Kyla's greed would win the day.

"Baby, just Evangeline and the girls," he promised with well-rehearsed sincerity, knowing that in a couple of months he would have to "reassign" her again. Why were women were so predictable?

Kyla Langdon forced a smile to mask the anger seething within. If she had only listened to Suzanne Weston and not crossed the line she wouldn't be in this predicament. Kyla kissed Duane and was enfolded in the bear-like hug of the WWF fighter. Had he used the exact same lying words on Karen and the others? And Evangeline would get payback ten-fold.

Casually, Duane Michaels began unbuttoning Kyla's blouse. "Duane's got ten minutes before he has to go. Show me that you can use that mouth of yours for something more than arguing."

* * *

Cassie Turner was leafing through the album of her wedding day. She hesitated at a lovely photo of the two of them exchanging vows at the altar. Phillip had been so handsome in his tux.

Life with Phillip Turner had been busy, frantic, uncomfortable, and disheartening. Being on the arm of a famous psychiatrist had opened doors and evenings were seldom spent at home. Phillip and Cassie Turner were feted, photographed, and written about. And their social calendar exploded when Cassie's book hit the best sellers' list.

Away from the madding crowd, restaurants, and Toronto life, their private time was very quiet and awkward. Phillip's pre-marriage charm and respect went out the window the minute he added Cassie to his collection. She discovered that her new husband had an obnoxious streak that included lecturing her and finding fault with every opinion she tried to express. Within months Phillip began criticizing everything about her. He took it upon himself to save pages from *Vogue* and *Vanity Fair* and firmly suggest she buy that outfit. Her husband spent more time with his collections of expensive cars, rare books, and wine bottles.

It wasn't any better in the bedroom, and Phillip's libido left a lot to be desired. Her husband readily admitted he found the thought of intercourse "messy." Foreplay was not in his vocabulary and once they were horizontal, anything lasting longer than a minute was a colossal feat. Discussions about children were not an issue. He agreed to begin the "process" when his wife turned thirty-two. With each passing year of marriage, Cassie realized that the only hope of pregnancy would be an immaculate conception. The twenty-five-year-old girl from Great Spirit Moon Lake went to bed alone wondering why she had married such a control freak of a bastard.

It went on like that for years until one day Phillip complained of excruciating pains in his stomach and back. At first he attributed the pain to playing too much squash. Then his Armani suits draped like they belonged on a larger man. When his skin lost colour and Phillip admitted having shed twenty-five pounds, he finally relented to seeing his doctor. A barrage of invasive tests showed the renowned psychiatrist had pancreatic adenocarcinoma normally associated with smokers, obesity, diabetes, and men over forty. Phillip was only thirty-eight but was at stage four of the tumour's growth. Knowing every head of surgery and oncology in the country only helped to cut wait times. Surgery was the only "cure" but not an option at stage four, even as a treatment to ease the pain or retard the cancer's migration to other organs. Phillip begrudgingly agreed to a therapy of chemo and radiation and unemotionally informed Cassie to prepare for widowhood. True to form, her husband remained obnoxious, rude, demeaning, and controlling to the very end.

After the funeral an emotionally decimated Cassandra Turner travelled overseas for a year staying with friends in London, Florence, Lisbon, and Athens. Upon her return to Canada, she immediately sold the Rosedale property, settled Phillip's insurance, liquidated their investment portfolio, and auctioned off his rare antiquities and all but two of his automobiles and his wine collection. When organizing Phillip's office she discovered the papers to her husband's vasectomy almost three years before their marriage. His agreement to start a family had been a lie. Ingrid's goddaughter packed up and returned to Great Spirit Moon Lake. Any thoughts of a follow-up book were shelved and she threw herself into a mind-numbing regimen of physical fitness. Her once-extroverted personality had been sucked dry and she accepted few visitors beyond her family and godmother.

When everything in her life had settled down and she had found peace and reconciliation, Charlie Langdon had shown up like an uncomplicated breath of fresh air. His arrival added a spark to her life and she felt alive and vibrant. Charlie helped Cassie rediscover that she was an attractive woman with desires and needs that had been driven to dormancy. She wasn't the priceless "collectable" Phillip had acquired to show off to the world. She was a caring, feeling, vibrant person who deserved more.

Cassandra closed the photo album and walked over to the fireplace. She removed one page at a time and set it on the top of the burning logs. Each sparked and burst into a colourful array of flames.

"Time to move on," she said aloud.

* * *

On one of her more coherent days in mid-December, Ingrid announced she wanted to see her friends on Christmas Day. So Charlie and Cassie made the arrangements. The special day arrived with a sprinkling of snow and one hundred guests including Meryl Patch's extended family, every cottage owner on the lake, and Niigaanii and Miigwaans' eldest son Ma'iingan and his family. Ma'iingan Cardinal looked so much like his father that Ingrid's mind was understandably confused.

"Niigaanii," she called out, "I have missed you."

"*Mindimooy*," the son replied, affectionately calling her "old woman." "You are mixed up. I am the boy who played with your children. I am the boy you teased about cutting my long 'girly' hair."

The celebration was bittersweet with songs and laughter and the unspoken understanding that this would be Ingrid Petersson's final Christmas. Everyone listened intently as their beloved Swedish gardener recalled her parents, their boarding house in Visby, and marrying Henko aboard the *Sleipnir*. Ingrid managed a private word with every visitor and her soul found peace. For that special day Ingrid's eyes sparkled for each friend she saw.

By New Year's Day, Ingrid's health had deteriorated rapidly and her final wish was to die in her home beside the lake. Around the clock nursing care was arranged but there was nothing to do but ease her pain and wait on the inevitable. Cassie and Charlie remained steadfast by her side as Ingrid lay peacefully beneath her duvet, conversing with Henrik in Swedish or in Ojibwe with her friends. Suddenly she would sit up and begin cursing at the elves and spirits she saw mocking her from beyond her window. To appease her, Charlie would stand outside in the frigid weather throwing acorns and curses at the scoundrels until his Swedish friend signalled they were gone.

On January 3rd, Ingrid began having a series of tiny strokes and her doctor predicted his patient would not last the night. Within the hour Ingrid's living room was overflowing with friends who sat in vigil. By midnight Ingrid was floating between consciousness and a dream world. An oxygen mask covered her face and a slow morphine drip eased any discomfort she might be feeling. Charlie and Cassie curled up on a sofa they had pulled into her room. Cassie slept in the curve of Charlie's arm. No matter how he struggled to remain alert and watch Ingrid's breathing, an emotionally depleted Charlie Langdon succumbed to fatigue.

It could have been minutes or hours when Charlie heard his name spoken.

"Charles Mikaeli, open your eyes."

Charlie slowly awakened to a darkened room. All the lights had been turned off and the nurse was gone. He looked down at Cassie who was soundly asleep.

"Charles Mikaeli, can you see me?" the familiar voice urgently asked.

There was a shapeless, shimmering light in front of him. He rubbed his eyes and stared as it intensified and began to brightly fill the room. He could see the ghostlike outline of something that seemed to be struggling to materialize. And then within the shimmering opalescent light appeared a tiny woman. The glow of the light intensified revealing a much younger version of Ingrid. She was breathtakingly beautiful and her green eyes sparkled as she smiled. "So, you can see me?"

"Ingrid, is this a dream?"

The vision within the haze of light moved forward and touched his face with the palm of her luminescent hand.

"Do not be afraid. Do not fear me."

Charlie tried to reach to her but was paralyzed. "I don't understand," he muttered, as tears overwhelmed him. "Are you really dead?"

Ingrid touched the tears streaming down his cheek. "I told you that I was going to be with those awaiting me."

Charlie sniffled. "We need to wake Cassie. She'll want to see you."

Ingrid shook her head. "No, Charlie, my godchild cannot awaken. Freyja has chosen you, not Cassie. My Goddess has answered my prayers. Odin has permitted that I will not be the last Stonecaster of my ancestral line."

The aura of light grew wider to his left and a second much larger spectre began to materialize. Momentarily, a giant figure appeared and stared intently at Cassie.

"This is the little Patch girl who ran faster than a rabbit? It cannot be. She is full-grown and beautiful."

Ingrid wrapped her hands about his huge forearm. "Yes, this is the child who sat on your knee and mischievously tugged at your beard."

Henrik Petersson turned to face Charlie.

"This is the one who will carry on your legacy?"

"Yes, this is the one who was prepared to give his life so that I might live. Charles and Cassandra will marry and raise daughters. Freyja will permit one of their five daughters to carry on the long line of my ancestry of Stonecasters. Charles will protect my runes and become the child's instructor."

"Children with Cassie?" Charlie repeated groggily. "We are going to have five daughters?"

"But he lied to you and pretended to deliver a message from Odin. That was deceitful."

The tinier spirit laughed. "Yes he did, but it was an act of love to ease my pain when I needed it most."

"Five daughters?" Langdon repeated, as if in a drunken stupor. "No son?"

The Viking looked towards his wife and placed a gentle hand on her shoulder.

"He is an unusual one with a spirit that is strong and courageous. I understand why Odin brought together your destinies. He chose wisely," Henrik avowed. Ingrid's husband removed two large golden amulets from around his own neck and placed them on the younger man's chest. "Boy, take these to protect you in your time of need. These will help you to believe in our world. Teach your daughter well if she is to follow in my wife's footsteps. It is important that you have faith in what Ingrid has told you or your child will never be a true Stonecaster. Do not fail or you will feel the wrath of the Gods."

Charles Langdon's head felt like it would explode yet he was still unable to physically move.

"I will not fail Ingrid, or Sigrid, or any of her ancestors," he responded deliberately. "Why would I ever do that?"

Ingrid Petersson leaned forward. "Freyja said you could meet my children."

Henko turned sideways, revealing two smaller orbs of light that had been sheltered behind. He motioned for them to move closer to the sofa. "Mikaeli and Birgitta," the big man introduced proudly, revealing a handsome young boy and the pretty blond-haired girl from the lake.

"We've met before," Birgitta whispered, in the tiniest voice, "when you bravely saved Momma from Nyykjen."

Charlie smiled at the children and his heart raced.

The little boy stepped forward. He had his mother's green eyes. "We have the same name."

Langdon nodded. "Yes."

The children looked up at their parents and Charlie felt himself drawing weaker by the moment.

"Ingrid, I don't understand. Am I dreaming?"

"You are not dreaming. You are having your own vision of another time and dimension. When you awaken, this moment will stay with you forever and you will believe that everything in the story of my life happened exactly the way I told you."

The ghostly spirit that was the Swedish gardener glided forward until their foreheads were touching. She spoke in Swedish like she was reciting a prayer or a sacred poem. Slowly, she raised her right hand palm upward and a tiny intense blue light about the size of a marble appeared above her fingers. Ingrid's face showed a great relief as the small blue orb glided towards him. He felt no fear and did not recoil as the orb of her spirit passed into his skull.

"Your five daughters, and the legacy of my ancestors, are now within you," she whispered, almost gleefully. "I must leave you, but we will meet again. Your destiny has been rewritten and it is rich with happiness and love."

The bright aura of light began to flicker and fade, removing the images of the children. Henrik held out his hand in a sign of friendship as his light diminished. Ingrid's voice sounded distant.

"I cannot remain. Freyja is calling. Charles Michael Langdon, I will be forever grateful that Odin chose you as his messenger and the father of the next Stonecaster of Gotland. *Jag alskar dig.*"

The room darkened as the last ray of light withdrew into the distance like a movie screen fading to black.

"Don't go, Ingrid," Charlie Langdon pled desperately, but his eyes closed and the Gods forced him into a deep, lonely sleep.

* * *

"Mr. Langdon," a voice said urgently, interrupting the silence. "Mr. Langdon."

When he opened his eyes, one of Ingrid's nurses, Lynn MacLeod, was shaking his shoulder. Cassie awoke with a start and sat upright.

"I'm very sorry, Mr. Langdon, but Mrs. Petersson has passed. Her aneurysm ruptured. It was likely brought on by a stroke. Please leave her exactly as she is and do not remove the sheets. I need to phone Doctor Harris," the nurse stated quietly.

Cassie was shaking and repeatedly asked, "Ingrid is dead? Ingrid is dead?"

The nurse nodded her head. "I'm sorry for your loss. I will inform the others."

Charlie felt such exhaustion as he stumbled towards the bed and touched the lifeless form beneath the sheets.

"Ingrid," he moaned, in that guttural sound that reveals an unbearable loss that crushes your soul. "Oh, Ingrid—"

Cassie approached the other side of the bed and wrapped her arms around the tiny frame. She opened her mouth to cry but nothing came out. Her grief was too great for sound and the room began to spin like a carousel.

Charlie ran around the bed and grabbed Cassie mid-faint. Protecting her from the fall he found himself sitting cross-legged on the bedroom floor cradling her in his arms. When she regained consciousness the two desperately clutched each other and rocked back and forth in unison. They sobbed inconsolably. An indeterminable amount of time passed and, as they stood, something hard on Charlie's chest bump roughly against Cassie's face. She tilted her head back.

"What's this?" she inquired through heavy sniffling, taking the two heavy golden medallions in her hands. "Where did these come from?"

Charlie's eyes glanced at Henrik's medallions.

"It can't be," he blurted out. "It just can't be."

Chapter Thirty-four

After collapsing unconscious on a busy sidewalk in the downtown Toronto business section, Terrance Greene was rushed by paramedics to St. David's Hospital. His weight had fallen below one hundred pounds, he was all but blind, and his concentration was suffering from what doctors termed AIDS dementia. Within an hour, the medical staff determined that he had pneumonia and was suffering septicaemia. Terrance overheard one nurse in the palliative care unit indiscreetly tell a co-worker, "This one's long gone. His bed will be available by tomorrow night."

A priest was summoned and after administering Last Rites asked, "My son, you must have family or friends. Is there someone you would like us to contact?"

"Evangeline," he whispered inaudibly, and his eyes clouded over.

It was evening when Terrance next opened his eyes. He had been dreaming about happier times when he awoke with the realization that there was something he needed to do. Pulling back the sheet and withdrawing the IV needle, heart monitor cable, and oxygen tubes took monumental effort.

"Evangeline," he moaned, as he crawled from the bed. No one on the palliative ward noticed him walk down the corridor and into the janitor's closet. Donning janitorial scrubs, Greene walked out the front door of the hospital and staggered into the parking lot. The janitor's key tag read BBKR 571. With only partial vision he found the old green Chevy. Within minutes heat was blowing into his face and he put the car in gear. A sharp pain struck at his chest and along his left arm as he drove out of the lot.

Twenty-five minutes later a near-comatose and mostly blind Terrance Greene miraculously managed to pull up behind the Michaels' estate. Across the street was parked a dark blue Escalade. It took a moment, but Terrance remembered the car and the bastard with the foreign accent who had nearly kicked him to death.

Dimitri Trechikoff was half-frozen as he patrolled the perimeter of the Michaels' estate during what would was supposed to be his last week of employment. Mr. Michaels felt he was a waste of money and terminated his contract. Duane might have had a different opinion if his wife had told him about the intruder. Trechikoff's backside was like a block of ice as he returned to his car to retrieve his thermos of hot coffee. After pushing the numbers on the keyless entry he hopped into the Escalade and turned on the ignition to get some heat. As he reached for the thermos, his peripheral vision picked up something in the rear view mirror. If Dimitri had been less cold, or if the inside light had been on, he might have reacted faster. But he was cold and it was dark and his head was violently jerked backwards. The security guard thrust his body upward to break the hold but that didn't prevent a completed depleted Terrance Greene from using the janitor's box cutter to slice across Dimitri's carotid arteries and jugular. Blood spewed, splattering against the inside of the windshield and along the light grey dashboard. Trechikoff could still breathe, and desperately grasped at his assailant's arms while struggling to reach his weapon. But it was for naught as the remaining pints of his blood oozed rhythmically with a diminishing heartbeat.

"1-2-3-4 for your keyless entry?" Greene slurred. "That was easy to remember, even for me."

Terrance removed the Beretta from Dimitri's shoulder holster and found house keys and garage door clicker in a jacket pocket. He stepped from the vehicle and stumbled across the snow-covered lawn, falling several times. Oblivious to the frigidly cold weather, he began coughing up blood and felt that sharp pain returning to his chest.

"Jesus," he muttered, wiping his mouth on the sleeve of the janitor's overalls. Standing up he clutched onto a branch of the hedge and momentarily forgot what he was doing. "Where am I?" Finding a clicker in his hand he depressed the button opening the garage door just ahead of him.

"Evangeline," he remembered. "Evangeline is my wife. I'm here for Angie."

After entering the garage, Terrance meandered along the row of cars and motorcycles until he stood at the back entrance to the house. The Russian had scratched the code into the plastic side of the garage door clicker and Greene entered the numbers on the panel disarming the security system. The Michaels' kitchen Terrance entered was bigger than the whole downstairs of the house where he and Angie had lived. There were bowls of apples, oranges, and bananas on the counter. There was even a fireplace in the corner.

Crossing the hallway, Greene walked up the wide-arcing, richly-carpeted stairwell. His lungs refused to refill and he feared his loud gasping for air would lead to his discovery. From all those nights of waiting for Angie to get home he knew every upstairs window and room. His wife's bedroom was at the far end of the hall. Like a dog, he padded down the hallway, stopping every few feet to gather his strength. After what seemed like an eternity, he reached the door of the master bedroom and pulled himself up to his feet. From within the room, Terrance heard the unmistakeable sounds of people having sex.

Quietly, the dying man opened the door and stepped inside the bedroom. Many candles burned brightly and the light stung his eyes. On the bed, two people were frantically making love and it hurt Terrance to hear his wife moaning in ecstasy. Angie's arms were clutched around the big man's waist and her long black hair whipped from side to side. Terrance Greene stared at them and his heart broke. As the lovemaking reached a crescendo, Greene realized that he had lost Evangeline. She would never come running to his arms. They would never live together and raise a family. Slowly, but very deliberately, he lifted the Beretta and began firing.

Neither lover's brain would comprehend what had ended their lives, given the incredible speed with which the stacked hollow-point designed bullets tore through their bodies. They might have heard explosions and seen streaks of light that resembled a photographer's flash. Bloody chunks of the mangled lovers splattered the walls and the ceiling. The two bodies continued to convulse until the Beretta's magazine emptied.

Terrance stared at the carnage and dropped the weapon to the floor. His shoulders shook and he began to sob realizing that he was no better than his younger brother. An overwhelming pain gripped viciously at his chest, crumpling him to the floor. The massive coronary took twenty seconds to finish him.

Chapter Thirty-Five

It was a beautiful sunny afternoon when Ingegard Signalda Holmberg Petersson was laid to rest. Despite the cold January weather, hundreds of mourners made the trek along the snow-covered forest trail. When they arrived at the family plot by the fork in the river their hearts were uplifted with the sight of sunshine reflecting through a thousand prisms that Barrett, Miriam, Phil, and Margery had hung from the thirty trees surrounding Ingrid's final resting place. Hundreds of thousands rays of light crisscrossed and flickered playfully like a computer-generated light show. And then as if part of the choreography a herd of twenty deer approached and stood undaunted by the large group of humans at the edge of the old homestead. It was obvious they were paying respect to their beloved friend. The forest awakened with the sounds of birds singing and cawing like a choir. Momentarily, a period of respectful silence ensued as the community offered their prayers for the woman who had been such a fixture in their lives.

And then those who had something to say stepped forward.

Phil Henderson spoke warmly about Ingrid and Henrik having financed his dealership when the banks had turned him down. He admitted how much Ingrid detested his toupee, and without hesitation, removed it.

A stream of people took turns sharing how Ingrid and Henrik had selflessly helped their families with friendship and financial support. Many had been able to attend university only because the Peterssons had paid tuition. Others praised Ingrid's compassion, love of nature, and unparalleled skills as a gardener. A few gently teased about her idiosyncrasies in believing in elves and sprites, and how the Norse runes had played such a major role in her life.

When it seemed that everyone was done, Barrett Sanford shyly walked to the front of the congregation and cleared his throat. All there understood how difficult it would be for Barrett to publicly speak. The lake's handyman walked to the grave and stared at the mound of dirt with flakes of snow falling atop it. He cleared his throat and then spoke loudly for all to hear.

"When I was much younger, I had a horrible accident. My body was badly damaged and my brain didn't work the same. I was unable to speak without people mocking or pitying me. I thought my life was over and hid away in our house. One night about a year after the accident I took Dad's hunting rifle and walked off into the woods. It was pitch black and I wandered until I was completely lost. I sat and placed the rifle's muzzle under my chin. My finger was on the trigger when a familiar voice gently spoke to me. Ingrid began to talk and I put down the rifle. We talked for hours until the sun came up. Ingrid took my hand and led me home. When I asked how she had found me so far in the dark forest, she said she had asked the animals to bring her to me. Ingrid then shared that everything in her runes told her that I was going to enjoy a happy life surrounded by friends who would accept me for the man I would become. I've never forgotten those words—'who would accept me for the man I would become.' We never spoke of that night again, and until today, not another person ever knew about it. Ingrid Petersson saved my life that night and gave me hope. I love Ingrid for that. I love her, and always will."

There was not a dry eye in the group of mourners as Margery Henderson stepped forward and wrapped her arms around her brother. Barrett was the only person in attendance unaware that while sharing his story he had not stuttered once. He also couldn't have known that from that moment on, he would never stutter again.

Off to the side, Charlie and Cassie stood quietly. Despite having so much to say, neither could find the words.

* * *

No one who knew the Swede was surprised at how Ingrid bequeathed her possessions. Barrett was so overwhelmed he broke into tears. Her goddaughter was thrilled that Ingrid had left the house to Charlie. Cassandra had always dreamed of living in Ingrid's house, and now she would.

Later that week as Charlie and Cassie were packing Ingrid's Ojibwe items to be donated to the library, her goddaughter opened a box shoved into the back of an upper kitchen cabinet.

"Oh my God, Miriam was telling the truth," she exclaimed, holding a red leather journal in her right hand. "Do you know what this is?"

Charlie looked over and instantly recognized Meryl Patch's red journal of Ingrid's predictions. "Yes, Miriam told me about it."

Cassie quickly flipped through the pages and then closed the book. "Is this something we should read?"

Just then Charlie's cell phone rang and the caller ID showed it was his lawyer James Clinton.

"Put it away until we agree what to do," he asked, before excusing himself to take the call.

"More crap from Kyla?" he asked, without saying hello.

"Charlie, have you been online this morning?" Clinton inquired.

"No, why?"

There was a momentary silence.

"There's a story that concerns you. A man killed a security guard and then broke into Duane Michaels' home last night and shot the place up. The shooter was the former husband of Duane's wife."

Charlie racked his brain. "Evangeline?" he added, remembering his conversation with Kyla.

"Yes, Evangeline Michaels. She dumped the shooter after he was imprisoned for armed robbery."

Again silence.

"And?" Charlie asked, as his curiosity peaked with what this had to do with him.

"Well, it's all over the Internet. Police have camera footage from the Michaels' security system showing how the shooter, whose name was Terrance Greene, gained access through the garage, disarmed the back door alarm, casually walked upstairs, and fatally shot the two occupants in the master bedroom. Greene didn't shoot himself. It appears he died naturally. Had disappeared from St. David's Hospital's palliative care where he was dying with AIDS. Somehow he managed to steal a car, and despite being half-dead drove to the Michaels' home."

Charlie's attention perked up.

"Jesus, that's incredible. So after killing a security guard he murdered Duane Michaels and his wife?"

Clinton's hesitation was frustrating.

"No. Evangeline had the flu and was sleeping in a bedroom down the hall. She was the person who called 9-1-1. The woman in bed with Duane Michael was Kyla."

"Come again?"

"It was Kyla. The man shot and murdered Duane Michaels and Kyla. Greene walked into a darkened candle-lit room and mistook Kyla for his ex-wife. It appears that Kyla was wearing a wig. It was a case of mistaken identity."

"He shot Kyla?"

"Yes. He shot Kyla. He killed her."

Charlie asked, "Are you sure? There's no mistake?"

"No mistake. She was positively identified at the scene by Evangeline Michaels," the lawyer confirmed. "Police have reviewed the security tapes and Kyla entered the house at 7:10 p.m. Her purse and identification were in the bedroom at the scene of the crime."

Cassie walked out of the kitchen, still clutching the red leather journal. The happy expression on her face melted to concern when she saw Charlie's intensity. He placed his cell against his chest and gently touched her shoulder.

"The woman I'm divorcing was murdered last night. I'll tell you in a minute," he explained succinctly, as a look of remorse stole over his face. Quietly retreating back to kitchen, Cassie put her godmother's journal back in the box and opened the fridge to see what there was to eat.

James Clinton continued.

"Anyway, the police see this as a straight-forward triple homicide but the coroner must conduct an inquest. As the not-yet divorced husband of one of the victims you'll be questioned and will need to make a statement. I've booked an appointment tomorrow morning at eleven. I want you to come to my office at nine so I can prepare you. I don't want you to discuss anything with anybody about Kyla, or your interaction with Duane Michaels. I don't care if Jesus Christ tries to ask you something. Keep you mouth shut. Am I clear?"

"Yes," Charlie responded, and he could hear papers shuffling on the other end of the line. His thoughts were far from any inquest or meeting with a coroner or a Crown Attorney. Kyla was dead. That meant Francine Powell was dead, and he could not put aside the heavy cloud of guilt that rested over his head. What if he had not been so focused on a career that took him away from the woman he married? What if his ego hadn't driven him for the next promotion? What if he had listened to Francine when she told him she missed him and was spending most nights alone in front of the television or her computer? What if "Kyla" had never been created? Charlie had a sick feeling in his stomach. How had he so easily forgotten how much Francine had meant to him?

* * *

It was early June and summer had arrived at Great Spirit Moon Lake. The lake was renewed with fishing boats and canoes as cottagers returned en masse. Phil Henderson's boat launch looked like a thoroughfare at rush hour. Builders were constructing two houses on the north side of the lake not too far from where Niigaanii and

Miigwaans had raised their children. The old lakeside road took a beating as gravel and cement trucks pounded their way to the construction site, spewing up dust and grit that stung eyes and turned lawns brown.

The water level of Great Spirit Moon Lake had risen a foot due to an unusually heavy spring runoff, which was the direct result of the heaviest winter snowfall in a decade. Ingrid's unsightly cement dock was now entirely submerged, and Charlie placed safety markers around it to prevent boaters running aground.

"You're going to have quite a time fixing that stupid dock," Cassie remarked. The two stared at the construction drawings laid out on the grass between their two chairs amongst the lavender bushes. All but one of the purple bushes had survived the winter. The roses had all survived thanks to burlap tent coverings.

Even though it was only June, the first five months following Ingrid's passing had been anything but dull. The whereabouts of the former CEO and CFO of NovaRose remained a mystery. Early reports that they had escaped to Dubai had been replaced with sightings in a variety of cities across North America and Europe. Charlie's disappointment with Alex lessened with a casual comment from Cassandra.

"Charlie, have you ever considered that your best friend was in an untenable situation? He couldn't contact you, or you might have been charged with insider trading and hounded by reporters. I wouldn't be surprised if when he left, he fully intended to make up your losses once everything died down."

And then there was the aftermath of Kyla and Duane, which unfolded like a Hollywood movie. The coroner's inquiry and the police investigation into the murders at the Michaels' mansion generated juicy headlines about wild orgies and rampant drug use. Kyla's reputation was dragged through the mud when it came to light that she had bartered sex to ink property closings. Terrance Greene was hardly excused for having committed a triple murder, but the press treated him with a sympathetic eye. The story of a good honest hardworking man who made one mistake that cost him everything.

"What goes around comes around," Clinton remarked, not attempting to hide his disdain for Charlie's deceased wife. "Everything Kyla wanted to take in the divorce now returns to you."

But the most incredible twist of that murderous night came back to haunt Evangeline Michaels. The inquiry exonerated her since there was no evidence to implicate involvement in the murders. But that was only the half of it. During their search of the premises on the night of the killings, Metro Toronto Police discovered a massive stash of cocaine, marijuana, hashish, and amphetamines in Evangeline Michaels' closet. Despite her defensive accusations that the drugs belonged to her husband for use at his private social gatherings, it was her fingerprints lifted off the boxes containing the illicit substances. Ordinarily, as a first time offender without any previous convictions, "drug possession" led to a fine and a suspended sentence. But the Crown Attorney had to look at the excessive quantity and street value of the drugs, which at $175 thousand was deemed far too high for private personal use. Under the Controlled Drugs and Substances' Act, the Crown charged Evangeline Michaels with fifteen counts of "possession with the intent to social traffic"—an indictable offense that carried a minimum sentence of twenty years and a maximum of life. Evangeline Michaels would follow in her ex-husband's footsteps and spend at least two decades in a federal penitentiary.

Charles Langdon took all of these events in stride. He often wondered what would have become of him had he not rescued the tiny white-haired lady. That day, his destiny changed, and his stars realigned. With Ingrid, he had been reborn to accept the reality of a supernatural dimension that existed no matter how hard it was to believe.

Cassie pled with Charlie to wait until the water warmed up in July. Although he intended to deliver on his promise to begin fixing the dock on the anniversary of their meeting in late August, he wanted to scope out the dock's foundation and take measurements required to order the building materials. Donning a wet suit, mask, weight belt, and snorkel he had borrowed from Tom Powers, Langdon inched into the seasonably cold water. Glancing back at Cassie, he opened his gloved hand and tossed five steel nails into the water. She nodded her approval.

"Bugger off Nyk," he commanded, as he gripped the snorkel mouthpiece between his teeth, turned on the underwater flashlight, and submerged. The sunlight from above and the eight pounds of lead weight on the belt around his waist made the job easier. The water was relatively clear and he saw a few minor cracks in the slime-covered concrete. He found that Henrik had poured the cement foundation atop a natural stone base.

The waterline dropped off abruptly twelve feet from the shore. That would allow a good draft for any sized motorboat to carry. It was deep enough even for a large craft like Phil Henderson's twenty-one-foot Malibu Wakesetter. The natural stone base continued twenty feet along the entire length of the dock. His flashlight reflected off something shiny when he reached the end of the structure. He dove and grasped the top of what appeared to be an old-fashioned dairy delivery canister, which was secured tightly against the base of the dock with a thick steel chain. His depleted lungs forced him to surface, but his curiosity had piqued.

"Don't dare get pneumonia, you idiot," he heard Cassie call from her vantage point at the water's edge. He saw her toss a handful of nails into the lake. Without saying anything, he splashed downward and counted a total of twenty-five cylinders. Ingrid had told him that Henrik had purchased old milk delivery cans to transport the trolls' gold. Charlie laughed giddily, and when he swallowed water he chokingly rushed to the surface.

"You've been in there long enough," Cassie concluded, as she helped pull him out of the water. After he dropped the weight belt to the grass, Cassie helped unzip the back of the diving suit. "So what's the verdict? Is the base in good shape?"

"You have no idea," he answered, choking back a giggle. "I need to sit down." The two strolled over and sat beneath an apple tree which was beginning to blossom beautiful tiny white blooms that looked like oversized snowflakes.

Charlie leaned over and planted a big wet kiss on Cassie's mouth.

"Ooh, you stink of scuba suit and snorkel," she complained, wiping her mouth with the back of her hand. "Go take a shower."

Charlie threw his head back and started to laugh.

"What?" she exclaimed. "It's not funny. You smell."

Langdon exhaled deeply and took a deep breath. "You're not going to believe what Henrik and Ingrid chained to the base of the dock. Now I understand why she was so insistent that I fix it alone."

"What did you find?"

Charlie stood up and stretched in a fake yawn. "I'm going to take a shower."

Cassie slapped his leg. "Come on. Spit it out. What was chained to the dock?"

Her mate turned and started walking towards their porch. He looked over his shoulder and glanced at her provocatively.

"I'm going to take a shower. You can wait 'til I get back—or you can join me, and I'll tell you then."

The gazelle was through the front door before Charlie was halfway up the porch steps.

Chapter Thirty-six

"For God's sake Momma, lower your voice or she'll hear you," Vito Carbrese asked. "She's in the bathroom next door, not a mile away."

Helena Carbrese reached across the dining room table and pinched her son's forearm causing him to grimace and pull away.

"Watch your mouth, little man," she chastised. "If your father were here, God rest his soul, he'd smack you across the mouth for taking the Lord's name in vain. All I said was she's pretty long in the tooth. What's wrong with that? She's been around the block a few times."

Her son rolled his eyes and wondered what had ever compelled him to bring the woman to Sunday dinner. It would be a miracle if she ever agreed to see him again. Momentarily, the toilet flushed and the bathroom door opened. His date smiled as she re-entered the room.

"You're not sick or anything?" Helena inquired genuinely, and the woman shook her head.

"No, I'm just fine, thank you. Dinner was delicious. The veal was fabulous. It's a real treat to have a home cooked meal."

Vito nervously held his breath for what would come out of his mother's mouth.

"You know I am not Italian? My parents were both Greek. My husband, Vito's father was Italian ... God rest his soul. My father was furious when I told him about Sergio. He threatened to disown me if I brought a wop into the house. 'Helena, what's wrong with a nice Greek boy?' he kept asking. But every time Sergio Carbrese looked at me, my knees went weak. Papa and Mama pretended to despise him, but Vito's father was very likeable. You know what I mean? He was just a likeable boy. In the end, my parents did not disown me, and Papa paid for our wedding. In four years we had three healthy boys: Vito and his younger brothers, Theo and Yannis, who we named after Papa. Sergio couldn't keep his hands off me and, in all honesty, I did not want him to."

Mrs. Carbrese stopped talking and motioned for her thoroughly embarrassed son to clear the table.

"No, I'll do it," Phaidra McTavish offered, but Helena Carbrese insisted.

"No, my boy will do it. He hasn't done a thing today. A little dishwater on his hands will do him good. Finish and come on back in when I call you," Vito's mother directed, and the full-grown man nodded obediently, knowing better than to argue.

Helena inched her chair closer. It scraped across the ancient hardwood floor.

"So, my boy says you are an alcoholic and have problems with drugs."

Phaidra's expression did not change. There wasn't much that could shock her anymore. Shortly after being released by their abductors, Tessa had made it clear she wanted nothing to do with her mother. Tessa told her to find a new place to live and to let the lawyer know the address for that time when she'd be expected to talk about her relationship with Fanning. Phaidra could only think of one place to go. Mr. and Mrs. Hatoyama listened to her story and opened their doors. Phaidra arrived with the clothing on her back, a desperate thirst, and a plea for help. Katsumi stayed with her day and night for two weeks until the worst of the demons had done their best. Then Phaidra attended an Alcoholics Anonymous meeting and found the encouragement she needed. At twenty-two days of sobriety, Phaidra was put to work at the dry cleaners' shop.

And then one day when one of her kidnappers arrived at the shop, she boldly confronted him and asked what he wanted.

"To have a coffee with you," Vito Carbrese had responded. "David asked me to look in on you and make sure you had enough money and were keeping off the booze."

Frightened for the welfare of the Hatoyamas she complied. That first coffee with Vito Carbrese led to a walk, to dinner, and then the beginning of a friendship. There were no questions asked or judgments passed. Now, three months later, she was still living with Katsumi and attending Alcoholics Anonymous meetings weekly. She had survived fifty-seven days without a drink or taking as much as an Aspirin.

"Your daughter will come around," Vito promised on their third date. "Tessa's a strong-willed kid. Just give her time."

And now Phaidra McTavish was sitting with Vito Carbrese's seventy-four-year-old mother who didn't pull punches. There was nothing to lose in telling the truth.

"Yes, Mrs. Carbrese, what your son told you is right. I am an alcoholic and I have a problem with drugs. But as of today at 4:27 p.m., I'm fifty-seven days dry and clean. But I could pick up a drink tonight or swallow some pill tomorrow morning, and part of me desperately wishes I would so this nightmarish aching would go away and my head would stop pounding like someone's hitting me with a hammer." Phaidra exhaled audibly, but wasn't done. "And you're also right about me being long in the tooth and having been around the block. I have a full-grown daughter, born out of wedlock, who would prefer me dead. I work at a dry-cleaning shop out of the kindness of the owners. I have no doubt that a wonderful man like your son could do a lot better than bringing home a broken-down wreck like me."

Helena lifted her glass of red wine and took a sip, knowing Phaidra's eyes were locked on the glass.

"This girl who hates you is the same daughter you tried to protect by offering your life?"

Phaidra stopped staring at the wine and looked at her hostess.

"Vito told you about that? You know what your son does?"

Helena Carbrese raised her hands like she was praying and scrunched her face. "My boy has no secrets from me. I am not proud of the life he's chosen and do not boast about him to our priest during confession. But my boy visits me every Sunday, makes sure nobody bothers me, and pays my bills. Sure, Vito got caught and went to jail. That made me mad. Not that he went to jail because he deserved that. It is that he was too confident and got caught. Now tell me, what kind of a woman gets knocked up, but does not have an abortion or give the child up to adoption? What kind of a woman offers her life to save that child? A good woman. That is the kind. A good woman."

Phaidra McTavish lowered her head and for the first time noticed the beautifully ironed lace tablecloth.

"I'm probably not any good for your son, Mrs. Carbrese. Lord knows I'm hanging on by a thread and the smell of your wine is absolutely killing me. Just sitting at this table is so exhausting I feel like fainting."

The mother of Greek origin looked across the table, reached over, and patted her guest's hand. She smiled warmly for the first time that dinner.

"My girl, there is a lot more to you than meets the eye. I can't imagine what you are going through, but I can tell when someone is lying and you are telling the truth, so let's not speak of any more of that unless you want to. And from now on, I want you to call me Helena. Vito," his mother shouted, "stop listening at the door and get in here." Her son hustled into the room and sheepishly looked at his mother.

"This lady I like, and from what I can see, she's far too good for you. And I say this as your loving mother. She has a good heart that has been kicked around long enough. You make sure you bring her back next Sunday for dinner. That will be day sixty-four, right Phaidra? And the Sunday dinner after that will be day seventy-one?"

* * *

Shortly after midnight, Cassie tossed a handful of nails into the lake and held tightly to the rope tied around Charlie's waist. The long-handed cutters worked and the three-foot aluminum dairy canister broke free from the chains. They used the wheelbarrow to transport it to the garage.

"Well, shall we take a look?" Charlie inquired giddily, as he picked up a crowbar to provide torque needed to unscrew the rusted top. One mighty twist unsealed the container and sent the top and dairy can careening across the garage floor dispersing its contents with each roll.

Cassie stepped forward and picked up a yellow chunk about the size of a large-sized jagged golf ball. She held it up to the light and her mouth fell open.

"There are twenty-four more containers like this?"

Charlie grinned. "Yup. Ironic isn't it? Ingrid leads me by the nose to this gold but we really don't need it. We already have a lot of money between the two of us."

Cassandra agreed. "She knew we didn't need this gold and didn't expect us to keep it for ourselves. Let's do something wonderful with it, like set up a foundation to help kids go to school. Ingrid and Henrik would like that. Don't you think?"

Charlie picked up the golden chunks and replaced them inside the dairy can. He started to laugh.

"What?"

Langdon grinned. "You know that I still have to fulfill my promise to Ingrid and fix the damned dock."

Epilogue

Two years later

The expansive, white, marble-stoned patio overlooked a rolling olive grove that stretched across a series of descending terraced gardens. The fields had been landscaped centuries before to allow the hilly topography of the region easier irrigation. The grove was bordered by a three-foot stone wall which separated the trees from forty acres of meticulously planted rows of jasmine. Upon harvesting, the aromatic white flowers would be sold to the Fragonard Parfumerie where Chanel and Coty would extract an extremely expensive essence for use in the perfumes they manufactured. The jasmine fields descended to the northern shore of the Mediterranean. Until 550 AD, wealthy Romans had lived on this estate west of Nice, harvested the olives, and transported them in urns to destinations in Gaul and Britannia. When the empire fell during the sixth century the Romans were destroyed, but not the olive bushes, whose thick roots outlasted even the most ruthless of Roman emperors.

This day, a stunningly beautiful young woman was sunning on a large flat-stoned patio just beside the crystal-blue pool. Dark brown hair matched her oversized sunglasses and swimsuit. Bronzed skin glistened beneath the lotion that protected her from the UV rays. Beside her was a glass table upon which rested a tall pitcher of lemonade, a glass with ice, her cell phone, and a fascinating hardcover book she'd picked up at the airport. It was number four on the *New York Times* Best Sellers' list and told a story about a Swedish mystic's life. Tessa picked it up and found the dog-eared page revelling at the thought she had an undisturbed afternoon to finish the book. The peaceful sounds of mourning doves cooing in the olive grove added to the ambiance of the day.

Tessa Conner looked across the top of the olive grove towards the Mediterranean Sea and saw a large white yacht moving slowly towards Nice. Sitting back into her chaise, she reached for the lemonade and took a sip. Tessa had purchased this estate fourteen months after the untimely suicide of Bettina Fanning. The paternity suit was won and Tessa McTavish was deemed one of two beneficiaries to the will. Half of the Fanning estate was released to her, but that amount was more than enough to satisfy her and the two men with whom she had formed an alliance. The remaining half was in limbo until the other beneficiary was prepared to come forward.

Tessa adored her new home en Provence. There was a peace to the south of France and so much to see. She loved to visit the Saturday farmer's market in the nearby village of Mougins, watch the local men at bolo ball, or sit in the café beside the old church drinking café au lait and eating something savoury. Her waking hours were no longer spent dwelling on how Ernest Fanning had ruined their lives. That was a closed book. Her mind was now filled with thoughts about her home, the olives, the jasmine, and where she might travel.

So much had occurred in the past two years. After much soul-searching, Tessa had reopened her heart to her mother and the scorn she had built up soon dissipated. As the daughter matured, the sins of her mother were more understandable. Phaidra sobered up and married Vito Carbrese, who aside from being a kidnapper, torturer, murderer, and extortionist, was a decent, family-oriented man. Vito helped

Phaidra find peace and serenity in his arms rather than in the bottom of a bottle. With his share of the Fanning "proceeds," Vito created an enviable life for his bride who could now quietly boast of 745 days of sobriety. The irony that their new lives had been made possible by Ernest Fanning was not lost on any of them.

Tessa had been saddened to learn from Vito about the death of their third partner. After the first instalment of the Fanning estate was released to them, the three celebrated "Plan B," and went their separate directions. David Fowler happily accepted his share, intending to retire to Florida and play the ponies. He never got the chance to pick even one horse or place a bet. David was walking from his bank when he happened upon a robbery in progress. As the two thieves ran from a jewellery store, the proprietor shot one in the back. His accomplice grabbed a passer-by as a human shield. Without any thought for himself, Fowler tackled the robber and shoved the hostage to safety. In the ensuing wrestling match, the thief's gun discharged into the Good Samaritan's heart. The shop owner shot the burglar and called 9-1-1 as the ex-cop bled to death on the sidewalk.

Vito Carbrese and his mother Helena wept at the loss of their friend. Helena Carbrese told her beloved daughter-in-law what a decent man David Fowler had been.

"Sure, he was corrupt, and used Vito to break the law for him, but look at how he saved that woman's life. You know what they say Phaidra: once a cop, always a cop."

A gentle, warm breeze from the Mediterranean wound its way upward across the jasmine plants and the olive orchard. It felt like someone had just opened the door to the sauna. That was the impetus for another swim. Tessa rose from her chair, dropped her sunglasses on the table, and dove into the deep end of the saltwater pool. The water had been cooking in the sun and gave partial relief to the scorching day. Floating on her back, Tessa looked at the twenty-foot tall hedge of rosemary that bordered the western edge of the patio. The rich aroma of the rosemary competed with wonderful smells of the jasmine.

"Your nose is beat red," a voice warned, as a slender, attractively dressed woman approached the pool. A large floppy sunbonnet completely shaded her face and shoulders. "You come out of the water and sit in the shade for a while." The woman picked up Tessa's towel and stood waiting at the top of the pool stairs. As her daughter stepped from the water, Phaidra draped the towel around her.

"I thought you and Vito had driven into Mougins," Tessa remarked.

Vito and Phaidra were spending two weeks with Tessa, which was the longest amount of time that her stepfather would be parted from his mother. Tessa had extended an invitation to Mrs. Carbrese who had refused, telling her son that she'd rather be found dead in a barrel of putrid, rotten fish than spend one minute in the house of the girl who had treated her Phaidra so despicably.

"No, we decided to go later when the sun's not so hot. Vito's making an afternoon watermelon salad for the three of us and told me to fetch you in ten minutes."

Tessa accepted the lotion handed to her and applied a generous amount to her nose and cheeks, all the while staring at her mother's face.

"What? What are you staring at?" Phaidra asked anxiously.

"Nothing," her daughter replied calmly, shifting her eyes towards the rear wall of the garden.

"Yes you were. Is there something wrong with my makeup?"

"No, your makeup is fine." Tessa smirked, and then smiled. "Don't get all freaked out or mushy, but I was thinking how beautiful you look. You're healthier and happier than I've ever seen. It's like you're a totally new woman and a different person. For the first time in my life, I'm seeing how you probably looked before I was born."

Vito called from the door that lunch was ready.

Phaidra glowed at her daughter's compliment. It was true that after years of ups and downs her life seemed to have found an even keel.

"I feel brand new," she responded. "Seeing you happy and relaxed like this makes it all the more worthwhile."

Tessa stepped into her sandals. "I'm reading this book that talks a lot about how our destinies are decided for us before we're born. But sometimes, we're able to change our destinies. Have you ever thought of that? Do you think we are able to change our destinies?"

Her mother took off the hat and ran her fingers through her hair. "I don't know. I've never really thought about it. If it is true then I hope whoever is writing our destinies leaves us alone to enjoy this new life we've found. I'm not sure why anyone would have written my destiny to be so harsh and unhappy for so long."

"Ahh, but then everything changed for the better. You have your health, you are sober, we have a lot of money, and you have a wonderful villain of a husband who adores you."

Phaidra laughed and placed her hand softly on Tessa's sunburned face. "And I have my daughter back, and that's the most important thing in my life. If this is my destiny, then bring it on."

* * *

The moonlight streamed through all the seashells, crystal prisms, and beads that Ingrid had hung across her bedroom window. The beam was then reflected upward across two Ojibwe dreamcatchers hanging above. Beneath them, in the duvet-covered bed, Charlie gently rubbed Cassie's lower back. His pregnant wife had been tossing and turning for hours trying to find a comfortable position but the rambunctious girls inside her would not settle down. After countless hours, the twins finally exhausted themselves and gave up on their tag team play. Certain Cassie was deeply asleep, Charlie crawled out of bed and tiptoed to the crib in the adjoining room. He stared lovingly at their beautiful eleven-month old daughter as he gently felt her diaper, glad to find it still dry.

"Daddy loves his little dove," he cooed, touching the dreamcatcher above the crib for good luck. "Your new sisters have been putting it to Mom, but they are finally asleep. Dream well, Inga."

After locking the door, Charlie Langdon donned a hoodie and quietly walked out onto the back porch. There was the plastic bowl of carrots and potatoes on the wicker table for Tomte.

"Eat up and watch over my wife and children," he demanded of Ingrid's house spirit, before making his way through the fruit tree orchard into the forest. The cloud-free sky shone with the full moon and sparkled with countless stars. Without the need of a flashlight, Charlie made quick time along the unmarked path keeping a wary eye out for forest elves. With every sound, his hand instinctively touched Henko's medallions hanging around his neck.

The faint rushing sound of the Pottawatomi River was the signal to turn northwards. Within minutes he arrived at the family cemetery. It was a far cry from the first time he had come across it. The tombstones were no longer hidden in the undergrowth of the forest. As Ingrid had requested, he took responsibility for it. The summer of the year that Ingrid died, Charlie and Barrett ripped out all the overgrown trees and bushes. They constructed a four-foot tall stone wall encircling the plots. Cassie and Miriam carved runic symbols on the stones. A steel gate opened to a walkway bordered with well-tended shrubbery. Edging the wall, Charlie and Cassie had planted lavender and climbing roses that flourished with wild abandon as if Ingrid was tending them herself. A marble bench was placed nearby so visitors could sit.

Charlie closed the steel gate with a clang and was greeted by the calming aroma of the knee-high lavender. Sitting on the bench he withdrew the charm pouch, held it to his nose and breathed deeply.

"I can smell you," he said aloud, as he began withdrawing runes and placing them beside him on the bench. One day he would discretely teach one of his daughters about the mystery of the runes. He would share Ingrid's story and the magical night that she and her family came to him in a dream. Charlie wondered if she would be given Sigrid's vision. Either way, one of his daughters was destined by Freyja to become a Stonecaster.

An owl hooted from the meadow off to the south where it would be hunting for bats and field mice. Overhead the prisms and shells swayed and played with the moonlight as a gentle wind crossed the forest. When Charlie looked upward at the dancing moonbeams, a shooting star streaked across the northern heavens, bringing warmth to his soul.

His Swedish mother was saying hello.

THE END

Afterword

To keep the record straight, for those of you who are history buffs, there are several dates in the prologue I adjusted to support the storyline of the fictional Sigrid Gustavson and the factual invasion of Gotland by the Danes in 1361. The first involves Valifrid Gustavson predicting the arrival in Gotland, of a deadly black snake in 1342. Her "snake," was a reference to the Bubonic Plague, which swept across Europe in 1346-1353 and appears to have reached Sweden and Gotland Island in 1350-51.

The invasion of Visby in 1361 was factual. Led by the ruthless Danish King, Valdemar IV, who retaliated against King Magnus IV of Sweden for reneging on a promise of allegiance against a common enemy. During his tumultuous reign Valdemar was a committed Christian and made a pilgrimage to Jerusalem. The thought of this Christian king siring five children by a "heathen" Stonecaster named Sigrid Gustavson would not have happened due to these religious divergences. I brought forward the timing of the invasion by ten years to create a more heroic character in the young Sigrid.

The prologue is dated mid-1300s by which time Christianity was firmly entrenched across Scandinavia, after centuries of religious turmoil and conflict between the diametrically opposed new religion of "one" God versus the Viking traditional beliefs of "many" Gods; including Odin, Thor and Freyja. As early as the beginning of the 10th century, King Harold Bluetooth of Denmark introduced the new faith espousing Christianity as the only true religion. Generations later King Canute of Denmark, who also secured the throne of England, saw the religious and economic benefits of one religion *and* one currency across England, Scandinavia and most of Europe. As the Viking trade network stretched eastward to Orthodox Christian Constantinople, the transition of Norsemen to Christianity took a firm hold.

Consequently, it would been unlikely that Visby's chieftain Jakob Pleskov would have entertained a rune reader, or Stonecaster, within the city walls. The old faith of sacrifices and many Gods was shunted aside and laws were enacted to exterminate any religious practises that contravened Christianity. If, in fact, either Valifrid or Sigrid Gustavson had made predictions about the future, it is a certainty that a bishop would have excommunicated them as sorcerers and condemned them to death.

This all would have made *The Last Stonecaster* a very short story, so to allow this tale to unfold, Gotland's conversion to Christianity was delayed under the premise that rune readers practised in the mid-14th century and then continued to exist outside the accepted Christian faith as generations came to pass.

On a different note, my sincere thanks and gratitude to the team at FriesenPress for their counsel, editing, design work and diligence. And last, but not least, to Martha Breen, Cathy Campbell, Winnie Tse, Jack Campbell and Rosalind Breen for the initial editing, thoughtful insights and encouragement…my deep appreciation to you all.

CPSIA information can be obtained at www.ICGtesting.com
Printed in the USA
BVOW06*2142221115

427812BV00007B/89/P